Tears
of the
MOON

Nicole Sharp

Tears of the Moon by Nicole Sharp
Copyright © August 2025 The Writing Moose
All Rights Reserved

Print: 978-1-966843-00-9
eBook: 978-1-966843-01-6
Cover by **A. M. Rasmussen**
Editing by **Ariane Kimlinger** at Owl Focus Editing

The WRITING Moose

For more information visit: www.nicolesharpwrites.com

The Simply Trouble Series:

Big Trouble in Little Italy
Simply Protocol
Worth The Trouble
A Simple Avalanche

Secrets of the Moon Trilogy

Tears of the Moon

Standalone Books

The Italian Holiday
La Bella Luna
Surviving Thirty

Novellas

Let It Snow
The Museum Guide
Italian For Christmas

This book is dedicated to my 'ride or die' friends:

The ones who show up whenever called, no questions asked, with proper pep talks loaded, alcohol ready to pour, and shovels poised...

Tears of the MOON

Doug MacRay: "I need your help. I can't tell you what it is, you can never ask me about it later, and we're gonna hurt some people."

James Coughlin: "...Whose car are we gonna take?"

-from *The Town*

Hello

Hello my friend,

Well here we are, another book and I'm giddy with excitement for you to begin, but before you do, I have a quick note:

In this book you will meet Gael, I just want you to hear his name the way I intended: Guy-el.

Now, pour your favorite cuppa, settle in and enjoy the adventure!

Chapter One

"**D**on't move, or I'll blow your fucking head off," Harper hissed, leveling her handgun at the disheveled man standing in the middle of a disintegrating building that had once been a deteriorating bar.

The man began to slowly raise his hands, fingers splayed, eyes wide and body tense as he tried to radiate his willingness to cooperate.

Renee, who stood behind her friend's left shoulder, rose onto her tiptoes in time with the man's surrender pose. Not wanting to interrupt the rising level of tension, she quietly breathed out the question, "You're not really going to kill him, are you?"

Harper clenched her jaw in answer. She had no *idea* what the hell she was going to do.

She had never been in a situation like this: In the middle of the Peruvian jungle; on the trail of the kidnapped friend of a friend; in possession of an illegal firearm. And now, steadily aiming *said* purchased gun and threatening the life of the last person to have seen the friend of a friend. (The person who had a hand in the treacherous kidnapping, but just how much remained to be seen.) All while desperately trying to figure out what the hell she'd do if this man *didn't* tell them anything. And consequently, what the hell she'd do if the greasy asshole *did* give them helpful information.

A whirlwind of actions and consequences thudded in time with her climbing heart rate. Of all the things Harper *didn't* know at the moment, there was one thing she was acutely aware of; she could *not* show any weakness. At all.

She squared her shoulders, wished her mouth wasn't so dry, and screamed an inner monologue through her entire body, insisting she was

Harper *fucking* Barrett. And Harper *fucking* Barrett could do anything!

"I said I'd blow his head off," Harper explained, "but maybe I wasn't talking about the one with the bad comb-over and sunken eyes." She cocked the gun and changed her aim to his crotch, impressed at how his eyes were capable of even more width and wondered how close she was to getting them to pop out of his head completely. Somehow, his growing fear inflated her courage.

She winked at him.

"¡Espera! Okay, okay. Just wait!" His voice wavered as he jiggled his hands, glancing down at his drab, olive green clad legs, then back at Harper's no-nonsense snarl. "Listen, just escucha ..." He licked his lips. "Cálmate. Okay? Be calm. Maybe you are not thinking clearly, you have hysteria. You are a little girl with a man's gun. It is not attractive when you threaten me that way."

Renee gave a disgusted scrunch of her face along with a sad shake of her head. "It's the twenty-first century asswipe. Demeaning a woman who's pointing a gun at you is just plain stupid." She elbowed Harper for verification. "Right?"

The insult fortified Harper's nerves even more than his fear had, and while her raging blood pressure didn't seem to be dissipating, the trembling was easing from her bones. Which was as helpful as anything else could have been at that moment. "Did you know, a man can survive having his penis shot off? I mean, if he can get to a hospital in time and doesn't bleed out."

Renee nodded encouragingly. "I hear they do some amazing reconstruction work if that happens."

"Wait! Mierda, just ... wait a minute." He pumped his hands higher in the air.

Renee lectured, "Maybe smelly little men with Napoleon complexes *shouldn't* be patronizing women. Should I remind you, all I had to do was smile to lure you in?" She shivered. "And I feel like I need a bath because of it."

Harper thought she needed to shit or get off the pot, and decided to push him. "I'm going to count to ten. If you don't have anything to tell us by then ..." she gave an impartial shrug, "that's fine. But I will shoot."

"And she doesn't fuck around," Renee verified.

Harper prayed she didn't fuck around. And like it or not, she was about to find out. "One—"

"Okay, okay!" He covered his crotch, hands crossed over each other.

Renee repeated their demands, "Tell us who took my friend. And why they took him. And tell us where they're going ..." she held her hands out to the side and cooed, "Then you can go and we'll be on our way."

"Two. Three—"

"Okay." His voice rose an octave. "I said okay!"

Renee put her hands on her hips. "You've said 'okay' a hundred times. What you haven't said is anything that could actually help us."

"I know! But maybe you stop pointing the gun at my ..." He thrust his hips forward slightly, to punctuate his argument.

Harper frowned at the action. "Four. Five—"

"Okay! I helped kidnap your friend. But I was *hired*. I was told to bring him here, then two other men met me and they took him. I don't know where."

"That's pretty shitty information. *Where* did they take him?" Renee demanded.

He gave a manic shrug. "I don't know! I was told where your friend was and to take him when it was easy. When he was alone in the taxi it was easy. Then they tell me to bring him here. That is *all* I know. I never ask questions. Nunca. You ask questions, you die." He was slowly trying to shift his body to the side, to make himself a slimmer target. "When a man has too many answers, that man gets killed."

Harper scoffed, "Sometimes *not* having the answers can get you killed."

"Okay! They left a few hours ago. This road goes only from Cusco to the coast of Brazil. I came from Cusco, so maybe they have to go este. East. That is the only other way."

No one moved for several long seconds. He'd given them a little information. Admitted he'd been hired to do the kidnapping. But now what? Harper slowly assessed the bar's forsaken relics – chairs, a pool table with one leg, a long wooden bar that had possibly been used for batting practice.

They'd tie him up. The idea came out of nowhere, but it had merit.

Harper commanded, "Turn around and put your hands behind your back." As he slowly accomplished her instructions, she whispered to Renee, "Zip ties."

Renee retrieved Harper's well-stocked backpack and dropped it next to Harper before she rummaged around, finally declaring, "Zip ties."

Harper told him, "I'm still the one with the gun. Don't try anything."

After Renee made quick work of securing his hands using two zip ties, Harper nodded to a chair and instructed, "Sit down there."

He quickly abided her instructions but in his nervousness almost missed the chair, until one glute caught the edge and he was able to slowly slip himself fully on the seat. Harper watched Renee attach each of his ankles to a leg of the chair, tugging on her work to make sure he couldn't get away. When it was evident he wasn't going anywhere, she stepped back. Harper returned the hammer of the gun to its original position, engaged the safety, then let it hang limp in her hand.

"Who are you working for?" the man asked.

"None of your business," Renee answered.

Harper shifted closer to Renee and said, "Get your phone out and pull up a map. Make him tell you exactly what 'east' means." She picked up her pack, exchanged the gun for a water bottle in one of the side mesh pockets and muttered, "I need a second ... You okay?" Though she didn't wait for Renee's answer.

She walked out the open door of the bar, hastily made her way across the small parking area, dropping her backpack halfway. When she arrived at the edge of the jungle, she bent at the waist and lost the contents of her stomach.

She spit several times, rinsed twice to get rid of the awful taste, then wiped her mouth with the back of her hand before she tested standing once again. Her heart rate and blood pressure had finally evened out, but of course that made way for the dull throb of a headache to take over. She took a series of slow breaths as she blindly gazed around the jungle butting up against the ruins of a dirt parking lot.

Unable to hold back a snort of hysterical laughter, she rolled her eyes and mockingly muttered: "Come to Peru Harper. We'll see the sights. It'll be the trip of a lifetime, Harper."

What the hell had she gotten herself into?

Chapter Two

Harper! Let's go to Peru!

This was the message Harper woke to in mid-January. When her heater had stopped working in the middle of the night, the news was calling for more snow to torment already freezing New Yorkers, and the previous evening she'd endured one of the stupidest dates she'd ever been on in her life.

The guy, a colleague's cousin, met her at an up-and-coming restaurant where her demure, quarter size fish filet had been covered with foams and micro greens. And while she tried to appreciate the lack of taste and ridiculous hip-ness of the place, she listened to the colleague's cousin cry about the love of his life that he clearly wasn't over.

When the server asked if they wanted dessert, Harper declared she was too full and the colleague's cousin grinned through his watery eyes and asked if they should take the momentum of the date back to his place or hers?

She stood, muttered she'd cover the tip (she wasn't about to pay for half of this ridiculous date, his cousin could reimburse him), told him to take care and texted her colleague: *I am going to need all the coffees and cakes and apologies after this debacle. Please tell me this isn't what you think of me.*

Then she hunkered down in her layers as she walked home and had a 'come-to-Jesus' conversation with herself about why she not only continued to allow herself to be set up, but persisted in using dating apps.

Because I'm lonely and tired of being lonely and tired of being a thirty-eight-year-old woman who is constantly asked why someone as amazing as me doesn't have anyone special in my life.

Inside the foyer of her building, she shook off the snow from her coat as her one-sided conversation continued, "I haven't found anyone because there is no one *out there*. Case in point: foam food guy."

As she washed her face and twisted her shoulder length auburn hair up, she studied her green eyes and complexion, pale from a long winter indoors. "You're fine," she told herself, then heated up leftover pizza and turned on the TV; opting for an action-adventure movie to take her mind off everything.

But that was last night, and this was a new day. She huddled deeper into her warm bed and read through the list of texts she'd missed:

Lena, her oldest sister: *Do you want to go in on a present for Mom and Dad for their anniversary?*

(The answer to that would be yes, because such a question meant Lena had already bought something.)

A message from her next oldest sister, the one in the middle, Luna: *Did you know Rome has 280 fountains and over 900 churches?*

(That message was a ploy to get Harper to visit Luna, who'd moved to Italy last fall. And Harper wasn't opposed to visiting, but it would mean spending time around Luna and Giovanni and their newly minted romance. Harper wasn't in the mood to be a third wheel.)

A message from her colleague: *I am so sorry! I owe you all the coffees and cakes and apologies and I'll show up to work with them on Monday morning first thing. I think you're amazing!!! I didn't know my cousin wasn't over his ex. Or had a recent ex. Call me when you can so I can properly grovel.*

And finally Renee: *Harper! Let's go to Peru!*

Harper only responded to that text: *When?!*

A fraction of a second after the message was sent, her phone rang. She happily answered, "Good morning, Renee."

"The first of February I'm going to Peru for a fashion shoot."

Harper yawned. "What will you be fashioning?"

"I've been hired to do hair and makeup for a fashion shoot in Cusco, Peru. A friend of mine, Gael? I've told you about him ... well, he's the photographer and we're going all over the place, like the Machu place and other really cool mountainous places." Harper felt warmed simply listening to Renee's excited spiel. "But I'm getting a free first class ticket. I already called the airline, and I can get the ticket downgraded to two economy tickets. And the whole shoot is for Gael's friend who has a clothing line, and *that guy* is getting free rooms for us for a month because he owns a hotel or something ..." She took a deep breath before continuing her enthusiastic pitch. "Anyway, the shoot is three weeks long, but if you come at the end, we'll still have a free place to stay for like ten days. So the whole thing would be free! Wanna go?"

"Let's see. Do I want to go to Peru where all I'm going to have to pay for is my food and souvenirs?"

"Yes! Can you get the time off?"

"How many people have told you they couldn't go?" Not that Harper cared if she was the second or even tenth on the list. Renee was the kind of person people flocked to.

"No one. You're the first call because I think it would be a blast. We had so much fun last fall when I came to New York. And this'll be the trip of a lifetime."

Harper pulled her phone away from her face, opened her calendar and scrolled to the requested dates. She had plenty of vacation days saved up. As a museum registrar who oversaw the transport of objects loaned to other museums across the nation for exhibitions, she got to travel quite a bit, so she rarely used her vacation time.

She had no upcoming projects, in fact her next oversight wasn't until May.

She put the phone back to her ear. "I'm in."

Renee squealed, "Oh my god, this is going to be the most fun! I'll start emailing you details soon."

"Peru." Harper gave a shiver of excitement (and maybe only a little of it was the cold now). "Just tell me it'll be warmer than a snowed-in New York."

"Highs in the seventies, occasional afternoon showers, fresh air and Incan history."

"I'm *definitely* in."

After excited declarations and goodbyes were traded, Harper did a preliminary search for Cusco, Peru.

Whether you are interested in nature, history, culture, or adventure, the vibrant city of Cusco won't disappoint! The city itself and its surroundings are home to archaeological sites, museums, marketplaces, viewpoints, and magnificent nature scenes.

She grinned. "Oh yeah. Let's go to Peru."

Chapter Three

Agent Nick Robbins needed a vacation. If he'd ever been certain of one thing, it was that.

He and his partner, Stills, had been called in at the last minute to surveil an intersection, two blocks away from where a joint task force operation was taking place.

Simple.

The bust had gone smoothly as DEA and CIA infiltrated a house and arrested over twenty notorious drug traffickers.

Then the call came; a runner headed their way.

Before they could intercept him, the escapee had stopped a woman unlucky enough to be driving past him and abducted her at gunpoint, using her as a getaway driver.

Luckily, the asshole didn't spot Robbins and Stills. So they stuck to protocol, following at a distance, keeping the operation informed of their location; eventually receiving instructions that the woman was first priority and if possible, the man be taken alive.

Several miles later, from cover at the end of a street, they watched the stolen car stop in front of a rundown house where the man ushered his victim inside.

They relayed the address, were told that the location was well-known among the group of men they'd apprehended and backup was on the way. Then the agents were instructed to proceed with caution if feasible.

Exiting their vehicle, Robbins and Stills began systematically moving down the block. Drawing closer, they reported through earpieces they were able to keep out of the house's line of sight by walking through the neighboring backyard which thankfully, had broken gate slats and overgrown shrubs.

They crept undetected to the back of the house and peeked inside the available windows. The first window was the kitchen with a view of the living room and the man pacing and screaming on his phone while his free hand agitatedly waved a gun. But the abducted woman wasn't with him. Robbins went to look in the next window over and saw her in a bedroom sitting on the floor, arms tied behind her back and feet tied together, desperately trying to free herself.

He relayed the information to Stills as the man inside continued to wave the gun and scream into the phone, "You set me up!"

Stills moved to the back door that led to a utility room off the kitchen. The door was open, so he left it ajar and whispered, "We could go after him."

Robbins reasoned, "Let me secure the hostage first."

Stills whispered, "I'll distract him, then you can get in and out. But you won't have much time if he decides to grab her and use her as a shield." Then he quickly snuck around to the front yard. Robbins watched through the kitchen window. When the doorbell rang, the man stepped out of his line of sight and yelled, "Fuck off!"

That was his cue; he pushed the back door open and hurried to the bedroom the woman was in.

He heard Stills' continued distraction as he yelled, "Let's talk this out man."

"Fuck. OFF!"

Stills yelled again, "C'mon man, let's chat!"

Reaching the room, Robbins quietly opened the door, slipped inside, then closed and locked it. He was turning to introduce himself when the woman threw her whole body at him. Wriggling for all she was worth, her erratic movements tore out his earpiece and she used her head to slam against his nose. He heard her intake of breath, she was about to scream. Using all his body weight, he wrapped one arm around her, pushing her into a corner away from the window while covering her mouth with his hand to stop the sound. She used that opportunity to chomp down on the fleshy pinky side of his left hand.

Then a gunshot echoed from inside the house. Robbins shielded her body as he willed her to be quiet, while hissing an even breath out between his teeth as pain shot through his hand.

A cacophony of shouting voices came from beyond the house; the backup had obviously arrived. The suspect inside answered with staccato gunshots. The abstract noises filled in moments that were elongated. Without his earpiece, uncertainty of the situation built.

These were the moments that were adding new gray hair sightings lately. He was too young for gray hair, too young to feel as tired as he did. The pain came again, harder this time, worse than the first time. He looked heavenward and let a silent curse escape as he admitted it was seriously time for him to take a vacation.

Nick heard the amplified assertion: "We have the house surrounded."

He took that moment to lean his mouth against the woman's ear and softly inform her, "I'm with the police."

And part of her did understand, because she stopped struggling but another scream from the winning orator in the front room, "Come and get me mother fuckers!" was punctuated with another round of gunshots and a renewed fearful bite down on his hand.

He felt warmth and knew her tears were running together with the blood she was drawing. He hugged her closer – an attempt to soothe her – and tried to recall the last time he had a tetanus shot.

The crash of glass from multiple windows was followed by a hiss of tear gas. Next, Robbins wasn't surprised when the asshole in the house unloaded the last of his clip in a last-ditch effort to defend himself. But when his screaming became coughing, the eruption of doors being knocked off hinges and heavy boots echoing against squeaky floorboards of the neglected house rang through the air.

"Clear!" The first call was a welcome sound and soon followed by a resounding chorus of the same pronouncement all around him.

The woman released his hand, her eyes wild as she looked at Nick. He took a step back and narrowed his gaze, slowly and loudly repeating, "I'm with the police." He urged her away from the corner and gently turned her, taking out his utility knife to cut her out of her bindings. After he freed her feet, he turned back and asked, "You okay?"

She nodded several times as her shock gave way to full-body wrenching sobs as she blindly reached for him. Nick hauled her against his chest, letting her soak his tactical vest.

"Robbins?" someone called.

"Clear," he returned, trying not to yell too loudly.

"Sorry," the woman sobbed.

Nick nudged her face up so she could see him. "You have *nothing* to be sorry for. You fought the whole damn time, and in my book, that's something to be proud of." She nodded and he squeezed her hand as he explained. "They deployed tear gas, so when we open that door, it'll start to get in the room; if you can pull your shirt up to cover your mouth and close your eyes, we're gonna move quickly to get outside, okay?"

She pulled her shirt over her mouth. He turned to go in front of her, but took her free hand and attached it to his belt. "Hold on, we'll go slow."

He reattached his earpiece and called, "Robbins, coming out of the back room." As soon as he opened the door, he covered his mouth and closed his eyes, then used his unhurt hand and memory as a guide to quickly move through the utility room to the back door. Once outside, they opened their eyes and let their shirts down. But they'd been unable to avoid all the dissipating gas, and started coughing. Nick put his hand on her lower back and led her around the front of the house where an agent and EMT, upon seeing them, asked, "Camilla?"

The woman turned her attention to them in verification as the paramedic offered bottles of water. Nick soothed, "You're in good hands now."

The EMT began to gently assess her and asked, "Is your mouth bleeding?"

Camilla glanced at Nick, eyes wide. He gave her a reassuring smile. "Nah, that's my blood," he explained.

The EMT glanced at him. "Do you need help?"

"I'm fine. See to Camilla first." He gave her a smile once more and took several steps away so he could cough and gulp down the water in peace.

"What happened to in and out?" asked a familiar voice.

Nick glanced over at his partner and shrugged. "She didn't let me get a word in edgewise."

"Sounds like most of the women you meet." Stills laughed at his joke.

"Well, I couldn't let you put yourself in danger, your fiancé would kill me if something happened to you."

"She would."

"She scares me," Nick admitted.

"It's not her you should worry about. It's her mom." Stills looked toward Nick's hand that hung by his side, drops of blood pooling. "What happened?"

Nick finally inspected the damage; it was already turning purple and the bite marks were impressive. And it hurt like hell. "She didn't know I was the good guy."

"Let's get you checked out." He pointed toward the ambulance.

Two agents were hauling the abductor out, hands behind his back; he was coughing, and in between, swearing and spitting. No one answered him, simply unceremoniously sat him on the curb.

"No one was hurt?" Nick asked.

"All pomp and circumstance to make sure we took him alive," Stills offered.

At the back of the open ambulance, Nick held out his hand to be examined. "When was the last time you had a tetanus booster?" the paramedic asked.

"Not sure really."

"Then you know what I'm going to suggest." He took out antiseptic and gauze.

"Do you happen to have a shot on you?" Nick asked. A shake of the head was the answer as the antibacterial cleaner was poured onto his hand. Nick hissed and thought once again, *I need a vacation.*

Chapter Four

On a blustery Wednesday evening, Harper left JFK headed for Peru. While she was aware that her ticket had a few layovers resulting in a long seventeen-hour affair; she underestimated possible hurdles in her travel to the city known as the gateway to Machu Picchu.

Her flight to Lima was delayed in Houston, but she welcomed it, reasoning it would cut down on the three-hour layover she was going to have in Lima.

However, sleep on the overnight flight from Houston to Lima was thwarted by the lack of room, continual shifting, and the raucous symphony of snores on either side of her. Turns out a first-class ticket, exchanged for two economy tickets = cramped middle seat with disrespectful fellow travelers.

Harper arrived exhausted at six thirty in the morning, Lima, Peru time, though the fluorescent lights and excited voices helped perk her up and shake off the rough flight.

She shuffled through the steps of checking in for her next flight which consisted of a trip through customs, waiting for her bags at baggage claim then re-entering the airport. But after all that, she was much closer — only one more short plane ride from her destination.

And that's when she was educated on the ways of travel into the high-altitude city of Cusco. Flights into the city that rested among the highest mountain range in the southern hemisphere were often delayed due to unpredictable weather.

As the ticket agent explained to her, "Weather has formed."

"Okay," Harper answered and waited for more instruction. When it didn't come, she asked, "What should I do?"

"We wait for a break in the weather. Then we will board the flight and take off quickly."

Harper blinked several times in reply, not wanting to ask the ridiculous question: *Do you know when there will be a break in the weather?* But also, *really* wanting to ask the question.

The ticket agent added, "Listen for the flight to be announced." But when Harper didn't move and studied the paper ticket she'd been provided, the agent said, "If you don't want to wait, you can purchase a ticket for the bus to Cusco."

"How long does that take?"

"Twenty-one hours." She shrugged. "A car rental would cut the time down. That only takes eighteen hours."

"It looks like waiting for the weather to clear is the best bet," Harper said, but it was more of a question.

"Yes. You can purchase some food or shop. But make sure you listen for the flight number announcement."

Harper followed the signs to the departure gates, and called Renee. When there was no answer, she left a message, then texted: *Delayed due to weather. As soon as we're in the air, I'll let you know my new arrival time.*

As tired as she was, the Lima airport was a shock. Not the foreignness of it, but the Americanization of it. Bright glass-encased stores sold designer purses, clothing, scarves and perfumes. There were the traditional book-magazine-candy-souvenir stores. But the food court where she meandered was the biggest surprise; the neon logos of McDonald's, KFC, and Duncan Donuts all preened their infiltration. She steered clear of the chains and settled on a more Peruvian restaurant for a breakfast sandwich and coffee.

Sitting in the crowded food court, she watched the hurriedness of the early traveling crowds.

She tried Renee again, but still no answer. When Harper talked to her three days ago, she'd been elated about the adventure they were about to share. So she wasn't worried, but it wasn't like her to not answer. Renee was the kind of person who didn't want to miss anything. Excitable was one way to describe her, but it was more than that, she had a compassionate happiness that was contagious.

Harper spent the next six hours walking through the shops. She grabbed another coffee and contemplated the 5-hour Energy drinks that were offered as impulse buys at the checkout counters of the souvenir stores, but settled on water.

She went to the restroom and studied her appearance. She had on a pair of comfortable well-worn jeans and a white tee that now had stains she could blame on seatmates from the previous flight. But if she zipped up her black hoodie, it covered the bulk of them. Her face was blotchy with jet lag, her hair a limp brown staticky mess. She retrieved facial wipes and moisturizer from her bag along with a Shout Wipe to clean her shirt, then put her hair in a ponytail.

Finally, the announcement came; her flight was taking off. Passengers were abruptly shuffled onto the aircraft where safety instructions, time to Cusco (an hour and fifteen minutes), and the fact that there would be turbulence was relayed. Then they were swept into the wild blue yonder, the hum of the plane seducing Harper into a quick nap. She missed everything until she was jarred awake by the overanxious slam of the wheels meeting the runway in Cusco.

Through sleep-fogged eyes, she stared out at the sea of red tile roofs cuddled in a valley surrounded by glorious green mountains rising in the distance.

She mindlessly accomplished the customary arrival to-do list: shuffled off the plane, stumbled to baggage claim, hoisted her small roller bag off the belt, attached her backpack to the extended handle, then schlepped to the arrivals area as her tired smile widened in anticipation of seeing Renee again.

She scanned the crowd back and forth, excited for the first glimpse of her short, possibly skipping, blonde friend who would be eagerly waving.

But she never showed.

And Harper called.

A lot.

And texted.

Even more.

After an hour of waiting with no answer, she consolidated her frustration, assumed there was a good reason, and hauled her fatigued ass to the taxi stand. She showed the address of the hotel to the driver and fell back against the seat, squinting her eyes in the late afternoon sun that broke through the clouds as the streets of Cusco tried to make her feel better about the confusing, if not disappointing, start to her vacation.

Chapter Five

Renee Young was a confident, self-possessed woman and the epitome of an extrovert. She didn't just walk to the beat of her own drum, she marched to an extensively populated, high-octane drum corps.

Renee often wondered if she would be so ... well, *her*, had it not been for her great-grandmother. She was in eighth grade when her visiting ninety-pound, four foot eleven great-grandmother shook her head and sadly said to Renee, "You have such a pretty face, it's a shame you're fat."

Renee stood five six, wore a C cup and was trying to come to terms with her curves in a world where anorexic magazine models were being hoisted on young girls as something to aspire to. To this day, she wasn't sure what came over her – maybe it had been a perfect storm of stress; perhaps having heard enough adult 'when I was your age' stories, or the latest friend drama – but she made a decision about who she was going to be and how she was going to stand up for herself in this life. She straightened to her full height, looked down her nose at her great-grandmother and countered: "You're surrounded by a loving family, it's a shame you're too much of a bitch to realize it."

Great-grandmother gasped, her hand flying to her neck in the same instant Renee's mom grabbed her daughter by the arm declaring, "I don't think so," and marched Renee out of the room.

But when they were out of earshot, her mom tugged her into her arms and kissed her cheek. "That's my girl." Then she gave her a shove toward her room, but Renee waited in the hallway, a grin splitting her face when she heard her mom say, "Grandma, you will never disparage my daughter's beauty, or anyone else's for that matter, *ever* again. Renee is an amazing force. And you owe her an apology."

There was a headiness and liberation that came with standing up for herself. From that moment onward, Renee embraced her body in all its ever-changing wonder – the way her curves came and went with phases of life and sports she would play; but she also became an ardent cheerleader for all women.

At first, she advocated for her closest friends. When they'd put themselves down with the tired one-liners: 'I'm so fat.' 'I shouldn't have eaten that cake.' 'I was trying to be so good today.' Renee's standard retort for the food bullshit was: "Food isn't bad or good. It's energy. What the diet industries have done to us is bad."

But when it was a personal insult along the lines of 'I'm so stupid,' Renee would delight in leaning close and demanding: 'Don't you *dare* talk about my friend that way.'

She began to pour over magazines and books that explained how to dress every body type for best effects; so she and her friends could feel comfortable *and* fashionable. She took several fashion design classes in college, but then moved to cosmetology school. Even then, she was finding more courses to take, actively seeking out the latest techniques and trends.

Then she took business classes and it was no surprise to anyone when she started her own business.

The idea was to use all her knowledge to empower women. She did hair and taught women how to do their makeup. She helped some create wardrobes they loved. And after a client came to her and asked to be taught how to walk and look sexy as a bigger-bodied woman, she started holding seminars on such topics. And her client list grew exponentially. She took on employees, but was very particular about who she hired; she wanted like-minded people who wanted to build up one another and each client.

With her success, and proximity to Los Angeles, she was hired to help on photo shoots. It was a good way to network, but as she was often pressed for time, she had to be selective in the jobs she took. And she would be forever grateful for a job she took three years ago as a stylist for a shoot at The Getty Art Museum. That was when she met Gael Torres.

Gael was an unassuming, down-to-earth photographer, never cocky or condescending. A true artist whose work held a magnifying glass up to humanity – at least, that's what *National Geographic* said about him.

Vanity Fair, Elle, and *Allure* laid their own accolades at his feet. But Gael never wore those around, he was easygoing and often said he was simply a guy who loved to take pictures.

The publicist for that shoot continued to halt the process due to rights that had to be obtained regarding the artwork visible in the background of shots. So with nothing but time, Renee waited on a bench taking in the panoramic view of Los Angeles, where she was joined by Gael who struck up a conversation.

When the long day wrapped, he asked her if she wanted to go to his favorite taco truck. They sat at one of the picnic tables beside the twenty-four-hour food truck and talked late into the night. When he found out about her business, he suggested adding body-positive photo shoots for her clients. Then offered his services. Their friendship continued to bloom and grow from that day forward.

It was New Year's Day when Gael called and asked, "Wanna go see my homeland?"

"Peru?"

"Yes."

"Sure. When are we going?"

He laughed and explained that a friend, who had gained notoriety with his sustainable clothing line, had asked him to take the photos for an editorial in a fashion magazine. "We've been working on this for a while," Gael explained, "but there were a lot of ducks to get in a row. I'm taking a small team, there will only be five of us. And everyone will have to pitch in and work in different areas. But you'll get to see a lot of southern Peru and it's all paid for."

Renee did what she normally did when opportunity knocked. She grinned at her big, glorious life, thanked the universe for all the adventure and opportunities and excitedly declared, "I'm in!"

"You'll have to do hair, makeup, probably some set designing, and help with clothing choices and packing things around."

"Gael, I'm in," she insisted.

"It will be a joint shoot for *National Geographic* and *Vogue.*"

"Why are you still trying to sell me on this?" She laughed.

His excitement over the phone was palpable. "We'd leave the first week of February. For three weeks."

"Okay."

"Okay?"
"Oh my god, Gael, yes! Let's go to Peru!"

Chapter Six

Bleary-eyed, Harper let her attention volley between her phone and the streets of Cusco. She obsessively checked to make sure the notification sounds and ringer were on high; then turned her attention to the swags of telephone and power lines held up by posts, racing beside the car. At intersections the lines were gathered together in ratty bundles, and between the posts were dark green, double-headed Victorian street lights. She had a feeling that at night, the light gave the illusion of stepping back in time.

The main street the driver followed had newer buildings painted with splashes of color: sky blue, earth red, butter yellow and natural brick. Many first floors of the buildings along the street had shops, while the second, third and fourth floors were apartments. There was the occasional graffiti, the kind that plagued most cities, but not an overabundance. And there was no trash. She realized this after a few miles, since she was so often aware of the trash build-up in her city; she wondered if she could get in touch with the officials here and see if they could email a few tips to the folks in her hometown. "Not even a wrapper in sight," she whispered.

When they entered older parts of the city, buildings began cuddling intimately closer to each other as streets narrowed. New buildings stood proudly next to older construction. Long stretches of brick walls were covered with artwork, creating vibrant murals.

The only time her driver spoke was to point out the stadium that butted up to the street. "Cusco Fútbol."

Harper gave an obligatory interested nod as they passed.

Soon, tour buses multiplied around them. When they drove through an arch, there was another change of architecture, an obvious sign they'd entered the historic city center.

They passed manicured plazas with benches, trees and simple fountains. The colors of Cusco, especially this part of the city, seemed to reflect the surrounding mountains. The asphalt roads became cobblestone; the terracotta rooftops happily topped white and beige buildings; while balconies and window coverings differentiated the structures from each other – some were black wrought iron, some light wood designs, and some primary blue.

Finally, the driver stopped in the middle of the street, next to a two-story white plaster building, the bottom half of which had been decorated with gray rock. He gave a declaration of "okay," and pointed to the cost of the ride on the display.

Harper used the last of the money she'd exchanged in Lima, collected her bags, and pushed her way through the half glass, half wooden door. Tumbling into the reception area, she was politely greeted by a young woman in a yellow cotton dress with long, silky hair swept over one shoulder, and bright eyes (*she'd* probably had some decent sleep recently). Smiling from behind the reception desk, she said, "Buenas tardes. Are you Harper Barrett?"

Harper gave an exhausted, grateful nod. She couldn't think clearly as it was, and having unearthed her high school Spanish a few days prior to the trip, she wasn't feeling very confident about using it yet.

"Yes. Buenas tardes, I'm Harper. My friend, Renee Young, was supposed to meet me but I can't get a hold of her. She was staying here with other people and I thought maybe she was still working? Maybe things had gone longer than expected?"

The receptionist gave an exuberant bob of her head. "Yes! It was very exciting. They used some areas of the hotel for their photos." Her voice had a soft lilt, her accent soothing. "I have a note for you." She began rummaging through papers on the desk.

That was good, a note for her and someone who was expecting her went a long way to ease the agitation and exhaustion that already hung on her shoulders like a wet, weighted blanket.

"Here it is!" She held up a notepad, then nodded to herself and cleared her throat to read aloud, "Miss Young is fine. She has requested that when Miss Barrett arrives, she is directed immediately to the police station to release Miss Young from jail." The woman reread the note, gave another nod and aimed a grin at Harper, having relayed the message so efficiently.

Harper blinked, her exhaustion might be affecting her more than she imagined. "I'm sorry, maybe I don't understand. My friend, Renee Young, has been arrested?"

"That is what she said when she called last night."

"Last night?" There's no way Harper was comprehending any of this correctly.

"Sì, Miss Young called last night, before I left to go home. She gave me this message. She asked me to write it then read it back to her before she ended the call."

Was being arrested something that happened all the time to the guests? Because this young woman seemed to be taking this a lot better than Harper.

"Renee Young," Harper began, "my friend, who is staying here with the people who did the photo shoot, was arrested last night and is in jail." It was a statement she needed to hear herself say as much as she needed to make sure she and the hotel receptionist were on the same page.

"Sì. It is a simple walk to the police station."

They stared at each other for several long moments. The young woman kept a smile in place, but Harper felt her frown indenting lines all over her forehead. Finally, Harper shook herself then pulled a Cusco guidebook from her pack and opened it to the foldout map of the city. "Where am I? What does a simple walk look like?"

The receptionist circled the hotel and police station, then drew a line within the boundaries of the streets that would lead Harper to her final destination. "See? Only four blocks away."

Could this be happening? Harper squeezed her eyes shut. After blinking them open again, she repeated the receptionist's words, "Renee Young; a bubbly blonde American woman, about three inches shorter than me, who was here working on the photo shoot; wants me, Harper Barrett, to go to the police station and get her out of jail?"

"Sì," the woman retrieved a key and set it on top of the open map, "but first maybe you want to put your things in the room?" She gave directions to the room, but Harper wasn't listening. She accepted the key, holding the book open with the map flapping down by her side, and frowned as she walked away, pulling her suitcase behind her. But when she made it to where the elevator and two hallways intersected, she turned, took several steps back and once more questioned, "Police station?"

"Police station. A la comisaría de policía."

Harper worried her bottom lip then her head shot up and she gasped, "Is there anyone else still here from the photo group?"

"No. Everyone has left."

"Oh." Harper glanced between the receptionist, who was now typing on the computer, and the hallway. Maybe she was dreaming. She was still asleep on the plane and hadn't arrived in Cusco yet.

She pinched her arm, frowning when it hurt. The woman in front of her did flicker slightly, but that might be the fatigue.

The receptionist looked up from her screen. "Is there anything else?" she asked Harper's frozen form.

"Where's the room?" Harper narrowed her gaze and really tried to focus as the directions were repeated. Then, as quickly as she could, followed them before they slipped from her disoriented mind.

She gave herself a congratulatory nod when the key worked. The room was quaint – a small living area, table, stove, sink and three doors leading to the bathroom and two bedrooms — but Harper didn't have time to be charmed.

She needed to look for clues.

She rolled her eyes, was she really doing this?

Yes! Now look for clues.

She dropped her things and walked through the rooms. Renee's room had clothes strung around and a novel by the bedside. Harper thumbed through to see if there were any hidden loose papers or secret messages. None. She found Renee's laptop, opened it but didn't know the password. On the coffee table was a piece of paper with Harper's flight numbers and times, but that was it.

With nothing else blatantly obvious jumping out at her, Harper really only had one option. To walk the short distance to the comisaría de policía to see if Renee was actually being held. She went back through Renee's room, looking for some sort of identification and found her passport in a purse in the closet. Harper chided, "Renee, you're not supposed to keep these things out in the open," but was secretly glad she had.

Back in the main room Harper picked up her backpack and put it on the table. She took out the heavier items; books and magazines she'd meant to read on the plane, and her camera. She grabbed a granola bar before adding Renee's passport, hotel key and a bottle of water from the fridge.

Putting the pack back on, armed with her guidebook map and granola bar, she headed into the streets of Cusco; trailed by wishes of 'good luck' from the receptionist, and regret that she hadn't purchased one or two of the 5-hour Energy drinks at the airport in Lima.

Chapter Seven

Renee bit her lower lip, tapped her foot manically and wavered between pacing, sitting and picking at her nail polish; or screaming at the top of her lungs for someone to help her.

When the officer who locked her up last night appeared in the corridor that led to the three temporary holding cells, she stopped her frustrated fidgeting and eyed him. When he didn't move, she crossed the distance between them, grabbed the bars and opened her mouth to start in on her demands again.

The officer immediately snarled, "You are to be let go. *If* you are quiet. I will release you to your friend who has arrived. But this friend will be responsible for you. If you begin to yell again, I will put *her* in this jail with you."

Harper. Thank god!

Renee's sigh of relief weakened her knees. She held up her hands in compliance. When he had the key fitted in the lock, she applied the calmest voice she could muster and asked, "But what about my other friend?"

He stopped abruptly and shot her a deadly warning look.

"I apologize." She ran her hands through her short hair, pushing the greasy champagne blonde mess out of her face.

He unlocked the cell and waved her out. She mentally ran through a list of things that needed to be done; since no one here seemed willing to listen to her, much less help her; she'd do it all herself.

After a short walk, they arrived back in the main lobby where Harper was signing paperwork. Renee gave a silent questioning look to the officer who was leading her, *could she go to her friend?* He nodded and waved her away like a pest.

"Harper!" Renee called and was across the room throwing herself into her friend's arms.

"Renee! What the hell is going on?" After a rough hug, she untangled Renee from her and held her at arm's length. "What the ..." she glanced around and lowered her voice, "... what the fuck! Have you been in a fight?" Renee understood how she looked; hair disheveled and a nasty cut on her cheek. Her jeans had patches of dried mud, and the lower right side of her black, button-down shirt had been ripped off.

"You look exhausted," Renee countered.

Harper frowned. "I am exhausted. Renee, what is going on?!" She quietly stressed the question.

Their attention was called by a clerk who slid a plastic bag with Renee's cell phone, a pack of gum, a few coins and a piece of paper with hectic writing at every angle covering it. "Sign your name," the clerk instructed.

"Did you have to pay bail?" Renee asked as she signed.

"There wasn't any bail. But they did say I'm responsible for you and if you disturb the peace again, *I'm* going to jail."

Renee snatched the bag in one hand, grabbed Harper's wrist with the other and tugged. "C'mon. We have to go."

Harper tripped behind her. "Go where? Renee, *what* is going on?"

But Renee didn't say anything, just kept walking until they were a block from the station where she aimed a wildly fearful look at Harper. "Harper, Gael's been kidnapped."

"What?!"

"He's been kidnapped and no one will listen to me or even believe me."

"How do you know?"

"He called me yesterday. He said two guys jumped him and put him in a trunk. He shared his location and I didn't think about anything. I took a taxi to some bar south of here. I banged on all the trunks I could find and listened for anyone who might be yelling inside of one of them, but nothing. And then ..." she licked her lips and held up her hands in defense, "I was *freaking* out. I didn't know what to do and Gael wasn't there. So I went into the bar and demanded the bartender, or anyone really, to tell me what they knew. Some chick got the wrong idea and punched me and the bartender threw me out then the cops were there.

And by the time they got me to the station and let me explain my side of the story, my phone was dead and they wouldn't plug it in, so I couldn't prove anything and they said I was drunk because they smelled alcohol on me, but that was from the fight … So they said I was going to have to wait in jail until I could get someone to bail me out."

"I have to be dreaming." Harper rubbed her eyes and muttered, "C'mon, focus." She shook her head. "Okay, why would Gael be kidnapped?"

"I don't know!" Renee's eyes bugged slightly as she threw her hands up, her whole body shaking with the declaration. "I'm sorry Harper, I … I don't know." She tried to take a calming breath, but could only manage a shaky one. "I don't know what's going on and I told the cops it was their job to figure this kind of shit out, but they told me I was mistaken and that's when I had the thought that maybe the cops were in on it too."

※ ※ ※ ※ ※

"In on what?" Harper's face scrunched with the confusion that was beginning to build an impressive headache around the circumference of her skull.

"I. Don't. KNOW!" Renee yelled, her bright blue eyes glassy with unshed tears.

"Okay." Harper took her friend's hands in hers. "Okay. We're gonna try to settle down a little. Let's … breathe." She demonstrated how, nodding when Renee mirrored her. After several breaths the manic look on Renee's face softened. But Harper's lightheadedness intensified.

Renee nodded and tried to let go, but Harper tightened her grip.

"You okay?" Renee asked.

"I'm a bit dizzy and unsteady."

Renee linked her arm with Harper's to stabilize her. "It's the altitude," she explained, urging her to begin walking. "I really don't know if the cops are in on it, it just feels like if they're not going to help me, then they're against me. They came to the cell this morning and said they looked into Gael and found that his bags had been checked at the airport in Cusco to go to LAX."

"But they weren't?"

"No. I mean yes. Gael checked his bags, but he left the airport to spend two more days with me. I tried to explain that and that they needed to check his passport, not a luggage tag, but I kinda screamed every time I opened my mouth so they said I was an unreliable source who couldn't be believed." She stopped and leveled a gaze at Harper. "But you believe me, right?" Renee's rising agitation was palpable.

"I believe you." Harper nodded, even though everything around her was feeling otherworldly, she still needed to have her friend's back. So she insisted, "*Of course* I believe you." Only, the world began to roll then, tilting her body sideways.

"Oh shit." Renee steadied her.

"Renee, I don't know what to do here. You don't look that great, I'm beyond exhausted. I want to help, but my vision keeps fogging over and I'm having trouble keeping track of my thoughts."

Renee slid her arm around Harper's waist to keep her upright and encouraged her to begin taking short, shuffled steps.

"I have some ideas, since the police won't help." She lowered her voice conspiratorially. "Last night, a woman in the cell next to me told me there is this bar—"

"Another bar?" Harper questioned.

Renee nodded. "This one is in a small town south of Cusco, one of the San somethings. The woman said it's easy to spot, has an Incan warrior painted across the front of it. She said I can find someone to help me there."

"Find *someone*?"

"A mercenary."

Harper pursed her lips and shook her head in adamant disapproval. (And to try and wake herself up.) This *had* to be a fever dream. Had someone put something in her drink on the plane? Because she'd come to Peru to buy woven things made from alpaca, hike Machu Picchu and listen to some flute music. Going to a bar to find a mercenary was definitely *not* on her to-do list.

"Renee, we can't ..."

"Yes, we can. You can nap on the way." Renee held up her hand as a taxi passed. When it slowed, Harper grabbed Renee's hand and lowered it.

"Wait a minute. Just wait a minute!" Harper waved the car away and forced a calm plan to the forefront of her mind. "Here's what we're going to do." She gave a soft shake of her head, trying to focus so she could come up with something that put hiring a mercenary on a back burner. "Okay. We're going to the hotel. *You* are going to take a shower. You said your phone is dead?"

Renee nodded.

"So you don't know if Gael tried to contact you again." Harper raised her eyebrows and congratulated herself on what sounded like, well ... top-notch reasoning. "Let's get as much information as we can before we go off half-cocked into the jungles of Peru."

"We're not going into the jungles, we're going to a bar," Renee defended.

"Fine. But first, you do some phone recon and maybe look at a map or a street view of the San-something town *after* you take a shower and let me try to sleep for at least thirty minutes." *Maybe an hour.* She waited with questioning eyes to see if Renee would accept the current deal on the table, but once again the world began to shift and she slipped against it.

"Shit." Renee straightened her again. "Okay. You're right. I don't even know why he'd be taken in the first place." They began to walk again and Renee repeated the plan. "You sleep. I'll shower, charge my phone and start calling the people we worked with the past few weeks to see if I can find anything out."

"There you go. That's what we'll do." The last word became a loud, wide-mouthed yawn.

Once in the room, Harper shuffled to the queen size bed muttering, "I know this is time-sensitive, but I'm no help if I can't focus." She fell onto the bed, hugged the extra pillow in her arms and thankfully closed her eyes.

Her brain had one more lucid thought: *If Gael really was kidnapped, wouldn't someone call with a ransom demand?* God, she hoped she could remember to bring that up to Renee when she woke up.

Chapter Eight

Harper was right. They needed information.

Renee fumbled for her charger, hands shaking as she plugged in her phone. She picked out a sports bra, a pair of dark gray hiking pants and white tank top then planned to break world records for showering. She stepped in while the water was still cold; but surprisingly, the shock to her system was exactly what she needed to calm down.

After hissing through the cold, once the water heated, she closed her eyes and took as many slow, deep breaths as she could before whispering to the spray of the water, "I'm not making this up."

Gael had called forty-five minutes after he left her; she thought he was calling to tell her he arrived at the airport. Instead, his voice was a whispered panic as he reported: "Renee, on the way to the airport two men rear-ended the taxi I was in and forced me into the trunk of their car at gunpoint. I don't know who they are or where they're taking me."

Time stopped with his frightened words. Renee had blindly looked around her as everything warped and twisted, what was he saying? How was she going to save him? How was she going to find him? The frantic thought led her to demand, "Share your location."

She heard the rustle before he was back on. "Done. But I only have thirty-seven percent battery left. I don't know how long it'll last. I don't know if they'll take my phone and I don't know—"

His phone was cut off. It took Renee several attempts to text: *I'm on my way.*

Looking to make sure he'd dropped a pin on his location, she quickly slipped on her shoes and grabbed her wallet, phone and room key; then took off at a dead run out of the hotel, down the amber lit streets of the evening, to where she knew she could find a taxi.

She insisted on sitting in the passenger seat of the cab so she could follow her GPS; it made her feel more in control, an attribute that was slipping. As they drove toward Gaels' last known location, she forced her attention to stay on the road and not the fact that *her* phone was now running on a very low battery.

She'd been manic by the time the driver pulled into the parking lot beside the bar. She banged on each trunk, her heart in her throat as she waited for an answer. When none came, she went into the bar and pounded on the worn, wooden counter to get the bartender's undivided attention. She showed a selfie she'd taken of her and Gael, asking, "Have you seen this man? Were there two men in here recently that looked like they could be kidnappers?"

"No inglés," the bartender scowled before walking away.

She opened the translator she'd been using throughout the trip and typed what she wanted to ask. Continually having to restart and delete because she was having difficulty focusing. Once she had the question translated, she walked the length of the sticky bar and slapped it again. "Señor." She faced the phone toward him, but her attitude had not created the best first impression. He wasn't about to focus long enough to read it.

So, she began going from patron to patron.

Everyone turned from her; one woman, drunk and thinking Renee was trying to hit on her 'man,' swung a ring clad hand and caught Renee's cheek with enough force to send her reeling several steps backwards.

Renee pocketed her phone, clenched her fists and was crossing the distance to finish the fight, when the bartender was suddenly behind her. Pinning her arms by her side, he lifted her slightly as he unceremoniously hauled her outside.

"No, wait! Please! I just need someone to answer my questions."

She was tossed into the muddy parking lot, falling to her hands and knees right as a cop car arrived. She tried to explain the situation, but when it seemed no one was listening, and because all she could think was that time was of the essence, she grew agitated in her demands.

And the language barrier expanded.

So off to jail it was. Cuffed and put in the back seat of the car; by the time she reached the station and was offered her one call, the only thought she had was to leave a message for Harper at the hotel.

As the warm shower washed the previous day from her skin, she tried a few more breathing techniques. When the tears came, she nodded that it was a good sign. Maybe it was good to rid her body of all the overwhelming emotions. Maybe it would help her focus more completely on helping Gael. But in order to do that, she needed to find some semblance of calm and control. She slid down the shower wall, pulled her knees up under her chin and let the tears fall. She would cry everything out. Let it rinse down the drain. Then, she'd start at the beginning.

She'd make a list of every interaction they'd had since they arrived in Peru, write down every place they'd gone. Maybe there were answers there, someone or something that explained why Gael would have been taken. When her list was made, her phone would be charged and Harper would have had some sleep.

Another well of angry, frustrated tears burned in her throat, but she wouldn't hold any of it back right now. She'd let it all tumble out.

Chapter Nine

"You're gorgeous!" Gael had to yell the compliment, as he was several feet from where Renee was backed up against the crystal clear water, falling into a pool several feet behind her.

She struck an exaggerated 'model' pose, then waited for him to take a few pictures, before calling back, "Is it the sweat-matted hair? Or my red face from exertion?"

The first five days of the trip had been scheduled for exploration, and the final scouting of locations that needed to be decided on. But altitude sickness had wiped out the other three members of the bare-bones crew.

In doing her own research before they left the states, Renee found her doctor could prescribe an aid in combating the altitude and she began to increase her water intake weeks ahead of time. The second they entered the hotel and were offered coca tea for the altitude sickness, she accepted that as well. Sure, she was exhausted and out of breath simply walking (even taking a shower was a bit of a workout), but the steps she'd taken kept her from succumbing to the exaggerated altitude of the ancient Incan city.

That's why the first few days of excursions were only attended by Gael, Renee and Victor Campos – the man whose clothing line had brought them to Peru in the first place.

Victor picked Gael and Renee up early on their first full day in Cusco, driving the trio an hour north to the city of Chinchero.

Victor was a few inches shorter than Gael, probably five ten. His eyes were light brown, and he had an infectious smile. Renee liked him instantly. The clothing he wore, she assumed, was part of his own design. A button-down shirt, beige with dark sienna stripes, complimented his skin tone and frame. His dark green pants had a slight wide leg and looked comfortable and warm.

"I love your clothing line," she shared honestly.

"Thank you. I'm very excited about this opportunity. I can't believe the time is finally here."

Gale clapped his friend on the back. This was more than a little photo shoot, she thought.

Victor had garnered a lot of attention for his clothing line and when he was approached by *Vogue*, he agreed to the editorial *only* if they would allow Gael Torres to take the photographs. The magazine readily agreed.

"Gael told me you were working on a few new designs for the shoot," she said.

"I shouldn't have, but when we were deciding on where to go for the photos, I was inspired." He shrugged.

She knew Victor had grown up around designers and creators. His family had been textile workers for generations. While he championed the traditional use of alpaca wool, when he began to branch out into clothing design, he wanted to infuse tradition with sustainability. So he used alpaca fibers, recycled fabrics and cotton; creating a comfortably soft material.

"I brought the catalogue, if you'd like to look at it," he offered, then urged them into the car.

Renee rejected the front seat, she'd let Gael and Victor catch up. As it was, she was stunned into silence. She was intoxicated as the car swayed up the road, and the mountain ranges played chameleon games, constantly changing shape and pitch. The rainy season had painted the tops of the vast ranges a rainbow of green shades. Every corner they turned seemed to hold a vista that she was tempted to declare, 'That would be a good place to shoot too!'

She mindlessly turned her attention between the pages of his catalogue and the scenery. During the planning stages, she had presented her carefully planned concepts to Gael and Victor in one of their many online meetings. But now that she was being ushered through the backdrops of Victor's homeland, those ideas seemed to be completely tangible.

Gael shared what he expected of his team; his vision, Victor's clothing inspiration, and the challenges they would face in the various planning meetings. He had shared pictures of the landscapes they would see, and while it excited everyone, Renee secretly worried she had built up her expectations. Now that she was close enough to see, and smell and hear it – she'd argue her expectations hadn't been substantial enough.

"Victor, I've only been in Peru for less than twenty-four hours, and I can already see the landscape reflected in your designs," she complimented.

"Thank you. That means a lot. I hope people see that. I wanted my designs to be a reflection of my country."

She ran her fingers across the glossy pages of his catalogue as he explained, "I used the earth tones of the surrounding mountains, and I wanted to use some of those jagged shapes in the lines of some of the shirts and pants. You see the sweaters that have knotted fringe?"

She turned to the page where one of those sweaters was on display.

"I wanted that to represent the Inca quipu writing system."

"The greens you use, are those the jungle shades or the green of the mountains I'm seeing?"

"All of it." The grin softening his face was reflected in the rearview mirror. "The deep orange-reds represent the terracotta roofs, and the pinks remind me of the summer sunsets of my childhood."

"I love that," Renee sighed. With the catalogue open on her lap, she shifted her attention out the window and allowed the conversational Spanish of two old friends wash over her.

The moment, the landscape, even the car was overflowing with magic and it was just the beginning.

Renee sat forward in her seat when they arrived in Chinchero, stopping at a stable where three horses, already saddled, were waiting for them.

"Surprise!" Gael grinned at Renee. "I'm sad the others are missing this, but we'll have other adventures with them." They climbed out of the car and Gael continued, "Victor's family has horses and a hacienda nearby."

"So we're ready to go?" Renee asked excitedly.

Victor said, "We have everything we might need in the saddlebags along with food and water and rain jackets."

Gael brought one camera, then as he closed the door, asked Renee,

"Have you ever ridden a horse before?"

She did a slight skip as she headed toward the horses, then slowed and approached calmly. "A long time ago." She began to coo as she got closer to the first caramel colored horse. "I went to summer camp several years in a row and learned to ride there."

Victor checked the horses and when he was satisfied, the trio climbed atop and headed out.

The skies were full of flawless white clouds, swimming across vibrant blue. In the afternoon, they would gather on top of each other and pour out their souls. But for now, it was bright skies and nonthreatening white cotton.

The weather was one of the challenges Gael had brought up early on in the meetings with the team. He'd intentionally chosen February because the temperatures would be mild – highs of seventies, lows in the forties. And because it was considered the rainy season, there would be an abundance of greenery. Also the ever-changing weather would allow for more dramatic lighting effects. Everyone was aware that plans on this shoot could pivot within a moment's notice.

They clopped along a dirt trail with high walls on either side, leading to sectioned-off yards and homes. Some walls were topped with threatening bunches of prickly pear cacti sprouting yellow buds. Others held stretches of bright green moss.

"This is unbelievable!" Renee grinned back at Gael, then said to Victor's back in front of her, "I think I'm going to get tired of exclaiming that."

People they passed greeted them with 'buenos días' or an offered wave of 'hola.' Wild dogs came and went beside them. Some gave a half-hearted growl at interrupted naps, while others kept up pace with the horses for a while until the call of their independent lifestyle beckoned them onto a different path.

Reaching the edge of town, they rode into a canyon, climbing a careful trail up into the mountains. On their left a creek ran parallel, covered with shrubs and trees. On their right, terraces and ruins rose. And even that view looked picture-perfect to Renee.

"It's so green. And stunning. And *gorgeous*." She couldn't decide which adjective to use. None of them seemed good enough. She turned in her saddle, again looking back at Gael. "Is it called Sacred Valley because of the greenery?"

"Actually, no." He grinned and urged his horse next to hers. "The Inca worshiped the sun and the moon and the stars. And the river in this valley, the Urubamba River, aligns with the Milky Way, which makes it a sacred place."

She glanced up as if she could see the constellations.

"The valley was also considered the heart of the Inca Empire."

"But you're from northern Peru, right?"

"Yes, the city of Trujillo."

"Will you see any family while you're here?"

"Not this trip. I'll come back later in the year."

"It's a big country," she said in wonder, then winked at Gael as she repeated information he'd already given the team. "Did you know, you can fit the entire state of California inside Peru, and still have enough room to drive all the way around the far outskirts of the state?"

"Thank you again," he said, smiling. "For agreeing to be part of this."

She threw out her arms as if she could hold all of Peru in them. "Opportunity of a lifetime! I have no idea how you narrowed down where you want to shoot. We could go right up there to those green terraces and ruins. Or on the street where our hotel is. Or at the restaurant we ate at last night ..."

"If you think those are impressive, get ready to have your socks knocked off."

She was more than ready.

The climb grew steadily steeper, keeping up with the rising wall of the mountains around them and forcing them back into a single file lineup. Victor, Renee then Gael.

"Are we on the Inca road now?" Renee asked.

"Yes," answered Victor this time.

"I thought they were closed in February?"

Victor turned his head so she could hear him as he answered, "Some of them are. The long trails, the most traveled hiking trails, like the one to Machu Picchu, those are closed during the rainy season. They are very dangerous to travel. Many of them have sheer drop-offs, are very slippery, and rock slides are common because the rain loosens the rocks."

"But going to Machu Picchu by train and bus is still fine, right?"

"Yes, that's how we'll get there." Victor waved to the path they were on. "This trail is short and faces more sun; it dries out faster and is well-maintained."

She turned and glanced back at Gael. "Have you been here before?"

"No," he wiggled his eyebrows, "but I've seen a picture of it."

"You moved to the states when you were twelve, right?" Renee verified.

The path widened, Gael rode back to her side and confirmed, "Mom was a cultural attaché to the Peruvian consulate in LA."

"That must have been something, to be a part of sharing your culture."

"Renee," he tilted his head, "think about when you were twelve. No kid cares about their culture then. I was the same; I just wanted to watch movies, crush on girls and ride my bike."

"Eat Doritos, try to get rid of my acne and scream-sing songs with my best friends." She chuckled as she listed her childhood angst.

"Exactly." He let his youth float past him. "I have to admit, though, my mom's job set me on my career path. Being around her constant production of art and watching the way she and Dad supported artists – not to mention all the art shows and festivals she curated to bring awareness to Peruvian culture – I was destined for the arts."

She knew that after his mother's time working for the consulate ended, his family permanently moved to California. "Did you come back to Peru a lot?"

"Once a year, actually. There's still family in Trujillo. Aunts, uncles and cousins."

"I know you've taken photos of Peru before and had shows in LA. But have you ever done anything like this?"

His face lit up and it took him a moment before he could speak. "This is the first time I've been hired for an assignment in Peru."

Renee turned and shot him an animated grin. "That is so damn cool."

"*So* damn cool," he agreed.

Wild green brush grew on either side of the raised, red dirt trail built by the ancients. Spindly trees stretched toward the sky. Birds sang old songs and the trickle of the stream rose and fell with the twists of the trail and the blush of the wind.

When the horses rounded a corner, Renee was surprised by the sudden steep downward grade of the trail. Where there was once the comfort of a mountian wall on the right, there was now an abrupt drop-off that tightened her core muscles when she glanced down. But all was forgotten as she focused on the stunning view ahead of them ... "Gorgeous," she repeated, not willing to look for another adjective; taking in the way the mountains continued their ever-moving angles and sought distant clouds.

From his horse, Gael took photos. Renee maneuvered her gentle giant so she could fit all three of them, and the view, into a selfie.

A short time later, the trail once again narrowed and began to zigzag in switchbacks downward. When they arrived at a large clearing, Victor guided them to the side, instructed everyone to dismount and tied the horses to a nearby post. He gestured to the trail. "You have to walk the rest of the way, my friends."

"C'mon," Gael encouraged Renee, "it's worth it."

She was certain every step she took over the next three weeks was going to be 'worth it.' They crept along a dirt path that dove into the jungle ravine. Out of breath, Renee laughed. "I don't remember being asked to be in shape to hike and climb in the paperwork you provided."

"You didn't read the fine print," Gael offered.

When they rounded a corner, she heard the rush of water and caught the first glimpse of the falls. Carefully, but quickly, she hop-skipped to the water's edge.

Reaching the pool created by the falling water, she tilted her head back as far as she could, looking past the jagged black rocks of the cliff, to pinpoint the exact place the water started.

The giant curtain had spent years washing the rockface; painting it with striations of rust, and green and teal algae, all while building up a mossy outer frame.

"Gael!" she exclaimed, holding her hands out to her side as the mist played in the natural light, streaming through the drops, illuminating everything. When she aimed her excited smile in his direction she wasn't surprised to find him taking photos, so she posed.

After she felt he had plenty of shots, she joined him and stood shoulder to shoulder. "You have to do something here."

"Honestly, it would be difficult to get all the equipment down here."

"This isn't one of the places you're going to shoot?" she asked incredulously.

"It was supposed to be a little adventure for everyone." His voice lowered slightly. "Today,the detour was only for us."

A slight eruption of butterflies liked the idea that this was just for the two of them. She let her head fall back as her gaze traced the waterfall. "Gorgeous."

Chapter Ten

Harper woke with a full-bodied jolt.

She blinked as the room came into focus, frowning at the surroundings when everything snapped into place and jerked her to a seated position.

Only the second her head was upright, a throb retracted like a rock in a slingshot, then let loose and slammed throughout her temple.

She moaned in protest, pressed her palms against her temples, then stood and somehow shuffled into the shared living area of the hotel suite.

She was glad to see Renee hunched over a computer at the small table because she really did half expect to find a scribbled note declaring her friend had gone to get help. It might have been the theme of a fitful dream.

"Advil. Alltheadvil," Harper muttered, carefully spilling herself into a chair. "Then I can help." She propped her elbows on the table to continue pressing her hands into her head, which seemed to bring a modicum of relief. "How long did I sleep?"

"An hour and a half."

Harper wasn't sure what was worse, her initial exhaustion or the party the heavy metal mob was having inside her skull.

Renee shuffled together a handful of papers she had strewn about the table before going to put a kettle on the burner at the kitchenette. "You also need as much water as you can stand. And after that, more water. You also need to drink this tea." She handed the requested pills and a water bottle to Harper. "It's the altitude. And we need you to get over it fast."

Talk about an understatement.

Renee fumbled through her makeup bag and pulled out a prescription bottle of medicine. "I didn't tell you to see a doctor to get a prescription for altitude sickness pills because I already had them. And this trip was supposed to start a little differently."

What do you call back-to-back understatements?

Harper took everything Renee gave her while silently gauging her mood. It seemed like a large portion of the hysterical edge had faded; though her eyes were red and swollen.

Renee pointed to her open computer. "I retraced our steps, made an itinerary from the past few weeks – where we went and who we met with. I emailed Gael's assistant to see if she'd already done something similar, but I forgot she was at her sister's wedding in the mountains, somewhere with spotty reception. I'm sure she'll send it as soon as she can, but I can't wait for her." She chewed her lip for a minute then admitted, "I didn't tell her Gael's been kidnapped. I didn't want to worry her. Yet."

"Good work." Harper meant it, but putting any real emotion into her voice right now hurt her head.

Renee added, "I saved it so I can get to it from my phone too."

"What's your password?" Harper asked. Renee frowned for a second so Harper explained, "To get into your computer." She left out the 'just in case' reason that prompted her to ask the question.

"Oh ... it's my last name, backwards. And actually," she turned the screen so Harper could see, "this is the document I'm working on and this file has a whole bunch of raw pictures Gael took as well as all the pics I took."

Harper blinked, because nodding hurt too much. When the kettle began to whistle, Renee unceremoniously prepared the tea and slipped it in front of Harper explaining, "It's kinda like green tea."

"Is this the coca Tea?"

"Yeah. Everyone gets all crazy about it because it comes from the same plant as cocaine, but that's refined and the tea is the same stimulant as drinking a cup of coffee." Harper's head was so bad, she was happy to follow the years of local wisdom. Renee continued, "Some people say it doesn't work, some say it does. It worked for me and like I said, I need you acclimated right now, so we're gonna try every trick we've got."

"Then I need my backpack. I also have headache pills." She stood but Renee waved her away. "I'll get it."

"Is there a piece of bread, or something to eat?"

Renee handed over the backpack, a box of crackers, some cheese and a half-eaten empanada. After a couple of crackers, Harper attempted to drown herself in liquids, hoping it would stop the massive ache.

"Harper," Renee sat down with the weight of the world on her shoulders, "I'm worried and scared to death. But I've been thinking, Gael *must* have been taken for a reason. And maybe that means there'll be a ransom call?" She'd been trying to be logical. "When my phone finally charged enough, I had another message." She opened her phone and played the quickly whispered message:

"They think I'm relieving myself. Stopped at an out of service gas station, the men who took me are splitting up. Said they're gonna cuff me, so don't know when I'll be able to get to my phone again, dropping a pin then turning off to save battery."

Harper took a long sip of the tea then stood on wobbly legs. "Give me five minutes and we'll go back to the station."

Renee pursed her lips and scrunched her face in reply.

Harper lowered again. "What did you do?"

"I ..." Renee cleared her throat, "I already went back. They've opened an investigation."

"Okay," Harper said slowly, "and what does that mean?"

"I swear, I was really calm this time," Renee insisted. "I told them I wanted to report Gael as a missing person and that I had proof he had been taken. I played them the messages and showed them the texts and locations."

⚏⚏⚏⚏⚏

The officer Renee had shared all the information with sat back in his chair and condescendingly explained, "These things do not happen in Cusco. Perhaps this Gael is at fault and bringing bad things into his life and into our country."

"He's from Peru," she said tightly.

"He *was*," the officer corrected. "He has not lived here for many years."

"He is the kindest, most honest person you'll ever meet. He was hired by Victor Campos, who *is* from Cusco. Victor and Gael are friends, and when his award-winning clothing line became the subject of an editorial for a fashion magazine, Victor insisted they hire Gael to do the shoot. And he's done nothing but capture this beautiful and diverse country for the past three weeks."

"And where is señor Campos?"

"Well ... he's on a celebratory trip."

"Have you contacted *him*?"

This was where Renee had to square her shoulders and look down her nose at the man. *Of course she'd thought of contacting Victor.* It had been her very first thought. She would have rather contacted him, but ... "He's on a ten-day silent retreat in the north of Peru. In the Jungle. With no phones or technology allowed."

The officer raised an eyebrow in disbelief.

She hurriedly continued, "I did some research, found the company the retreat is with and ... they have a satellite phone they use only in case of emergencies and the team will check in on the fifth day of the retreat."

"When did this group leave?"

"Two days ago," she muttered.

"Maybe Victor Campos is perhaps doing illegal work? He used Gael and now needs to dispose of him? Perhaps the entire job was a lie and instead you were all moving drugs or other illegal substances."

"What? No!" She held up her hands in apology from the outburst and tried again. "No, the only things we moved were clothes that were constantly steamed and tried on and hung back on hangers. Victor and Gael are friends. It is a very real company and I'm sure it's in a Better Business Bureau database or something. And while we were working, we had proper work visas for the entire crew and for each location that was used. I know those had to be filed with the Peruvian Embassy and Consulate. Can't you just search for those? I'm sure you have access. If you did, you'd see both men and both of their jobs are legitimate."

"Perhaps."

She picked up her phone and found the file that held several of Gael's untreated photos from the past three weeks. "These are a few of the photos Gael took. And Victor Campos has brought so many jobs to this city. *Please*, can't you look some of this up?"

The officer, obviously not liking being told what to do, frowned as he wiggled his mouse and took steps to search something on his computer. Renee tried to look at the screen, but a snarl from him pushed her back into her seat.

After clicking around and reading for the longest five minutes in the world, he gave a sigh. "Okay, I will open an investigation." He clicked around some more and asked questions about Gael to fill in his report.

"You say you remained in Cusco because your friend," he looked at his notes, "Harper Barrett, was meeting you to continue your vacation?"

"Yes. Harper Barrett. The woman who came and got me earlier. Today."

"Why did señor Torres not leave with the rest of his crew?"

"We ... I thought he was leaving. I went to the airport with everyone and he checked his bags, but then, he surprised me and stayed," she explained. "So we could have time alone and celebrate how well everything had gone."

The officer narrowed his eyes. "You are romantically involved with him?"

"No. Kind of. Yes. But only for this trip." She shook her head. "He's one of my best friends. We were having fun." She held out her hands as she searched for a way to explain this quickly and succinctly. "Haven't you ever had fun for the sake of it because you realized life is short and life is for the living and the moment you were in the middle of was so magical...?" *That* was not succinct.

The officer's expression darkened as he continued to stare Renee down but answered honestly, "No." Then he typed a bit more on his keyboard. When he seemed satisfied, he told Renee, "We have a small staff, but I will start the investigation."

"How long do you think ...?" Her calm was slipping because she wanted to scream that someone needed to get in a car *right now* and find Gael *TODAY!*

"I cannot say how long this will take. A few days, possibly longer."

"Possibly longer..." She was going to explode. She swallowed and shifted forward in her seat, trying to exude any and all the goodwill she possessed as she begged the officer, "What if he doesn't have a few days?" The sentiment made her sick to her stomach.

He shrugged. "If he has been kidnapped, there will be a ransom. You should be thinking about who would be called in such a case?"

Jesus, Renee had no *idea* who would be called. She supposed Gael's parents? Should Renee try to get in touch with them? Or his family in Trujillo? And how did she find that information? Had he been kidnapped because his mother once worked as an attaché? But that had been *years* ago and as far as she recalled Gael telling her, his parents hadn't worked for the government since then. And she wasn't sure a cultural attaché even had important information. So what good was information they may have from twenty-three years ago?

Gael's assistant could get his parents' phone number for her. But then, how did she go about explaining the situation? Maybe she was wasting her time with the police and she should go to the US consulate. What was she expected to do? Maybe there was a website with a checklist of who to contact and what forms to fill out and how to explain to your friend's parents (you've never met) that their son had been kidnapped.

Instead she feebly answered, "I'm not sure who would be called in case of a ransom."

"Do you have the contact information for any of his family members?"

"I don't."

"If you do find it, please give that information to our office. We have your information. We will contact you if there is something you should know." He took his card from his pocket and handed it to Renee. She stared down at it. It was too small and too light a piece of paper that held no promise; the moment was a very heavy dead end, but she still muttered some semblance of thanks.

She didn't recall her feet carrying her back to the hotel, but when she arrived, Renee had made a decision.

Now, she had to explain her plan to Harper.

She swallowed. "I searched for Gael's parents, found their home number. When I called, a woman answered and explained she was a friend who was house sitting while they were on vacation. In Europe. Until the end of March." Two more people to add to the list of humans she was unable to get in touch with.

"Harper, I'm not going to sit around and wait for the police to slowly get around to doing something." She shifted in her seat. "So that means the only chance Gael has is for me and you to save him."

Harper let her head drop back into her hands and began to deeply massage her temples.

Renee hurried, "I think we should go to his last location, and if we can't find anything; if there is nothing there—"

"Renee, Gael said the men who took him were splitting up. That he had been at an abandoned gas station. What do you hope to find there?"

"Him!" she growled impatiently. "I don't know Harper. I only know I need to *go*. And if we don't find anything there, then I think we need to go to the place the lady in the jail told me about and hire a mercenary."

"Jeeee sus ..." Harper breathed out.

"You don't have to come." Renee had been resolute in that decision as well; if Harper decided not to go, that was fine. But Renee wasn't going to be stopped.

"Don't be ridiculous, of course I'm coming with you."

Renee let out half the breath she'd been holding, but she wasn't completely done with her plan. "I also think we need to get a gun or something!"

The exclamation of weaponry needs echoed and stretched around the room.

Renee called Harper's name.

"Renee, I need to let a few more heartbeats pass, because the words *mercenary* and *gun* are throbbing inside my head." She pressed a few more massaging circles against her temples.

"Harp ..."

"Renee, I'm about to utter a question I never expected I'd be asking on this trip. Exactly how do we go about acquiring a gun?"

Chapter Eleven

T he first thing Harper did was insist they research the legalities of American citizens carrying a gun as well as getting a license to carry a gun in Peru.

It was as expected: Peru had strict gun control laws. (Which, any other day, when a friend hasn't been kidnapped and time wasn't of the essence, was a really great thing.) Harper and Renee would need a special permit – which was extremely difficult to get. And in order to get said permit, there were super strict procedures. As it turns out, foreign citizens were rarely able to obtain the necessary licenses.

If they had time, Harper would do everything by the book; consult legal counsel and contact the Peruvian consulate. And if her headache wasn't so violent, she'd try to talk her friend out of doing this ridiculously illegal thing. *But,* Renee wanted to go after people who'd kidnapped someone she cared about, and heading into that sort of situation with nothing but attitude and determination seemed like an even worse idea.

"Think like a criminal," Renee instructed.

Harper scoffed, "I bet we could go on some list site and find whatever we need." She was being facetious, but when Renee searched one popular world-wide site, it had listings for machetes, knives, and several pistolas.

None of this was making Harper's head feel better. "Have you ever held or fired a gun before?" she asked.

Renee was single-minded, her answer confident. "We'll figure it out." She translated their request to purchase one of the guns and hit send on the message. "Have you?" Harper nodded sadly and wasn't surprised when Renee's eyes lit up. "You have?" The message pinged a reply too quickly for Harper's comfort, but Renee saw it as a sign. "It's ours! We can meet and pick it up in an hour." She mapped the location on her phone.

Another whirlwind of emotions throbbed in time with Harper's headache.

Why yes, your honor. I did willingly participate in illegal activities but I wasn't thinking straight at the time and my friend was going to do it with or without me so I figured ... you know ... peer pressure. Why yes, sir, I do realize I am a thirty-eight year old woman.

An hour later, while other people were heading to restaurants or home for dinner, Harper and Renee were taking about a hundred dollars in Peruvian soles to an alley. (A bargain, Renee had insisted.)

So what could possibly go wrong? Harper frowned at the question and waved it away. She did *not* want an answer.

Somehow, it helped that she was having problems breathing in the high altitude, her lungs fighting to expand and gather oxygen as she sucked in air. And she'd be remiss if she didn't give some appreciation to brand new feelings washing over her: slight confusion and a lot of fuzziness. A result from the mixture of medications she'd taken. And possibly her continued exhaustion.

"Renee, I think I need to talk us out of this."

"It'll be fine."

"Why don't we buy mace and a taser?"

"We'll get those too. But I just think we need something a little more intimidating," Renee reasoned. "We're never going to use it."

"Then why are we buying it?"

"It makes the most sense," she insisted passionately.

"Does it?" Harper stopped and put her arms up in the air, an attempt to make more room for her lungs. She took as deep a breath as she could muster.

"The woman ..." Renee cleared her throat, "in jail. She said I should get one if I was going to try and find Gael myself."

Harper muttered, "Maybe we should find *her;* have her broker all these deals for us."

"Harper ..." Renee begged.

"Renee. We're taking actions based on the advice of a stranger; who was also arrested," she tried to reason. "And this isn't something I do on a regular basis ..." they turned a corner, "or have ever thought of doing." They were now on a street less populated, its already closed shops adding to the ominous atmosphere. Halfway down was the alley they were headed to.

Renee's head was on a swivel, checking their surroundings as she mumbled, "Think of the story we'll have to tell at dinner parties."

Harper put a hand on Renee's arm to stop her. "Okay. Listen. If we're going to do this, then *I'm* the one who's going to go do this." She opened her pack, fished out a small bottle of eye drops, tilted her head, and waited for relief from the burning caused by the exhaustion.

"No," Renee put her hands on her hips, "we both go."

"Renee, this is probably a sting operation," Harper waved, "and whoever makes this deal is probably going to end up in jail." She blinked her eyes several times and added more drops. "Since you've already been arrested, it's my turn to have a first offense."

"No, I'll go. Gael's my friend."

"We both know I'm right. If you end up in jail again, the bad guys get further away with Gael and the cops probably won't let you out this time." Harper thrust the backpack to Renee and put her cell phone in her back pocket. "One of us needs to be available to pay bail." She gestured to the bag. "My passport's in there." She took several steps backward and aimed a smile and two thumbs up at Renee, not giving her a chance to argue.

Then Harper turned, the smile immediately falling while under her breath she added, "And if I'm kidnapped, she'll be able to add my name on the cop's list of things to look into."

In the dim, early evening light, the shade from the surrounding buildings darkened the alley even more, but Harper could still make out the form of a young woman. Short, a bit disheveled. She wore a beanie, a large sweater that needed a wash, dirty pants and a drawstring bag slung over her shoulder.

The woman tilted her head and in a shaky voice said, "Hoy el cielo está azul." *The sky is blue today.* In the email to set up this sale, the seller explained a set of 'clandestine' phrases that should be used. Harper butchered her part of the answer, "Creo que está nublado." *I think it's cloudy.* And tried not to roll her eyes.

With that, the woman removed a dirty dish towel from her bag and folded back part of it to show off the gun. Harper nodded, took the money out of her pocket and held it up. They slowly edged toward each other. Once Harper had her hand wrapped around the gun, and the woman's hand grasped the wad of bills, they each released their hold, backing away to check the validity of their trade. After a quick count, the woman pocketed the bills and hurried away.

"Buenas noches," Harper mumbled as she unwrapped the gun. She made sure the safety was on and checked the magazine; it was full, but there was no bullet in the chamber. As she wrapped it back up, she hated the silent thanks she gave to an ex-boyfriend who thought a shooting range made for a fun date. And who'd spent an exorbitant amount of that time teaching her how to 'respect the weapon.' While shooting the gun she held was another issue all together, her respect for the illegal item was quite handy at the moment.

"I'll be sure to send him a thank you note when I get home." She made the snarky promise out loud, hurrying back to Renee who was pacing in circles, her head volleying back and forth, tracking every angle around her.

"Harper!" Renee called, jogging the rest of the distance toward her.

Harper glanced behind her again to make sure she wasn't being followed. And with no one around on the street, a new set of worries took over.

"You have it?" Renee asked.

Harper nodded as her frown increased, and she again looked around.

"What?" Renee followed her gaze.

"*Why* isn't anyone following me?"

Renee tugged on her arm. "Who cares. Let's get a cab."

"That seemed too easy."

"Maybe it was just *easy* and we found an honest seller." She tugged again. "Come ON."

Harper snorted then pulled her arm away from Renee. "Hold on a second, okay?"

She took her backpack from Renee and buried the gun in the very bottom before putting it over her shoulders. "Renee, let's think about this. We're a few hours from Gael's last location. At this point, we won't get there until like nine o'clock. I'm not sure two women in a foreign country should be so hasty ... running off to an unknown location."

"I've waited long enough," Renee insisted.

A multitude of possible problems rushed past Harper. She scrubbed her face and sighed. "Reneé, god love ya, but you stand out. With your blonde hair, blue eyes and big boobs ..."

Renee looked down. "I'm wearing a sports bra and baggy clothes."

"You could wear a sack and be covered in mud, you're still gorgeous and have big boobs."

"Thank you?" Renee frowned.

Harper gave an almost unhinged laugh. "I'm trying to say ... that whatever we do, whoever we talk to, wherever we go, we are going to be very obvious, *very* memorable."

"I realize that."

Harper spread her hands out in front of her to try and explain. "Before we go running around like chickens with our heads cut off, I just think we need to be a little more prepared."

"We have ..." Renee stopped herself, glanced around as she stepped closer to Harper before whispering, "a gun, cash and a location."

Harper had the gun. Renee only carried cash and her phone on her person. And maybe it was because of that, Harper found herself wanting more. "I'd feel better if we had a few more things."

"What kind of things?"

Backup. An army. Peru's version of the FBI ...

"I don't know, Renee." She let her exhaustion and frustration vent. "I'm not sure what *things* we need, but I feel like we need something substantial and helpful for this sort of ..." She fumbled to find the right word for the excursion they were embarking on. "Can we go to a store first?"

"There's a mercado about two blocks away."

"Okay." Harper took her hair out of the ponytail then ran her fingers through the greasy mess before gathering it back in the hairband. "Yeah. Let's go there."

The mercado was a large warehouse sort of building where individual merchants had set up stalls with their goods for sale.

Harper tried to be methodical as they rushed up and down the aisles formed by vibrant vendors on either side. Each stall varied in the goods they had for sale. She bought dried fruit and nuts: food that could last a while. Renee bought chocolate, cookies and sunscreen. Then she asked if Haprer wanted a fruit juice.

She didn't.

Harper growled internally, *I thought we were in a hurry.* Then she asked out loud, "I thought we were in a hurry?"

Renee nodded. "You're right. What else do we need?"

Harper scoured the stalls and bought antibacterial wipes. Baby wipes for possible bathroom emergencies. A a small sewing kit, a paracord, a bottle of antibacterial spray and cream. She figured it was the best she was going to do.

The last stall they stopped carried more hardware goods than souvenirs or food. Harper put a pair of tweezers, duct tape and a multi-took on the counter.

Renee asked, "Are we really going to need all this stuff?"

"I don't know." Harper let out a frustrated grunt, she was getting tired of that answer. "I feel like we need to be prepared for whatever comes with saving someone who's been kidnapped."

Renee picked a pair of pliers off the hook of a pegboard and added them.

Harper added scissors.

Like a game of hand stacking, Renee added a magnet that said Cusco and two pairs of knitted gloves.

Harper added zip ties.

Lastly, Renee added two more chocolate bars, a bar of soap and a hand fan.

Harper stopped them. "That's probably good."

"I'm spiraling," Renee excused.

Once paid, they headed to the street and Harper organized things as best she could in her pack while Renee hailed a cab.

They never did find a place to buy mace or a taser.

Chapter Twelve

"**S**eñor ... nosotros tenemos un problema." *We have a problem.* The man Nick hired to transport him up river, slowed the boat's engine to a stop and pointed a few hundred feet away to where the river bent, where he could just make out several motley motorboats hugging the riverbank. The kind of boats and men that weren't always welcoming when you 'happened' upon them.

"It's not a problem. No es un problema," Nick assured. "That's who I'm looking for." He hadn't necessarily explained to the guide what he was doing, but figured the large sum of money he handed over for the ride would deter any questions, and leave him open to certain directions when the time came.

And the time had come.

"You can drop me off up there," Nick instructed.

"Drop you off?"

"Yup. Just drop me off and head back home. This ride was all I needed." Nick took off the worn green baseball hat he was wearing, nodded toward his destination and nonchalantly added, "Eso no es importante." *That's not important.*

The man gave a worrisome nod, but lurched the boat back into action; if not a little slower than previously.

Nick made his way to the bow of the small boat, casually holding his hands far enough away from his body to signal to the men on the beach he wasn't a threat.

Still, the five men stood in a relaxed, somewhat guarded formation. They all wore khaki pants, various dark t-shirts, sunglasses and not a smile between them. Nick knew if they thought he was a threat, a few of them would produce a gun to dissuade any recklessness.

As the boat chugged closer, the man standing at the head of the group let out a gruff laugh, signaling to the rest of the men behind him everything was okay. "Robbins?" he called, crossing the distance. "What the hell are you doing here?"

Nick tossed two duffle bags onto the rocky beach, slipped his pack on his shoulder and jumped off the boat. He waved the boat pilot away with a quick "gracias."

Not waiting to be told twice, the driver reversed, then hurried back the way he'd come.

"Shaw." Nick held out his hand to the dark haired bear of a man that greeted him. "I needed a vacation."

Duncan Shaw, an old friend from Nick's youthful days in the military, accepted the hand and pulled Nick in to slap him on the back as he teased, "And then you got so bored on vacation you decided what you really needed was an adventure?"

Nick shrugged. "Vacation hasn't started yet. A *friend* found out I was taking a few days off and suggested I take my vacation in Peru. Then he asked me to do a favor since I would be headed down here anyway."

"Man, why would you let Wilder choose your vacation spot? Don't you know that frugal bastard would try to rope you into something? Get a two for one." Duncan laughed.

Sean Wilder was a mutual friend they'd both served with. He helped run a company which contracted security teams for humanitarian organizations operating in areas that might face dangerous circumstances.

"I didn't have a concrete destination set in stone, just time off and a vacation looming. Did Wilder con you into this gig?"

Duncan glanced around. "What gig? I'm on a fishing trip with some buddies."

"Well then, if you'd be so kind as to take the tackle I've brought for you off my hands, I've got a beach and a drink with an umbrella waiting."

"What's her name?"

Nick flexed his hand, still sore from his last female interaction. "Solitude."

Shaw made a sound between an entertained snort and a growl, then slapped Nick on the back again. "How are you getting back to this solitude?"

Nick crouched to unzip the duffels. "I was told you'd be open to giving me a ride."

Duncan scratched his beard as he squatted beside Nick, fishing out one of the tactical drones. Holding it aloft, the proper operator collected it.

Nick unzipped his pack next and handed Duncan a satellite phone. "These aren't the kinds of things I'd think you'd forget."

He gave Nick a knowing side-eye. "Things haven't gone according to plan."

"Fish aren't biting?"

"You know how these trips go. One minute you're trying to find the biggest Arapaima fish you've ever caught, the next thing you know, someone forgot the damn fishing poles."

Nick chuckled, catching the nervous foot to foot shifting the man standing farthest from the group was doing. "New guy?"

"Forgot the fucking tech," Shaw growled then stood and stretched. "At least this trip is only planning and logistics. Lucky you were in the area." He tilted his head. "Are you really taking a vacation?"

"Wanna join me? I'm headed to some prime beach in northern Peru."

"Who knows, crazier things have happened."

Nick nodded. "Okay, tell me what you need."

"Like I said, merely gathering intel."

Nick scoffed, "Shaw, the past two days I had to finagle a car and a motorcycle, then hand over a hefty sum of money to find a boat to bring me to this location."

"Is there a question there?" The other men had retrieved the bags and begun to talk among themselves as they divided the items.

"It's quite a long way to go just to drop off a few things for a recon trip."

Duncan jutted his chin. "That's because you've been sitting in front of a computer for so long, you forgot what real work is like."

"Well, let me give you a little taste of what sitting in front of a computer has done for my observational skills." He nodded toward the boats. "You have five boats."

Duncan sarcastically replied, "Good job Robbins, we *do* have five boats. What else would you like to count?"

Nick snuffed. "Okay asshat, where am I headed?"

Duncan took out a handheld GPS from one of the bags and walked Nick over to a twelve-foot aluminum boat with a trolling motor; it was nothing special, but it would keep afloat. "Right now we're running through a variety of practical escape scenarios. Times. Distances. Obstacles – human, animal or natural. You know the drill." He opened a map on the device and traced the path Nick was to take. "You'll end up at a little bed and breakfast called El Mirador."

"The Lookout?" *Wasn't that a little too on the head?*

"It's supposed to have great views," Duncan said. "The owner, Ian, is expecting you. He'll take care of the boat, put you up for the night and have made arrangements for you to continue onward to that umbrella drink."

Nick knew enough not to voice his opinion that this sounded easy. Part of the superstition when working an operation was to not congratulate yourself until the job was completely over and you'd signed your name to the paperwork.

But really, a little boat ride up a river in the Peruvian jungle ... it hadn't been so bad on the way out. He had his fair share of mosquito bites, but his gray pants and long sleeve button-up beige shirt kept most of them off. And even though it had been a puzzle to coordinate with Shaw, Nick had the opportunity to see some new country, eat some great local food, practice his Spanish and use someone else's money for quick, 'no questions asked' transportation. So all things considered, the detour was a decent start to his trip. He shook Shaw's hand and once again offered, "When you're done here, you know where I'll be."

⁂

As Nick puttered up the river, he was accompanied by the sounds of birds, animals he wasn't familiar with and the buzzing of insects thriving in the rainy season. The changing greens of the trees along the riverbank fluctuated between looking ethereal to dangerous, all depending on how the sun peeked through.

He logged the information and times on his satellite phone as he traveled, slow and steady. When he was less than a mile from his final destination, the clouds began to gather quickly to perform their daily afternoon shower duties. Fitting his ball cap lower on his head, Nick welcomed the water that dissipated the bugs. When the dock was in sight, he used his body to cover his phone so he could log his final report.

He tied up the boat, lugged his pack onto his back and grinned as he followed the arrow shaped sign, 'El Mirador,' that marked a path climbing up a slope from the boat dock to the house above; thinking that this time tomorrow, he'd be beachside.

Lush blooms of trees and flowers showed off on either side of the path as the elevation steadily rose. He heard soft music and laughter drifting from the front of the large two-story bed and breakfast. He imagined a covered porch and dancing while waiting for the afternoon rain to dissipate.

The path ran beside the house, then disappeared around the front. He stopped and turned around to take in the view. The lookout indeed. He could see far into the distance. The treetops below, and across the river, looked like a sea of green flowing upward into a cresting wave of vegetation that covered mountains in every direction. It wasn't the beach, but there was a breathtaking beauty to it.

He turned, tripped over a rock but caught himself with the branch of a tree which dropped an unsuspecting snake onto his shoulder. But before Nick could whip the shocked snake off his own shocked self, it lunged for his shoulder and sank his needle-sharp fangs through his shirt.

"Fuck." He grabbed the snake's head, forcing it to release his shoulder, and held it back so he could find out what kind of snake it was. And as the angry eyes of a forest pitviper came into focus, Nick hissed an elongated *"fuuuck"* this time.

The green asshole was venomous. He kept a hold of the snake's head, knowing he was working against the clock now. Red hot pain began to sear into his shoulder as a dull throb started to build in his head. He hurried along the path to the front of the house, and when within eyesight of a few people on the large porch, he yelled, "¡¿Hola?!"

A woman gasped when she saw the wriggling beast he was holding aloft as he began to stumble on the path leading to the house. The pain was growing, his head was pounding, and a lightheadedness was washing over him.

A man hurried forward asking, "Señor, ¿le mordieron?" *Were you bitten?*

Nick held up the snake when the man was close enough, which stopped him from coming any closer. "Forest pitviper?" Nick asked. "Bosque ... verde ..." He was trying to communicate with the man his question, so he shook the snake, a silent question, *did he see what kind of snake it was?* Because Nick knew that was going to be the most important part when it came to helping him with anti-venom. Oh god — if they had some nearby.

"Sí, ha sido una víbora del bosque." *Yes, it is a forest viper.* The man nodded emphatically, he understood.

Nick gave the snake another shake. "¿Tiro?" *Throw?* he asked, questioning what he should do with the little beast.

"¡Sí, sí!" the man called and gestured where he wanted Nick to fling the snake.

When it was done, Nick pulled the collar of his shirt aside to show the man where he'd been bit. He felt like he was walking through a dream, sluggish, his feet stuck in mud. "Hospital?" he asked, trying to remember the Spanish word for hospital. "Oh yeah," he slurred, "el hospital."

The man nodded, slipping Nick's arm around his shoulder to keep him upright.

Nick grimaced but asked, "Ian?"

"Sí. You are the friend of Señor Shaw?"

Nick nodded as he began to slip, his body no longer cooperating with him. Ian called for more help, "Ayúdame." Soon another man was there, propping up Nick's other side.

The pain and fogginess was making it hard to concentrate. But for some reason he couldn't let go of one idea; he opened his mouth several times, trying to push out the words, licking the roof of his mouth, his brain obscured from rational thinking because of the pain.

He used all his remaining fortitude to focus, even as the areas around the light were growing dark, becoming a pinpoint. And he wasn't sure if, before he closed his eyes, he was able to finally get out the words stuck in his mind. *"I just needed a vacation."*

Chapter Thirteen

"I have to tell you something." Renee's whisper smelled of the emotional chocolate she'd eaten after she convinced the driver to take them the hour and forty-seven minutes south of Cusco to an abandoned gas station. (Granted, the sturdy tip she handed over to begin the ride helped.)

Harper glanced up at the upholstery lining the interior of the cab and silently asked all unseen deities to give her strength for another of Renee's exhaustive confessions. Then she cracked open a bottle of water and took out the herbal pill one of the vendors at the mercado promised would help her headache.

Normally, Harper wouldn't take pills that came in capsule form, in resealable baggies, from strangers. But she also wouldn't normally buy illegal firearms. And she was desperate. Every few seconds she found herself reaching for her head, to make sure it was still attached, because it felt like it was trying to remove itself from her body. Mostly she wanted the world to stabilize and make sense once more. Or at the very least, she wanted the light tracers to stop and the fogginess to dissipate. Pill swallowed, she dropped her head to the side and gave Renee a questioning glance.

Leaning toward Harper she muttered, "The driver said he'd wait for us, but only for ten minutes."

"Okay."

"We don't know what we're going to find," Renee bit her lower lip, "though the map doesn't show anything else near the station for a few miles in each direction." She took out her phone and for the umpteenth time, checked Gael's last location, applied the satellite filter, zoomed in on the street view (as if the photo had somehow just been taken) and captured a glimpse of him.

For Harper, looking at the street view was a reminder to lay off the water for the next few hours. The abandoned gas station didn't look like it had available facilities and if it was in the middle of nowhere ... "Eh, that's why I bought the baby wipes and know how to squat."

"What?" Renee frowned.

Harper returned the frown. "What?"

"You have baby wipes and—"

"Shit, did I say that out loud?" She was not in control of all her faculties anymore. She squeezed her eyes shut then changed the subject. "You've always said you and Gael were just friends. But you told the officer you were romantically involved?"

"With the officer?" Renee made the joke, then sighed out a deep breath. "Gael and I tried dating once, when we first met. We made out a little and it was nice, but we were both so busy and it seemed like life was in the way and it wasn't meant to be, but we worked really well as friends; which was fine, because there was never the big moment, you know?"

Harper did know. She'd had her fair share of one night stands with guys who were nice enough, and friends she'd jumped into the 'friends with benefits' zone, because she was lonely and needed human contact. But each experiment never had one big 'Aha!' or 'Oh my' moment.

"When we got to Cusco, everyone was so sick," Renee went on, "it was just Gael and Victor and me for the first few days. We traveled to *so* many places, and I swear each new place was better than the last. It was magic, and it kept growing and growing and it got under our skin." She smiled and Harper imagined the memories bumped up against her worry, pushing it aside for the moment. "Harp, we were riding horses, finding waterfalls, gazing up at the unforgiving Andes Mountains, following the path of ancient Incas ... and we were doing these things because we were at *work*. The three of us had followed our passions in life and we'd been brought together because we were doing our *jobs*."

Harper gave a soft smile. "That's pretty amazing."

"I think Gael and I, being in such close confines without everyone for a few days, sharing all of that ... there was this need to express everything we were seeing and feeling physically." She gave a frustrated laugh. "I don't even know if this is making sense. But having someone to hold and be held by, in the middle of all those amazing circumstances, didn't ruin the trip, it enhanced it. We held hands, laughed, talked a lot, worked tirelessly, flirted and didn't put any confinements on what we were doing." She scrubbed her face. "Does any of that make sense?"

"The moment was like a comet," Harper offered.

"Exactly! Gael is a really, really good friend." She gave a breathy snort. "And hot and ..." she tilted her head as she looked for the right words, then blurted, "exuberant in bed."

Harper's stomach gave a twinge of jealousy. (Of course, that could be the pill she took.) But she couldn't recall the last time she had someone exuberant in bed or even considered herself exuberant. Hell, she couldn't even recall an exuberant make out session. "So was there something 'there' this time? A moment?" she asked.

Renee nodded. "Something."

"We'll find him." Harper gave the no-nonsense, fervent promise in the form of a squeeze to Renee's hand. Renee returned the squeeze, as if she could soak up all the positive vibes.

The driver turned on the radio and began whistling along. Harper's head thankfully began to reattach to her shoulders and everything around her started to come back into focus. She took a deep breath and slowly blew it out.

With a moment of clarity, she reached into her bag and moved the wrapped gun from the bottom to the front pocket.

Then, because she'd nonchalantly moved a gun so it was more accessible, she hugged the bag to her chest and let out a softly muttered chuckle. "Jesus ..."

"What?"

Harper closed her eyes. "Nothing." If she was going to be waving a gun around and running all over a foreign country, she needed to take the opportunities that arose for catnaps. "Wake me up if anything happens or when we're fifteen minutes away."

As she tried to even her breathing, she found herself thinking that her jeans were tight enough for her to tuck the gun in the front waistband and hide it with her hoodie. She clenched her jaw in an attempt to dismiss logistical thoughts about carrying a gun and tried to catch the attention of the deities she'd bothered several moments ago. *It sure would be cool if I never had a reason to use this gun.* Amen.

Chapter Fourteen

As the driver pulled the car into the abandoned gas station, Renee leaned forward and told him they'd be quick. He nodded his reassurance several times and replied, "Sí, sí, sí."

They took less than ten steps before he broke his promise and drove off.

"Wait!" Harper yelled at the same time Renee screamed, "Asshole!" at the taillights.

They glanced around the middle of nowhere they'd knowingly asked to be taken. A sad lamp post swathed the area in shades of horror film, prompting Harper to move the gun into the waistband of her jeans; which made her feel better while at the same time heightened her distress.

Another sudden moment of clarity hit. They should not have come here. There was no reason other than Renee's need for momentum – her need to keep going while she waited for 'clues' or another phone call or something more substantial to drop in her lap. That need, along with Harper's exhaustion and inability to reason, were the only reasons they'd ended up here.

"Well," Harper said, mainly to hear her voice.

Renee squared her shoulders. "We came here to see if we could find any trace of Gael, so that's what we're going to do."

"Okay," Harper agreed standing frozen in place, really happy her headache had dulled for a moment so she was able to appreciate how awful and stupid this idea was.

Still, she was going to try and be pragmatic about it. Harper held her hands out to the area in front of them. "What do we know? This is where Gael last shared his location and he sent a text because they let him go to the restroom."

"Yes. So we know we have cell service." They both took out their phones and verified they had service.

Just then, a car slowed and pulled into the station. They turned their attention to the lights. "Is that the taxi driver?" Renee asked, a dash of hope in her voice.

But the car rolled to a stop right next to them. The driver rolled down the window as the passenger climbed out and headed to a dark corner to relieve himself. The driver didn't smile but greeted them with a nod. "Buenas noches."

This! Harper swallowed, *this was why they should have stayed put for like ... five more minutes and thought through their actions.*

Renee gave the man a half nod in return.

His skin had a slight sallow tinge, though that could be the overhead light, but he exuded an air that suggested he was not to be trusted. (Or messed with.) It could be his unsmiling light brown eyes, or the two-inch scar on his left cheek or possibly the scar that intersected his left eyebrow.

"¿Americanas?" he asked.

They didn't react positively or negatively to the question.

He scanned the area that surrounded them, then back to where they'd made statues of themselves. "¿Necesitan ayuda?" *Do you need help?*

Harper cleared her throat. "No."

He jutted his chin and with pursed lips gestured to the area and said, "Not safe."

The other man, tall and lanky, wearing the same no-nonsense facial expression as the driver, returned. He stood in the open door, resting his hands on the hood of the car. When he asked, "¿Necesitan ayuda?" he instilled a fear that made Harper and Renee take a step back.

"No," Renee said as Harper added, "We're fine."

The driver responded, "Tengan cuidado." *Be careful.* Then he grunted to the other man to get in the car. When his partner was in, the driver looked at the women once more, opened his mouth, but seemed to change his mind about whatever he was about to say and started the car. After moving a fraction of an inch, he stopped and again nodded to the surrounding area. "Not safe," he reiterated.

They watched the car disappear into the night and only then did they both release the breath they'd been holding.

"I'm sorry," Renee said, "I'm not thinking very clearly, am I?"

"Neither am I, otherwise I don't know that I would have let you talk me into this late night adventure."

"I need to keep moving," Renee admitted. Harper tugged her friend to her side, an acceptance of her apology and understanding of how she was feeling.

"Okay," Harper gestured, "let's search for something." *In the darkness. At this run-down gas station, with a two-story building missing a front door that looks like zombies will most likely appear through it at any moment.* Harper used the flashlight function on her phone. Still, neither of them moved. They took their time studying the scene before them.

A u-shaped, crumbling white plaster wall created the entirety of the station. Within its confines was the covered pump area, the pumps having been removed. Against the back left corner was a two-story building, and in the back right sagged an old pick-up held together by rust.

The rest of the space was a forgotten, unsupervised construction zone. A stack of rubble was covered with a tarp. A pile of tires sagged together. A gathering of oxidized trash cans were holding an endless meeting. And a dangerous looking game of Jenga, using corrugated tin, was happening in the center of it all.

"What are we looking for?" Renee asked as she turned on her flashlight app.

"I'm not sure but I feel like we'll know when we see it." Harper had absolutely no expectations of finding anything.

Renee suggested they search methodically, walk from the street to the back of the lot in straight lines. When they were halfway done and nothing had been found, Harper began scripting a pep talk.

So she wasn't ready for Renee's gurgling sound of dismay and triumph as she picked something up from the dirt and thrust her hand in the air. "It's Gael's! We bought bracelets from this woman in the Rainbow Mountains. I picked this out for him." She hopped in a circle. "Harper! He's leaving breadcrumbs!"

Harper tried not to frown in reply, because wasn't that what the text messages had been?

Renee held the bound pieces of string lightly in her fingers. "We went to the Rainbow Mountains in the south. The hike was muddy, but when we reached the peak for the view of the colorful mountains, it had all been worth it."

⁂

The wet season had deepened the lush greens that blended with the striations of mineral deposits – a deep copper, an almost pink-beige, and chocolate browns. The vibrant colors against the dramatic, rolling cloudy skyline was Gael's photographic paradise. Some of the most captivating shots had been constructed from the blend of color from Victor's clothing, the light that peeked through the ever-changing clouds and the mountains.

There had been an older Peruvian woman dressed in traditional clothing nearby, sitting with her llamas, offering to pose for photographs with tourists for a minimal fee. She also had blankets, hats and woven bracelets for sale. Renee had picked one with the colors of the mountains for Gael. While he'd chosen a vibrant rainbow of pinks, yellows and blues for her, saying it was her personality captured in a woven piece of art.

She twisted the bracelet on her wrist as her elation faded. "But we knew he'd been here. That's what the texts were for."

"Yes, but now we have tangible proof," Harper encouraged.

"I'm sorry, I thought this would be more …" Renee glanced around her at the abandoned station, "telling." She gripped his bracelet tightly in her hand. "Harper, I don't know what to do now."

"Well, we can either stay here tonight in that building," she pointed, "or in the cab of that truck."

Renee gave a snort.

"Or …" Harper opened her map app. Renee looked over her shoulder as Harper found their location and zoomed out to find the nearest hotel, motel or place with a rentable bed. She found one in a town that was half an hour away by car. When she clicked on the option to find out how long it would take them to walk, the result was three hours. "What the hell?"

Renee's phone screamed a notification. It was so unexpected, she dropped it. Once she had it back in her hand, they both stared dumbfounded as a new shared location from Gael glowed in the darkened night.

Renee quickly mapped to the location. "Only two hours away by car! We need a car." She glanced around as if she could find one.

Harper was zooming in and out on the map Renee had pulled up, studying the road. "Even if we had a car, I don't know that we should drive that road in the dark."

Renee looked at the twisting mess of elevation gains and descents until eventually ending at the edge of the jungle and thought it did looks like a child's scribble of what a road should look like on a fantasy map.

"I'll drive. Slowly," Renee reassured. "How do we get a car?"

"I don't know." Harper glanced back at the rusted truck. "Wait! I *do* have an idea. Holy shit, I think I'm feeling better." She gave Renee a tight grin. "Let's look up twenty-four-hour car rental places."

There were several, all in Cusco. Harper called the first one on the list, put the phone on speaker and with the help of the English to Spanish translator app on Renee's phone, explained they were stuck and needed a rental car. And they were willing to pay for someone to deliver a car to their location.

The woman on the other end of the phone made it seem like this was a common occurrence and promised the car would be delivered to them in three hours. Harper relayed her card number to the clerk, then hung up and muttered, "If a car doesn't show up in three hours, I'll cancel the card."

"You're amazing." Renee hugged her friend.

"C'mon. Let's go see how bad it is in that building."

"Why?"

"I need to sleep. I'm dizzy again and I think that good idea zapped all my energy."

They stealthily peeked inside the building, it was as deteriorated as the outside, but it offered cover and a view of the area, in case anyone other than the rental car people showed up.

They found a few old newspapers, cleared a spot and sat with their backs against a wall.

Harper yawned, hugged her bag against her chest, and closed her eyes. "Hey Renee? Don't let any zombies get me, okay."

"I won't." After a moment, she added, "And I'll wake you up if anymore scary scar-faced men drive up."

Renee took a deep breath and moved closer to Harper. She was about to settle in for a few more hours of helpless waiting. She hated it. So she tried to focus on Harper and how she was supporting her. She needed to tell Harper she appreciated her more than she could ever know.

Chapter Fifteen

The car would get them where they needed to go.

At least, that was the shrugged promise they were given by the young man who delivered it at three in the morning. Along with the explanation that since it was such late notice and the rental company had to find two drivers, (one to drive this car and one to take the delivery driver back) this car was the only option: a light gray, off-brand, two door model. No bells, absolutely zero whistles. The driver side door had been hit at some point, the dent obviously hammered out rather than the door replaced.

Harper signed the paperwork and was given a copy. She mumbled her thanks as she stared down the rental. At least she had asked for every form of insurance she could on the ridiculous little beast.

The young man opened the passenger door of the car that was taking him back to Cusco and called to Harper, "Next time, you should hire a driver for your trip. It's cheaper."

She nodded, but as his ride, a brand-new Toyota Rav 4 drove past, she snarled at the telltale rental barcode on its back window. "Yeah, we got ripped off."

"I'll take the first shift," Renee offered.

They climbed into the car and arranged their seats. The car had a cup holder attached to one of the vents in the center, which was actually the perfect place to put a phone so the driver could follow GPS.

Harper tried to stay awake, but her exhaustion won, and she patted Renee's arm. "I'm just going to close my eyes for a minute."

Left alone with her thoughts, Renee carefully followed the intense switchbacks, allowing the car to crawl its way through the night. She used the slow weaving of the road as a guide for her breathing. It did help a bit.

She reminded herself that she would see Gael again soon. If anyone could find Gael, it was her. If anyone was *going* to find him, it was her.

She imagined how it would feel to be in his arms again. His taut body pressed against her softness, his arms around her waist, her head against his chest as he said, "Mi reina."

She breathed out, "mi reina," and let the memories of the first time he used the endearment wash over her.

When the time had come for the shoot at Machu Picchu, the crew and models stayed at a boutique hotel built mere steps from the entrance to the historical monument.

Gael and Victor obtained special permits that allowed the team access to the stunning ruins for the duration of their stay, all hours of the night and day. They did have a preservationist who would accompany them, but still, the rare opportunity was beyond amazing.

Their proximity to the ruins from the hotel made the shoot much easier. For one thing, Renee could ready the models inside the hotel room before they had to walk the short distance through the lobby, out the door and into the entrance of the ruins.

After arriving the first day and packing all the equipment into their rooms at the Machu Picchu Lodge, everyone went to the ruins to explore and talk about logistics for the shoot.

Ten minutes after looking around, as others' ideas floated around her, she had a lightbulb moment of inspiration. "I'll be back," she promised and took one of the tourist buses that shuttled passengers up and down the expansive switchbacks from the ruins to the small town of Aguas Calientes. She walked through stores and the outdoor markets, her head on a swivel until she found what she was looking for. Or, at least something that could be manipulated into her vision: sunburst mirrors.

The wall of one vendor's stall was covered with the hanging mirrors.

The mirror itself was no bigger than the palm of her hand, but she was after the halo created by the sunrays. Hammered aluminum had been painted gold to create rays of various sizes, and was exactly what she had in mind.

The vendor understood enough English that when she explained what she wanted, he shrugged, popped the mirror out and cut the sun in half, leaving her with a basic golden headband shape. She picked out five different designs and requested the same cutting be done for each one. She was so excited, she overpaid for his efforts then searched the market for earrings that would compliment the bands.

When she returned to the hotel, the first person she found was Gael's assistant who said he was still at the ruins. She wandered with her bag of goodies until she found him, sitting on a stone, camera held loosely in his hand, his attention on the shapes and light and angles.

She grinned at him and explained her idea, realizing she should have explained it to Victor as well. But so far, Victor had been supportive of the additions she'd made to enhance his clothing. She put on the earrings and donned one of the headdresses meant to resemble something regal and sun-like; held her hands out to the side and wiggled her eyebrows asking, "It'll work, right?"

Then, the sun peeked out of the clouds. Gael's gaze narrowed intently on her, and Renee thought she'd never felt so powerful or *seen* in her entire life.

He stood, took a blind step back from her, aimed his camera with a whispered "mi reina," then began shooting. He instructed her movements, explaining where to look, and how to hold her head and smile. But when he told her to lick her lips and hold them slightly apart, he lowered the camera for a moment. The look of unadulterated desire in his eyes stole her breath. The camera back in place, he took several more photos, before unceremoniously slinging it over his shoulder. He crossed the distance separating them, drew her against him, then shaking his head in wonder, lowered his lips to hers.

She swore the winds carried ancient, intoxicating murmurs. She drowned in his attentions, unable to get enough of him. And felt powerful as he clung to her, just as captivated.

When they separated, the sun slid back behind the clouds; Gael held her face gently in his hands, grinning down at her. "It's a great idea."

She reached up and touched the side of the sunburst. "I thought it would look very regal."

"Mi reina," he repeated once more then stepped back, desire still radiating off him as he gave her a slight bow and translated, "My queen."

Renee gripped the steering wheel, swallowed the tightness in her throat, squeezed her eyes shut for a quick second before promising herself that soon she'd hear him call her his queen again. But for now, she needed to focus. On anything else.

She'd only been driving for an hour, but her hands were as cramped and tight as her nerves. She looked at the map and felt relieved to see a small town ahead.

Renee welcomed the lamplit town. The clean main street was a mix of old colonial-era buildings, new three-story structures, and remnants of brick – all of them hugging each other. When she saw a yellow and blue building with a painted name, Mercado Central, sitting next to an open courtyard, she parked in a space under a streetlamp.

Harper jerked awake as the car stopped, quickly trying to get her bearings. "You okay?"

"No," she answered honestly as she stretched and wiggled her fingers. "I need you to drive. But go ahead and keep sleeping for a little while longer. I'm going to pace that courtyard for a few minutes and stretch."

She did just that, shaking her body out, doing some deep backbends and declaring to the surrounding sleepy town, "I've got this."

Chapter Sixteen

R enee let Harper sleep another hour. By then, the mercado was opening, so they sat at a small counter and had a fried egg, juice, coffee and roll for breakfast. Harper thought it might be the best breakfast of her life. But that could be because her headache had dulled and her exhaustion had been downgraded from extreme to moderate.

After using the restrooms and buying more water bottles, they were on their way. Harper wondered if Renee might want to drive now that she'd had something to eat and a chance to stretch; but because she was clutching her phone the way a child tightly held onto a security blanket, Harper retracted the idea.

Day two of vacation found Harper Barrett in a crappy rental car, watching as Peru yawned and stretched awake; coming to colorful life with the rising sun. The vibrant blue skies were clear, intermittent towns slowly waking as they passed.

The road twisted up the side of the mountains that remained more barren, before dipping down the other side, lush with the first glimpses of jungle. Overlooks showed blooming stretches of green that slid up and down, creating mountainous formations while the peaks in the distance were hidden in the bellies of clouds. They crossed a river and the road took on the gentle yaw and curves of the water.

"God this is dazzling," Harper whispered in wonder.

"This wasn't how you were supposed to see it," Renee muttered.

Harper reached over and gave Renee's hand a squeeze of reassurance then insisted, "We are going to find Gael. Then you two can have some celebratory, exuberant sex. And *then* we'll send him home and start this trip over."

"Do you know how to ride a motorcycle?" Renee asked.

"I know how to ride *on the back* of a motorcycle," Harper said. "Why?"

"Victor wanted to have shots of the models in his clothing posing on motorbikes with jungle foliage in the background. So much travel in Peru is done on motorbikes or tuk-tuks, he wanted to highlight that part of life here. And there are a ton of touring companies that do motorcycle tours. So we all learned how to ride." She inclined her head. "It would be fun to do when we are finally back on schedule."

"If we have to go over roads with these kinds of hairpin turns, I feel like the only thing I'd be able to do is lay a bike down and slide."

"Nah, you'd be great. And it feels really good. Like a really cool accomplishment." She mindlessly glanced at her phone. "And you'd look like a badass."

"Can I look like a badass on the back of a bike *you* drive?" Harper asked.

"Sure." Renee found a soft smile. "Or, we could find you some sexy ass man to drive you around."

"What's a tuk-tuk?" She changed the subject.

"Like a rickshaw, it's a three wheeled taxi, the front is a motorcycle where the driver sits, the back is a covered seat with room for two people."

"Oh, I did see those in Cusco."

Renee checked her phone again. Harper turned on the radio to try and sidetrack her. The station was spotty but the energetic percussion rhythms lightened the mood.

"What ever happened with that guy?" Renee asked. "The one your oldest sister set you up with?"

Harper sighed, she'd been set up on so many dates recently, and none of them had been memorable. Actually, that wasn't true; they had been memorable, but for their ridiculousness and lackluster.

"You remember Mr. Collins from the *Pride and Prejudice* movie?" Harper asked.

"Eww," Renee groaned, "which version?"

"BBC."

She gave a more dramatically exaggerated groan.

Harper laughed. "He was really nice. Very smart, successful. But he was nervous, fidgety, and every time I talked, he talked over me with an antidote about *Star Trek*."

"So, no second date?"

"Definitely no second date." She gave an involuntary snort. "Though I did give him a Vulcan salute and told him to 'live long and prosper' instead of a goodnight kiss."

Renee spat an unexpected, contagious laugh. They rode out the laugh until it petered out, ending with simultaneous sighs.

"I'm not saying relationships make a woman. And not having one makes you any less ..." Renee waved the explanation away. "You know how I feel about all that. But I just don't understand why there isn't a line around the block of people who are desperate to get to know you because they see how amazing you are."

If Harper had a dollar for every time she heard that.

"I waited too long." She muttered what she feared was the truth, but shook it off and forced a smile. "It's fine."

"No. It's *not* fine." Renee turned her full attention to Harper. "And it's okay that it's not fine. But I think you should also remember, it ain't over til it's over."

Harper gazed at her out of the corner of her eye for a second. She'd love to believe that. That there was love and connection and exuberance still out there waiting for her. So she repeated Renee's words as if she were wishing on a star. "It ain't over til it's over."

"Exactly!"

⁂

The jungle growth on either side of the road was impressive, but a little worrisome. They passed an occasional, half visible dirt road that gave off shady, if not dangerous vibes. But, in their current situation, those were games that Harper's imagination was playing. As time ticked by and the only traffic they passed was one motorcycle rider, and it had been an uncomfortably long time since they'd last seen any sign of habitation, her worry grew.

"Here we go." Renee straightened. "We're about a mile away."

And because Harper wasn't in the mood to get 'there' too quickly, she slowed her speed. Still, soon enough, they rounded a corner and found a small, rundown one-story building set back from the road. Not the kind of building that looked like it was still in business or had seen any inhabitants recently.

To the right of the building was a small cleared trail. Obvious tire tracks led the way to the back of the building, where the space opened into a dirt lot – quite similar to the gas station the previous evening – where various piles of forgotten debris and rubble thrived.

"I don't know what I expected." Renee let out a breath. "I didn't want to stumble across a whole bunch of threatening people, but I thought maybe at least we'd find ..." Harper knew she wanted to say 'Gael,' but instead finished, "I don't know."

The building was butter yellow, pockmarked with peeling stucco, topped with a rusted corrugated roof, the single entrance missing its door. A faded strip of paint across the top might have once had the name of the establishment, but now it was merely a memory.

Harper made a wide circle in the lot, which gave them the perfect view of a three wheeled cargo van, its back covered with canvas, backed into a space along the opposite side of the building. The windows of the cab were rolled down and the driver was leaning back against the seat, head back, eyes closed. Harper slammed on the brakes, and they both held their breath waiting to see if the crunch of tires on dirt would wake him.

Renee whispered, "How do you want to do this?"

Harper choked back a laugh, but whispered back, "Do what?"

"He might know something," Renee said.

Harper shook her head in disbelief. "We don't know who he is. And we sure as *hell* don't know if he has anything to do with Gael. You said Gael said he was in a trunk."

"He was." She eyed the driver. "At one point."

"Renee, I want this to be something. I really do. But why would this guy still be here? Sleeping if he had just kidnapped someone?"

"I don't know." She chewed on her lip thinking for a moment. "I'll distract him, and you check the back ... area of the van."

Harper's eyes grew fiercely wide as she whispered a demand of, "What?"

But Renee already had her door open and was motioning for Harper to do the same.

"What the fuck?" Harper hissed, hurriedly retrieving her backpack from the back seat. She briefly closed her eyes before opening her door, and when it didn't squeak, left it open and hurried in a wide arc behind the van.

Grabbing the gun from her pack, she put it in her waistband and tried to settle her breathing, then peeked around the vehicle just in time to watch Renee fluff her hair and adjust her breasts before cheerfully calling, "Hola?"

In his rearview mirror, she saw the man shoot up in his seat, glance around until Renee came into focus, at which his confused frown eased into a wide grin.

"Hola, señor?" She waved.

"Ho-la," he said slowly, licking his lips, letting his gaze drift over her body.

"Hablas inglés?" she asked, cringing apologetically, as if she'd asked the most offensive question. "I know I should know Spanish, but ..."

"Sí. I speak good English." He smoothed his hair with the palm of his hand to make sure what thin hair he had left covered his bald spot before climbing out of the van. He stood only about an inch taller than Renee and leaned back on his heels; and while Harper could no longer see his face, she was pretty sure the way Renee was trying not to let her upper lip curl into a snarl meant he radiated lechery.

Harper peeked inside the free flying canvas flap that covered the back. It wasn't a high step to climb in over the low gate, but she was glad the man was out of the vehicle as it rocked slightly with her weight; at least it didn't make any sound. She shook her head in disbelief that she was even here and 'searching.' But she was going to give it a once-over on the off chance ... Her heart began to pound in the back of her throat, because there on the van's floor was the 'off chance.' She picked up a leather bracelet and found the name Gael pressed into the soft material.

How many bracelets does this guy have? She'd ask Renee later, now wasn't the time.

She backed out, peeked around the corner and caught Renee's eye, shaking the bracelet, indicating they were on the right path.

Renee's friendliness grew as she leaned into the charade. She stepped closer to the man. "I'm *so* glad we found you. We are seriously lost and haven't seen any buildings or anything for*ever*, and my friend had to go to the bathroom and we saw this building ... but look how lucky we got! We found you *and* you speak English. That's so cool," she cooed, reaching out to touch his arm.

He nodded his head encouragingly at her words and the bat of her eyelashes over those shining bright blues. Harper was impressed how easily Renee had trapped the fly in her web. "Oh my god, you have to meet my friend." Tugging on his arm, she headed toward the building. "She went in there to see if there was a bathroom."

Harper kept the van between her and Renee, tiptoeing around it.

"What's your name?" she heard Renee ask.

"Luis."

Taking him in the building was a good idea; with only one entrance/exit, Harper could stand between it and Luis until he gave them whatever information he had.

"Fuck," she breathed out as she hiked the backpack onto her shoulder and touched the gun. She mentally ran through the lessons she'd had on the proper handling of a gun. Of course, the memories were spotty because the reality of what she was about to do had her raised heartbeat screaming wildly between her ears.

When she was close to the entrance, her steps stuttered. He wouldn't know she had a gun, but how was she going to know if *he* had one?

A stupid idea presented itself, so she didn't stop to think too long about this spur-of-the-moment plan. She put the gun in the side mesh pocket of her bag, entered the room and quickly took in the two windows covered in yellowed newspaper, chairs and broken pool table.

When the man and Renee turned toward her, Renee declared, "Look, I found someone to help us! This is Luis."

Harper dropped her bag right inside the building, gave an exasperated release of breath, then crossed the distance and hugged the man as she exaggerated, "I thought we were lost forever!" He was a head shorter than Harper and smelled of BO, soured clothes and bad breath.

Renee caught her eye and mouthed 'what are you doing?' To which Harper replied with a wide-eyed expression as she tried to subtly (if not awkwardly) feel the areas of the man where a person would hide a gun.

Renee caught on and gave a silent 'oh.'

Obviously, Luis really enjoyed the attention and held Harper close to his body, wiggling himself against her.

Happy with the lack of a weapon on his person, she pried herself free, then held him by his shoulders and pushed him away. His clothes were stained, food on his t-shirt (hopefully it was food) and mud on his pants.

The few taut muscles, slightly visible in his shoulders and chest, seemed the result of daily labor with a definite lack of cardio.

Harper affixed the least snarling smile she could muster. "So, now you can help us."

"Yes," he replied with his own slimy smile, "I love to help beautiful women."

Harper walked back to the bag, tried not to shake as she pulled out the gun and was glad Renee had sense enough to follow and stand behind her.

"Good, because you have a lot of explaining to do." Harper pointed the gun at him.

"¿Qué demonios?" *What the fuck?* He frowned, glancing between the women and the gun. "What are you doing?"

"You took my friend, Luis," Renee accused.

"What? Me?" He seemed truly shocked.

"In my pocket," Harper said.

Renee retrieved the bracelet and when she saw Gael's name, she ground her teeth and held it up. "This was in the back of your van," she hissed, then double-checked with Harper. "In the van, not on the ground, right?"

"Yes," Harper verified, picking up her narrative. "Which means *you* were responsible for helping kidnap him and you know where he is so you're going to tell us exactly where that is."

Luis took a step forward and Harper leveled the gun at him. "No," she snarled. "Don't move, or I'll blow your fucking head off."

The man slowly raised his hands, keeping his fingers splayed, the universal sign he would cooperate.

Renee whispered, "You're not really going to kill him, are you?"

Chapter Seventeen

Nick found that if you can get anti-venom for a snake bite almost immediately after being bit, it fights the worst of the effects within thirty minutes.

Had that been the longest thirty minutes of Nick's life?

Well, yes, but at least he *was* passed out for the first fifteen. When he woke, he'd been moved to a bed inside The Lookout. His shirt had been removed and a woman was cleaning the puncture wound while Ian, the man who had come to his aid, stood by looking down at him with a frown.

His shoulder still felt like he was being seared with a red-hot ice pick, and the cleaning didn't help. Even though they assured him it was soap and water, the woman had to squeeze the skin to clean it properly. He ground his teeth and clenched the sheet under him so he wouldn't fly off the bed or rip the rag from the woman's hand or throw the pan of water at Ian's head.

Ian pointed out that at least Nick wasn't going to die. It kind of helped, and after thirty minutes, the burning eased tremendously. He was given his body weight in water and instructed to stay in bed. Which was fine with him, he was exhausted.

Before he fell asleep, he called Duncan to do a final check-in.

"Did you get sidetracked? Meet someone in the middle of the jungle?"

"Yeah," Nick groaned, "the kind that bites. And not in a good way."

"What?"

Nick muttered, "I got bit by a forest viper."

A roar of laughter. "No shit?!"

"No shit. Hurt like a bitch."

"Where were you?"

Nick sighed. "Around the corner from the front door of The Lookout."

"Lucky for you."

"No kidding."

"Well," Duncan cooed, "do you want me to send someone to help kiss and make your boo-boo better?"

"Ain't no one on your team I want near my boo-boo."

"Ha! Glad you're okay, man," Shaw offered, but quickly added, "I'm gonna give you so much shit about this later. I might show up to your little vacation just to do it."

"Whatever. Now fuck off. I'm signing off and vacation bound."

"Heard." He hung up.

✦ ✦ ✦ ✦ ✦

Nick was up early, but he'd slept for twelve hours and felt like a new man. Or a hell of a lot better man after having deadly venom running through his system; his shoulder no longer felt like it was being dislocated from his body with fire. He was tired and a little sore, but anxious to get moving.

He made his way to the dining room and found pan con chicarrón, a pork and potato sandwich that had been prepared for the guests' breakfast. Ian asked him to consider staying one more day for his health, but Nick assured he was well enough to travel. So Ian begrudgingly gave him instructions for his continued well-being; and the promised vehicle to get him to Cusco, a motorbike, along with the address where it was to be dropped off.

Nick's grin spread as he zoomed around a corner on the little 150cc motorbike – it's manual transmission the only thing keeping it from being a scooter. Still, it was fun to ride. As he twisted along the dense tree-lined road in the cool morning, squinting through his sunglasses, his hat on backwards so it wouldn't fly off, his button-down shirt billowing, he thought it was a great day to be alive.

It was a great day for about ninety minutes.

That's when the bike died; sputtering with an ungrateful cough, lurch, then nothing. With a resigned grumble, Nick climbed off and pushed it to the side of the road, which wasn't far as the jungle continued to grow over the attempted pruning.

What little he knew about motorcycle repair wasn't much, but he knew you needed fuel, air and spark to make the things work. He set his pack on the ground to retrieve the generic Swiss Army knife he'd purchased, it wasn't really going to be helpful with this problem, though. He checked the tank, there was gas. Followed the fuel lines, no apparent leaks. He couldn't check the spark because he didn't have the proper tools to get the spark plugs off. He also needed a socket wrench to take off the panel that held the air filter.

He gave a chuckle as he studied the bike, of course this model didn't have a kickstart; so if the problem was starter related, there was nothing he could do about that either. He gave the bike time to cool off, tried to turn it over once more, and while the lights came on the small dash, nothing else happened. Which meant it was time for him to also recognize the fact that in the past two hours he hadn't seen another soul. "Looks like you're hiking back to The Lookout, Robbins."

First, he stepped into the trees to relieve himself. Not more than two seconds passed when he heard another bike approach. "Yes." He hurried to finish, then happily called out, "hey!" as he burst out of the trees.

Only his friendly greeting became a warning "hey!" when he saw a kid, mid-teens, crouched over his pack, rummaging through it.

The young man stood, but picked up Nick's pack.

"That's mine," Nick said sternly.

The young man's eyes darted between his bike and Nick. He must have decided he couldn't get to his bike fast enough so he let the bag slip down to the ground. "Lo siento, no quería ..." *Sorry, I didn't mean ...*

Nick nodded, holding his hands out to the side as he slowly began to cross the distance. "¿Dónde está ... el pueblo más cercano?" *Where is ... the nearest town?* He glanced down into his bag, the envelope of money he'd been using (of which there was still a sizeable amount left) sat on the top and open. The kid had obviously seen it.

What happened next was his own damn fault. He was craning his neck so far to the left, looking in his bag, and the kid was, well ... a kid. So he didn't think he was a threat, and figured he'd be fine for several seconds while he assessed the situation in his pack.

His head sure as shit spun back to the right when something slammed into his right thigh.

"What the fuck?!" Nick roared, looking down to find a lightweight, black gripped handle of a folding utility knife sticking out of his thigh. He turned his shocked frown toward the kid and reached for him, but the young man crouched and pushed Nick off balance.

While he tripped a few feet in the opposite direction, the teen grabbed Nick's bag and in two steps was on his bike. Nick hissed as he hop-stepped across the distance, reaching the kid just as he kick-started his bike and pulled away, leaving Nick swiping at air.

He did a circle in the road, his eyes filled with fear and shock.

"You little shit!" Nick screamed.

The kid probably hadn't started his day thinking he was gonna stab someone and steal their stuff, anymore than Nick thought the day would see him robbed after being stabbed.

"¿!Dónde está el pueblo más cercano!? Where's the next town?" Nick seethed the question loudly, taking another hobbled step in the thief's direction. The young man pointed the way Nick had come, "unos kilómetros más allá," then sped off in the opposite direction he'd pointed

"A few kilometers that way," Nick growled, then screamed after the disappearing kid, "What's a few?!"

He glanced down at the knife; it wasn't very big, two maybe three inches. He reached to take it out, but stopped, recalling something about having a better chance at survival if he left it in.

He rumbled, "Mother fucker." How had that kid gotten the best of him? Maybe he should have stayed at the B&B, maybe the snake venom was lingering, clouding his judgement.

He took another exploratory step. It didn't hurt that bad, though anger and adrenaline could be masking the pain at the moment. And if he were being honest, the snake bite had been worse. "Not that I ever wanted to be able to compare the two." He gave his exasperated grievance to the jungle.

He had a choice to make. Continue up the road or wait for someone to come by. He decided to hedge his bets. He'd head up the road, the way the boy had gone, for thirty minutes while *hoping* someone with more scruples than the young man had, would drive by. Sooner rather than later.

He checked his pockets, nothing. That little shit had his passport, wallet, a nice little wad of cash, his satellite phone and the GPS (thankfully, both were encrypted), his water bottles and change of clothes. At least Nick had his watch. He checked the time, so he'd know how long the knife was stuck in his leg, then rubbed the back of his neck and laughed. "I mean ... I might have done the same thing." He'd been young and stupid once too. "But why stab, why not slash?" It was a better defensive move. Unless that's something the kid picked up in movies and video games?

He bent and retrieved the only possession he'd been left with, his green baseball hat.

"Little shit'll probably tell all his friends he was in danger and the fight was so dramatic; he barely escaped with his life."

He reminded himself, "You've been through worse." Then began a slow, steady hike along the roadside, armed with only his wits and a little bit of hope. "What part of vacation is hard to understand?" he asked the world beyond him. "It's your own fault Robbins, you didn't have to answer Sean's call and you didn't have to admit you were open to options for your vacation destination, and you sure as shit didn't need to go make that delivery."

In another few steps, after the berating of himself swirled a few more times, he told himself to "shut up."

Nick stopped and looked at the knife, it wasn't a heavy blade. If it had been, the handle would be wobbling with every step and cutting him more. If that were the case, then why leave the knife in place? Maybe that's what you were supposed to do if you sat still and waited for help to arrive. Should he stay still and wait for help? Maybe he *should* pull it out. But what if the little shit had nicked an artery and he started to bleed out as he walked? What if the moving blade nicked an artery? Maybe he should tie his long sleeve shirt around the knife, to keep it from moving around while he walked.

"Christ, Robbins," he groaned, "make a decision."

He would keep his leg as straight as he could and walk for fifteen minutes; if there was no sign of anyone by then, he'd use his shirt and secure the blade but even that idea wasn't ideal because then he'd be left a bare-chested feast for the mosquitos.

He was sweaty again, the mugginess beginning to set in. The bugs were beginning to arrive as well, but hopefully the bug spray he put on would hold a little while longer.

After a few minutes, he glanced down to inspect the wound. There was a little seepage and it hurt, but he was able to keep going. He hoped that meant the kid didn't hit any major arteries or veins. He assumed more blood would mean something had been nicked.

"You've been through worse," he reminded himself again as he began to slowly walk once again. "Like that accident when you flipped the car, crawled out the shattered window and sliced your hip open on a piece of metal." He'd lived through that, he'd live through this.

He just needed to keep thoughts about important arteries and veins being sliced at bay.

Suddenly, an echo stopped him. He thought he heard a voice, though he couldn't be sure. He stood still and thought he heard movement a few hundred feet away, echoing through the thick vegetation. He studied the area surrounding him, finding a small animal path leading toward the sound.

He pursed his lips, it was a bad idea. Then, the sound of someone vomiting had him compromising with himself. He'd go slowly. To keep from having another encounter with something that wanted to kill him.

As he made his way down the path, he wiped away unseen spider webs and slapped at his neck as phantom mosquitos found areas of his skin to feast on. In all reality, maybe it was the sounds causing him to think he was being covered in creepy crawly bitey things. Hopefully most of the feelings were phantom.

He slapped at his neck again, berating himself for coming this way, but when he heard the distinctive sound of someone talking, he knew he was close. He put his head down and pushed forward for the most important reason:

At least whoever was at the other end of this path was human.

Chapter Eighteen

Renee squared her shoulders and gave herself a quick internal pep talk: *C'mon Renee! You built your own company. You're amazing and tough and a badass. YOU are one hell of a Badass Boss Bitch!*

Because what she really wanted to do was kick this slimy asshole in the crotch several times before melting into a pity ball on the floor and crying. She was one step closer, yet felt so much further away from Gael.

It *was* helpful that when she'd jumped out of the car with a ridiculous scenario to get information, Harper was hot on her heels, playing along. Harper was her damn rock in this storm and there was going to come a time Renee would need to heap magnitudes of gratitude on her; but not right now.

Right now, Renee needed to tap into some of Harper's badass energy.

Renee would continue to tap into the impressive power she felt when Harper aimed the gun at Luis' crotch and said, "I wasn't talking about the head with the bad comb-over and sunken eyes."

Renee's hands trembled as she tied him to the chair, but when it was finished, she looked down at Luis and felt pretty amazing. She didn't know she had it in her. She aimed a smile at Harper, who'd lowered the gun, picked up her pack and asked, "You okay? I just need a second ..." She didn't wait for Renee to answer, though.

Renee turned her attention to Luis and let a snarl raise her lips. "Oh, I'm fine. I have lots of questions for my new friend."

Luis tried to jerk his body into a standing position, but Renee pushed against his chest and he fell back with a grunt. "This is uncomfortable." He tried to look over his shoulder at his hands behind his back.

"Were you thinking about Gael's comfort when you kidnapped him?" Renee scoffed. "Give me more information about my friend and maybe

I could help your comfort."

"I told you, I don't know anything. I don't want to know anything. I only do little jobs here and there. This time I drove a man from one location to another. I got paid. That is all."

"How much?"

"What?"

"How much do you get paid for a little drive?"

He shrugged and she narrowed her gaze, hoping her grin was viciously happy enough. "Where's the money?"

He swallowed and she quickly pushed him to the side of the chair, raising his right glute; when he tried to fight her, she found his wallet. After tugging several times, she extracted it from his greasy pants while Luis protested, "No, no!"

Inside she found a rather thick stack of cash. She counted a little over thirty-five hundred soles and did some quick math. It was about a thousand dollars.

"I'm gonna take this."

"No! You bitch!"

"Yeah, definitely keeping it." She pocketed the money and tossed his empty wallet at his feet. "So, let's start at the beginning. When you got a call and were asked to pick up my friend."

⁂

Harper slipped the gun in the side pocket of the pack and retrieved a bottle of water. When she was halfway across the parking lot she dropped the bag, barely making it to the jungle's edge before she lost the contents of her stomach.

She cleared her throat several times, spit, used the water to rinse out her mouth and gargled to clear the awful taste.

She righted herself and tried several deep breaths as she mindlessly gazed around the intruding jungle. A stress-filled laugh bubbled out. "Come to Peru Harper. It'll be the trip of a lifetime."

She gargled again then continued her diatribe. "As long as you can shake your altitude sickness and my boyfriend doesn't get kidnapped for reasons that aren't clear, it'll be awesome." She let another unbalanced laugh slip, but stopped abruptly when the vegetation to her right began to rustle.

Stumbling back a few steps, she waited for a dangerous animal to come barreling out — because that made sense with everything else that was happening.

Her fear radiated in time with the trees and she opened her mouth to scream, when the unseen beast grunted an expletive.

The tension flowed from her shoulders and out through her feet until the realization that a deep male voice in the middle of nowhere was just as deadly as a wild boar (or whatever beasts were nearby), so now new terror refilled her body, toes to head.

Another grunted expletive and Harper raised an eyebrow, at least the beast *did* curse in English; but so what? She knew how to cuss in at least three other languages.

Merde, French. Scheiße, German. Mierda, Spanish.

Shit. And English.

She took another step back from the originating ruckus and was truly shocked when the owner of the voice burst through the underbrush with a relieved, "Damnit!"

Harper's eyes widened as the tall man stomped in a circle, knocking his baseball hat off as he manically brushed the sleeves of his beige shirt before starting to scrub his short, dark hair with his fingers. When that was done, he caught sight of Harper as he began to brush his neck, demanding, "Do you see any bugs on me? Any spiders? Or snakes?" He brushed his arms again.

She was frozen in place as she studied his twisting body, his neck craning right and left, attempting to look over his shoulders, making the muscles in his back flex beneath his tucked shirt – showing off a healthy, athletic ripple of muscles and a taut stomach.

Since she still hadn't answered, he took a few steps toward her, eyes wide with concern, arms held out to the side. "Anything? ¿Vez algo sobre mí?"

Harper was having trouble finding her voice, not only because of his unexpected arrival, but because of the sight before her. His eyes were honey brown; he had about a three-day stubble; and the top of his shirt was unbuttoned, showing off tempting tanned skin. The entire visual was dangerous and sweaty in a spectacularly sexy way. Hell, even the dappling effect of the sun through the trees showed him in a halo of light with shadows that added to his shocking magnetism.

She blinked instead of answering, so he made another twisting circle, begging, "Hey beautiful? I'm dying here, do you see anything?"

"No," Harper finally rasped. "I don't see anything."

He stopped turning and looked skyward, closing his eyes for a moment as he took a deep breath. He scrubbed his head, then wiped his neck, arms and chest once more.

When he finally faced her full on, she pointed to his lower extremities, an eyebrow raised. "You *do* have a knife in your leg, though."

He nodded, glancing down at the protruding knife. "That, I know about."

"You speak English," she voiced the obvious.

"I do." He wiped the sweat from his brow with the sleeve of his shirt. "So do you."

"I'm from the East Coast," she muttered, then frowned as she turned her attention to the foliage behind him. Would the person who stabbed him be tripping out next? And if she had to, could she get to the gun in time?

"I'm from the other coast, Los Angeles." He glanced around at where he'd ended up.

Harper eyed the knife. "Why didn't you pull it out?"

"I was going to, but then I remembered a wilderness show I once saw. The guy said if you're ever stabbed, you should leave it in so you don't bleed out."

She inclined her head but her attention oscillated between him and the area behind him as she asked, "Who stabbed you?" But then she scrunched her face at her conversational tone. *Sure, why not talk about a knife sticking out of some stranger's leg in the middle of nowhere. Add it to the growing list of ridiculous situations she was already steeped in.*

"It was a misunderstanding." He glanced down at his leg. "It's a small blade really."

She looked at the thick black handle. "It doesn't look small."

"The handle makes it look bigger. You know what they say, it's not the size, but how you use it." He winked.

She scowled.

He licked his lips before changing the subject. "Where am I?"

Harper tilted her head and frowned. "Peru?"

He gave a quick snort of laughter and hobbled a few feet to the side where a tarp covered stack of bricks sat. "I know the Peru part. I was in a town east of here and was headed to Cusco." He grunted as he took the weight off the leg for the first time.

"Were you walking there?"

He adjusted his leg as he muttered, "It's a long story."

She looked back to the trees. Usually, the person who was stabbed – unexpectedly handsome or not – tended to be the bad guy. She slowly nodded. "I'm very open to hearing the story, long or not." She took another step toward her bag.

A smile tugged at the corner of his mouth, easygoing sexiness radiating across the distance that separated them ...

She cleared her throat and reminded herself: *Sexy or not, he has a knife sticking out of his leg!* Then she reasoned, "I think you'd want to hear the whole story if someone tripped out of the middle of the jungle with a knife sticking out of his leg."

"Maybe." He pushed his sleeve out of the way to check his watch. Harper waited, but it didn't feel like he was about to start story time.

She took a deep breath and sighed. "What are you doing alone in the middle of the jungle with a knife sticking out of your leg?"

That awarded her a wide charming grin. "Sightseeing?" He laughed at his cleverness then signaled to Harper. "I could be asking you the same question. What are *you* doing in the middle of the jungle alone?"

"Sightseeing." She pursed her lips against the unexpected smile that threatened.

He wasn't glancing over his shoulder, so maybe she should take that as a sign *he* didn't think anyone was following him. He did, however, let his gaze nonchalantly scan the two cars parked in the open lot.

Which brought her back to the ridiculous plight she was already embroiled in, and the fact that she didn't have time to pencil a new one on her to-do list.

She needed to get rid of him.

Fast.

Though, the knife wound was a bit of a hiccup. The area around the knife hilt didn't look too bad, there wasn't much seepage and he'd made it this far. Maybe she could tell him to head up the road and she'd call him a ride.

"You know–"

"Harper!" Renee's voice echoed from inside the building.

Or, she could zip tie this guy as well.

"Harper! He talked!" Renee came jogging out. "He told me where to go next!" Only when she caught sight of the new situation, she skidded to a stop in the dirt, pointing. "Who's that?"

"Not sure," Harper answered honestly.

"He has a knife sticking out of his leg," Renee stated, but before she received a response, added, "Oh Harper, you didn't stab him, did you?"

The man chuckled as Harper defended, "*I* didn't stab him." She eyed her friend. "I might help him though." She took the opportunity to retrieve the backpack and felt a lot better having it in her arms.

"It would be really handy if you could help me," he admitted, then shrugged. "But if you can't, I suppose I've been in tougher scrapes."

"What kind of tougher scrapes?" Renee asked, but Harper cleared her throat.

Renee cocked her head at the stranger, then stepped close to Harper and quietly asked, "What do you want me to do about ...?"

Harper turned her back slightly on the man and matched whispers. "Keep the current situation intact. I'll help him then send him away."

Renee turned and gave the man another once-over before elbowing Harper. "He looks like he'd be fun to help."

He gave an appreciative wink.

Harper growled which brought Renee's attention back. She gave Harper's arm a squeeze and excitedly relayed, "We have a location." Then she skipped back toward the ramshackle bar.

Harper gritted her teeth and turned her attention back to the man. With a wry smile pulling at his lips, he tilted his head and assessed, "So. No sightseeing alone?"

Chapter Nineteen

Harper stared at the problematic new arrival for several long moments. He didn't look away, didn't flinch, but allowed the study. Finally, she asked the question foremost in her mind. "Is someone else going to come crashing through the jungle any minute to ..." she gestured toward his leg, "finish the job?" God, that sounded ridiculous.

"No. It really was an accident. I've been shuffling for a while now and when I heard a voice, I walked directly toward it because I needed help," he said matter-of-factly.

"If I help you, are you going to hurt us?"

He shook his head as he gave an exhausted exhalation. "In the past ten days, I've been bitten by a woman, a deadly snake, midges and mosquitoes. Today, my bike broke down and I was stabbed by a misled youth who stole all my worldly possessions." He gave a hollow laugh. "And hearing all that out loud sounds comical."

I bet I could top that, Harper thought, but instead said, "That doesn't really answer my question."

He held out his hands as a sign of goodwill. "No one is chasing me. And if you would be so kind as to help me; I promise to leave you to your information and location. No questions asked."

She let the sounds of the jungle – the breeze that only reached the tops of the trees, the Peruvian bird songs and active bugs – fill the expanding time. She narrowed her gaze, attempting to see the truth of his words somewhere on his face.

He did look tired, a hint of jaundice maybe at the edge of his eyes; eyes that were slightly sunken from his professed adventures. But when he mindlessly licked his delectable, slightly chapped lips, an unexpected twinge punched low in Harper's abdomen. She reactively licked her lips, then pressed them together, steeling herself as she inwardly rolled her eyes. *You are looking for possible threats; not delectable lips!*

The shadowed stubble of dark hair on his jawline perfectly complimented his olive skin. (Still not the kind of 'noticing' you're looking for, Harper.) He probably kept the beard trimmed shorter when he wasn't in the middle of the jungle with a knife sticking out of his leg.

Okay, that helped ground her, the realities of where she was and what was happening.

But then the bastard wiped his neck with his hand, which brought her attention to the undone buttons, revealing his chest, where a dusting of dark hair and defined pectoral muscles peeked.

"I'm Nick, by the way." He broke through her concentration. "Nick Robbins."

"Harper," she returned, and having decided she'd help him, took out a new bottle of water from her bag and closed the distance between them, handing it over.

He groaned thankfully before chugging the contents, allowing a few stray drips to follow a path down his throat to that chest ...

"C'mon, Harper." She muttered the demand as she made sure to position her bag so he couldn't see the gun. Then retrieving antibacterial wipes, spray and the roll of duct tape, she placed them on the bag and stood with her hands on her hips.

"Whoa," Nick said impressively as he watched her, "is that a magic bag?"

"I was a Girl Scout." She frowned at his leg, "How do you want to do this?"

"I guess just pull it out." He reached for the knife, but she waved her hands and yelled, "Wait!"

He stopped, aiming a questioning look her way.

She sighed. "Let's figure out the best way to do this first. Like, should we cut the pants away so we can clean and tape the wound? Or pull out the knife then you slip your pants off ...?"

He glanced down, realizing what she was asking. Since it was higher up on his thigh, he figured pants down was the best bet. He stood and directed, "I'll pull the knife out, then take the pants down. If you could hit the wound with some antibacterial spray ..."

"If it starts bleeding we'll need something to stop it." She reached back in pack and brought out a baggie of folded napkins. "At least they're sterile ... ish."

"That works," he said approvingly, as he shifted his weight between his legs to steady himself. He glanced down at the knife and started to reach for it.

But again Harper stopped him. "Wait!" She frowned, then knelt in front of him and asked the knife, "If it starts to bleed, should we keep the napkin against the wound, then duct tape over it, or just duct tape on the wound?"

"I think the napkin and duct tape over it?"

She put everything in order on the backpack turned triage table. Wipes, spray, napkin, duct tape ...

"Hold on." She fished out her multi-tool and opened the scissors.

Nick unbuckled his belt, lowered his pants slightly around his hips, and asked, "Ready?"

Harper didn't answer, because she was in no way, shape or form ready for this.

He moved to take a hold of the hilt when Harper stopped him again. "Wait."

"Now what?" Nick asked, gritting his teeth.

She could see that the wound had bled a bit and she knew they needed to get the knife out. (Of course, a few other logistics bounced around too. Like, how long could a knife be kept inside a human body? How far were they from a good hospital? What kind of snake bite did he get? Why hadn't she thought of finding a way to buy some anti-venom and was anti-venom something that could be purchased over the counter?)

"Harper?" Nick called softly.

She cleared her throat and explained what she was thinking. "I think I should pull it out, so it comes out straight, like, the exact way it went in?" She glanced up at him and thought he paled, but caught the slight jerk of agreement.

Harper glanced at his thigh and hovered her hands at different angles, not touching him, but trying to figure out the best way to grasp the knife and get some leverage.

In the end, she moved to the side so she could hold the back of his well-formed upper thigh, encircling her hand around the hilt of the knife. Before she grabbed the knife, she looked up at him with wide eyes and nodded: *Was he ready?*

Nick didn't say a word, because unexpectedly staring down into Harper's upturned face was a bit more arousing than it had any right being.

He'd been shocked when he finally stopped looking for deadly bugs and really took her in. She was striking. That had been the first word that slapped him upside the head. Her auburn hair was in a ponytail, green eyes wary of him; calculating but in a self-assured and intelligent way. She wore a t-shirt with a black hoodie partially zipped. And he would have to be without a pulse not to notice her stately stature and the mouth-drying curve of her hips in those well-worn jeans that hugged her so so well.

She was right to be cautious of strangers, and even though he promised to leave once she helped him, he wasn't really in a hurry. Hell, maybe there would be a reason he could stick around, get to know her better.

"Nick?" She brought his attention back to where she was on her knees in front of him. Her warm hand pressing into the back of his thigh at the base of his ass, her other hand hovering over the handle of the knife blade in such a suggestive way, his inner Neanderthal was dragging his mind solidly into the gutter. Which caused involuntarily tensing of his muscles.

She patted the back of his leg. "I think you need to try and relax."

He closed his eyes, tried to think of the smell in his apartment when he'd accidentally left dirty dishes in the sink for a month when gone on assignment. The hairy mole on the face of his middle school librarian. The way the latrine backed up in the middle of the hottest summer when he was in bootcamp. And the fact that he was about to have a knife pulled out of his leg.

That all did the trick. "Okay," he said then looked down again. Into her smoky jade green eyes looking up at him through dark lashes and that tempting bubble gum pink mouth that was so very close to his–

"Shit!"

"Got it." She held the two-inch blade up as proof, then dropped it on the ground. He studied the blade while his leg throbbed.

"Nick," she said irritatingly. And he gazed down once again, immediately lost in her eyes.

"Your pants," she insisted.

Pants?

"Oh. Yeah, yeah." He lowered them carefully past the wound to his knees. Any unwanted daydreams dissipated when she sprayed the antiseptic, pulling a hiss of pain from him.

"I think," her frown increased as she told the wound, "we should wash it with a wipe too. Just in case."

She sprayed her hands before pulling out a wipe. As he watched, he muttered, "I recently updated my tetanus ..." As if that would help the situation. But Harper only nodded, then wiped the wound several times.

"Goooohhhh ... damnit," he hissed.

She nodded, allowing a faint smile, seeming happy with her sanitation. Then picking up one of the folded napkins, she pressed it against his leg instructing, "hold this," and cut a large strip of duct tape.

When she paused with the tape held above his skin, he asked, "What?"

"It's gonna rip the hair when it needs to come off."

"That's a problem for another day," Nick encouraged.

She put the duct tape in place then blew out a breath of success as she sat back on her heels and aimed a grin up at Nick.

⁂

Harper became aware of her current position. Blinking, she let her gaze drop to Nick's well-formed thighs and short black boxer briefs that were not ashamed to brag about their contents. She swallowed hard as her gaze ran back up his length to his face, where a sly smile suggested he definitely knew she was checking him out and what she was thinking.

She fell to the side with an *oomph,* caught herself, then did a strange roll and pushed herself to her feet, brushing the dirt off her clothes.

Thankfully, when she was able to focus again, his pants were up and he was securing his belt. "Can I have another piece of tape?" He pointed to the hole in his pants in explanation.

She handed a piece over, then picked the knife up and cleaned it with a disinfectant wipe before closing it, and put it in her backpack.

"Souvenir?" Nick asked.

"I thought it might be a good idea to have a bit of your DNA; just in case." Her eyes lit up at her joke when he laughed. She took out a bottle of pain reliever and held it up in offering.

"God, yes," he said appreciatively.

After handing the pills and another bottle of water over, he held out his hand for her to shake. "Thank you so much, Harper. You're amazing."

She took his hand, warm and calloused, which sent unnecessary shock waves up her arm. With a frown she wiggled her hand out of his, cleared her throat and pointed up the road. "You're about four hours from Cusco."

"My bike broke down," he reminded her.

She licked her lips and glanced at the rental car and three wheeled van behind her. She could give him the van; he could even go pick up the bike. Everyone wins. He'd be one less unexpected worry out of their hair, then she and Renee could get back to their interrogation.

"Take the van," she offered.

"Are you sure?"

"Sure." She hoped he wasn't picking up on the fact that she was trying to dismiss him. But she was trying to dismiss him.

"I can help ... with anything ... if you need any help." He glanced around the area, looking for an excuse? She wasn't sure. But it might be time to remind him that he promised to leave her alone once she'd helped him.

"I don't need any help." She gave a tight grin. "Give me a second and I'll get the keys."

Just then a loud commotion erupted inside the abandoned bar.

Chapter Twenty

Nick's instincts kicked in and he hobbled to place himself in front of Harper; only she cursed, dropped her bag and took out a gun from the side pocket.

How had he missed seeing that?

He watched Harper angrily march toward the noise, intrigued as everything turned to slow motion. A short, stocky Peruvian man hobbled out of the building with pieces of a broken chair bound to his legs and his arms tied behind his back. The blonde was close behind, yelling, "Get back here, asshole!"

The man turned and glanced behind him as he hobbled, so he wasn't aware that Harper had moved to stand a few feet in front of him. When he did turn his attention back, he slid to a stop, stomped the ground and muttered a litany of Spanish expletives.

The blonde did her own sliding stop but slammed into the man, causing him to fall on the ground, while she took several uneven steps around his prostrate body before she caught herself.

"You okay?" Harper asked.

"I'm good," she assured, "He rocked on the chair and when it fell, it broke." She looked down at the man who was obviously trying to get away.

The man rolled over onto his side and whined, "I told you everything. Let me go."

Harper took a few steps closer and aimed the gun between his legs.

Nick crossed his arms, impressed. He liked her style.

"Where are the keys to your van?" Harper asked.

"What? Why?" the guy demanded.

"He's gonna take it." She nodded toward Nick.

"No! It's my truck," he yelled, then frowned following her gaze. "Who is that?"

"A friend," Nick said.

The blonde walked over to the truck. "They're in the ignition."

"No," came the cry from the ground.

"Nice meeting you, Nick. Have a good day," Harper excused without looking at him.

He weighed his options as he glanced between the van and Harper. None of this had anything to do with him. She seemed to know how to handle a gun. She said she didn't need any help. He could leave.

But he was also only human (and his job aligned with helping in situations just like this.) And, okay, he was also pretty damn curious why two American women were in the middle of the jungle holding a man – who'd they'd apparently zip-tied to a chair – at gunpoint

Nick, he warned, *being curious about such things can get a man in a lot of trouble.*

Yeah, but look at her. No-nonsense, in charge. Intriguing as hell.

Men who play with fire get burned.

The image of her on her knees in front of him flashed once again, those damn seductive eyes looking up at him and—

She cocked the gun, bringing him back to reality. A twinge of sympathetic pain at the horrific thought of what a gunshot to a man's genitals would do to the area made him adjust himself.

"Hey, Harper?" Nick casually called her name as he slowly edged toward her.

He'd made his decision.

She shifted so she could see him out of the corner of her eye.

"We're good," she said. "We've got everything covered."

"I see that." He kept his hands extended slightly out to the side as he stepped closer. "I thought I'd check to see if I could be of any help."

"I don't need help, Nick." The frustration was evident in Harper's voice.

"I need help!" the man declared. "They kidnapped me!"

The blonde kicked the dirt by his side. "Because *you* kidnapped my friend."

Nick stopped moving, no longer too concerned about the man's well-being. "Who did he kidnap?"

"No one," Harper muttered at the same time the other woman said, "My friend, Gael."

"Renee," Harper hissed.

Nick took the opportunity to move toward the blonde, his hand held out. "I'm Nick Robbins."

She didn't accept his hand but verified her identity, "Renee. You already met Harper. And this," she kicked the dirt again, "is Luis. He was hired to kidnap my friend. But Gael is smart, he's been texting me when he can, letting me know where he is."

"Really?" Luis stopped wiggling around in the dirt.

Renee grinned at him. "And you just told me where to find the assholes who hired you."

"Is that right, Luis?" Nick asked.

"No!" Luis yelled. "These two, están locas."

"He called us crazy?" Harper asked, stepping closer as Renee confirmed, "Yes he did."

Luis let out a whimper and Nick sighed, slowly inserting himself in the situation again. "Harper," he said softly, "can I help?"

"No."

"I am the man in the middle," Luis insisted. "No sé nada. But the men, the ones who hired me, they have a usual meeting place. Outside the gasolinera. Cerca del pueblo Quince Mil. I told her." He eyed Renee.

Renee pointed. "See? That's what he told me and hasn't changed the story. C'mon Harper."

"Wait a minute," Harper said at the same time Nick did.

She finally gave him her full attention.

"I can help," he offered calmly.

"I don't know you. And I don't want to get to know you, because we have our hands full as it is." She moved so she could see Nick and Luis at the same time.

"I'm supposed to be on vacation," he muttered, more to himself than anyone else.

"Great. Get in the van and continue your vacation," Harper encouraged.

He aimed a lopsided grin in her direction as he softly admitted, "I have a special set of skills ..."

But before Harper could comment on his ridiculous movie phrasing,

Renee gasped excitedly. "Are you a mercenary?! The woman in jail with me said there are certain places where it's easy to find mercenaries for hire."

"*Places*," Harper corrected. "Not randomly in the middle of jungles."

"It's a place," Renee shot.

"Jail?" Nick asked.

He made a quick list of red flags that should be deterring him from getting involved with this situation: One – the growing crazed look in Harper's eyes. Two – the gun. Three – the man they'd allegedly kidnapped but most definitely tied up. Four and five would be the mention of jail and that there was an active pursuit to hire a mercenary.

Did you hear that Robbins? None of this will get better. Get in the van and go.

"It wasn't *real* jail." Renee waved the idea away. "They only put me in holding until I cooled off."

And that would be number six on the list.

"I was so upset about Gael being kidnapped that I went to a bar, one of the locations Gael shared with me. I got in a fight." She gestured to the bruise and cut on her cheek (*number seven on the red flag list*). "And then in the police station, I demanded they do their job, and when they didn't take me seriously, I may have begun screaming and throwing a few things."

Hey asshole! That's number eight on the list.

"She went back and apologized," Harper defended. "And they've opened a proper investigation."

Renee added, "But they aren't moving quick enough and we've been getting more information than them so we're going to find Gael ourselves."

And we'll add delusional right here.

But then Harper made eye contact with him and he knew, beyond a shadow of a doubt, he was about to stupidly, knowingly, willingly, jump on board this crazy train.

"I can help," he insisted.

"I told you, we don't need help." Harper glanced at his leg. "You have a knife wound." Out of the corner of her eye, Luis slowly began to snake his way across the dirt, away from her. Renee stepped toward him and kicked him in the side. Harper retrained the gun on his crotch.

"Maybe you should help *me*, eh gringo?"

"Harper, I swear, I can help. And my leg's fine, I'm good to go," Nick assured. He pointed at her as he told Renee, "This formidable beauty already saw to the knife wound."

Renee gave a snort of a laugh. "Formidable sex goddess."

"That's not what he said." Harper swatted.

Nick finished crossing the distance to her and when close enough, lowered his voice and said, "I mean, it's not too far a leap from beauty to goddess, that definitely works too."

Renee mockingly swooned, "Oh my god!" At the same time, Harper scoffed and gave an exaggerated eye roll. "Oh my god."

"*Are* you a mercenary?" Renee asked.

"Looks like I am today." Nick took another step closer. He was within an arm's length of her now.

Harper frowned. "What makes you think you can help us?" She quickly followed that question with, "What makes you think we should *accept* your help? We don't know you."

He reached out and lightly put his hand on her arm and she seemed open to allowing his fingers to trace her soft skin to where she was holding the gun as he admitted, "I'm not asking you to trust me, I'm willing to earn your trust. But I'm dependable and I'm here. And when I'm not trying to go on a vacation, I work for a three-letter government agency that I'm sure you're both familiar with." He cupped both her hands in his; when she released the gun, he took it, put the safety on and tucked it in his waistband.

Renee let out a whoop, jumped up and down then threw herself into his arms. "Thank you!" He grunted from the force of her lunging into him and tried to gauge Harper's reaction.

Luis had taken the opening to stumble to his feet and take floundering steps.

"He's getting away." Harper crossed her arms over her chest, nodding in Luis' direction.

Nick removed Renee and called, "Luis? I'm a really good shot, man." And in case he didn't understand the English completely, repeated, "Soy un muy buen tirador."

Luis slowed and turned in a circle, his frown deepening. He kicked at the dirt, then as it rose up he coughed and let out a string of curses before plopping down in defeat.

"Nick Robbins?" Harper asked.

"At your service."

"You said all your things were stolen."

"I did."

"So we don't have any way of knowing if that's your real name. We don't have any way to check what you do for a living. All we have is your word and the tangible fact you showed up with a knife sticking out of your leg."

He took the gun out and handed it back to Harper as a gesture of goodwill. She tucked it in the back of her pants. "You know, this is my illegally purchased gun."

He shook his head. "I didn't hear that."

Harper let an accidental grin flash.

"As soon as I can, I'll prove I'm who I say I am," he said. "In the meantime, I can help and I *want* to earn your trust."

"I trust him." Renee winked at Nick. "I have a sixth sense about these things. Harper, he has good juju."

"Bad luck, though," Harper muttered. She tilted her head. "You said you got bit by a woman and a snake?"

He held out his left hand where the clear indentation of a set of teeth could be seen, then unbuttoned his shirt and pulled the collar to the side so they could see the snake puncture wounds.

"Man," Renee said, "you're a mess, Nick."

He agreed.

Harper frowned. "I don't know."

Renee stepped closer to Harper and squeezed her arm. "He's a good guy. I promise. Right, Nick? You're a good guy?"

"I try to be."

"Fine." Harper sighed. "Help us. Just don't ... fuck us over or anything, okay?" It was the best threat she could give, because her headache was returning.

"I give you my word," he said softly, "I won't." He hoped the seriousness behind his oath helped.

Nick clapped his hands together. "How about we all go sit in the shade and maybe you can start at the beginning."

Renee shook her head. "Sorry buddy, we're racing against time here.

We'll tell you in the car."

Chapter Twenty-One

Harper thought the small rental car was perfect for a single woman in a small town who did grocery shopping on Saturday afternoons or occasionally drove a friend to the doctor. *Not* following the directions of a man they'd kidnapped, who'd assured them he knew where 'bad guys' hung out.

Harper drove, Renee beside her. Luis and Nick were in the back. And since Nick was behind Harper — his distracting ruggedness so perfectly visible in the rearview mirror — she had to work doubly hard to keep her attention on the road.

But luckily, four people crammed into the little two door seemed to overpower most of its capabilities, and helped Harper refocus. Especially when the air conditioning died and it began to pull to the right slightly. At least when it turned a corner, the added weight kept it firmly in line.

A few miles up the road Nick pointed, "there's my bike," and they all watched it float by.

As Renee finished the final recap of the major events in Gael's kidnapping, Nick nodded appreciatively. "That's really smart, making a list of everywhere you went. Do you have any idea why Gael was taken?"

Renee made eye contact with Luis as she reproachfully answered, "I have *no* idea."

"*I* don't know why." Luis pouted, then declared, "I am hungry."

"You're lucky you aren't tied up anymore," Renee shot, still disappointed Nick hadn't allowed it.

"And I need a drink," he added childishly.

Harper admitted, "I need something to eat too."

Renee fished out the dried fruit and nuts and passed them around, then handed a bottle of water to both her and Nick. (Harper was secretly happy when he drank half of it before passing it to a disappointed Luis.)

An hour into the ride, as the road rose in elevation, Harper wondered if someone needed to get out and wind the little car up before continuing. Next, the unavoidable, but expected, afternoon showers began. Clouds dipped low to make sure they completely emptied their bellies.

Harper turned the windshield wipers on high, and the car lost more power. When the windows fogged and she tried the defroster, the damn vehicle slowed to almost a crawl. She began to laugh, several short snorts in the back of her throat before she opened her mouth and let the riotous sound out.

"You okay, Harp?" All Renee had to offer her friend at this point was an apologetic half smile.

Harper shrugged her shoulders as far up as she could get them. "I don't know." She cracked her window and asked Renee to do the same.

When Nick gave her shoulder a friendly squeeze, she gazed at him in the rearview mirror and thought about pulling away. But his warm, strong hand lingered and began kneading her tense muscles. And it felt really good; the empowering nod reflected in the rearview helped too.

"There!" Luis yelled, his mouth full of nuts.

Harper slowed (which was an oxymoron), turned into the empty modern yellow and black painted gas station, drove under the covering, parking next to a pump. It might not be a bad idea to get gas while she was here.

"Do they work here?" Renee asked.

Luis smacked his lips and leaned forward between them, saying, "They meet here sometimes." He pointed his fist, full of dried fruit, at the building. "There." Next to the two-story convenience store, in the back corner walled in space was a covered patio with a table, sofa and several mismatched chairs.

But there were no nefarious men taking refuge under the covering and planning more kidnappings.

Renee rubbed her eyes and gave a grunt of frustration. "Now what?"

In answer, Nick shifted, pulling Harper's attention to the mirror. He turned his body so he could face Luis; then all he did was settle back and give the man his undivided attention.

Harper was fascinated as she watched Nick silently build an

uncomfortable, foreboding threat. She wasn't sure how Luis was reacting, but Nick hadn't moved, hadn't blinked; just stared at the slimy creature. The car rocked with Luis' nervous shifting as the heaviness expanded.

When Renee took a breath to speak, Harper gently reached over and squeezed her arm, giving a slight shake of her head to deter any talking.

And they all waited, their breathing fogging up the windows. Nick a damn statue. Luis continuing his nervous movements at various intervals.

Finally, Luis gave an exasperated grunt. "What? I told you everything. Esas dos locas, they pointed a gun at *me*. Threatened *me*." Still, no one moved.

Harper found she was not only enjoying this, she was truly intrigued by the sheer power Nick could emanate simply through a look. There was no slight raise of an eyebrow, no flicker of movement around the edge of his mouth. His eyes homed in on their prey as he simply waited.

Luis gave another groan. "All I was told to do was pick up a package. The package is a man. My partner and I took him when he was on his way to the airport. We put him in a trunk. We needed a drink and stopped to celebrate. Then we went to a gas station and put your friend in my van. My partner ... he had to get home." He snarled. "I tied your friend up so he didn't jump out of the van, for his own safety. Not the way *they* tied me up!" he accused.

But when he received no reaction, he added, "I drove him to that old bar. Then two men, one with a scar on his face, and the other man, who hires me sometimes, they take your friend and put him in the back seat of their car and paid me. That was all. That was everything."

His grunt of anger was audible. "I have said too much." He ran through a range of animalistic sounds. "Maybe ... quizás," Luis stretched the word out, "I saw the license plate on the car. But that information is no good. The car is probably stolen." He gave a definitive *humph,* as if saying *that* was the extent of the information he'd give.

Nick still didn't move, so neither did Harper or Renee. Luis' fidgeting, on the other hand, was reaching manic levels. The silent intensity from Nick was unlike anything Harper had ever witnessed, and it wasn't causing her to be fearful of him; quite the opposite, she was unexpectedly captivated.

Then, Nick's upper lip gave a microscopic twitch of a snarl, and Harper felt like she'd been physically pressed against her seat. Her eyes widened in wonder. She knew Luis felt it too.

"Fine! I heard them ask your friend a question. Maybe I heard them ask him ..." Luis paused. "They asked him ... where is the killa waqay. The moon tears."

The pressure in the car released like a balloon losing air. Nick said, "Good job, Luis. Hey Renee, can I see your phone for a minute?"

Renee handed it to Nick, who opened the video app and hit record. "This is Luis ... do you want to give me your last name?" Luis, wide-eyed, blinked several times before shock turned to anger and he looked away, holding his hand up to block the video. Nick continued, "He has given us a lot of information on the abduction of Gael ..." Nick looked at Renee. She supplied Gael's last name, "Torres."

"Luis was complicit in the abduction of Gael Torres and has given us the location and names of the men who hired him."

"Vete a la concha de tu madre," Luis hissed.

"Whoa." Renee snorted as Harper asked, "What?"

Nick explained, "It means we've hit a nerve." He turned off the phone and handed it back to Renee. Luis tried to grab it, but Nick slapped his hand away. "Luis, is there anything else you'd like to tell us?"

He seethed. "No."

"Do you know what moon tears are?"

"They use the Quechua words. I have never heard of this. I think your friend was confused too. He said he didn't know what they were talking about."

Nick requested, "Renee, can you open a note on your phone or something?" While she did that, Nick asked, "What was the license plate number and the make, model and color of the car?"

Luis hissed and cursed under his breath but sputtered the information out; Nick clapped. "Great. I need to stretch my legs."

Harper climbed out of the car and slid the front seat as far forward as she could to give Nick room. But when he unfolded himself from the small space, his wounded leg buckled, causing him to stumble.

Harper reached for him at the same time he reached for her. She tried grabbing his waist, but he slipped his arms around her back, pulling her against him for leverage while trying to stabilize himself; pushing her off-kilter and forcing her to take several awkward steps backward while gripping his body against hers. He sucked in a wheezing breath of pain and finally, they found their footing; both still upright, holding tight.

Harper was acutely aware of every firm inch of his warm body and where it was pressing enticingly against hers.

"You okay?" he asked into her hair.

"Yeah," she leaned back so she could look into his eyes, "you?"

He breathed "*yeah*" as his eyes took on the intensity that had been aimed at Luis only moments ago; only this time there was a different fiery passion to it, a new level in this close proximity. The force of him was all encompassing and she felt the rest of the world around them begin to fade away around the edge.

He moved a hand to her hair and bushed a few of the strands that escaped her ponytail away from her eyes. And Harper rose up on her tiptoes—

"Nick!" Renee yelled. "A little help?"

They looked over and saw that Luis had a hold of Renee's arm, but she was moving to keep from allowing him to get a better grip. "He's trying to get my phone." She pulled out of his gasp and when he lunged toward her again, she was in the right position to get one good slap across his face.

He seethed and raised his hand, giving Nick time to reach him and grab him by his upper arm. "Adiós and hasta luego," he said, hauling him toward the building.

"What?" Luis asked, trying to shield his head from the rain.

"I think we have everything we need from you. Time to part ways."

Harper discarded the idea of putting gas in the car as she watched the interaction. "Renee, hop in the back."

"Yup." She followed directions, leaving the passenger side door open.

Harper started the car and they both continued to watch the scene in front of them, but Renee leaned forward, hugging the seat as she conspiratorially whispered, "What the hell was that with Mr. Three Letter Government Agent?"

"He lost his balance," Harper muttered.

Renee grinned. "About time a real man *fell* for you. And Mr. Three Letter Agent looks to be *all* man."

"Renee," she chided, because internally the part that wanted to hold *all that man* against her again was nodding emphatically.

Luis was yelling at Nick, "You can't leave me here! I need my truck."

"I'm sure you'll find someone to help you," Nick said, heading back to the car as Luis hissed a loud threat, "When I get my car, I'll come for you and esas locas."

Nick stopped. He turned back toward Luis, causing the short man to take a step backward. Harper and Renee didn't need to see the look on Nick's face, Luis' face said it all. Nick caught up to him, grabbed the scruff of his shirt and yanked him onto his tiptoes. "Luis, I'm offering you an olive branch here. That means I'm giving you a chance to find a ride back to your car and get back to your life." He waited until Luis gave an indication he understood. "If I see even a remote shadow of you or get the feeling that you're following us or trying to disrupt my friends' lives, I won't even have to call in favors to have you hunted for sport. I know guys who will do it for free."

Renee gurgled a laugh as she breathlessly whispered, "Holy shit."

Luis snapped, "Okay. Okay." He was trying to pry Nick's hands off his clothes.

"I'm not the kind of man who fucks around, Luis. I need to know we have an understanding."

"We understand each other," Luis said fervently. "I swear."

"Good." Nick dropped him, causing him to trip backward a few steps; and while he regained his footing, Nick was already walking toward the car.

Harper pulled forward a bit to intercept him; he barely closed the door and she was off.

"Thanks for anticipating." He grinned at Harper.

"Thank *you*," Renee stressed. "That was amazing." She mimicked, "I'm not the kind of man who fucks around Luis." She clapped and threw herself back against her seat. "God, I needed that."

"Glad I could help." He put on his seatbelt. "Okay, how do you two feel about a darling B&B on the river overlooking the jungle?"

"What?" Renee's voice filled with distress. "No, we need to keep going. We need to get more intel or something. We still have enough daylight."

Nick turned in his seat. "Renee, I'm starving. My leg hurts. I don't think I'm completely over being bitten by a snake either. I'd like to talk through all of this information in a place where we know we'll be dry and safe. And I need to make a few phone calls."

"Phone calls? Are you going to call for backup? Guys who will hunt for sport?" Renee asked hopefully.

"Was it too much?" Nick asked.

"No, it was perfect." Harper swore she could hear Renee's eyes sparkle with the declaration.

Nick asked Harper, "Are you okay if we hunker down?"

"I'm exhausted, I've had only catnaps for three days now. My headache is back. I'm hungry. And I would really love to brush my teeth."

"Great, it's decided," Nick said.

"What about Gael?" Renee asked softly.

Nick calmly focused on Renee. "Luis said the men who took him asked for information. They think he knows something. When people think you have information, you stay alive."

She swallowed hard, but repeated the difficult truth, "When people think you have information, you stay alive."

Nick inclined his head, then turned his attention to the road and gave Harper directions. Though it wasn't that difficult. There was only one road.

"What if Luis finds the guys who hired him and they come looking for us?" Renee asked.

"The B&B has a garage, we'll ask if we can use it. And I wouldn't worry about Luis. In order to get someone to help him come after us, he would have to admit he was overpowered by two women, and he seems like the kind of man who isn't in a hurry to share that story."

"No," Renee replied as Harper nodded in agreement, both letting the information soak in.

They drove through a small town and on the outskirts, Nick filled the silence explaining they were only about five minutes from their destination.

A police car passed them and the irony pulled a strangled laugh from Harper.

Chapter Twenty-Two

Ian, the owner of El Mirador, was walking into the house with an armful of fruit from a nearby tree, when he spied Nick. He shot him a curious questioning smile.

Nick raised an eyebrow and joked, "Te extrañé." *I missed you.*

Ian put the fruit down in a basket just inside the house as Nick explained about the motorbike, that his new friends had given him a ride, and they all needed a place to stay for the night. Ian apologized profusely about the bike and told Nick he'd send someone to pick it up, then said he'd find him another ride to Cusco.

Nick waved the offer away, the women were already headed that way and would take him.

Ian handed over keys to two rooms and informed them they were invited to dinner in about two hours.

Nick's thigh burned as he climbed the steps to the second floor where they had rooms across the hall from each other. Renee went ahead to the room she and Harper would be sharing.

Harper stopped in the hallway and turned to Nick. He thought she looked the same way he was feeling, weighted down with exhaustion from the day.

She licked her lips. "Thank you. For your help with Luis."

He squeezed his hands into fists to keep himself from reaching out to brush the loose hairs from her face; not that he minded them, he merely wanted to touch her.

Touch her? His inner voice gave a scoffing laugh.

He didn't just want to touch her, he wanted to spend time with her. He wanted to sit across from her over a candlelit table so he could find out what color her eyes turned in the flicker of the low light. He wanted to walk on a beach and hold her hand. He wanted to lay on a blanket next to her at sunset, her head in his lap so he could run his fingers through her hair and study the auburn hues. He wanted to see those green eyes when they were filled with desire and heated with anger. He wanted to get to know the little intricacies of her gestures. To listen to her talk about her day so her voice, full and round with a slight depth and a hint of light, could wash over him.

Fuck.

He shook his head to dislodge the wave of thoughts.

"You okay?" she asked.

"Just tired," he replied.

"Well ..." She glanced at her room.

"Thank you for saving my life." He hurried the comment, attempting to prolong the moment.

She turned back and brushed away the thanks. "I didn't save your life."

"Then, thank you for fixing my problem a lot sooner than I was going to be able to get it fixed," he reasoned.

Hmmm.

Renee poked her head out the door. "I'm gonna take a shower unless you want to go first?"

"Go ahead," Harper said, "I'm going to lay down." Nick felt like he was watching the last of Harper's energy slide out of her body.

"Harper?" He reached out and gently touched her elbow. "Are you alright?"

Her eyes were half-mast when she blew out a defeated breath and feigned a smile. "Not really. I landed in Peru and was immediately caught up in all of this and I don't feel like I've had a minute to think. My head hasn't stopped throbbing and I'm beyond exhausted, I'm surviving on short naps and adrenaline."

He gave in to his urge and let his hand drift from her elbow up to her face, brushing a few stray strands of hair behind her ear. He knew he was pressing his luck when he let his hand linger, but when she closed her eyes and leaned her cheek against his warmth, he felt his world expand. When a small sigh drifted out of her full lips, he also knew he was in deep shit.

He dropped his hand and swallowed hard. "I'll be across the hall if you need anything."

She blinked her eyes open, gave a disoriented nod, but without any words, went into her room and gently closed the door.

Nick stood where he was rooted, clenching and unclenching his hand, still able to feel the heat of her cheek against his palm. Releasing a soft snort of disbelief, he eloquently summarized his current state of affairs. "You're in it now, Robbins."

When Renee joined Nick for dinner, he felt a pang of disappointment that Harper wasn't with her; but she'd fallen asleep and Renee said she wasn't about to wake her.

"So what do we do?" Renee asked. "How do we find Gael and kick the kidnapping assholes' asses?"

Nick wouldn't mind some of her animated vitality. He'd taken a shower but his last two days had left him a little low on energy.

They sat at one of the five tables in the large room, at the back of the house, that had been converted into a dining area. Maroon walls were decorated with bright Peruvian blankets hung at various angles for their color. Nick figured this space was most likely chosen as the dining room because of the large windows across the back wall that showed off the view of the jungle and river. The view that gave the B&B its name, The Lookout. A view barely visible now in the deep blue hues of the coming evening.

He took a sip of his beer and cleared his throat. "First, we start with intel. We need to gather as much information as possible."

"You're gonna make a few phone calls," she repeated the plan he'd laid out earlier.

"I am. Normally I'd use my phone, but it was stolen."

She slid her cell phone that was sitting by her fork across the table. "Use mine."

"Renee, I won't lie to you ..." he promised.

"I'd appreciate that."

"So, in that spirit, I can't use your phone because we should assume that whoever took Gael knows about you, and if that's the case, your phone might be compromised."

Her face fell, but only for a moment before she shook it off. It helped that both of these women were formidable.

She asked him, "Want Harper's phone?"

"Thank you, but no. Same assumption." He mindlessly added, "And my phone was encrypted."

"So do we need to find your phone first?" She frowned. "Find the guy who knifed you?"

"When that gets out ..." he would have said 'if' but he knew how life worked. "Finding the kid would be a waste of time. We have bigger problems, but we also have options. I'll use the landline here to call a friend once we're done with dinner." He took another sip of his beer. "Do you have *any* idea what moon tears might be referring to?"

"No." She frustratingly threw herself back against her seat. "Nick, can I be honest with you?"

He nodded, though highly doubted there was a time in her life she wasn't honest with people.

"I want to *go*! I feel like movement is the best thing to do in this situation. I want to find a string of clues and people and ... hurt someone, until we find Gael."

"I understand," he assured.

"All we're doing is sitting here eating dinner and I feel like we're getting too far away from him. Like, it's been too long. And I keep wondering what will happen to Gael if he can't give the kidnappers the information they think he has ..." Her eyes glazed over with the possibilities.

Nick leaned forward. "I told you this in the car, and I mean it. The fact that the people who have Gael want something, is *really* good," he confirmed. "Now, while our top priority is to find him, we have a new piece of information and if it's possible to figure out what moon tears are; then we'd have leverage."

Renee dropped her forehead onto the table and told the worn wood, "This all sounds so daunting."

Nick understood that feeling of hopelessness, but he also needed her to understand how to tap into her perseverance. "Renee. Look at what you've accomplished. When all this started, I bet you didn't give yourself time to think of how discouraging the situation was. You continued to move forward."

She straightened as he continued his pep talk.

"The detailed timeline you pieced together is brilliant. And it wasn't the cops who found Luis, that was all you. You've been doing good work, you even figured out how to have a rental car delivered to you in the middle of nowhere in the middle of the night."

"That wasn't me, that was Harper." She took a deep breath, held it until it was too much, then blew it out. "Nick, I keep flip-flopping between being okay for a minute then trying to figure out what I need to do. Because sitting here drinking a beer with you? It seems *so* ridiculous while Gael is in trouble."

"I know those feelings well. I've had them often when I'm working."

"How do you handle it?"

"I understand that I'm no help to anyone if I'm not operating at a hundred percent."

She gave a grunted *hmmm*.

"Renee, if you aren't well-rested, well-fed and hydrated, then you won't be thinking clearly or making solid decisions." He gave her an encouraging smile, "I *know* it sounds trite; but if you want to help Gael, you have to rest and eat and drink plenty of water so your body and mind can keep up when you have to push yourself and think clearly."

He wasn't sure if it was his instructions or the weight of the past few days that pressed her back into her chair. "Okay." Her eyes were glassy again. "I don't know what the universe did to put you in our path, but I'm pretty grateful."

He raised a curious eyebrow. "Universe?"

She reached for her beer bottle and rolled it between her hands. "A while back I went with some friends to Europe. One of my friends is a yoga teacher. She's always talking about opening ourselves up to the universe. For the entire trip she challenged us to open up and had us all saying mantras aloud." She mockingly repeated one of them, "'The universe is working to support our needs.'" Pursing her lips, she went on, "I kinda hate it because it sounds so privileged. But we promised her we'd be 'open to the possibilities,' at least for the duration of our trip. And I'm not saying I believe it, but Nick, some *amazing* experiences crossed our paths." She motioned to him. "And I've been trying to stay positive and Harper keeps helping by insisting we're going to find Gael. And maybe you could say I've been open to the possibilities again, and maybe it's not the universe, but it sure is interesting that we needed help and here you are."

"What if I'm not really a good guy?" he challenged.

She scrunched her face to dismiss the idea. "You're a good guy."

"How do you know?"

"I feel it."

Hmmm.

She straightened as much as she could in her seat. "Okay Nicholas Robbins. I am now well-fed, so it's time to get some sleep. And first thing tomorrow morning ...?" She aimed the open question at him.

He filled in the answer, "We'll go into town and have some fresh juice."

She frowned. "And that's going to help?"

"Big time. We'll leave at seven."

She didn't move. Nick reached across the table, took one of her hands and gave it a squeeze. "Kidnappers need to sleep too."

Her entire face lightened. "Kidnappers need sleep too," she repeated, squeezing his hand in return. She took another sip of her beer then clapped her hands and rubbed them together. "Okay, let's talk about Harper."

The switch of attitude and subject aligned with her energetic spirit, although the change in topic shocked and twisted his stomach. "Okay. What do we need to say about Harper?" He tried to sound nonchalant.

"She's single and I see how you two have been looking at each other."

So much for nonchalant.

Nick felt thrust right back to eighth grade – first crush nerves, shaking as he approached the girl's best friend to get intel on if his crush liked him back or not ...

He took a casual sip of beer as part of his lackadaisical act, but was met with a pointed finger aimed between his eyes as Renee verified, "Yeah, you like her."

He shrugged. "Of course I do. She helped me out of a difficult situation."

"Ugh, really Nick? Don't slip into the jerky macho crap."

Yup, that was exactly what he was doing. He let a slow smile spread across his face, his pulse quickening as those green jungle eyes sparkled in his mind. He allowed himself to concede, "I would be lying if I didn't admit I am intrigued by Harper."

"She is *amazing*. Hell, look what she's done for me. She negotiated the sale of an illegal firearm and until today, I know she was trying to figure out how to approach people to find out if they were hireable as mercenaries. So I might be biased, but she's an incredible friend. Super smart. And not bad on the eyes." Renee wiggled her eyebrows at him.

"No, she isn't bad on the eyes," he agreed.

"Are you single?"

"I am."

"And there's something about you Nick Robbins that makes me think you're pretty cool too."

"Is there?"

"Only a few type of people would be willing to help two women after finding out they've tied someone to a chair and kept them at gunpoint."

"Creeps and deviants?"

"A good guy," she insisted.

"You have a fascinating brain, Renee."

"I know. And I know you're the kind of man who steps up to the plate when faced with a challenge, but I think you've got a decent moral compass. Otherwise, you would have let me keep Luis tied up."

His eyes widened but before he had a chance to sputter a response she clapped her hands again. "So Harper is amazing, you're single; she's single. There was a spark between you two and I think you need to get to know her. She's the best person you'll ever meet. You'd be stupid to let someone like her slip by."

"Noted." How else was he supposed to answer her?

"Once we find Gael, you need to take her on a date and rock her world. You seem to have some exuberance to offer." She laughed at the comment and Nick felt a little taken aback. When had this conversation gone from trying to comfort Renee and plan next steps, to being told to rock the world of a woman? (Granted, rocking the world of said woman was something he *really* wanted to do.)

"And Nick, you've got to know you're easy on the eyes too. And it's clear you think she's sexy, so ..." Renee pushed herself away from the table, yawning as she stood.

Nick blinked several times as the conversation caught up to him. "You don't hold back any punches, do you?"

"Neither do you. And life's too short for it anyway; don't you think?"

She rounded the table, hugged him around the neck and said, "Thanks for the pep talk."

He patted her arm, glad to be back on familiar conversational territory. "If ever there was a time you need to be okay with taking care of yourself, it's now."

"We'll be ready to leave at seven." She wished him goodnight.

Nick watched her walk away and sat back exhausted in his chair. Taking a swig of his beer once more, he began to rummage through the events of the past two days, the new situation he found himself, and the laundry list of information he now had. What he would do if he had just met Harper under ordinary circumstances, how he'd wedge his way into a conversation to get to know her better; where he'd take her, somewhere with low lighting and excuses to accidentally brush his arm against hers–

"Nick?" Ian interrupted, asking after clearing the dishes. Nick nodded and asked, "¿Tienes un teléfono que pueda usar?" *Do you have a phone I can use?*

He was directed to the front room's check-in desk. Nick leaned his hip against the desk as he made a collect call, checking his watch; he had no idea what time it was in Seattle.

"Calling collect?" Sean Wilder answered.

"I think I'm going to place blame squarely on your shoulders for the past two days." The green eyes floated through his mind – okay, it hadn't been all bad; but he wasn't about to admit that to Wilder.

"What happened?" His friend from his military days sounded tired.

"I need a favor. Or four," Nick said.

"That's what a collect call normally means. What've you got yourself into now?"

He wouldn't answer that question yet. "The first favor is monetary."

"What's her name and how much did she take you for?" Sean laughed, but Nick heard the click of his computer in the background, he was getting ready to make arrangements.

"My bag was stolen. And before you give me a hard time about it, I was stabbed in the process, so my pride has already suffered enough."

"You okay?" Sean asked, sounding genuinely concerned.

"Two-inch blade," Nick admitted and rolled his eyes.

"And Shaw reported a little snake bite?" Sean's deep laughter rolled across the miles.

"Yeah, I'm having a blast in Peru. Look, I'm still at El Mirador. I need some cash if I can get it, from the nearby town. Then I'm going to need some help, but I'm not sure exactly what that entails yet. I'll have a better idea in about twenty-four hours."

A few moments of silence accompanied clicking computer keys before Sean answered, "There's a small market that will do a Western Union, but only two hundred." He gave Nick the address.

"That works for now. I need you to put the money under the name Harper Barrett." Even as he said the name he cringed. Now he was going to have to explain that he saw the luggage tag on her backpack, and how he also needed her to remove it.

"Ohhh," Sean drawled, "so it is a woman."

Nick ignored him. "I'll need more cash when I get back to Cusco as well."

Sean's good-natured laugh grew. "Holy shit, not willing to give me any more information than a name. She must be something."

"She's on vacation with a friend, their mutual friend has been kidnapped."

"You *are* having a blast in Peru."

"Remember when you promised me I'd be in and out quick, and on a beach even faster? For my well-deserved vacation?" Nick handed over the guilt trip.

"How much money do you want sent to Cusco and what kind of backup can I send?" Sean atoned.

"Two thousand for now. I have a feeling most of it could be bribe money. And I really do appreciate the offer for help, but I don't know what I need. Once I do, you'll be my first call."

"Who's flipping the bill for this outing?"

"Well," he gave a laugh of disbelief (Renee would appreciate this), "I suppose I'm doing a little mercenary work."

"Harper Barrett." Sean whistled. "Want me to do a background check?"

"Not yet." He knew it was a professional suggestion, but it felt a little intrusive.

"Money's transferred. I'm here when you need me."

"Thanks."

"And Nicky," Sean drew the nickname out, "at the rate you're going, try not to get shot next."

"Ass." Nick hung up.

With that chore done, it was his turn to follow his own advice and get some rest. His leg throbbed as he took the stairs. When Ian had first checked them in, Nick requested rooms on the second floor because he could hear the movement of those coming and going better from there. With little information, he needed to be on guard in case someone was also following Renee. He told her he'd tell the truth, but that bit didn't need to be mentioned just yet.

He stopped in the hallway with his hand on the doorknob of his room, though he turned to the door opposite as Renee's words whispered, 'you need to take her on a date and rock her world.'

Yeah, he confirmed confidently, *at this rate you* are *gonna get shot next.*

Chapter Twenty-Three

It took Renee two hours of tossing and turning before she was finally able to fall asleep. Then she dreamed she was standing at the edge of a large hole, reaching for Gael, their fingers touching momentarily but she couldn't hold onto him. She was powerless as she watched him descend into the darkness, arms and legs flailing, eyes wide, his mouth open in a silent scream as all she could make out was her own scream.

She woke with a jolt, blinking wet eyes as she regained her senses. The room was shrouded in darkness, the muted sounds of nocturnal animals and soft patter of rain on the roof mixed with Harper's soft breathing.

She rolled over to check her phone for any missed messages. Nothing. At this point his phone was most likely dead.

"Gael, where are you?" she whispered into the darkness as her mind drifted to their last night together.

Renee planned to have two days to herself to recoup before Harper showed up. She went to the airport to see the small crew off. Everyone cried and hugged, knowing the magic of the three weeks they'd spent together was ending and the good work they did was already twisting into memories.

Gael checked his bags. After pulling his assistant aside for a second to give her several instructions, everyone gathered for one last group photo at TSA. Renee waved everyone off, a wide grin in place.

Only, Gael didn't go through the checkpoint.

When Renee looked up at him expectantly, he slipped his hand in hers. "I want to show you something."

And she followed him. She was still draped in the magical fabric of the trip that had been woven from the sustainable clothing of Victor Campos; the clouds and the rain that washed the jagged mountains green; the earth tones that painted cities golden ochre, sienna sand, copper brown and rose quartz; and each spectacular Peruvian person they'd had the privilege of meeting.

He hailed a cab, gave directions and slid his arm easily around her shoulders. The radio played music that may have been created to make sure the wise secrets of Peruvian ancestors were continually passed down.

The ride through the streets of Cusco, winding back into the Sacred Valley, was punctuated with long, delicious, lingering kisses, and an exploration of hands twisting and caressing where they could; while maintaining a modicum of respectability.

An hour later, in another small town, on another lone dirt path, the driver stopped in front of a traditionally built home. Brick had been covered in plaster and whitewashed. A thatched roof made from palm leaves and grasses had been constructed into a weather-tight covering. A small garden showed off its bounty on the side of the house, and beyond it, were lush green shrubs and trees. But she had a feeling that wasn't their destination.

If she'd learned one thing the past few weeks, Gael loved surprising people. Several times, he'd given the crew a list of what they needed to wear and bring, but never the destination. Because he enjoyed watching his friends and their looks of shocked wonder when they viewed the almost otherworldly beauty of waterfalls in the jungle or rode horses into a turquoise lake at the base of a glacier peak.

Gael told the driver they would see him 'mañana,' then guided her through a trail, cut into the overgrown trees behind the house. It led to a large man-made pool filled with water from a hot spring. A tent was set up in a grassy clearing next to the pool, along with a table draped in a bright Peruvian cloth with a basket of food and cooler next to it. Twinkle lights swagged among the trees, and as if the sky knew it had to behave, there were no clouds. They'd be tucked in under a blanket of stars.

"It's ours for the entire night," he informed, breathlessly.

She stepped into his arms, reached up on her tiptoes and whispered, "I wanted one more night, just the two of us."

The night had been perfect. They took time luxuriating naked in the hot waters, making love under the stars and eating the carefully prepared picnic. The flavorful food was almost as outstanding as the rest of the evening. Sea bass ceviche marinated in lime juice was served with red onions, boiled corn and sweet potatoes. Skewers of spicy marinated meat was alongside a dish of seasoned mashed potatoes that acted like a 'bun' for a mix of shredded chicken, mayonnaise, avocado, and carrots. And for their sweet tooth, sandwich cookies filled with dulce de leche.

All the while, she and Gael relished the extra gift of time.

"Renee?" Harper's voice broke through the fog of memories. Renee wiped at her cheeks, she didn't realize she'd been crying.

"I didn't mean to wake you," Renee apologized.

"It's fine." Harper yawned. "My headache is worse. I think I need some of that tea and Advil and aspirin and water. And maybe a shot of something."

"Pisco," Renee offered.

"Pisco?"

"It's the official alcohol of Peru. Or is it the official alcohol of Cusco?"

"I don't care, I'll take a shot of that too." Harper turned on the light between the beds and swung her legs over the edge. She pressed her fingertips into her temple, but narrowed her gaze on Renee. "I know you're worried ..."

"It's okay. These are good tears. I was thinking about my last night with Gael."

"Exuberant?" Harper winked, pulling a smile from Renee.

"*So* exuberant." Renee got out of bed and retrieved the required elements from Harper's bag, then added water to the tea kettle – a staple of the room.

"Nick's single, by the way."

"Renee." The name was a guttural groan.

"I told him you were single too and in need of a good man."

"Why would you do that?"

"Because I think *you* should do *that*." She pointed at the door of their room, an arrow to Nick's room. "Because I'm not stupid and I felt all that heat between the two of you."

"The air conditioning wasn't working in the car," Harper muttered.

"Fine, but I see how you look at him."

"I was looking at him like he had a knife sticking out of his leg when he jumped out of the jungle; then I kept an eye on him because we don't know anything about him," Harper defended, accepting the bottle of water Renee handed her, along with the requested headache fighting pills.

"You haven't really eaten anything substantial in a while." Renee felt a pang of guilt.

"I'll eat a huge breakfast in a few hours."

Renee opened the coca tea bag and twirled it in her hands. "Nick said we'll go get juice tomorrow morning."

"Okay ..."

"He said he was going to call someone to get help. I should have pushed him to give me more information." She frowned.

Harper gave a grunt and said, "Look. How about we give him one chance. If he doesn't come through with something that helps us, we'll dump him off on the side of the road."

Renee eyed Harper.

"What?"

"I don't think you want to throw him away yet."

"I don't have a vested interest in him."

"He's hot."

"Duh. I'm exhausted and have a headache, I'm not blind. You can't *not* notice his looks." Harper fizzled into a mutter; "It doesn't matter. We have bigger issues at hand."

Renee handed her the cup of tea. "He likes you too."

Harper held the cup of hot tea with both hands and breathed in the steam. Renee cooed, "Ohh, I see you Harper Barrett, was that a little roll of excitement that washed over you, hearing that sexy ass man likes you?"

Over the rim of her cup, Harper eyed Renee and changed the subject. "Tell me about your last night with Gael. And don't leave anything out."

Chapter Twenty-Four

Renee hurried Harper out of the room and downstairs for breakfast. On their way past the front desk, the owner was working on the computer so Renee asked if she could pay the bill.

"What are you doing?" Harper asked.

"I want to be ready to go."

"You said Nick said we'd leave at seven. It's six fifteen."

Renee tried to explain, "Harp, I need to *do* something, and be ready."

Harper patted her on the shoulder. "I get it."

Nick was already at breakfast; he toasted the air with his coffee cup in welcome when they entered the dining area. He looked good. Not like a crazed maniac who jumped out of the jungle worried he was covered in bugs, but fresh. As if he'd gotten a good night's sleep. The short dark strands of his hair stood slightly on end. Less sunken around the eyes, less jaundice as well. A whole lot more handsome.

"Harper?" Renee tugged on her arm to get her to move. She cleared her throat as they crossed and sat opposite Nick at a table next to the window.

"Did you sleep?" he asked Renee.

"I did."

"Good." He let his gaze drift over Harper. When he didn't say anything right away, she reached up to squeeze her damp hair she'd left down to dry. He cleared his throat, but his voice was deep as he quietly asked, "How did you sleep?"

"Good," she fumbled, "like the dead, but good. Good." She swallowed and rearranged the silverware set in front of her. "I just can't seem to stay in front of my headache."

"It's the altitude," Renee and Nick offered simultaneously.

She gratefully accepted the coffee that was handed over and closed her eyes as she sipped the hot beverage, thinking this was going to go a lot further than anything else.

Breakfast was a selection of breads, butter and jam, fried eggs, some fruit and sweet corn tamales. They ate quietly, or, more accurately, Renee quickly ate then waited as long as she could before finally demanding, "Okay, what do we do first?"

"I need to go pick up a wire transfer," Nick responded.

"I paid the bill already," Renee said.

"I'll pay you back," Nick promised.

"Why? I'm using Luis' money."

"What?" both Harper and Nick asked.

"Oh." She swallowed as she glanced between them." Didn't I tell you? I took the money he made for kidnapping Gael."

"Atta girl." Nick smiled. "Still, I need to pay my own way."

"Whatever." She pulled out a large sum of money from her pocket and gave it to Harper. "Though you should probably put this in your bag." She waved to the table. "Okay, we're fed and caffeinated and rested. It's almost seven. So can we go?"

After their goodbyes and thanks to the owners, they were back in the small car. Harper followed the directions to a small convenience looking store a few minutes away. The building was near the center plaza of the town.

Nick got out but when he pushed the seat forward to make room for Renee to get out, Harper said, "I'll wait here."

He bent over so he could make eye contact with her and scrunched his face slightly. "If you don't mind, could you come in with me? I don't have any ID, so I had my friend do the transfer in your name. Harper Barrett."

She felt a rush of warmth; but with a raised eyebrow, asked, "How do you know my last name?"

"It's on the luggage tag on your backpack." He cleared his throat.

"Oh, shit." She reached into the back seat and grabbed the bag. Why hadn't she thought about that? She unclipped it and put it inside the bag. Though, maybe she shouldn't have it in there either.

She nervously looked at Nick. "Do you think Luis saw it?"

"I don't think he's that smart," he said honestly.

She hoped he was right, and followed him into the store.

Renee rummaged through the small aisles as Nick greeted the man behind the counter. "Hola, buenos días. I think you have a money transfer, hay una transferencia. For Harper Barrett?"

"Sí." The owner of the store nodded hearing her name, then slid a few documents to sign across the counter. "¿Identificación?"

She handed over her passport. After stamping the proper paperwork, he produced a few hundred soles. Harper pocketed a hundred for herself, not sure of the exchange rate (*because this hadn't been that kind of trip yet*).

"Fair enough." Nick put the rest of the money in his pocket. "C'mon." He gestured to the plaza near the store and told Renee, "I'll show you what juice has to do with information."

They walked through the charming plaza with intersecting sidewalks lined with palm trees and other native greenery swaying in the slight morning breeze. Nick's slow gait with a slight limp wasn't lost on Harper. She sighed as she watched him and muttered, "Infection."

"What?" he asked

She stopped him with a hand on his forearm. "Does your leg feel hot, the area around the wound? Did you have a fever or anything last night?" She touched his forehead with the back of her hand, frowning, then tried his cheeks. "You don't feel hot."

He took her hand away from his cheek and gave it a squeeze, "I'm okay."

She pointed. "You're limping."

"It hurts." He gave a 'what are you gonna do?' shrug then pointed at the colorful tourism sign with the city's name in six-foot-high letters. He looked up at the perfect backdrop behind the letters, the plaza and rising jungle covered hills. "Wanna take a selfie?"

"Not really," Harper said, but Renee had moved so she could aim her phone at her and Nick. "Say 'what the hell.'"

Nick grinned, Harper frowned.

Renee viewed the picture. "Good one."

Nick pointed the direction Harper was to go, but she lingered and waited for him. "Not ready to trust me just yet?"

She wanted to trust him; hell, when she walked into the breakfast room and saw him, laid-back, an easy smile in place, his short stubble adding a darkening allure ... Then he made eye contact with her and her whole damn body hummed. She *wanted* to trust this man. She recalled how he'd told her he was going to earn her trust, and she was ready for that declaration to come to fruition.

Had Renee not elbowed her to get her to move to the table, she would have stayed where she stood, *could* have stayed and let the moment wash over her.

But she was also trying to be pragmatic. Sure, he'd called someone and had money transferred, but he'd also done something to cause someone to stab him. And bite him. (The snake probably *was* an accident.)

And looks aren't everything. There were plenty of bad guys who were handsome and could look through lowered lashes with amber honey eyes and ignite flutters and have money sent to them no matter where they were. Those men were usually drug dealers and thieves.

"Let me know what I can do to help," he said.

"Your actions and time will tell," she replied honestly.

They walked up to a cart on the outskirts of the plaza and sat on the provided stools in front of the folded out bar. The vendor amplified her product by promising the fiber would help Harper's headache and altitude sickness. Harper had already proven (when she took that pill the other day) she was willing to try anything.

As they sipped from their juice glasses, Harper watched Nick as he watched the sleepy town's morning activities. She swatted a few daydreams that passed, caused by being so close to him. She needed to stay focused, not study the way his shoulders looked broader this close, how she could spy into his shirt for a better view of his chest *this close*, or how he smelled of soap and heat and jungle and want. *THIS CLOSE.*

When he triumphantly muttered, "here we go," she was snapped out of her dreamy study.

He stood too quickly, hissed in apparent discomfort, but did an awkward hop step to shake off his stiffness, before continuing across the street.

"What's he doing?" Renee asked.

Harper shrugged.

"Should we follow him?"

"I feel like we should wait until he wants to let us in on his plan." Harper took another sip of her mango-banana juice. (Which was so good she wanted one a day, regardless of the healthy consequences that came with an uptick in fiber. But having daily fresh juice seemed more like something that would happen once she got back to vacation norms. Maybe she should start making a mental list of things she'd like to do when that time came.)

They watched Nick happily signaling a short man – in his early thirties maybe, wearing a nice button-down shirt and dark slacks – who was about to enter a two-story municipal building.

"Who ...?" Renee started her question but didn't finish when the man squinted at Nick, the universal sign that the man had no idea who Nick was.

Nick donned his nonthreatening, unhurried attitude. The kind of guy who'd be happy as a clam while a Jimmy Buffet cover band played "Cheeseburger in Paradise."

Another thing villainous men were capable of, Harper reasoned, *flipping from handsomeness to possible wickedness.*

Nick then gestured to Harper and Renee, waving and nodding his head, encouraging them to wave back.

"I guess we wave?" Harper was skeptical but they each held up a tentative hand in greeting.

After another brief exchange, Nick made his way back to the stand with the strange man in tow, and introduced, "Estos son Harper y Renee."

The man gave a curt nod in their direction.

"This is César," Nick started. "I was telling him how we're sorry we didn't make an appointment with his office and how everything has fallen apart on this trip. That we didn't even know until two days ago we were coming here to start the preliminary information gathering for the road infrastructure." He casually beamed at César while he wove his lie. "Did I tell you that we are partnering with Inter-American Development Bank?"

That caught César's attention. "Ah, yes. I have worked with them before."

"Great. We don't want to take up too much of your time. We have so much to do and Harper is still suffering from the altitude." He reached out and began to gently rub her back.

Bad guys can rub backs really well too, she chided, mainly because she wanted to melt into his warm touch.

Get a hold of yourself, Harper! He's in the middle of lying to a stranger!!

César tilted his head in understanding.

Nick continued, "If you don't mind. We only need fifteen minutes of your time. Maybe thirty? We were asked to only count cars." He laughed. "It shouldn't take three people, but ..."

"Count cars?" César frowned.

Count cars? Harper internally repeated the question.

"We were told you have a traffic camera at the weigh station on the outskirts of town? And I assumed you have the footage?"

"Ah, sí," César said.

"If you don't mind allowing us to see the footage, we only need to count the number of vehicles that passed by within one week's time."

"Ah!" The entire reason Nick had accosted César dawned on him and he nodded his head. "Muy bien. Todos vengan conmigo." *Everyone come with me.* He ushered them to follow into the municipal building. "But you will need to do this many times?" he asked.

Nick sighed. "Yes. So many little things like this need to be finished and studied before we can move forward."

Within a matter of fifteen minutes, César had shown them to the small room where they could crowd around the screen to do their surveillance work, before excusing himself.

Harper insisted Nick sit to rest his leg, while she and Renee stood behind him.

"Did you know, this road will soon be the only one you can drive from the coast of Peru to the coast of Brazil?" Nick asked. "I read an interesting article a few days ago about all the studies they've started. For example, one of the preliminary studies for infrastructure is to count cars?"

"Juice." Renee smirked, obviously impressed.

"Yup. I stopped there yesterday morning and noticed the people coming and going from the municipal offices," Nick confirmed. "Renee, can you pull up that license plate number and car description?"

After twenty minutes they'd reviewed a week's worth of cars, never finding one that fit the description Luis had given.

Renee gave a frustrated grunt. "Now what?"

"We're going back to Cusco. Like Luis said, there are only two directions and since they didn't come past here; and they're looking for something, it might stand to reason they went back toward Cusco."

Renee headed out the door, muttering, "I need some air."

"That was pretty good," Harper admitted, pointing to the screen in front of Nick.

"How far does this go on the trustworthy scale?" he asked.

She shrugged with her arms folded across her chest, her lingering headache a frown still etched on her forehead.

Nick said, "You've been put in a really difficult situation, you know you're handling it with some real tenacious chutzpah."

She let the comment melt her aloofness a bit. "It also says a lot about me that I don't blatantly trust a man who jumped out of the jungle with no identification, claiming to be a special agent."

"I never said special agent."

She smiled. "That's right. I believe you said 'three-letter government agency,' which we still can't verify."

"Exactly. Once we get back to Cusco, at the very least, I promise to prove my identity."

"Not your trustworthiness?"

"You already said that was going to take time and action. I'm good with that."

Harper took a deep breath, then cleared her throat and dropped her arms. "Nick, we need help. And I need to trust someone right now. It looks like you're it." She pointed to the screen again. "This was a good call."

He stood with a flinch of pain, took a step and said, "I have one more trick up my sleeve."

"You gonna pull a rabbit out of a hat?"

He grinned and she hated how his smile lit up his face when she was this close, or how much she could *make* him smile, or how her insides fluttered *when* he smiled.

"We're going to see if César can run a license plate number for us. You know," he winked, "since our rental car was stolen."

"Ah, nice."

They found César and he was more than happy to run the plate. "It's an address in Lima, not a rental car company," he said, confused.

Harper played into the shock. "Do you think the rental car company gave us a stolen car?"

César offered to do a more in-depth search, but Nick shook it off. "We have taken up too much of your time. If you could print out the report with the address? Then we can give it to our bosses and the car rental company and let them all deal with it."

Appreciation given, Harper quickly followed Nick's exit. They found Renee, and together, hurried to the car. Once again, Harper was trying to get the ridiculous car to pick up speed and take them back to Cusco.

"Now what?" Renee asked from the back seat.

Nick shifted so he could see her. "I know you've already told me a lot and recapped everything. But could you tell me more about the past three weeks? What does a photo shoot consist of? I thought it was always one guy and a camera."

Chapter Twenty-Five

"A lot goes into a professional photo shoot." Renee started her explanation for Nick. "The first time I worked with Gael, I was shocked at the number of people it took to get the perfect shot. A professionally controlled shoot normally has about twenty or thirty people working on it. More if agents and producers show up."

"For a photo shoot?" Nick had never thought about who was standing behind the camera of a photo in a magazine.

Renee bobbed her head, she understood his shock. "What we did the past three weeks, was quite different. Gael wanted this work to have an intimacy, and he wanted to achieve that organically. His idea was to start the entire process by hiring a few trusted people he thought would work well together. There were only five of us and we understood that we'd fill in across several areas. For example, I did hair and makeup, was a partial wardrobe stylist, prop stylist, lighting assistant and all-around pack mule."

"Those jobs are usually held by separate people?" Nick wondered.

"Yes," Renee verified, "Gael was the travel agent, tour guide, photographer, producer, location scout, and artistic director. His assistant did everything from reservations to finding doctors to keeping us somewhat on schedule. A photography assistant who was really a jack of all trades; drove, hauled equipment, set up lights, held reflectors and made sure we never forgot anything. And finally there was our digital tech, who took care of anything with a sim card or battery."

Nick asked, "Did you have several cars or a service that drove you?"

"We had two vans with all our equipment and the clothing. Victor, Gael and the photography assistant took turns driving."

"Show him some of the photos," Harper encouraged.

Renee pulled a series of photos up on her phone and handed it to Nick. "Now, keep in mind, these are the raw photos. He's still going to edit them. But it's pretty easy to appreciate his talent and see why he's so highly regarded."

Nick's eyes widened as he scrolled. "These *aren't* edited?"

Renee grinned. "Even after all this time, I'm still impressed by him."

Nick had been approaching the current situation as an 'operation.' A problem that needed to be worked, and in the back of his mind, he had been applying protocol that he'd go through if he were working a kidnapping. But looking at the pure, unadulterated talent of what one man with a camera was capable of; made Gael more human, not just a concept. His work, viewed on a small screen no less, was wild and unburdened, but also grounded.

He'd captured Peruvian men and women standing on the edge of jungle landscapes and rugged mountainous drop-offs. In the midst of Machu Picchu, his subjects gazed off into the distance, surrounded by rainbow colored elevations. The clothes were the focal point, but Gael had captured the wild land and the intimate lives in the eyes of the models.

In an awed voice, Nick explained, "My sister is an artist and because of her, I've been around a lot of art in my life. She often explains what I'm looking for in art is actually a feeling. These ..." he shook his head again in wonder, "his work is spectacular." He scrolled through the photos again, slowly. Letting each one land this time. "And the clothing was created by his friend?"

"Yes, Victor Campo, his clothing–"

"Holy shit!" Nick interrupted. A notification popped up and the name was a shock.

"What?"

"It's him!" he exclaimed, fumbling to hand the phone back to Renee. He twisted his body as she leaned forward to show what had been sent.

"It's another location share." Her voice rose in pitch. Nick read the: *1% bat want tears of moon think I know but don't.*

"What's his location?" Renee's hands shook as she fiddled with her smartphone, her voice quivering as she muttered for the inanimate object to cooperate. "Take your time," Nick said. She wiped her eyes with the back of her arm. Nick knew she was trying to focus.

Finally, in a hoarse whisper she relayed his location, "Ollantaytambo." *Oh-yahn-tai-tam-boh.*

Harper pulled to a stop on the side of the road and plugged in the new location on the GPS. Nick glanced at the phone when she angled it toward him, showing the time to the destination: six and a half hours.

"This is good. Really good." Nick turned around and reached for Renee's hands to give them an encouraging squeeze. "As long as someone thinks he knows something, he's got leverage." She tried to nod in agreement, but her fear and worry were plain on her face and with one hitch, all her pent-up emotions came tumbling out, in a sob, her voice small as she said. "But he's so far away again."

"Your turn to drive," Harper told Nick, opening her door, and climbing in the back seat, hugging Renee to her side.

Nick got behind the wheel and after Renee was settled down, he began asking more questions. "Renee, did you come this way during the past three weeks?"

"I think the closest we got to this area was going to the Rainbow Mountains." Nick glanced in the mirror as she conferred with her phone. After a few moments said, "But that's five hours from where we found Luis."

Nick frowned as he questioned out loud, "Why take him from Cusco, come all the way out here, only to go back through Cusco, then north?"

"Because they're assholes?" Renee muttered in despair. "I don't know."

"We'll figure this out," Harper said, meeting Nick's eyes in the mirror. He leveled his gaze and repeated her words with conviction, "We'll figure this out."

Chapter Twenty-Six

As they drove north, Renee let her thoughts ebb and flow through her memories of the past few weeks. Of all the places she'd visited in her short time in Peru, Renee felt Ollantaytambo was the *most* Peruvian.

Maybe because it was part of the first adventure she, Gael and Victor had taken. All she knew for sure was that there was something about the small town tucked at the base of the Andes Mountains that had completely and utterly enchanted her.

During her first adventure, after they returned from the waterfall and returned the horses, Victor drove them further into the heart of the Sacred Valley to Ollantaytambo.

The town overflowed with charisma as the car twisted down worn cobblestone streets that butted up against neighborhoods of butter yellow homes. All roads lead to the large plaza in the middle of town, its square shape surrounded by stores and restaurants all aimed at the tourists. Some came to visit the town's archaeological sites, others boarded the train to get to Machu Picchu.

As they drove past shops, she was charmed by the colorful wares hung outside the doors. Purses, jackets, scarves and hats fought for attention, but when Victor turned down one particular street, the stores moved out of the way to reveal the well-watered mountains rising out of the earth in ancient terraces, layered with green growth and mossy plant life; all of it clinging to the sides of the sharp, earthen slopes. And at the base, unbelievably large gray stones had been fit seamlessly together without mortar, a precision achievement of engineering by the Inca. This particular structure was the Ollantaytambo Sanctuary.

Victor pulled out of the narrow street into an open area where the entrance to the sanctuary could be reached, but also where a mercado area was set up, with rows upon rows of covered stalls displaying an explosion of color.

"I'll drop you here and meet up with you in the mercado," Victor said.

Gael climbed out of the car, backpack in place, camera slung across his chest. He held out his hand to help Renee, which she gratefully accepted. She didn't want to concentrate on such simple things as watching where she was going. She wanted to allow her eyes a lifetime to take in the beauty surrounding her as she attempted to figure out how to explain the way the mountains emerged from the earth, serrated and stark and overpowering and glorious in each direction.

She kept hold of Gael's hand as they explored. Her head on a swivel, taking in the rich bounty, she saw so many textiles made from alpaca, showing off traditional designs: tablecloths, sweaters, hats, gloves, shawls...

But when they were in the middle of the market, Gael turned her, revealing his vision – swags of yarn in primary colored rainbows hung between the tops of the stalls, creating a celebratory atmosphere. The color and goods became an elongated runway that perfectly framed the devastating mountains, dramatically protruding into the sky their impressive elevations.

"That'll be everything!" She aimed the full power of her excitement toward Gael.

He squeezed her hand, but suddenly, it didn't seem enough for him. And it wasn't enough for Renee either. So it made perfect sense when he wrapped the hand he was holding behind his back, forcing her close enough that he could easily lower his lips to hers. Though he hovered for a breath, smiling into her eyes. She felt her enthusiasm for everything — this moment, life, her surroundings — reflected in his gaze. Rising on her toes was all the urging he needed to close the distance; capturing her sigh that held the sights, sounds, and smells of their shared adventure.

After more exploration of the town, Gael, Renee and Victor had dinner and too much to drink, so they got rooms and stayed the night. And in the wee small hours, she lay stretched out under Gael's warm, lithe frame as his lips and hands caressed and blatantly worshiped her.

She was jarred out of her reminiscences when the car dramatically bumped over a worn section of road as the rental car drove through

Ollantaytambo.

"You can't park by the market," Renee explained to Nick as the car wobbled slowly along the cobblestone streets. "Victor parked by the plaza ..." She checked the location for the hundredth time – the center of the market.

But that had been almost seven hours ago and the sun was on a quick descent. They had less than an hour of light, and for some reason, that fact made Renee nervous. It seemed less daunting trying to find a trace of Gael while there was still light; right now the darkness held too much of an added threat.

Of course, chances were that Gael was long gone.

※

Nick found a parking place in the plaza and once they were all out, Harper watched as Renee scanned their surroundings. Harper didn't know what to do for her, wasn't sure if there was a point coming here seven hours after a text message. She felt like they were chasing their tails now, but when she held Renee's shaking body, Harper knew she was willing to stay on his trail, even if they were always seven hours behind.

Harper took a deep breath, stretching backward, putting her hoodie on and zipping it halfway. She took out her ponytail and ran her hands through her hair before putting it up again.

She pulled her backpack out of the car. It was heavier than she remembered. Not physical weight, it was weighted with responsibility that grew each time she went to put it on. She closed her eyes, but then Nick's hand slipped on top of hers.

When she blinked up at him, he gave her an encouraging nod — a silent offer that he was willing to take the weight and responsibility for a while. And she needed that. After he had the bag on his back, she stepped close enough for him to hear her soft reminder, "It's in the front pocket." He squeezed her upper arm and let his hand slide down the length of her arm before releasing her. Such a simple action, meant for reassurance, released confused butterflies.

Butterflies she did *not* have time for.

"My phone only has ten percent left," Renee interrupted.

They'd tried to charge phones in the car, but each time one was plugged in, it stole so much power the top speed dropped by ten miles per hour. And driving faster was more important, so they let the hours eat up their phones' batteries.

As Renee pointed where to go, her attention bobbing back and forth, Harper wasn't sure she was seeing the tourist shops or the road that led to the majestic flaunting of Incan ingenuity in the looming mountainous terraces before them.

But Harper was having a hard time *not* being amazed.

Renee pointed out the ancient structure at the end of the road and muttered, "That's the Ollantaytambo Sanctuary."

"Renee," Harper linked arms with her and promised, "we'll come back later and do this the right way."

"This isn't how I wanted you to see this place." She gave a frustrated laugh. "Definitely not what I imagined we'd be doing when we came here."

"I get it."

"It's still amazing though, huh?" Renee squeezed Harper's arm against her side.

"It is. And while we're talking about things I find amazing, I can't catch my breath."

"You haven't had a chance to acclimate properly," Renee's voice waivered, "I'm sorry."

"It's okay," Harper lied.

Nick kept pace on the other side of Renee. "Tell me about your time here," he encouraged.

Harper knew he wasn't asking for a tour, he was looking for some kind of missing piece. *Hell, they were all looking for some kind of missing piece.*

From where they stood, Renee pointed at the dramatic terraces ahead of them. "Do you see the stairs on the left there? I think someone said there are about two hundred steps, but we climbed to the top and there was an entire view of the valley. Gael shot up there." She gave a slight shake of her head, and Harper could have sworn she watched Renee physically push aside her melancholy fear and take on a businesslike demeanor.

She then detailed each of their trips they'd made to this city. "The first time we came, we went up and down each of the aisles in the market.

Went into the sanctuary. We walked through the oldest neighborhood." She gestured toward where the area could be found. "The cobblestone streets there are so narrow, two people walking shoulder to shoulder could barely fit. And one of the streets still has the drainage system carved into it by the Inca, and it still carries water." She cleared her throat several times.

Harper was sympathetic. "There are a lot of memories here that are probably bumping around with your worry."

"You have no idea ..." Another throat clear. "The next time we came was for a photo shoot with everyone. I spent my time doing models' hair and makeup. I have the list of models on my computer ..."

"How did you do hair?" Harper immediately waved the question away and corrected her vagueness, "I know *how* you do hair. But didn't you need electricity for curlers and hair dryers and stuff?"

"I did everything out of the back of one of our rented vans. We had a small generator and I sat the models in a chair near the open back doors. It's pretty cool to be able to make magic using the tools at hand and getting the job done when you have to improvise." A soft smile eased the worry from her forehead but didn't necessarily meet her eyes. "A lot of the time, I had an audience while I worked."

"Did you ever notice anyone watching any of you that looked like they weren't tourists or locals?" Nick asked. "Anyone who seemed a little off?"

Renee pursed her lips sadly. "No, nothing comes to mind."

The street opened up to the market then, and all three stopped abruptly. "Wow," Harper said in wonder, "this is amazing." It was an explosion of trinkets, tourist trap offerings and master craftsmanship. Harper wasn't sure where to look; the shock of color was so great, she forgot for a few seconds why they were here. She thought Nick was having a similar reaction as he shook his head at slow, random intervals, taking in all of his surroundings.

When Renee began walking again, Harper blinked a few times to realign herself with the issue at hand. Renee led them through the aisles, stopping when she reached the point where Gael had shared his last location. She turned a frown at Nick. "There's no way they drove a car to this spot."

"That's a good sign; if they're letting him out." Nick glanced at the four sellers that surrounded them. "But why would they be *here*? And you can't recall anyone talking to Gael who looked off or made him look uncomfortable or nervous?" He winked at her. "No sixth sense stuff?"

Renee pursed her lips. "I wasn't always nearby. But when we were in places like this, he always attracted attention. When I did catch people talking with him, it was mostly photography; cameras he was using, settings. And asking what we were doing here."

Nick did a slow circle and asked, "Why these vendors?"

"We bought so much from local vendors. Sometimes it was for the shoot, sometimes they were personal souvenirs." Renee matched his slow circle. "I mean, we bought *a lot* of things, often at the last minute."

"Why last minute?"

"Gael or Victor or I decided that the addition of something — a hat, blanket, or earrings — was needed for a shoot." She pointed to one of the four stalls with a large jewelry selection. "I know I bought jewelry from here. Several pairs of earrings, necklaces, bracelets. All used in the photos." She touched one of the necklaces.

Nick did another circle, only this time, his attention was on the surrounding buildings and higher angles.

"What are you looking for?" Harper asked.

"Cameras."

Renee followed Nick's gaze. "I suppose we could start going from tourist to tourist and asking when they got here and if we can see their selfies," she said facetiously.

"That's actually a good idea," Harper responded.

"I was joking?" Renee mused. "I'm not accosting tourists."

"But what if we show Gael's photo to the vendors. See if they saw him or remember anything?" Harper amended.

The idea seemed to add more steel to Renee's spine. She pulled up a photo of Gael on her phone and asked a nearby vendor if she'd seen him.

Harper touched Nick's arm and whispered, "It's been so long since she got that message."

"We'll do what we can," he assured. "Actually, Renee. Can you send a picture of Gael to Harper? We can split up."

After Renee sent the photos, Harper handed her phone to Nick. "I'll be right back. I need to use the restroom."

Renee pointed to the buildings behind them. "There's a coffee shop called Bus Stop Café. They have a really clean bathroom. But you have to pay to use it." She fished a coin from her pocket and handed it to Harper.

Before she left, Nick drew an imaginary line down the rest of the market. "Renee will go right, I'll go left. We'll meet back in the middle." He hadn't even finished before Renee began a slow jog in the direction he pointed her.

Before he left, he turned to Harper. "We'll meet you in the middle."

Chapter Twenty-Seven

The Bus Stop Café's subliminal advertising was on point. Harper bought a large coffee because the dancing coffee cup looked so happy and carefree, without a kidnapped friend of a friend in the world. And really, caffeine did make sense. While she was at it, she bought the shiniest bag of chips. The visually enticing display of American brands promised not only to take the edge off her current emotions, but the crunchiness might also help alleviate some of her worry.

As she stood at the edge of the tables set up outside the café, she took a deep drink of her coffee and closed her eyes. That's what she needed. She thought about going back and having the barista add two or ten more shots to get her through whatever else the day had in store, but decided to finish this coffee first, then see where she was.

After opening the chips, she held the bag and cup in one hand as she began to crunch. Loudly, going against propriety and chewing with her mouth open. It worked so well, she added another chip, ignoring the crumbs that fell out of her mouth onto the ground.

The indication for vendors to start packing up came when the setting sun ducked behind a mountain. The clouds bumped together, blanketing the sky; begining to tuck the small town in for the night.

Slowly scanning the crowd still meandering among the stalls, she found Nick first and with her mouth full chided, "Of course you did." Then she tried to lie to herself and reasoned, "He just stands out."

He walked slowly, the limp only evident because she was looking for it. (Maybe she should make him go to a hospital. Or look up how long it takes a knife wound to heal.) He arrived at another stand and grinned amicably. Her lips twitched to mirror his action. His handsomeness was still a shock. Though he was tall, he didn't tower. His button-down shirt was tucked in, fitted against his athletic build. As she knew from her recent up close and personal view, his muscles weren't bulging.

But Harper, there was one 'bulge' that impressed you. One you had a difficult time ignoring.

She scoffed but began choking on the dust of the chips she inhaled with the action.

She stepped away from the tables and lingering patrons so she could cough alone while she sipped on the hot coffee to try and fix the situation.

That's when she caught sight of Renee. (The blonde hair helped.) Now, she *did* stand out. Harper kept an eye on her while trying to stop the cough; but when Renee's quick walk became a run, Harper frowned, eyes narrowing as the scene unfolded. Renee dodged a few people while yelling something then was suddenly throwing herself into Gael's arms.

"Holy shit!" Harper dropped everything she was holding. The warm liquid splashed on the ground, ricocheting up onto her jeans. "Shit!" She glanced down at the mess, hastily picked it all up then blindly shoved it in a nearby trash can as she attempted to refocus on where she'd last seen Renee.

But the couple wasn't alone. Renee and Gael were being hauled apart by two vicious men, who then marched them toward a car parked at the very edge of the market.

"Holy shit!" Harper yelled and began running, not sure what she was going to do once she reached the car.

There were so many people in her way, she started to scream Nick's name. He'd been on the other side of the market, too far away from Renee. "Nick!" she screamed, not sure if he could even hear her.

Harper saw Renee and Gael forced into the vehicle. Harper frantically pushed through the crowds to get to the car, but it had already begun to move; causing a disruptive path. It swerved into tables and stalls, throwing some vendor's colorful clothing into the air, while crushing the livelihood of others.

"Nick!" Harper screamed again as she pushed through shouting people, trying to change her trajectory. The car had nowhere to go but down the street they'd walked in on. She was almost there.

Almost... there! She reached the car, but only had a moment to slap her hand against the passenger side window as she ran alongside, exchanging astonished frozen gasps of disbelief with Renee. Harper attempted one more heroic effort by jerking on the door handle, but it was locked. She slapped at the window two more times before the car picked up speed and slipped away, causing Harper to trip over her feet and fall hard on the rough, uneven cobblestones; momentum sliding her along the dirty road.

Pure adrenaline picked her back up and panic forced her to run again, screaming after the car, screaming for Nick.

She caught the last glimpse of the car as Renee turned around in the seat, pressing her hand against the back window, wide-eyed, her mouth open in wordless communication. Rounding a corner, it sped away, but still Harper ran as her lungs burned and her ability to breathe dissipated. The car was gone. She gave one more hoarse, distressed roar, her run becoming a jog as disbelief twirled with crushing shock.

Chapter Twenty-Eight

"Harper!" Nick called after hearing his name being screamed. He looked for Renee, but when he couldn't find her and his name echoed again, he pinpointed the direction and saw Harper running, screaming his name once more before she turned down the street, out of sight.

He followed her at a dead run. He watched her fall, yelled her name, but when she was back on her feet running again, he roared even louder, "Harper!"

She didn't give any indication she'd heard him, though she slowed, jogging to a stop. He caught up and put his hand on her arm, calling her attention once again. "Harper?" Her breathing ragged from the exertion, she blindly turned, but it took several long seconds for her eyes to truly focus on him. Once they'd cleared, he nodded but she pointed and with a look of disbelief demanded, "Did you see that?!" Though, she didn't give him time to answer. "What the ever-loving *fuck!*" She slapped Nick's hand off her arm, thought twice about it, then took his hand and pulled, him down the street, insisting, "We have to go."

"What happened?"

"It was Gael," Harper said breathlessly and tugged Nick's hand again. "They're getting away."

"Harper." He needed her to focus so he could understand what was happening.

"Renee saw him, I watched her run to him. Then there were these guys and one grabbed Gael and one grabbed her ..." A half sob, half grunt of anger, and another attempt at catching her breath mingled. "Nick!" She tugged. "They're getting away. We need to get to the car." She dropped his hand and began to jog again; he figured it was the best she could muster with the exertion and altitude.

He squeezed his hands into fists as he began to follow but the hand she'd been holding was wet, a little sticky. He looked down and saw blood. His gaze shot to Harper's back. She was bleeding?

He shouted, "Harper!" in an attempt to stop her, but to no avail.

He jogged awkwardly after her. His thigh had been on fire when he began to run before, but he'd pushed the pain down and now it was a dull throb. Once they rounded a corner and found the rental, Nick swore under his breath. The two tires he could see were flat and when he walked around the other side, those too had been punctured.

Harper stood blinking in disbelief, trying to catch her breath. "Nick ..." her voice cracked, "they're getting away."

"Harper." He caught her attention as he crossed the distance between them and gently turned her hands so he could see her palms. She wasn't looking, her focus still on the direction where the car carrying Gael and Renee had gone; as if it would somehow keep her telepathically connected — knowing where to go and how to help.

Nick frowned. "Harper, you're bleeding."

At that, she did look down, giving Nick time to assess her palms that had been badly scraped from her fall. She shook her head, still trying to catch her breath. "I can't comprehend what happened. I don't understand." Her breathing started to hitch in waves, and he worried she was moving past exertion and into a panic attack.

She jerked her hands away. "Nick, they took Renee and Gael. What do we do?" she demanded. "I don't have *any* of the information she has. She said her phone was almost dead when we got here. What were they doing, Nick? What were they doing here for the past like ... seven hours?" She began to pace in a woozy circle. "Were they waiting for us? For Renee? How do they know who she is? Was it a coincidence? How are we going to find them? Did they slash our tires? What the hell have Renee and Gael gotten themselves into?"

Nick knew spiraling, and Harper was caught in the swirl. She shook her head in disbelief, her ragged breathing coming as fast and furiously as her thoughts had.

Calmly, Nick tried to break through. "Harper, I need you to calm down."

"And I need my friend to not be kidnapped," she shot. "I was supposed to help her, and now if something happens to her—"

"Harper," Nick bit, using the deep, jarring no-nonsense tone he had for spiraling occasions like this.

"Nicholas," she snarled back.

He raised an eyebrow and hid an impressed smile; his tone had pushed several grown men into line during difficult situations. He was taken with the fact that it didn't seem to hold any power over Harper Barrett. But if that didn't work, he wasn't sure what would.

She took several steps in the direction the speeding car had gone, then stomped back to Nick. Eyes wide and wild, she demanded again, "What the hell are we supposed to do? We don't have transportation. I don't have *anything*. Renee had everything and I was so stupid! Nick, I didn't even try to get the license plate." Her chest rose and fell dramatically with the constricting panic.

In an attempt to stop the unraveling, Nick slipped his left hand into her hair, snaked his right arm around her waist and unceremoniously hauled her against him, attaching his lips to hers. He didn't close his eyes so he was well aware that as her arms stayed limp by her side, her eyes widened even more. But it was all he could think to do to shock her a bit, help calm her down.

So he definitely did *not* expect the intense spark of electricity, he didn't expect that it would be him who was shocked and so damn captivated. He twisted the back of her shirt, pressing her tighter against him. When she melted slightly, angled her head and parted her lips, Nick took the offered taste.

Then he released her slightly; slipped his hands down to her waist and watched her eyes flutter, confused but no longer on the verge of hysteria. When he was assured she'd be able to stand on her own, he released her, holding his hands up in front of him, fingers splayed as he took a step back. Not sure if he was surrendering or asking for forgiveness.

"Why did you do that?" Harper whispered.

"To help calm you down?" He tilted his head and shrugged.

An entire repertoire of soundless expressions played across her face while her mouth tried to form several words. He waited for her anger at him to spill out, but in the end, all she said was "okay."

He gave a nod of relief and was ready to begin a dissertation of how they could pragmatically look at the situation when she stepped back toward him and tiptoed to meet his height. As the action already had him looking down into her upturned face, it was easy for her to brush her lips against his for a long, powerful kiss.

All too soon she backed away and bit her lower lip. Her face screwed up, looking as confused as he felt. An internal stampede took the plan of action he was concocting away and left him with a few simple questions about what the hell that kiss was all about. But he felt like he needed to come up with something. So he cleared his throat and said, "Okay." It was a question, statement and verification all in one.

"Okay," Harper repeated.

They blinked at each other, and when she took a step toward him again, Nick let out a low groan, slid his right hand around her waist and roughly drew her pliable, willing body against his. Their lips searched to come together, and when they did, those unexpected sparks ignited once more. He teased her, tasted her and each time he thought he should let go, convinced himself just one more second, one more brush of building heat.

She broke them apart, pushing against him, taking a stumbling step back to where they'd begun the strange faceoff. After a few wobbles of her head, she whispered the word that seemed to be keeping the entire situation from falling apart. "Okay."

He volleyed it back. "Okay."

His erratic breathing matched her own. Her hooded eyes took him in and when her gaze swept the length of his body, she stopped at his chest, and took a step back. The fog of the past few moments faded away. "Sorry about your shirt." She jutted her chin in the direction of the bloody handprints she left on his chest.

Nick again cupped her hands and studied the blood that was almost dried. She glanced up at him and took a deep breath. "Okay. Now what?"

Chapter Twenty-Nine

Gael was taken by two men he'd categorize as petty criminals. They'd overpowered him simply because he was shocked by the situation.

From the trunk, he listened to them argue about who was better at abducting people. Argue about the time it would take to get where they needed to go. Argue about who was better with women. Argue about who had set this particular job up. And argue about needing a drink.

Lucky for Gael, when the car — and the arguing —stopped, he knew he had a few minutes to try something. Unfortunately, all he could do was send a message.

When they finally let him out, they were at an abandoned gas station. He tried to ask questions; the biggest one: What did they want with him? But no one answered, they roughly transferred him from the trunk to the back of a canvas covered van. His hands bound behind him.

He never thought he'd miss a trunk so much as the van twisted and turned its way along the zigzag roads, throwing him around like a rag doll on the floor (where he tried to stabilize himself) in the back of the vehicle.

When they stopped at another abandoned establishment, he was handed over to two men who were straight up thugs.

The intimidating kind.

As his hands were bound in front of him this time, Gael repeated his questions: "What do you want?" (And his latest theory), "Did you kidnap me for a ransom?"

One man sucker punched him in the kidney and replied, "This is so much bigger than ransom."

The other lit a cigarette and asked why Gael had been shipping things from Cusco to the town of Quince Mil.

A confused frown filled Gael's face. "It was clothing. Just clothing."

The smoker asked, "Where is the killa waqay?"

Gael's frown intensified, he knew a little of the Quechua language and that the words were moon tears, but not what '*they*' were. "I don't know what you're talking about."

"That's fine." The man put out his cigarette. "We're close to Quince Mil now. You can't hide what you were shipping."

They were close to Quince Mil? What the hell did they think Gael was involved in?

Still, once they handed over a wad of cash to the idiot who'd delivered him, they roughly coerced him into the back seat of their car. And honestly, Gael saw the new position as a win. Even if it was only for a short while.

They drove onto one of the unmarked dirt roads into the jungle, to a run-down house. Gael was tied to a chair in one of the rooms and asked the same question over and over; where was the moon tears?

He frustratingly continued to answer that he had no idea what they were talking about. A variation of punches were used to accompany the questions.

Exhausted and hurting, Gael spit the blood pooling from cuts inside his cheek onto the floor and insisted, "Maybe you idiots could ask me another question, like put it another way or something. I don't know anything about killa waqay or moon tears."

In reply to that, they left him alone for several hours.

Gael moved his head a fraction to the left and right; what he'd give for some pain reliever. He couldn't decide which hurt worse, his head or his body. The mistreatment of both over the past few days (in cars and by fists) had left their marks. His stomach churned too from hunger, and his mouth was dry with the need of water. But maybe the pain, thirst and hunger were a blessing in disguise; it didn't leave much room for fear.

It was human nature that caused him to try and escape when he was left alone, while the house was so quiet. Only, one of the men opened the door and grumbled, "We're still here, stupid." He dragged Gael back to the center of the room. He snarled down at him for a moment, left, then returned with a bottle of water. He tilted it for him to take a few drinks then left again, slamming the door.

Gael wasn't sure how much time passed, but pain and hunger eventually put him to sleep.

A splash of water woke him.

"Okay." One of the men had brought a chair and sat across from Gael. "There were only clothes in Quince Mil."

"I told you that's all I was shipping. I was here to do a fashion photo shoot, and Quince Mil is where some of the clothing is made. It was an important shoot and the designer wanted everything to be perfect. So there were a lot of packages sent between us." He wished he knew what the hell was going on.

The man who was standing gave a backhand slap to Gael's face.

He didn't know how much more abuse he could take, it felt like his brain was dislodging from inside his skull. He let his head hang as he muttered, "I don't understand what you want."

The man in the chair facing him said, "You were in Ollantaytambo."

Gael confirmed the statement with a nod.

"You picked something up at the mercado," the man led.

Gael glanced up and frowned. "In Ollantaytambo ... we picked up a lot from the mercado."

A slap across the face was his reward. He worked his mouth to try and find his voice, but it took a few moments. "I was leading a photo shoot. We bought things everywhere we went. My whole crew did. So yes, I picked up a lot of *somethings*," he elongated the word, "at the mercado."

"Did you ever mail the things you bought at the mercado in Ollantaytambo to Quince Mil?"

Gael felt like he was going crazy. "Clothes. Just the clothes from the clothing line I was taking pictures of."

"Would anyone send anything else? Who packed the boxes?"

"Nothing else would have been sent. *I* packed the boxes or the designer did. I felt like it was my responsibility to make sure they were always handled properly." He swallowed the urge to scream that he had no idea what the fuck they wanted from him.

The man in the chair lifted a gaze to his partner who made a phone call and gave a replay of Gael's answers. And the volume was turned up loud enough that Gael heard the replies of an English accented voice who demanded the caller ask Gael, "Who else would buy jewelry?"

"We all did." Gael tried to lie when the question was relayed to him.

The unattached voice said, "I bet it was the blonde woman Luis was talking about."

Gael's head began to pound as his stomach churned.

"Luis said the woman has been receiving text messages from him. Did either of you assholes check his pockets?"

The man in the chair raised an eyebrow, pulled Gael into a standing position and began patting him down. He found the phone in Gael's sock, held it up with a sad tilt of his head and tried to turn it on. He showed his partner the dead phone.

"We found it."

The English voice ordered, "Lure the woman to Ollantaytambo. Take her by force and bring them both to me."

The conversation over, Gael was unceremoniously returned to the back seat of the car, while in the front, the thugs plugged in his phone so it could charge.

Gael had hoped Renee was getting his messages and had gone to the police, but apparently, she was taking matters into her own hands. Which was admirable and so stupid he was going to wring her neck when he saw her again.

He swallowed his fear at the thought, and silently encouraged, he *would* see her again when he was finally free from all of this.

⁂

Gael tugged on Renee to turn around from the back window she had her hand pressed against, as the car sped away from Harper.

She finally turned her attention to Gael and gently cupped his face in her hands, squinting as she studied every inch of his swollen bruised cheeks and forehead, along with the cut next to his right eye. "Jesus, Gael–"

"I'm fine." He covered her hands with his, turned his face and brushed a kiss against her palm, and repeated, "I'm fine, mi reina."

Her voice cracked. "No, you're not." She pulled away from him, tugged his shirt up so she could see his chest. He tried to stop her but she glimpsed the bruises. "Renee." He squeezed her hands, and she released his shirt. He rearranged them, hauling her to his side and brushed a kiss against her hair as he softly admonished, "I was trying to tell you to get away from me, you know."

His captors had successfully lured Renee to Ollantaytambo. With the help of his photos and the selfies he'd taken with her, they knew who to look for.

They stayed in the car most of the time, Gael's face inviting the wrong kind of curious stares. He spent a hungry day half asleep in the back of the car. The men took turns watching and walking through the shadows.

It was almost dusk when one of the men returned to the car, an evil grin in place as he showed the photos he'd taken to his partner. "I found her, she's traveling with another man and woman. I slashed their tires once they were out of sight."

Gael was taken out of the car, and the three waited in a blind spot as they watched the group arrive. Gael willed Renee to turn around and go the other direction, but leave it to Renee to do the opposite of what he'd like and be more contrary when she split away from the group.

The men seemed genuinely happy at how well things were working out and pushed him into her line of sight, but not before threatening him. "Don't try anything." To reinforce the threat, he was shown the gun that would be trained on him and the one aimed at Renee.

Still, he tried to melt into the surroundings and will her away from him. Then she saw him and her whole damn face lit up – he felt like the setting sun had returned to the center of the sky in full force. He also made a very small motion with his hand by his side; and he *knew* she saw it. He knew *she* knew it meant 'go away.'

But she got that look in her eye, the one that meant she wasn't about to listen to anyone, and ran to him. And he hated that her life was in danger, but having her in his arms was almost worth it.

He needed to touch her again now, to make sure she was real. "We could talk about what's on your face." He gently brushed his fingers across the bruise and cut on her cheek.

"Oh that," she waved him away, "it was just a little bar fight."

He grunted, then in an attempt to lighten the mood asked, "How is your visit with Harper going?"

"Good, I've shown her a few sights. Got to go shopping at the mercado near the hotel."

"Buy any good souvenirs?"

"Chocolate, coca tea, zip ties, a multi-tool, and pliers."

He let a gruff laugh escape, then moaned when the pain shot through his body.

Renee began to gently rub his arm as she continued, "She met a guy. He's actually helping us save you."

God he *missed* her. "And how is that going?"

She gave him a sideways glance. "I think we're gettin' close."

The man in the passenger seat grumbled "cállate," the order to shut up.

Gael picked up her hand and brushed a kiss on her knuckles, then began a slow, stuttered, whispered conversation. "They want the moon tears."

"What is that?"

"No idea. They think I know. And now, mi reina, I worry they'll use you to make me talk about things I have no knowledge of."

She squeezed his hand and in the barest of whispers said, "Then we play along til we can get away."

While Gael did *not* like the fact that Renee's life was in danger; he had to admit, her assurance that they would get away was beyond comforting.

"You can do anything you set your mind to, can't you?" he asked in true wonder.

"Of course." She winked then gestured to the man in the driver seat. "I've seen him before."

"What?"

"At an abandoned gas station, when we were looking for you." She softly added, "I remember his scars." He didn't have time to stop her as she leaned forward slightly and asked, "Where are you taking us?"

To say Gael was shocked when the man in the passenger seat answered "Choquequirao" was an understatement.

Shock was quickly followed by a fearful concern; did he tell them where they were going because they wouldn't make it back alive?

Renee aimed a questioning frown at Gael. He gave a small shake of his head and watched as she slipped her phone from her pocket. He knew this was their one chance to get information to someone and his job was to make sure the two thugs didn't see what was about to happen.

He put his hand on her thigh and gave her a squeeze, the coast was clear. She quickly typed out a message. His warning came when she'd already turned the phone off.

He took a deep breath. "Thank you for looking for me. I've got you into a lot of trouble, though. They were waiting for you because they found my phone and messages."

Another demand of "cállate" was grunted from the front seat.

Renee snuggled closer to Gael and put her head on his shoulder. "I got your back. Let's get a catnap so we have energy for whatever's coming."

He chuckled and slipped his arm around her shoulders. "I'm glad you're here, mi reina."

Chapter Thirty

Nick helped Harper sit down on the curb next to the car; it was his turn to retrieve antiseptic spray and wipes from her pack and kneel in front of her.

She held her hands out showing how her palms had taken the brunt of the damage. He met her eyes and gave an apologetic tilt of his head.

"Just ... do it." She knew it was going to hurt.

She drew in a deep hiss of breath with each spray of antiseptic, but at least he was quick and methodical. He gently cupped her hand to keep it still while he wiped away the dirt, debris and blood.

"Do you only have the duct tape?" he asked.

She bit her lip before admitting, "I have a variety pack of band-aids. There should be some big ones."

He held up the box once he retrieved it, accompanying it with an entertained, if not incredulous look. "You had band-aids and I got duct tape and a napkin?"

She held back a smile. "You were a stranger who showed up out of nowhere, stabbed. I wasn't gonna waste good band-aids on you."

He grunted as he opened the packaging.

"How's your leg?" she asked.

"We probably need to change my duct tape." He winked.

When he'd bandaged both her hands as best he could, he put everything back in the bag except for one of the larger band-aids. He held it up in front of Harper. "I'm keeping this for myself," he said, then pocketed it.

"I suppose you're allowed to keep *one* band-aid." She stood and flexed her hands. "The last time I remember scraping both hands this bad, I was skating around the block with my sisters and they tripped me."

"How many sisters?"

"Two. Both older."

"I have a younger sister," he offered.

Harper didn't want small talk. "Nick?" The question was obvious.

He stepped close enough that he could narrow his gaze and force her to focus only on him. "I told Renee this same thing I'm going to tell you. We are no good to her or Gael if we are starving and exhausted. And being hurt doesn't help either." He reached out and gently touched her elbows. She appreciated the connection as he calmly laid out his plans. "We are going to get some delicious, hot food. We're going to get someone to put new tires on this car. We're going to get a place to stay for the night. I'm going to make a few phone calls. And tomorrow, we're going to feel like we can take on the world."

He waited for the plan to soak in and for her to give him a nod that she not only understood, but more importantly, that she would accept it.

"Good." He slipped his hand to her lower back, moving next to her as he eyed the plaza. He pointed to a restaurant directly across from them. "C'mon, we haven't had anything since breakfast except nuts and dried fruit."

"I had chips," she muttered, allowing herself to be guided. His warm hand was an unexpected comfort.

"Harper, they took Renee for a reason. That's a good thing," he assured.

***

The restaurant glowed in the early evening. Welcoming light spilled out of four large windows that ran the length of the restaurant, the half window walls allowing each table a view of the breathtaking mountains that surrounded the city.

Inside was a fairly large space with exposed, dark wooden beams stitched across the ceiling. Square cherrywood tables all had matching chairs. And the wall directly across from the front door was black with a painted white tree blooming out of it.

They were guided to a table and when their waitress arrived, Nick did a lot of gesturing toward Harper and then his shirt. She figured he was giving their sob story, and their server's properly applied facial expression of concern aimed at Harper, verified her theory.

Nick made jokes with the waitress and touched her arm, sending an unexpected spark of jealousy through Harper. When Nick glanced at her to ask what she wanted to eat, she blinked several times to soften her frown of confusion and mindlessly pointed to an item on the menu.

After another round of obvious flirting, the waitress left but quickly returned with two Cusqueña beers and frosted glasses. Nick poured Harper's into the glass. "She said it's a local beer. But I have a feeling it will help you with … everything." His smiling eyes had gone amber in the dim light of the restaurant.

He wasn't allowed to flirt then tell her what to do. Though, the frosty beer did look good. She took a hefty swig, and between the altitude and lack of water and food, the liquid eased her bones as quickly as it passed her lips into her stomach.

At the waitress's next pass, she gave Nick a beguiling smile, stopped and made more small talk. When she batted her eyelashes before she walked away, Harper pursed her lips and was sure her nostrils were flaring with anger.

Nick's brow furrowed as he leaned across the table. "You okay?"

Harper waved his concern away. He could flirt with anyone he wanted. He was nothing more than a stranger to her. Sure, the kiss had been nice and it felt good when he'd held her last night. And she now felt like she was between a rock and a hard place and he was the only help she had; but she *could* find someone else. The waitress would be stupid not to notice his rugged handsomeness, and easy smile and how strong his forearms looked when he rolled up the sleeves of his beige jungle shirt. Or how all his undivided attention aimed her way elicited a flutter … she swallowed and gave a slight shake of her head.

Let him flirt with another woman.

In front of her.

What did she care?

He hadn't stopped watching her with concern, so when their food was delivered, she bit, "I'm fine. Are you okay?"

As Nick continued to flirt, Harper withdrew and put all her angry attention on her food. And since holding a fork hurt, that too fueled her anger. Except, the marinated strips of beef that had been cooked with onions and tomatoes, served with a side of rice and french fries, was so good – warming her and filling her up – she fluctuated between sated and resentful.

Food finished, the waitress brought a plated dessert of flourless chocolate cake. Harper was sure he hadn't ordered it, and when she handed him a piece of paper with a number and address written on it, she wondered if he *had* ordered *that*.

When the waitress squeezed Harper's arm and offered a smile as she walked away, she felt like she'd been slapped across the face.

Nick didn't owe her anything, but he said he'd help her and she hated that she needed his help. Maybe she should leave and go back to Cusco and give the cops all the new information she had.

Nick aimed a triumphant smile across the table. She tried to hide her hurt and gestured to the paper. "You gonna see her again?"

A frown creased his forehead. "What?"

"She's cute." Harper took the last swallow of her beer.

"Harper," he leaned forward trying to capture her attention, "I thought you spoke Spanish."

"Forgotten high school Spanish," she muttered.

"Barrett," he reached across the table and caressed the back of her hand, "are you jealous?"

"What?" She pulled away from him. "Of course not. Why would I be jealous? *What* would I have to be jealous about?"

He slid the paper across the table. "This is the address of a place to stay tonight where the owner's son has a mechanic shop and the ability to fix our tires."

"Oh."

"So you didn't understand when I told her that you deserved a romantic vacation, not to get hurt."

Yeah, she'd missed that.

His voice lowered as he continued, "Or how you deserved a really nice place to stay for the night."

To be fair, she hadn't been paying attention at that point. Probably.

Yet another lowering of his voice. "And how we were celebrating on this trip," he pushed the plate toward her, "so she brought this for both of us, to make our adventure better."

"I wasn't jealous," she shot.

In reply, he took a bite of the cake and with his mouth full said, "You should try this. It's good."

She dug into the cake, and took a bite. Then, his voice — still tuned into those lower sultry tones — offered another view of the cake. "It doesn't taste as good as you, but still not bad."

Her eyes sought him; she felt like she didn't know which end was up anymore. She'd traversed such a vast set of emotions over the past hour; she barely felt like she'd found any semblance of solid footing. Then, Nick lowered his voice and aimed such an unexpected seductive look her way (a look she didn't even *know* was in his repertoire), *then* had the audacity to make a comment like that ...

The universe, however, took that moment as a challenge, having her phone ping with a message.

She checked it and her throat immediately burned with tears. She reread it and wearily sagged her head, but at least had the wherewithal to slide the phone across the table so Nick could read it.

The message from Renee read: *Taking us to choke a key rouw SAFE don't worry.*

Chapter Thirty-One

"I think she spelled that phonetically," Nick suggested.

Harper felt the room squeezing in on her, she had to swallow several times to ease the building lump in her throat. She wiped the few tears that attempted to fall. When Nick called her name, his voice filled with concern and tenderness, but she knew she couldn't look at him yet, or she'd be a puddle. She needed to stay strong right now.

So Harper waved down the waitress and forced a smile. "Our friend wants us to meet her at a place called choke a key ..." She shrugged off the rest of the word and Nick took over the translation. The woman apologized, but she had no idea what they were talking about.

"Excuse me." An older gentleman with a thick accent leaned over from his table next to them. "I heard your question. Choquequirao." The pronunciation sounded the way Renee had phonetically spelled it. "It is not a city. It is una zona arqueológica."

"Archeological?" Harper asked, to hear herself speak (it was more of a grounding exercise at the moment).

"Yes, and there is no way to drive there. You must walk."

A frown in place, Harper finally looked at Nick. She was glad to see he wore a similar expression.

"Do you mind spelling that for us?" Nick asked the man, thanking him when he finished.

Harper transcribed the name, then searched for the archeological site. She read: "To reach Choquequirao, the only way is by foot, making it a multi-day trek. The trek typically starts from the town of Cachora. From Cachora, it's a challenging hike through rough terrain to the ruins ..."

She looked up directions from their current location to the city of Cachora. "It's almost five hours from here." Another burn of tears in the back of her throat began, the continual cycle of two steps forward a hundred steps back was not conducive to keeping a level head.

Nick caught the gentleman's attention again. "Excuse me, does the phrase moon tears have any significance in Peru?"

"The Inca called silver 'tears of the moon,'" he replied. "Is that what you mean?"

"I'm not sure but thank you. Gracias." Nick turned a raised eyebrow toward Harper. "Tears of the moon?"

Harper watched numbly as the waitress brought the bill and rattled off a few well wishes, squeezing Nick's arm and patting Harper's shoulder before she left. Nick translated, "They are expecting us at the hotel."

"Nick ..." she had been trying to make sense out of the new information, but there wasn't enough information, "what does Incan silver have to do with a photographer?"

"That's the million-dollar question," he muttered.

Harper leaned forward, whispering, "Is our current theory that the men who took Renee and Gael think they know where silver is?" Just making the statement sounded ridiculous.

Nick gave a slight shrug, took the last bite of cake then pushed himself up with a grunt. After two cautionary steps to test his own soreness, he held out his hand for Harper. She gave him her forearm then followed his example, standing with a grunt of pain. The muscles in her legs were throbbing from her unexpected sprint and rough fall.

"I'll wait outside," she mumbled, leaving Nick to pay the bill.

She took a deep breath of cool air. The temperature had dropped dramatically; she shivered but wasn't convinced it was all due to the cold.

The plaza and surrounding buildings were lit with amber bulbs and strings of lights. Sounds of diners spilling out from surrounding restaurants, music from a few other open windows, and soft conversation from people walking through the plaza, all resonated off the surrounding walls. It had a calming effect, enough for her to find a laundry list of questions and theories by the time Nick joined her.

"Do Gael and Renee know where a horde of silver is? Did Gael bring silver with him? Does Gael know where to find silver at some random archeological site?" She began to blindly walk as she talked. "It has to be about a lot of silver if he hasn't been ransomed and now Renee ..." She couldn't finish the thought, 'had been taken,' because it threatened to undo her. "Does Gael own a silver mine or something?"

"Harper," Nick gently caught her attention and gestured with his head to a street behind him, "the hotel is that way."

She corrected her direction, and when she was close enough to Nick, he stopped her, touching her elbow to get her attention again. She swallowed hard and looked up at him, "I'm okay." Hearing herself say the words helped steel her spine.

"I *was* going to tell you not to worry." He tilted his head. "But then you look at me with those eyes," his voice lowered, "and all I can think about is how your eyes change color throughout the day."

His deep voice reverberated through her body, unexpectedly clearing out layers of worry.

"When I first saw them, I thought they were smoky jade, but they've run through a color wheel since then. Every time I look at you, your eyes are a different shade of intoxicating green."

The smooth baritone compliment pushed her fears away even more, allowing her time to contemplate him. She admitted, "I've had a few thoughts about you myself." Intruding thoughts that pushed through at random moments. How rich honey color continued to be the best way to describe his eyes; confident was the way he walked, and attentive was how he approached other people. She reached up to touch his face, and instead caught sight of her bandaged hand. It fell to her side with the weight of the situation.

Nick was quick to push reality away. "Do you know what that does for a man? Knowing an attractive, intelligent, powerful woman thinks of him?" He brushed a stray strand of hair behind her ear. "And it's not every day a man stumbles out of the jungle to find a resourceful, courageous vision willing to help him."

Good lord!

It had been a very, very, *v e r y* long time since someone looked at her, touched her, or spoken about her in such a way. And she was enthralled. Who wouldn't be? He'd captured her in a web of compliments, and that attentive, leveled gaze. She mindlessly licked her lips, he looked like a man who was doing everything in his power not to kiss her.

"Harper, I know you're worried—"

So much for stepping away from reality.

She stepped away from him, but he stopped her, gently holding her shoulders. "Harper." It was a caress and a plea, "I *know* you're worried," he reiterated, "but we have a plan."

"We do?" she asked skeptically.

He winked as a lopsided smile lit up his face. "First order of business, Renee said not to worry. So we're not going to worry."

"I'm still gonna worry," she muttered.

"Not tonight." He was asking her to trust him. "Tonight, we're not going to worry. We're going to drop all our worries at the front door of the hotel and I promise, we'll pick 'em up on the way out."

She licked her lips and after a second, offered, "I'll think about it."

⁂

Nick had more reassurances to help her feel better, but for the life of him he couldn't recall what he was going to say - those full pink lips were glistening. He settled on saying her name, "Harper."

"Nicholas."

He thought about asking her out, right then. He would say they could wait until all of this was over, but he had the strangest urge to dress up, shave, make reservations, take her out and flirt with her over candlelight; finding reasons to touch her arm, her waist, her lower back, kissing her until she asked him to come back to her place ...

"We have a plan?" she reminded him.

He cleared his throat. "We have a place to stay for the night and we know Renee and Gael are being taken to an archaeological site. We also know moon tears might have a correlation to the Inca calling silver tears of the moon ... with all that, I now know who to call."

"Ghostbusters?"

Her deadpan reply was so impromptu, so unexpected, Nick barked out a laugh and felt his whole face light up. She bit her lower lip to keep from laughing but let a smile escape. It helped to deflate the buildup of worrisome tension, and Nick's attracted tension; both fading as he repeated his plan once again, "Harper, we're not going to worry tonight." He gave a slow nod, an indication he wanted her to repeat his words.

"We're going to *try* to not worry tonight," she corrected.

"I'll take it."

Only he didn't move.

And neither did Harper.

Time stretched until Harper broke through with a soft remark, "You can let go now."

But he didn't want to let go. He wanted to wrap his arms around her and capture those lips in a kiss that would send them spiraling. He wanted to feel her body against his and take her hair out of that pony tail and slip his hands through the silky strands.

He tilted his head slightly, daring her, daring himself for another kiss. He knew she understood what he was thinking because she licked her lips again.

But she didn't lean in for a kiss; instead, she slipped into his arms the way she'd done the night before; pressing her cheek against his chest while wrapping her arms around his waist, hugging him tightly to her.

He returned the hug, resting his head on top of hers. "It'll all be okay." His fervent promise elicited a shiver from her. It was probably a culmination of all they'd been through in such a short amount of time that really caused her reaction.

But for Nick Robbins, in that moment, he felt part of himself opening. He couldn't quite explain it, but he knew he would always remember the night he stood in the middle of the Andes, in a small Peruvian town, and held a powerfully intriguing woman who made him realize there might be something in his life he'd been missing all these years.

Chapter Thirty-Two

I t took them an hour to actually get into their room. Not because the hotel was difficult to find, but because when they arrived, the proprietors were eagerly waiting for them. As the waitress had shared some of their story, they were immediately ushered into the front room and given a cup of tea while they visited and waited for Rodrigo, the owners' mechanic son, to show up. When he did, Nick led him to the car while Harper stayed behind. Where she was informed by Rodrigo's mother that she and Nick made a very nice couple and they'd arranged the best room with a large bed. (That last part was offered with a knowing grin.)

Since the owners were being so helpful, Harper didn't correct the assumptions. Who cared if she slept in the same bed as Nick? They were adults. Sure she didn't mind the way his arms felt wrapped around her, or how he looked at her, or how he kissed her, but they were in the middle of a nightmare, not some rom com.

Besides, the building throb of pain in her legs and hands was all it took for any attraction to Nick Robbins to dissipate.

Of course, when she opened the door to the room, she was met with a room that was *all* bed illuminated in hues of cuddle-up cozy. Soft peach colored walls were lit by the diffused glow spilling from lamps on two bedside tables. There was a thin dresser to the right, and across the room in the corner was a small square table with two chairs.

And the bed.

The inescapably big bed.

The-large-tempting-her-to-roll-around-with-that-rugged-manly-body-unabashedly-size-bed.

Thankfully, before the room was given the chance to envelop them in the inviting romance, Nick asked "Do you have a pen and paper and can I use your phone?"

She handed him her phone and sidestepped the bed, pressing herself too far against the wall (eyeing the bed; it knew what it was trying to do), as she made her way to the safe table. She sat down and pulled out the requested items.

Nick followed, not hiding his conversation. "Hey Sean, it's Nick." Though when he declared the number he was calling on wasn't a 'secure line,' any romantic ideas about the room were quickly diffused. "I still don't have a lot to go on. But do you have any way to contact Sophie Keen?" He gave Harper an encouraging smile as he asked the question. After a few minutes he wrote down a number and ended the short conversation by saying, "When I know more or need more, you'll hear from me."

He tapped the phone number and explained, "I worked a case several years back where we were helped by a civilian consultant who has doctorates in archeology and anthropology. When the man at the restaurant said Choquequirao was an archeological site, I thought of her, figured it's a starting point."

He didn't leave time for her to ask questions as he quickly dialed the number, turned the phone on speaker and pushed it to the center of the table. She wondered if it was one of the ways he was trying to get her to trust him.

"Hello?"

As ready as he'd been, he cleared his throat before he began, "This is Agent Robbins." Nick glanced at Harper. While she'd offhandedly referred to him as a 'special agent' yesterday, he hadn't exactly verified the assumption. *Another attempt to gain her trust?*

There was an exasperated exhale from the woman who answered, "I don't know how you got my number, but I don't work for that organization anymore."

"Sean Wilder." Nick seemed happy to throw his friend under the bus. "He helps run the Salus Protection nonprofit. He gave me your number."

"Fuck," she grumbled.

"But I don't need to talk to you in an agency capacity," Nick hurried. "Dr. Keen, how's your knowledge of Peruvian archeology?"

An elongated pause stretched until her curiosity must have outweighed her natural urge to hang up on the 'agent.' "Peru, huh?"

Nick waded in. "I don't have a lot of information."

Wasn't that the truth!

"By the way, you are on speaker with my friend Harper Barrett as well."

"Hi," Harper lamely piped up.

Nick continued, "Harper's friends were kidnapped. The reason we're calling you, Sophie, is because the kidnappers seem to think her friends have knowledge about something called moon tears, or maybe tears of the moon ...?"

"Tears of the moon?" A shuffle of movement was static through the receiver. "Hold on." They heard typing, then an interested *hmm*. "In Incan mythology, gold and silver were sacred and associated with deities as well as the sun and moon. The 'tears of the moon' refer to silver."

"Do you think if someone was looking for tears of the moon, they would be looking for ... well, this is where we're at a loss. What do you think someone would be looking for?"

More sounds of a computer in the background as Dr. Keen continued her preliminary search. "The 'tears of the moon' could also refer to the tears of the Goddess Mama Quilla. Mama Quilla is the moon goddess and the protector of women."

"Quilla!" Harper snapped. "Luis didn't call it tears of the moon, he used a word like key-ha; the men who took Gael asked him where the key-ha something was."

"Well," more typing sounds from Sophie's end, "Spanish isn't the main language of Peru." More typing. "Quechua is the most widely spoken indigenous language. And tears of the moon in Quechua is killa waqay." She grunted under her breath. "I bet I didn't say that right." Another long pause suggested Sophie was reading; or weighing the pros and cons of doing a favor. "Okay, Agent Robbins. Let me do a little research for you and I'll see what I can find."

He let out a breath. "You have no idea how helpful that is."

She sternly instructed, "Don't let it get out that I did something helpful for one of you people. Do I call you back at this number?"

"Or you can email me. It's in the directory." His voice was teasing.

"What if I don't have access to the directory anymore?" she shot back.

He laughed. "I have it on good authority you're a genius."

"Ass," she snarled. "I assume this is time-sensitive?"

"The sooner the better," he verified.

"Fine. I might have something for you in a few hours." Her voice lost its agitated edge. "And Harper, take care of yourself, don't take any crap from Agent Robbins." Sophie hung up without waiting for a reply from either of them.

Harper sat back. "She's ... something."

"I've heard stories."

"What can an archeologist do for the CIA?" This was her chance to verify who he worked for.

Nick didn't deny it, but gave her a wink. "Did you know that during World War II, archaeologists were recruited and served as spies?"

"Really?" She truly was surprised at the information. "I had no idea. How did that work?"

"All they had to do was go about their normal activities during a dig but pay attention to the comings and goings of caravans and troops."

"Were they legitimate digs?"

"They were; just not funded by universities."

Harper shook her head in wonder. "Was Sophie a spy doing digs?"

He shrugged. "It's worked before."

Since he was being forthcoming, she pushed forward with her questions. "You said your friend works for a protection nonprofit?"

"Sean Wilder," Nick confirmed. "The nonprofit is called Salus Protection."

"And how does a nonprofit offer protection?"

"It's actually the brainchild of a friend of ours." He rattled off the mission statement; "Vetted, retired military professionals can be contracted as private security for various humanitarian organizations."

"That's ..." She gave a sound of disbelief. "And we just *happened* to run into you?"

"It's the universe."

Her frown increased.

A lopsided grin pulled at his lips and he appeared to blush as he admitted, "That's what Renee told me. She said it was the universe's fault we ran into each other."

It was Harper's turn to tease. "But I wasn't running anywhere. You, however, ran into a clearing screaming about bugs with a knife sticking out of your leg."

"It was more of a limp than a run."

"Okay, so you have a friend who works for a protection agency. But it's different from where you work? With the …"

His response took so long she thought maybe he wouldn't admit which three-letter agency he worked for. But his eyes softened and the look he gave grew; sexy, soft, tempting … "You were correct, I work for the CIA."

"Are you in Peru on a job?"

"I was dropping off a few things to some friends before heading to a beach city in northern Peru for vacation." He held her attention, tempting her to believe him.

She was getting there. "Were you meeting someone?"

"Someone like a romantic friend?" he asked, clarifying the question, forcing that awful jealousy streak to tingle down her spine.

She tried to shake off caring about such a thing, but before she had a chance to wave the question away, Nick slipped his hand across the table and touched her wrist. "I was going alone. I'm not seeing anyone."

She pulled away and sat back in her chair, but said, "I'm not seeing anyone either."

He mirrored her position. "Renee told me."

"What do you do …" she paused (finishing the sentence 'what do you do for the CIA?' sounded juvenile), and cleared her throat, "for … the work?" That didn't sound any better.

"In all reality, it's a lot of information gathering."

She nodded, not sure what else to ask; and before she could formulate any other questions, Nick inquired, "Where do you work? I'm sorry I haven't thought to ask until now."

"We've been a little preoccupied," she excused. "I'm a museum registrar."

"I'm sorry to say, I don't know what that is," he admitted happily. "I do know enough to figure it has to do with a museum?"

She gave her usual spiel, "I oversee the transportation of museum items when they're on loan to other museums. I get to travel with them and make sure they are handled properly throughout the shipping, unpacking and display process, and once again when they are packed to be returned."

"That's ... fascinating." He tilted his head. "Before you even answered, I had this thought that Harper Barrett would have a job as fascinating as she is."

This damn man was dangerous, he continued to spread her emotional state from one extreme to the other. Though, that *could* also be a result of her current situation. Because at any other time, if he looked at her across a table with eyes exuding dangerous attraction, giving her his complete attention (and no one had recently been kidnapped) ... well ...

"So cool," he reiterated.

"Not really." She cleared her throat. "I basically do a lot of organization. A lot of spreadsheets and cataloguing of items for scratches and knicks before they are packed to be moved." She gestured between them. "Comparatively; I would argue my job is pretty boring."

"Not at all." He shook his head, then frowned as he thought, "Should I have let you contact some of your people?"

"Nah. The people I know specialize in American history, not a lot of help with what we're dealing with."

"What have you overseen?"

"That's a long list. I've worked with a little bit of everything. Dinosaur bones, photographs, small sculptures, artifacts from Theodore Roosevelt's expeditions ..."

"That's ... incredible." He gave several small nods of his head. She liked how shocked and interested he was in her job. "Do you have a favorite?"

She moved her head from side to side, considering, "That's a tough question. Once I work with a collection, I end up having more insight and appreciation for it, which at that point suddenly makes it one of my favorites. Sorry, that's really not an answer ..."

"I suddenly have so many questions," he admitted, but went with, "What are you working on now?"

"The next collection I'll work with is a set of original photos taken by a woman named Frances Benjamin Johnston. She was a journalist and photographer in the 1880s. They'll be on loan to the Getty Museum in Los Angeles."

"And you'll travel with them?"

She nodded.

"You know, I live in LA. When you're there ... Renee said I should ..."

He trailed off, and Harper could only imagine what Renee said. Nick licked his lips. "It isn't important," he finished, tapping the table to end their conversation. "I think we probably need to get some rest."

She glanced at the bed and muttered, "I don't know how I'm going to get any rest."

"Harper, I'm going to tell you what I told Renee. You need rest to keep going and bad guys sleep too."

She was relieved that he misconstrued her 'bed' concerns. "Okay, then I'm gonna take a shower." She awkwardly used her forearms to push herself into a standing position, wincing at the pain that throbbed in her knees. She looked at the dried blood on her jeans; the fabric had stuck to her skin and she knew the wounds had scabbed over. "Nick ..." there was no getting around it, "I might need some help."

"Sure, what do you need?" he asked with concern.

She pursed her lips, her attention still on her knees, trying to figure out the best way to deal with the problem. "Well, I scraped my knees pretty bad, and I think the dried blood fused my pants to my legs. I don't want to just take them off, I think I need to get them wet first, but ..."

"You want me to start the shower for you?" He stood with his own grunt of pain and shuffled in front of her to the bathroom.

"Actually ..." She hadn't even gotten to the favor yet; but she let him ready the shower. He pulled back the curtain, turned on the water, and put a towel on the sink counter that butted up to the shower.

He checked the water temperature, nodding it was warm enough. He took several steps toward the door while she gathered her courage enough to call, "Wait ..." She cleared her throat. "That wasn't the favor."

He turned and raised an expectant eyebrow.

She opened and closed her mouth, he seemed much bigger in the small space. She held out her hands. "Can you take the bandages off?"

"Oh, sure."

"They hurt a lot too. It was hard enough to hold a fork at dinner."

"Why didn't you say something?"

"What were you gonna do," she scoffed, "feed me?"

"If it would have helped." He turned his attention to her outstretched hands.

Harper rolled her eyes; she still hadn't gotten around to the favor. *Just say it,* she mouthed to the top of his bent head. "And I don't think I'm going to be able to get my hoodie and shirt off. Or unbutton my pants," she rushed.

She'd been trying to figure out the best way to go about this. If he helped, she could leave her bra on in the shower, let it dry overnight and she'd at least have a dry shirt – if not a clean one – to wear to bed.

(And now was the moment she finally understood her mother's continued insistence that no matter what purse or bag or backpack her girls left the house with, they should always have a clean pair of underwear in a plastic bag on hand. Harper and her sisters used to tease their mother that she was teaching them some promiscuous lesson; but they'd each been in situations where the clean underwear wasn't something sexy, but very much a practicality. And sure, once or twice it had come in handy after a one night stand ... but she was trying not to think about sex with Nick standing so close.)

"I can help with that," he said nonchalantly, all his attention on the bandage he was attempting to slowly lift up from one side. "It's going to hurt when I take these off." Nick stopped, frowning. "If we get them wet first it might help, but that'll probably sting."

"Six one way, half a dozen the other." She glanced between the shower and her hands. "I think I'll soak them, so, could you take off my hoodie and shirt first?"

He nodded and she was grateful for his business-like manner.

She tried to match it, by *not* noticing the warmth of the back of his hands against her skin.

And it was probably safe to say they both tried *not* to notice her beige bra edged with white lace, the flash of fascination that crossed his face, or the shiver that ran through her body as his hands brushed her skin.

Of course, any titillating buildup was gone when she put her hands under the warm spray of water, sucking in a deep breath. After several seconds she moved one hand to Nick. He slowly rolled back a side of the bandage, then without warning, quickly removed it. She gave him the other hand to repeat the process.

With the bandages off, she let her hands fall to her side, throbbing in pain.

She watched Nick clench his jaw as he reached for the top of her jeans, unbuttoned them and pulled down the zipper. Averting his eyes, he started heading toward the door, but said over his shoulder, "If you need anything—"

"Wait." She stopped him again, her voice tight with pain.

He glanced back, in time to watch stray tears tumble down her cheek. She wiped them with the back of her hand. "I'm tired and I'm hurting and I'm worried and I want to wash my hair but ..." She shrugged in explanation. "That's what the tears are all about."

His answer was to silently add an extra towel to the counter, put a washcloth on the soap holder next to the complementary toiletries, unbutton his shirt and slip out of his pants. He walked into the shower, stood opposite the shower head and held out his hand to her; an invitation.

She took a deep breath before stepping under the spray, her back toward him, the water burning her knees when it came in contact. She let another round of silent tears fall. Nick didn't touch her, he let her have time. When she thought maybe the fabric and scabs had been softened enough, she wiped her eyes, and turned toward Nick. The warm water felt good on her back, it was the encouragement she needed to tentatively ask, "Can you pull them down?"

· · · · ·

Nick slipped her pants down carefully (trying not to be a jackass by noticing the matching underwear, curve of her hips or the delectable way they flowed into graceful toned legs.) But when he peeled the fabric off her knees, they began to bleed again and revealed dark bruises – any temptation was doused with concern. "Shit Harper. Why didn't you tell me it was this bad?"

She rested her fingertips on his shoulder as she stepped out of her pants. "I think my hands hurt worse, I didn't really notice."

He studied the area. "The fabric kept any debris from getting into the scrapes."

She reached for the washcloth and handed it over. "But can't be too sure."

He tried to be gentle, but mostly tried to be quick. That's what he would want. Finished, he stood and saw her eyes red with tears.

He didn't give her a grimace in solidarity or try to wipe her eyes, but instead helped her tilt her head back to get her shoulder length hair wet before massaging in the shampoo.

Nick lingered as she closed her eyes; he'd just been thinking about running his hands through her hair. There was only the sound of rushing water as their bodies brushed against each other intimately. But the scrapes and stab wounds shared between them doused the opportunity of any real building sensuality.

When her hair was shampooed and conditioned, she used her arm to brush away the water dripping down her face. "I need another favor."

He gave his 'happy to help' nod.

But she didn't say anything.

"What do you need?" he asked.

She sighed and rushed the favor out. "I stink. I need help washing my armpits."

He grabbed the soap, lathered up his hands and poked her arms with his knuckles to get her to raise them. She followed his directions but saw the flash of a smile too late, and realized what she'd opened herself to as he actually began to tickle her.

She squealed, "Nick!" Trying to twist her body away from him, she sucked in a breath when the spray hit her knees, so turned back into the circumference of his arms as he continued his assault.

The laughter was a balm they both needed and when he stopped trying to tickle her, he danced her around until he was under the spray. He gave a moan of relief when the warm water rushed over his body.

He picked up the soap and lathered his hands again. "Anything else you need cleaned?" he asked, and meant it as a joke. But the prospects of other parts he could clean made his mouth go dry.

Attempting to push the implication away, he closed his eyes and tilted his head back to wet his hair while he washed his chest.

⁂

Harper's mind swirled past a few sexy answers to his question, so she was appreciative when he closed his eyes and let the issue wash away down the drain. And she'd be lying if she wasn't equally appreciative of the unobstructed study she was able to make of his physique as his hands and water covered spots that would be perfect to trace with fingers or a mouth.

Dark hair slicked back, his right ear protruded a fraction more than the other. His neck, straining to keep his head under the spray, was strong and vulnerable; perfect for pressing lips against, or playfully nibbling. Although, near his collar bone were the reddened puncture bites of the last creature that nibbled on him.

He had powerful shoulders, not corded with muscles, but defined. His skin was golden where the sun touched it, olive where it had been covered. His chest and stomach taut, slightly sculpted with a trail of dark hair that dove to a distracting vee. High on his right waist was a long, angry welt of a scar that wrapped around his side. She frowned, wondering if it was a remnant from his job. But his briefs pulled her out of any momentary stall. She'd already been introduced to those, she bit her lower lip as her attention traveled to the duct taped rectangle on his thigh. "We're a pair, aren't we?"

He opened his eyes, followed her gaze and touched the tape. "Yeah, but I think we've handled ourselves pretty well."

She should get out.

She nodded toward his neck. "You really did get bitten by a snake."

She didn't want to get out.

He rubbed the area with his hand. "I did. I don't recommend it."

She pointed to the healing teeth marks on his hand. "And someone really did bite you?"

"I highly suggest biting your attacker if it's the last defense you have, but not in the fleshy part." He pointed to the thin skin between the thumb and pointer finger. "If you can bite this area here, it will break the skin and hurt a hell of a lot more." He muttered, "Not that this didn't hurt like a bitch."

"Noted."

They stared each other down, the water spilling around Nick's strong shoulders. She gave an involuntary shiver.

"Shit, get back under, warm up," he said.

"No, I'll get out. Unless ..." She cleared her throat and shook off the 'unless' part. "I'll get out." Harper stepped out of the shower, then closed the curtain and picked up a towel. But when she reached behind and tried to maneuver the clasp on her bra, she clenched her teeth; *her damn hands.*

She sighed. "Nick," she held the towel against her chest, aiming her back toward the open curtain, "can you unclasp this please?"

He did, but she swore his fingers lingered for a moment. "There you go," he offered, his voice ragged.

When she heard the shower curtain close, she took off the bra, hung it on the small towel hanger and wrapped the towel around her chest. As she bent to slip off her underwear from underneath, a hiss and muttered curses began to accompany the duct tape removal.

Grabbing her shirt, she went into the room and fished her baggied underwear from her pack; slipped them and her shirt on then awkwardly wrapped her hair in the towel. Her hands were a dull throb now, but she felt tremendously better.

She was sitting at the table when Nick entered; his hair freshly scrubbed dry, slightly standing on end, towel slung low on his hips and tucked on the side. "Check it out." He pulled part of the towel out of the way and at first, Harper blinked wildly wondering what he was happily trying to show off, then realized it was his wound. There was a little redness around the edge, but it had scabbed over. All in all, it looked like a scratch, not like a knife had been plunged into his leg. Actually, the skin around it only looked worse due to tape residue. But the important thing was that there was no swelling or redness.

"Oh, that does look good," she responded.

He nodded and went back to the bathroom, then returned wearing his pants. No shirt. *Which was fine. Distracting, but fine.*

"I squeezed out our clothes and hung them up," he explained. "Hopefully they'll be dry-ish by tomorrow."

"We need more clothes," she stated.

"I've been thinking about that." He sat across from her. "According to the map, we have to go back toward Cusco to get to Cachora, the town where you start the trek to Choquequirao. I know Renee had made a list and had it on her phone. Did she have it anywhere else at your hotel?"

Harper nodded. "She saved everything on her laptop."

Nick pondered, "There's something we're missing. If someone thinks Gael has information about the tears of the moon, whatever that means, then Renee was on the right track making lists of where they'd been and we need that information."

"But how far behind them would that put us?" she worried.

"We won't linger, but we can grab clothes while we're there."

"Okay."

Nick gave a loud yawn, causing Harper to follow suit.

"We've had a long ass day and tomorrow will probably be just as long." He nodded to the bed. "Right or left?"

"Right?" *I guess.*

Nick nodded, but before he headed to the bed asked, "Is the gun in the backpack?"

"It's in the dish towel."

"Dish towel?"

"When I bought it, the *'seller'* gave it to me wrapped in a dish towel."

"I'd like to put it on my bedside table, if that's okay with you."

She retrieved the gun and handed it over. He checked the cartridge and safety before putting it on the table. Then, he flipped the covers back, climbed in and turned the lamp on his bedside off. Harper did the same but was glad he'd left the bathroom light on and the door cracked. Sure she was a grown woman, but when a grown woman finds herself chasing down friends who've been kidnapped, a night-light doesn't hurt.

She quietly laughed at herself and thought, *I'll be sure to have that stitched on a pillow for myself.*

They pushed and prodded pillows into place, fumbling about until they'd found comfortable positions. Then the world was completely quiet. Not something Harper was ready for.

She filled the void. "Thank you. For the help ..." She sighed with gratitude. "All the help," she corrected.

"Are we even now?"

She smiled into the dark. "Probably not. I saved your life. You just got to see me in my underwear."

"Not long enough." He didn't give the honest rumble time to properly settle over her. "To be fair, you got to see me in my underwear twice now."

"Well, who knows what tomorrow holds. Maybe we'll tumble down a mountain side and ruin all our clothes."

"It's a date."

She closed her eyes that burned from the tears, worry and exhaustion. But all she could focus on was their uneven erratic breaths; it was almost comical, like they were both trying not to notice it while waiting for their breathing to even out. A small laugh began in the back of Harper's throat, but she couldn't stop it, so it grew. And Nick shocked her with his growl of a laugh. It was the kind of contagious laughter that came with snorts and wheezing, erupting into more nonsensical puffs of amusement.

The bed shook as Nick shifted his position and slipped his arm around her waist, pulling her against him. And she found herself snuggling into him as the laughter faded.

He buried his nose in her hair and in a whisper admitted, "Harper, I'm exhausted. I want to sleep with you in my arms. But I realize it's a pretty forward action for a stranger, so if you want me to let you go, I completely understand. I just thought I'd make a move." The vulnerability in his voice was blatant.

She laid her hand gently on top of the arm slung around her waist. "Tell me about yourself," she said softly, closing her eyes.

"Well, I'm the oldest of two kids. My sister, Nina, is two years younger than me. We're actually not blood-related; our parents married when we were young but Mom and Dad proved that sometimes you don't have to be blood to be thick as thieves."

"You said you live in LA?"

"Most of the time, but my parents kept an apartment in San Francisco where my sister lives. I stay there when I'm in town. Our folks are in southern France."

"Really?"

"Yup. They both took early retirement so they could enjoy their lives."

"Do they spend afternoons drinking wine and eating charcuterie while watching the wind blow across long fields of lavender?"

"Something like that."

"How old are you?"

"Thirty-eight. You?"

"Thirty-eight," she said, then after a second, "What's wrong with you?"

This time his laughter reverberated inside her. She pushed against him. "I didn't mean it in a bad way. It's just not that often you meet a single man of a certain age ... who ..."

"Who?"

She snickered. "I was going to say who seems to have his shit together, but you're lying here with two bites and a stab wound."

"And who left home with the simple intention of going on vacation."

"And suspiciously agreed to do mercenary work for two strangers."

His voice seemed to lower in register even more. "One stranger who he's quite captivated with."

She swallowed hard, if they kept this up ... "Have you ever been married?" she blurted.

"No. You?"

"No."

"Then *I* could ask what's wrong with *you*?"

"Two older sisters," she answered. Then, probably because she was tired and it was dark, she expanded, "Two older sisters who taught me how to steel myself against love rather than open myself up to it." She cleared her throat, what was it about darkness that tempted honesty? Rather than worry about that, she decided to continue. "Lena, that's the oldest, she married for security and she has this photo-shoot perfect life and is so ... pretentious. And I don't get it, but she seems happy. She's always organizing and fixing things. We have fights because she sees my life as something that needs to be fixed. She wants me *fixed* with a house, kids and a husband. In that order I think." She thought about the truth of that statement. "As a sort of rebellion against her, I've been single in a rented apartment in New York." She handed over her confession to the dark. "My other sister, Luna, fell head over heels in love, but her husband died when she was young. She shut down and became a shell of a woman for a long time; that scared me away from the head over heels stuff. I think I've been a little messed up in between all that." She squeezed her eyes and tried to cover the information dump with a dismissive laugh. "And that was way too much information when it was me who asked *you* to tell me about yourself."

"I've had a few relationships," he began, rather than comment on her shared vulnerability. "I let work get in the way too much. I'd take long assignments, like big two-year assignments and it was my fault when things fizzled out. And I probably kept people at arm's length so they wouldn't get hurt, as a byproduct of my job. But the truth is that I never met someone I wanted to build something with."

"So we've both got some good, colorful baggage," Harper said.

"Sounds like it."

"Where was your last big, two-year job?"

"Italy."

"Are you allowed to tell me that?"

She felt him shrug. "Sure, why not?"

"It's not top secret or anything?" she joked.

"Tons of people go to Italy every day. I'm allowed to tell you I went to Italy. It's not like you know any other details."

"My sister Luna recently moved to Rome. She wants me to go visit."

"You should."

"First things first, we get some sleep, get some clothes, find Renee and Gael, then finish our current vacations. *Then* I'll think about going to Italy." She yawned, the loud, extended sound echoing in the room. "Have you been to France to visit your parents?"

"I have."

"Tell me what it's like."

"Well, they live in the south, in Montpellier. And you're not wrong about drinking wine and eating cheese. But they don't look over fields; they bought this three-bedroom apartment in the middle of the city to be close to the action. Their words, not mine."

Harper fell asleep listening to the deep rumble of Nick's voice as he painted French daydreams for her.

Chapter Thirty-Three

"Jesus ..." Harper blew the word out as she scanned the ransacked Cusco hotel room in disbelief.

Nick did tell her to prepare for the possibility when they were informed by the hotel clerk that Gael's 'cousins' had stopped by.

All clothes had been ejected from drawers and suitcases. Blankets, sheets and pillows had been stripped from the beds, furniture turned upside down. The sofa cushions had been sliced open. Renee's computer was gone, as were all the papers she'd used to retrace her trip. And whatever assholes had done this, emptied all available cosmetics, shampoo, conditioner and body soap in a heap on the bathroom counter.

Harper was dumbfounded as she walked through the suite. In the kitchen, Nick was moving the contents of the fridge that were blocking the door from closing, muttering, "Now that's just wasteful."

Harper's phone rang and she answered with a dejected, "Yeah?"

There was a *tsk* before Sophie Keen said, "I *told* you not to take any crap from him."

Harper found a half smile, but assured Sophie, "It's not him. Yet."

"I think I've got something," Sophie jumped right in.

Harper turned one of the chairs right side up and sat down with the phone in the center of the table. "Okay, you're on speaker."

"So, there are a lot of legends and myths in Peru about stolen silver and magical healing silver and lost silver and silver that was gifted to the people of Peru through the tears of the Goddess Quilla Mama. But most interestingly, and most plausible for our purposes when it comes to tears of the moon, is the legend of Atahualpa's ransom.

"Time to get comfy kids. I've got a story to tell." She took a deep breath. "Atahualpa was the Inca emperor, abducted by Spanish conquistadors in 1532. Pretty quickly, he realized he could barter for his life with a crap ton of silver and gold. The conquistadors agreed and let the emperor send messengers throughout his entire kingdom, calling for his people to bring treasure to save his life. When some of the treasure was delivered, the conquistadors figured they'd made a pretty good haul, but instead of releasing Atahualpa, they killed him. And they didn't go home right away. They waited a little longer for more silver and gold to arrive.

"The thing is, the Inca Empire's road system helped news spread quickly that the Emperor had been killed. If you had been transporting treasure and found out the reason you were doing it was dead, chances are you'd stop." She cleared her throat and her voice rose with excitement. "Well that's exactly what one group did. They were being led by a renowned Inca general and upon hearing the news, they stopped. Only they had a problem; they were far from home and weighted down with treasure. The general decides they'll hide everything. Now this is how legends are made. Turns out the general wasn't transporting a few trinkets; it's been theorized that he was transporting over seven hundred *tons* of gold, silver, copper and electrum."

"Electrum?" Nick asked.

"A natural alloy that contains gold, silver and copper," she explained. "So the general hides this treasure in a cave, and he and his men never tell anyone where it's been hidden. Only the general was eventually taken by the conquistadors who demanded to be told where he'd hidden the treasure. The general never breaks and unfortunately, he too was killed.

"Now, it's fifty years. A poor Spanish adventurer falls in love and marries a local woman of Peru. But after the marriage, he suddenly wasn't very poor any longer. He's got some money. A lot actually and he starts to flaunt it. It wasn't until he was on his deathbed that he wrote a three-page letter explaining that his wife's father was one of the men who helped the general hide the treasure. In the letter, he draws a crude map with the location."

Harper glances at Nick who's listening intently, forehead drawn in a frown.

Sophie continued, "As you can imagine, people go crazy over this story and treasure hunters come out of the woodwork and spend years searching; but mysteriously, everyone who goes looking dies or has tragedy befall them.

"Okay. Fast forward to 1886, a treasure seeker from Nova Scotia named Barth Blake thinks he's cracked the whole map and letter. He sets out on an epic adventure and supposedly, he finds the treasure. He wrote a letter to the backer of the expedition, here's a little of it:

"It is impossible for me to describe the wealth that now lays in that cave marked on my map, but I could not remove it alone, nor could thousands of men. There are thousands of gold and silver pieces of Inca and pre-Inca handicraft, the most beautiful goldsmith works you are not able to imagine, life-size human figures made out of beaten gold and silver, birds, animals, cornstalks, gold and silver flowers. Pots full of the most incredible jewelry. Golden vases full of emeralds."

This time, Nick and Harper exchanged matching frowns.

"On Blake's return to raise money to expand his expedition, he falls overboard and dies. No one ever found his gold, no one ever found proof that he'd found any treasure." She paused for another breath. "Okay. Now, let's leave that treasure behind and jump over to Quilla Mama. Like many gods and goddesses, she had temples dedicated to her. And there are legends that her temples were sanctuaries made of silver, as it was her tears that left behind the silver found in the earth. One of the lesser known legends regarding Atahualpa's treasure is that his general put everything in a temple of Quilla Mama, because it was nearby. Then, he and his men spent a few years designing traps around the area, planting fast-growing foliage so the jungle would also help to protect and keep the treasure from ever being found."

They heard some clicking of a keyboard before she went on, "That legend is based on another deathbed letter confession left by a man who claimed he was the engineer of the traps. In his confession, he detailed the location of the treasure and made a map of every single trap. But this has been dismissed because treasure seekers are convinced the treasure was buried in northern Peru, closer to where the conquistadors were keeping the emperor. The basis of the Quilla Mama temple theory is nowhere near northern Peru."

She had been talking quickly, speeding up as her excitement grew. "Okay, here's why you're getting a very long-winded, but summarized history lesson on treasure. Because in the letter the engineer left behind, when he used the term killa waqay, he wasn't referring to a goddess, but an entire structure that was named Tears of the Moon."

The hairs on the back of Harper's neck stood on end.

"And," Sophie's breath rushed out, "*that* treasure, if it really was over seven hundred tons, in today's market, is worth over thirty-seven *billion* dollars."

Nick gave a low whistle as Harper rubbed her temples and hissed, "Jesus ..."

Sophie asked, "Were your friends kidnapped because they know where thirty-seven billion dollars' worth of buried treasure is?"

Harper had to swallow hard to find her voice, "If they do, they don't know they know."

"I don't know if this helps, or if this is the right track ..." Sophie trailed off.

"It helps give us a few more theories to work on than we had before," Nick said. "I can't thank you enough for the help."

Sophie added, "I did reach out to a colleague, Sonia Herrera, the director of the National Museum of Archaeology, Anthropology and History of Peru. She's the one who told me about this history; though I didn't tell her exactly why I'm interested."

"You said the man who left the letter on his deathbed, the one that referred to the whole structure as the Tears of the Moon, also said the location wasn't in northern Peru. Did he say where in Peru it was?" Nick asked.

"The director said some think it's near an archeological site that is very difficult to get to. It's hard enough getting a minimal amount of equipment there, so not a lot of work has been done in the area. She also said the locals say the place is cursed, and while she doesn't believe in such things, there are a lot of tragic events that seem to befall those who try to work there. But ..." they could hear clicking from her computer, "she gave me the name of the site."

Harper's voice was barely audible when she supplied the name, "Choquequirao."

"Yes! How did you know?" Sophie's voice was elated, then it fell. "Oh my god, your friends did find it."

Harper gazed in disbelief at Nick, trying to reject the headache that was trying to creep back in.

Nick replied, "Like Harper said before, if they 'know' about it, they have absolutely no idea."

"Well, there is good news here, Harper. If someone thinks your friends know the location of the Tears of the Moon, then they are *very* valuable. They won't get hurt," she reasoned pragmatically. "And I don't know how you stumbled across Robbins, but he has a reputation of making sure the job gets done right."

"He stumbled across me," Harper mumbled.

Sophie gave a *humph*. "Interesting. Well, that's all I've got for now. If you need anything else, let me know."

"That's more than helpful," Nick replied.

"Oh, and Robbins," her voice took on a warning tone, "if you do find out that the people you are helping have found a lost treasure, you need to make sure your first call is Sonia at the museum. I feel like she would be more helpful than any other *agency*."

"I'm on vacation, Dr. Keen. This is pro bono work, no one else needs to know what's happening," he promised, but followed up with the clause, "*If* something is happening."

Sophie laughed. "Nick, has there been a ransom yet?" She didn't give him time to answer. "With the information you've given me and what I've found out; something *is* happening." She gave a click sound and instructed, "Harper, don't let the man get you down." And just like before, hung up without saying goodbye.

"Nick ..." Harper tilted her head, unable to give voice to any one of the tornado of questions:

What the ever-loving fuck?

Did she say someone has thirty-seven billion reasons to kidnap Gael and Renee?

Peruvian treasure?

Really?

What do we do now?

What the hell do Gael and Renee know?

In the end, she finally voiced the one question that insisted the loudest. "What the fuck?!"

Chapter Thirty-Four

Renee stood in the middle of the room where she'd been unceremoniously deposited, and stared at the door. She was teetering on the edge of several different emotions. Each one seemed like a good idea. She could go for anger – start screaming and pounding on the door, making demands while she raged. She could spill onto the ground in a mess of tears and snot and feel sorry for herself as she produced groans of 'why me?' She could try to escape – although a glance around the room revealed a lack of windows, back doors or John McClane sized air vents.

Thankfully, Nick's voice came back to her with pinpoint precision, so she voiced it aloud – "You're no good to anyone if you aren't rested and hydrated Renee."

Option four it was.

She'd use the facilities in the room, take a shower and get as much sleep as she could. Then, when the moment came, she'd be ready to run.

She threw a few punches in the air as she waited for the shower to heat up. When it was ready, she climbed in and repeated the things Nick had told her several times; the most important being that these assholes thought she and Gael had important information. And when people had vital information they stayed alive. And a bonus, Nick and Harper knew where they were headed next.

⁂

Once Renee and Gael had been abducted, they drove.

And drove.

Eventually, the boredom and the relief of knowing Gael was alive lulled her to sleep. She was awakened by an arm pulling her across the back seat and Gael's string of Spanish curses as he was hauled out the other side of the car.

They were in a town, but Renee knew 'town' was a stretch. Village seemed more accurate. It was dark out, but on the right side of the road, street lamps every hundred feet attempted to push the dark away.

The muddy road glistened, reflecting the light, the tale-tell sign of a recent storm. As she was pushed, her shoes (meant for casual city walking, not mud) slipped; she held out her hands to block her fall when the goon who'd hauled her out of the car caught her. She slapped at him as he tried to right her, grunting until he succeeded. Then he muttered a curse and released her. Renee returned her own curse and snarled at him, "I remember you, ya know." She touched her face, mimicking his scar.

He didn't reply, merely pointed for her to walk.

Renee shivered against the cold, damp night air. After a quick assessment of their surroundings, she glanced up at thin wispy stretches of clouds here and there which allowed the vibrant, starry night to show off.

"Vamos," the man who had a hold of Gael's arm called, his voice echoing off the two-story buildings on either side of the sleepy street.

The only other car was a small van that looked like one of those late 80s Toyota vans, sagging halfway up the street. Two windows from the surrounding buildings glowed with light. But they were ushered away from that direction and prodded to follow Renee's scarred 'goon' to a large wooden door. He entered while Gael's goon, who stood behind them, made sure they followed.

Renee thought she should come up with names for their abductors; she was getting tired of referring to them as Goon 1 and Goon 2 in her head. She decided to call hers Scarface; really, the only appropriate name. The one that was pushing Gael ... she shrugged, she supposed she'd call him Kyle.

Sure, why not? Scarface and Kyle.

She had to swallow unexpected laughter that attempted to escape. Already imagining the TV show about two unlikely paired thugs and thinking, *I'd watch that.*

Once again, Renee and Gael were close enough to touch, so she slipped her hand into his as they shuffled into the warm, brightly lit room.

Looking around, they were shocked by their surroundings. It was the lobby of a hotel with cheerful yellow walls; exposed, dark wood beams; and a bar, made out of light gray rock, that acted as a reception desk. Two sofas sat facing each other in front of a fireplace, and beyond the front part of the room, was a dining room with about eight tables.

A man entered from an office behind the reception bar.

Scarface cracked an easy smile and began talking.

Renee quietly asked, "What's he saying?"

Gael frowned. "They have a reservation for us?" Renee thought it wasn't a question about the man's words, but a question about the civility of a room for the night.

She muttered, "Kidnappers need to sleep too."

Gael frowned down at her, but she winked at him.

As Scarface continued, she understood a very English name: Jacob Smith. She shot a sideways glance at Gael who gave an almost imperceptible shrug, but she didn't miss the way the man at reception prickled.

The short conversation over, they were pointed to the tables in the dining area.

"He said they'll bring out dinner?" Gael blurted another astonished non-question, question. "God, I'm hungry." And as if to prove his statement, she heard his stomach growl.

Scarface and Kyle sat Gael and Renee at a table where the only escape route would be passing them.

"Is it nice to be doing something normal in a very uncommon situation?" Renee asked, sitting down across from Gael. "I don't know what I'm feeling right now. Trepidation. Exhaustion. Relief?"

"Most of that is just in reaction to me," Gael joked.

"Probably. Did you miss me?"

"Eh," he shrugged, "you do know that I arranged all this because I was worried you'd get bored."

A grunt from Kyle suggested they stop talking. Which wasn't difficult as hot food was delivered. A large portion of poached chicken coated in a spicy, creamy nut-based sauce, served over white rice and boiled potatoes.

She took a few bites, glanced at the men, then with her mouth full, softly said, "I don't think they speak English."

"They might, but not a lot."

"So should we use considerable language as we construct an actionable scheme?"

Gael's face lit up at her attempt but was followed with a grimace of pain.

She reached across the table. "Sorry."

"Mi reina, we don't even know where we are."

"So you're saying any constructed actionable scheme will be done flyin' by the seat of our pants?"

He tilted his head. "That's what I'm saying."

"Gael," she whispered, wiggling her eyebrows, "Those tend to be the best kind of plans."

Scarface and Kyle had two helpings of dinner. When they spoke, Renee remained extra quiet so Gael could overhear, in case they were saying something important. When he never translated anything, she figured they were talking about superficial things; the way two unlikely characters, tossed together by their life choices, would, in the middle of a job.

She'd add that line to the pitch for the TV show.

Scarface and Kyle took their last bites, stood and signaled for Renee and Gael to follow them up a set of stairs to where their rooms were. Only when they reached the top floor, Renee was taken in the opposite direction as Gael.

She tried to pull away from Scarface, but he tightened his hold on her arm. "C'mon asswipe, at least let us stay together. It'll be cheaper."

"It's okay," Gael reassured softly with a wink. But she knew it really wasn't, his face a testament of how mistreated he'd been when she wasn't there.

She wasn't allowed any more arguments as Gael was pushed into a nearby room and she was led to the opposite end of the hall. Scarface pointed her into the room, then stood in the doorway, and let his coat slip aside so she could see the gun he carried. He narrowed a deadly gaze at her. "Be good, no escape. Then, tu novio, we no hurting him."

She snarled at him in answer and when the door was closed she used both hands to flip him off.

Then she took her cell phone from her sock and was about to try and turn it on, when she began to wonder why they hadn't taken it from her. If they used Gael's phone to lure her, would she be luring Harper and Nick if she used her phone? But Nick could help in this sort of situation.

She decided not to try anything and leave it off. She might have one more chance to send a message later, so she needed to make it a good one.

After her shower, she took a glass of water to the bedside table as she scrunched her short blonde bob to give it some wavy texture before she laid down. It was comforting to do something monotonous. She was concerned she wouldn't get to sleep, but when her eyes closed, instead of counting sheep, she counted punches to Kyle's ugly mug and imagined Scarface wetting himself out of fear.

It worked like a charm.

Chapter Thirty-Five

Slam!

Renee shot up in the bed and groggily looked toward the resulting sound.

Scarface stood in the doorway, his usual congenial attitude in place. "Vamos."

She cleared her throat and took a drink of the water she'd put on the bedside table. "Do I have time to visit the restroom?"

"Fast."

Oh, she was going to go so slow.

She was glad she'd kept her cell phone hidden in her sock while she slept. After taking her time on the minimal morning routine she could accomplish with a washcloth and water, she exited and found an angrier Scarface.

He stood in the hallway and pointed her in the direction she was to go. Toward Gael's room.

"Will we be having breakfast first this morning?" She hoped it sounded as if she saw him as the help and she was some spoiled, high-class woman on an extravagant cruise. When Scarface angrily grunted in reply, she smiled at the little victory.

But it was just that, a little victory.

Her smile was immediately hijacked when he opened the door to Gael's room, revealing him tied to a chair, his head hung low. He looked up when the door opened and, in that instant, Renee took in the new cut on his lip and the blood running down his chin. He began to struggle as she tried to rush to his side, but was stopped by Scarface grabbing her arms to keep her in place. Renee frantically fought while releasing a litany of derogatory names.

"Such a display for a friend," a voice interrupted, pulling her attention.

A new addition to the team stepped behind the chair Gael was tied to, and rested his hands on the top rail. He was tall, late fifties (if she had to guess); and clearly had a good hair stylist, who covered the gray seamlessly with a light brown shade and gave a cut that minimized his balding. His eyes were dark, almost sunken above a crooked nose. He gave her a leering smirk and she frowned in reply.

"Gael told me you were just friends, but I'm not so sure." He had a smooth English accent, but there was an underlying depth to it. "I do hope you slept well." A dangerous depth.

He walked over to her so he could look down his nose at her from his height, forcing Renee to crane her neck to look up at him. "I'm Jacob Smith, charmed to meet you Miss Young." He didn't offer a hand, not that she would (or could) take it – Scarface still had a hold of her.

Smith tilted his head studying her, then reached out and took a strand of her blonde hair between his fingers. She leaned as far away as she could to get him to release it.

"You're a pretty little thing." He gently caressed her cheek with the back of his hand, and again she pulled away, shooting him with an angry gaze. He chuckled. "Fiery too." He continued to inspect her while Renee tried to keep her ground; chin jutted in defiance, even when his expression darkened. When he stepped away, she felt like she'd been holding her breath and the air around her cooled.

"The two of you have interrupted my timeline and made me very angry. You have something I want, but for some reason, you refuse to give it to me." He pointed at Gael. "I tried to beat it out of him, and I was thinking that today, in front of him, we could try to beat it out of you. Get one of you to talk."

The words were a bucket of ice water, dampening her ability to hear properly. She was barely aware of the empty threats Gael spat, all the sound in the room becoming white noise ricocheting between her ears.

Smith nodded with a grin in Gael's direction. "Thank you for proving my point. But we are working against time. I will give you one more chance to give me what you have stolen from me." He gave a nod.

Renee missed it, her attention was on Gael. It was only seconds after the pain sank in that she realized Kyle had punched her in the side. She would have fallen, her feet failing her, but Scarface kept her standing. She thought she heard Gael yell but the second thick fist interrupted any concentration. She stopped trying to hold herself up and Scarface released her. She slipped to the ground, folding onto her knees, grunting and wheezing, trying to replace the air that involuntarily left her lungs.

She thought Gael might still be yelling, and Smith laughing; but her ears were ringing and she couldn't focus. She wasn't given long to collect herself before Scarface yanked her back to her feet. She still had trouble telling her brain to keep her legs locked so she could stand on them without needing to grip Scarface's forearms. And it took Smith asking a question twice for her to understand the words. "Do you have any information you'd like to give me?" The open-ended question was meant for either of them.

Renee tried to focus on Gael, who gave a soft smile, his attempt to comfort her. Renee softly bit, "We have no idea what you're talking about."

"That's what I feared." He stepped toward her again, cupped her chin and when she tried to pull away, gripped it harder. "Since you refuse to produce the Tears of the Moon, you will be put to good use. We need someone who is disposable." He stepped away and slapped his hand against invisible dust on his thick jeans. "We're leaving in fifteen minutes." He nodded to Scarface and Kyle, then left.

Renee and Gael were given the hospitality of a few more punches before Gael's restraints were cut and Renee was left alone to crumble to the ground. Gael fumbled to her side as she tried not to cry and push herself into at least a sitting position. His jaw was clenched as he searched her face. He opened his mouth to apologize, and as she saw it coming, she put her finger against his lips to stop him.

Kyle relocated an unseen duffle onto the bed, unzipped it and took out woven hats, gloves and rainproof jackets. He tossed the items at their feet, then handed over a set of each to Scarface before taking his own.

"Vamos," Scarface instructed.

They held their bundled warm clothing as they were ushered into the back seat of a van this time. Scarface and Kyle sat in the middle seats, while Smith sat in front with a driver, a new addition to the growing group.

"You okay?" Gael's voice was thick with emotion.

"As good as you," she said honestly. "We should have gone with Victor on that silent retreat, huh?"

"You think that would have been better?" he tried to joke.

The ride began and they turned their attention to their surroundings. Gael elbowed her after a few moments, covertly pointing to Smith, who was holding what looked to be a very old map. A copy obviously, because it had extensive writing covering it. On the top left side was a symbol that seemed familiar to Renee; but they'd spent three weeks exploring Peru and seeing so much history, it could be anything.

The driver rumbled down the muddy streets. The clock on the radio of the van said 7:14. The sky was already filled with low gray clouds. The surrounding mountains had been brushed neon green from the abundance of rain.

Gael pulled her to his side, both grunting from the pain in the effort.

"Don't apologize," she instructed. "I know you want to. But this isn't your fault."

"Then what should I say?" he asked.

"I don't know ..." She took a few seconds to watch the overcast sky as the van drove up into the surrounding mountains. "Wanna talk about how much you missed me and that we probably need to admit we like each other a lot more than we let on in the past few weeks? And that it wasn't just a fling?"

"Weird place to have the relationship talk."

"Are you worried because Scarface and Kyle speak more English than we thought they did?"

"Who?"

She gestured with her head to the men sitting in front of them. "I call them Scarface and Kyle."

A strangled laugh led to a cough which was followed by a moan. "Nah, not worried about that. They already said they were going to use us against each other." He scrunched his face. "But I suppose since we have all this time ..." He looked down into her eyes and she took the offered moment to drown in their warmth.

"Good," she finally said with an accompanying definitive nod. "I like you a lot too."

"Good. I think I'm falling in love with you," Gael admitted softly.

Renee's body rolled with butterflies. "Good."

"Good," he repeated.

She patted his knee and laughed. "Glad we had this talk."

For thirty minutes, the van wobbled along dirt roads, up and up in elevation. The sheer drop on their right had Renee clenching all her lower extremities. Gorgeous if you were a tourist, devastating when you were continually working on a way to escape in the back of your mind.

They came to a stop when the road was no longer able to be traversed by vehicle. The driver pulled over in a flattened area carved out of the side of the mountain. There was a closed store, several small storage sheds, and to the side of all that, in a clearing on the edge of the mountain, were six A-frame wooden huts with thatched roofs. One had its door open, showing two beds and a window with an awe-inspiring view.

The only other vehicles parked in the area were two trucks with horse trailers. When Smith climbed out of the car, he greeted the team of men already waiting. Four more men. Renee did *not* like the continual addition of people to whatever venture they were headed.

Although, these men didn't look very dangerous. They were congregated next to four horses and looked as if they were the guides. An assumption she made from their actions; all of them were busy strapping items into place on the pack animals. A lot of rope, shovels and what looked like metal detectors.

Out of the car, she and Gael were careful of their sore bodies as they slipped on the jackets; putting the hats and gloves in their pockets. Scarface came over and handed them each two lukewarm empanadas. He scowled at Renee but asked, "¿Estás bien?" *Are you okay?*

She scowled back at him. "No. What do you care?" Then she held out her free hand. "Can I have two more?"

He handed them over and walked away. She raised an eyebrow at Gael but opened her empanada. They stood next to each other and ate their breakfast as they watched the group ready itself. It didn't take long before Scarface and Kyle were thrusting pre-packed backpacks into their arms.

Gael nodded for her to look up at a sign, several feet in the air, near the A-frame huts that read:

Choquequirao 40km —>

"How far is forty kilometers?" she asked.

"About twenty-five miles."

They weren't looking at each other but adjusting the straps and packs on their backs as they surveyed the rest of the group.

Renee stated the obvious, "Looks like we're walking."

Smith put on his pack as he stood near the driver of the van and one of the men who'd been giving orders about the handling of the horses. They were all huddled over the map they'd seen Smith studying on the ride.

When the three seemed to come to an agreement, Smith put the map in his pack and glanced around. He met Renee's gaze for a moment and she wondered if it was the natural sunkenness of his eyes that gave him a deadly air. But then again, the asshole did have her beat up as a reminder that he was in charge and held all the power. As if he knew what she was thinking, he smiled and cocked his head, touched the top of his hat and called, "Vamos."

The men guiding the horses went first. The 'horsemen.' She'd refer to them that way, but she wasn't crazy about the fact that there were only four 'horsemen.' Smith and the driver were next, followed by Gael and Renee, then finally Scarface and Kyle.

Renee took a deep breath, hated how badly her side hurt but gave Gael an encouraging look.

He met her attempt with his own. "So, ready for our first adventure as legitimate boyfriend and girlfriend?"

Chapter Thirty-Six

"Grab an extra set of clothes. Warmer the better. And extra socks." Nick glanced around the mess. "In fact, whatever socks you have, bring 'em. I need to borrow a pair."

"Want a pair of sensible cotton undies as well?"

He shrugged. "If they don't have any at the store we're going to, might not be a bad idea."

She blinked, it had been a joke, but his reply meant they were in the thick of it now (*but what the hell did that mean she thought was going on the past few days then?!*). This was a new layer of stress, though. She tried not to think about it and grabbed what she could from the floor that would help, stuffing everything into one of Renee's overnight bags.

"Do you have a bigger t-shirt?" he asked. She went back to the pile of clothes and found her black AC/DC shirt she wore to bed because it was too big.

He pulled his shirt off, the simple action causing her to blink quickly, swallow hard and try not to look, while *never* wanting to look away.

Jesus, she'd stood in a shower and studied that chest up close, knew how the muscles rippled and how his naked torso felt pressed against her back – so very good …

Should she be so fascinated (and attracted) by such a casual action? These were the moments that continued to push her off-balance.

The fear and worry — those were emotions she understood. She'd been steeped in them from the moment she landed. But this unexpected arousal should not be so enticing while everything else around them was coming undone.

Should it?

It was like drinking orange juice after brushing your teeth.

She let a sound rush out. *God, that was exactly what it was.*

Nick scanned the suite once more and picked up her bags. "You don't know if anything else is missing? Other than the computer and loose papers she left laying around?" he verified.

"My time in this suite was very brief and spent sleeping," she admitted.

"Okay then, if you're ready, let's go."

On the way out, the front desk clerk stopped them. "Do you need your friend's things?"

Harper slowed and turned a shocked smile at the young woman who had also given her the news about Renee's incarceration. "My friend's things?"

The woman pursed her lips and glanced between Harper and Nick. After a moment she sighed and went to the back room, returning with Renee's computer. She slid it across the desk and apologetically said, "I did not trust the *'cousins.'* I said I would go see if you were in the room. I hid the laptop."

"That is ... brilliant!" Harper declared. She opened the computer and when she saw the full battery, shut it down and hugged it to her chest. "Thank you."

"I did not let them into the room. But they must have returned, I saw ... the mess. I should have cleaned it, but ..."

"You did the right thing," Nick assured.

"We'll deal with it later." Harper dismissed the apology.

Harper put the computer in the backpack but took out her and Renee's passports. Holding them up to Nick, along with a questioning look, he nodded, confirming her idea.

Harper turned towards the clerk. "Can you put these somewhere for safe keeping?"

"Of course."

Back in the rental car, Nick adjusted the rearview mirror, asking, "Did you get insurance on this?"

"I added shit they didn't even know they offered." She laughed. "We can drive it into a ditch and it's covered."

"Atta girl." He started the car and asked her to pull up an address.

"Where are we going?"

"Shopping," he answered, pulling into mid-morning traffic on Cusco's cobblestone streets.

They retrieved the money Sean wired Nick, then separated to make the most of their time. Nick went to an electronic store and bought himself a phone, two smartwatches and three battery packs that were already charged. Harper went to a typical tourist shop and bought two large alpaca wool sweaters, a brown and tan one for Nick, a green and white for herself. (Not that she was thinking about what he'd said about her eye color.) She also found a package of boring yet functional men's underwear. In white. Which was fine. Even though she really did prefer those tight, black boxer briefs and how they showed off his assets.

As she headed back to the car, she found a woman on a corner selling pastries and tamales. Harper grabbed a few of each, keeping one out for herself. She found Nick by the car, parked in front of the electronic store, unwrapping his phone, the packaging resting on the hood of the car.

"I found you some clean underwear," she said. He barely nodded, distracted. But then seeing the pastry she was holding up, he gave a groan. Nick gently captured her wrist in his hand, pulled it toward his mouth and took a bite. Finished, he let go and licked his lips appreciatively. Harper stood wide-eyed and frozen at the sensual act.

Orange juice and toothpaste.

"You okay?" He frowned and put the back of his hand to her forehead. "You look flushed."

She took a step away from him but when seeing his concern, she kept eye contact with him while taking a bite of the pastry; then licked *her* lips and made an appreciative groan.

He slowly hissed out an impressed "*damn*" as she climbed back in the car.

Before they left, Nick shared his number and location with Harper, and she did the same. Then he opened his GPS and typed in their destination: 'Cachora.'

The rest of the setup was done on the road. Harper opened the watches Nick had bought and paired them to the phones. Then Nick called Sean, letting Harper virtually meet the famous man.

Sean started the conversation. "You finally picked up the money."

"And used it wisely," Nick said. "I have two smartwatches I need you to keep an eye on. I'm driving, Miss Harper Barrett is working on the watches."

"Hi, Harper. I'm Sean, and sorry to hear about your friend. But you couldn't have bumped into a better man to help you."

"That's what I hear."

He walked her through setting up the watches so he could monitor them from his side, explaining that the watches could be tracked in a way cellphones couldn't.

"Okay, those are good to go." Sean cleared his throat dramatically, but didn't say anything else.

Nick took up the exchange. "Harper," he gave her as steadying a gaze as he could while driving, "for situations like this, we always collect as much information as we can. It's for worst-case scenarios."

"Information?"

"About you," he explained. "Your address, license number, stuff like that."

"Okay." She frowned slightly.

He winked at her, lowering his voice to make sure she understood the connotation of their newly acquired inside joke. "Okay?"

She let a quick flash of a smile flicker and repeated, "Okay."

"We're ready, Wilder."

Sean asked her full name; driver's license number; height, hair and eye color; as well as her address. Then it was her employer, her parents' full names and their address. Harper was fine with all the questions, but when Sean asked her what her blood type was and whether she was a donor, it took her a few seconds to get the answers out.

Nick reached over and gave her arm a reassuring squeeze.

He asked the same questions about Renee and Gael. She had less information on them, but supplied what she could.

"Harper, I'm going to give you a number to call if you need help. It would be best if you could memorize it, in case you don't have your phone." She added the number to her phone and Nick let out a barking laugh when he looked over and saw that she'd put the contact name under 'Ghostbusters.'

"Last thing, once we're done here, could you send a photo of yourself, Renee, and Gael to that number, and label them please?" Sean requested.

She nodded her head, whispering her agreement. The seriousness of the situation, which hadn't been lost on her, continued to grow and expand in ways that she hadn't been prepared for.

"What else do you need, Robbins?" Sean asked.

"That's all for now."

"Stay safe," Sean said, before adding, "And don't take any crap from him, Harper."

Another ribbing about not taking any crap from Nick helped calm her down. "When this is over, I'd love a longer conversation about why I'm continually getting warned about not taking crap from Agent Robbins."

Sean laughed, and Nick hung up on him.

She stared at her phone for a few moments before saying, "Nick, I should have asked this before I gave out all my worldly information, but you're the good guy, right? And Sean's a good guy? For real?"

He didn't answer, but pulled off to the side of the road. Once the car was in park he twisted his body to give her all his attention; she looked at him expectantly. Then he aimed his intense gaze at Harper.

The air in the car grew thick and she felt a burning begin in the back of her throat. He reached out and gently cupped the side of her face as he vehemently swore, "I *am* the good guy. We met under strange circumstances. But I am going to do everything in my power to help you find Renee and Gael and I'm not going to let anything happen to you." She swallowed the building ache and bit her lower lip when the unexpected tear slipped. He brushed it away with a finger then tilted his head. "Since I'm being so honest, I think you should also know that while I would have helped you regardless, a very small part of me is helping you because I find you pretty damn attractive. And I'm also using the circumstances to be with you."

Harper shrugged as she rolled her eyes. "Oh, that's a given."

He shocked her by lunging forward and capturing her lips in a kiss, but before she could register what was happening, he pulled away, flipped the blinker and steered back onto the road.

"Can you open a note or something on your phone?" Nick asked.

She nodded when she was ready, thinking he was going to have her make some CIA shopping list. Instead, he began giving her all his information. Full name, date of birth, addresses in LA and San Francisco, parents' names and address in France, as well as his sister's.

She stared at the long list of information. "Nick, don't get me wrong, thank you for this, but ..." She gave a soft laugh.

"But?"

"I have no way of checking any of this information to see if it's real."

"That is a problem." He glanced at Harper then nodded. "I have an idea." He punched in the number he'd given for his sister.

"Hello?"

"Christina," he said in a singsong voice.

"Nicholas," she returned angrily.

"Whatcha up to?"

"Working, Nick. I thought you were on vacation."

"I am. I met someone. She doesn't think I'm trustworthy. So you're on speakerphone with Harper Barrett. Harper, this is my sister, Nina Robbins."

Nina gave that sisterly chuckle that Harper knew well, the one only younger sisters can give, that meant they had been given all the power. Nina instructed, "Run, Harper."

The tension from answering Sean's questions loosened, and Harper said, "I tried, it didn't work."

"That's a shame." She gave a dramatic sigh. "Well then, I guess I should tell you this much. Nicky has never called about a girl, *with* the girl on the phone before. I guess he's trying to impress you. But don't be impressed. Keep your guard up." Nina's laugh was tangible. "Hey, Harper. Is he doing that intense look thing while clenching his jaw?"

Harper looked over at Nick; he winked at her, a smile in place. "Not yet, but I know the look you're talking about."

"Oh my god, he really *is* trying to impress you." She loudly sighed. "Fine. I'll be nice. Harper, you won't find a more honest, loyal guy out there. He's not too broken, he's a hard worker, has a good sense of humor and he's pretty laid-back."

Harper looked at Nick and thought about a few other attributes she could add to that list.

"Did you hear me, Nicky? I was nice."

"Thank you, Chrissy."

She gurgled at the nickname, "Nicholas, note to self. When you call your sister on speaker to prove you're a good guy, it's kinda creepy. I'm going back to work. Be nice to Harper."

"Do good work."

"Harper, nice chatting with you. Tell Nick to give you my number and I can text you all the stuff he doesn't want you to know."

"I am *definitely* going to take you up on that."

She hung up and Nick asked, "Wanna get my folks on the phone next?"

"We've gotta save something for tomorrow."

"True."

She slid down in her seat. "Nick. It *is* kinda creepy calling your sister to prove you're a good guy."

He wiggled his eyebrows in answer and turned on the radio allowing Peruvian music to accompany them on their drive into the Andes.

Chapter Thirty-Seven

As the road twisted into desperate switchbacks though the mountains, the sky darkened with cloud cover.

Harper glanced at the GPS on Nick's phone that sat in the cupholder, when he took a wrong turn off the main highway into a small village; but he wound around a few streets then was back on track.

She didn't think anything of it until he did it a second time. She frowned, but once again, he wound around an area the size of a block in New York and was back on the main road just as the inevitable rain began to fall.

She was about to ask him what he was doing when he turned the wipes on to clear the torrential amounts of water, which slowed the car considerably.

"This car ..." Harper sighed.

"It's fine," Nick said, but he was sidetracked and she noticed he'd slowed down even further. Maybe he was having difficulty seeing in the heavy rain. "Fine," he repeated, only this time there was a distracted edge to his voice.

"What's going on?" she asked.

"Take my phone and pull up the satellite map. I need you to find a road, any kind of road we can turn onto."

It didn't take a brain surgeon to realize something was very wrong. "Um ... where, and ... ah, how far away?"

"The first one you can find."

She turned on the satellite imagery, zoomed out and in on the map, looked up and stared out the watery window. "We're on the side of a mountain," she whispered. Not that she wasn't aware of the fact, she just needed to say it out loud.

"Yes."

She wasn't ready to ask what was wrong, so she attempted to stay laser focused on the task he'd given her. "Okay, well ..." She followed the curves, three more and then it looked like there was an area that leveled out and had a small road. It didn't go far, though. "How long of a road? I found something; a dirt road maybe. The whole thing looks like it's only about a quarter mile long, but then it goes off a cliff. I think."

"That works."

"That works?" she asked doubtfully.

"Set it as the destination," he instructed.

Her hands were unsteady, but she did as instructed then placed the phone back in the cup holder on the dash where he could see it.

"Harper," the eerily steady calm of his voice was unnerving, "we're being followed. They're probably waiting for a good opportunity to try and run us off the road."

"How ...?"

"It's what I'd do." He reached out and squeezed her arm, but she slipped her hand to feel the warmth, and squeezed back, not minding the pain. "I'm not going to let that happen, but I'm gonna give you a whole lot of instructions at once. Ready?"

"K." She was not ready.

"Take the gun out and put it on the dash for a second. Put whatever you can reach in your backpack. Take your seatbelt off, put the pack on backwards, across your chest, then buckle again."

"In eight hundred feet, turn left," the suddenly not so comforting GPS announced.

Harper's hands shook as she shoved the bag of clothes and food she'd bought into the pack, along with her phone. She forgot how straps on a backpack worked as she failed twice to shove her arms through the straps and hug the bag to her chest. It was an awkward reach around to finally buckle herself in place. And she hated how small her voice sounded when she whispered, "okay," letting him know she'd finished all his directions.

"Is the safety still on the gun?"

She checked it. "Yes."

"In five hundred feet, be prepared to turn left."

"Put the gun in the side pocket of the bag so you can reach it quickly, put my phone in the other side pocket. Once I turn on the road, I'll go a short distance then I'm going to slam on the brakes; you unbuckle then, get out of the car, and run directly for cover."

"What cover?"

"Whatever cover you can find."

"One hundred feet ..."

Harper's breathing was shallow, she clutched the seatbelt between her hands, the roughness biting into her palms. When he pulled the parking brake to make the sudden turn down the dirt road, Harper prayed she'd read the map right; because she couldn't see a road through the fogged up windshield, spotted with drops of downpour.

She held her breath and when the car stayed grounded, she let it out, but glanced out her rearview mirror. A car passed them and seemed to immediately slow and skid to a stop.

At the same time, she was thrown forward against the seatbelt as Nick slammed on the brakes and instructed, "Go."

With her head pounding, she somehow did everything he told her. Unbuckled, opened the door, clocked cover to the side – trees and bushes – and ran, slipping and sliding as she hugged the backpack to her chest as her lifeline. The rain made it difficult to see, but she narrowed her gaze on the bushes and pushed her way into them. When she maneuvered herself around to peek out, she could make out the taillights of the rental car, only, it wasn't stopped. It was still going. She stood and squinted through the rain in disbelief as it rolled over the edge of the cliff. She opened her mouth to yell when a hand clasped over her mouth and an arm wrestled her down into the covering. "I'm here," Nick said loudly against her ear then demanded, "Gun."

Her body was having a difficult time processing the cycle of horrific alarm, fear and elation. Her hands trembled violently in her attempt to grab the gun. She managed to retrieve it on her third try and handed it to Nick. He held a finger over his lips to be quiet, then crouched in front of her, shielding her body with his. It was darker due to the gray clouds and rain, but there was still enough light to see, even in the obstruction of the deluge.

From the cover of the bushes, they watched as the following car pulled to a stop. The passenger got out, hurried through the rain and looked over the edge. After a moment he turned and jogged back, yelling at the driver, "¡Necesitamos ayuda!" *We need to get help!* After climbing in the car, it reversed quickly back to the main road and sped away.

When Nick was sure the car was gone, he stood and watched the road for a few minutes, then held out his hand to help Harper. "You okay?"

"The car ..." She ran her hands through her wet hair, slicking it out of her face.

"You said you had insurance."

She nodded, that was true, but that wasn't her point. They were only an hour into their almost five-hour drive. "We needed the car to get to Renee and Gael."

He nodded, still watching the road.

"I suppose faking our deaths might help too," she reasoned aloud.

He didn't nod his head in agreement.

"Nick?"

"We have to go, that man yelled they needed to get help."

She glanced out at the mountains that dove into each other on the horizon, green with brown splotches; low clouds obliterating most of their peaks. In the distance, a white spec of a possible house could be seen. Other than that, the landscape was vast and empty. And going back on the road was obviously not an option. She pulled out Nick's phone to find out where they were, but there was no signal.

She shook her head, letting laughter escape. "I'm beginning to sound like a broken record, but what do we do now?"

He swept her into his arms. Pausing briefly, he glanced into her eyes as the water dripped from his matted hair to his cheeks and off the end of his nose. He raised his eyebrow, a silent question. She reached up and took his face in her sore hands and brought his lips to hers, tasting him and the rain.

The brief kiss electrified everything. She reluctantly let go, and Nick brushed her hair and the rain off her forehead. "Okay?"

"Okay." She nodded.

"We gotta get going, Barrett."

"Didn't think we had much of a choice."

"Let's look for a trail that leads down." He frowned.

She voiced her previous concern, "We need to stay off the road for a while, huh?"

"Yeah, just in case."

Nick took the backpack as they searched. Eventually they found a switchback trail.

It was a trudge, their shoes weighted with the muddy buildup. When they were halfway down, Harper slipped, finding a much faster route to the bottom.

Even with losing her footing, she still had the wherewithal to sit down on her behind as the water and mud slipped her down the mountain, past bushes, plants and grass; all of which she tried to grasp. But nothing caught her, though everything tried to sting her. Finally she stopped. Laying on her back, eyes closed, water pelting her face, her hoodie slipped up around her chest. She heard Nick yelling her name over the rain and held up her hands to give a double thumbs up.

"Harper!" he exclaimed when he was close enough. She sat up, immediately twisting to her left as pain shot through her other side. Looking at the culprit, she wasn't shocked when she found the palm sized pad of a prickly pear cactus stuck to her, its long needles pressing into her skin.

She held out her hands for Nick to help her up, but when he gripped them, she pleaded, "Wait. Let go." In explanation, she showed her hands, they were torn up again and bleeding a little where the scabs *had* been. He reached under her armpits and pulled her to her feet. She kept her arm pressed against her hoodie to keep it up so Nick could see her side; to which he exclaimed, "Shit!"

"We need to take it out," she explained, "some people can have a bad reaction to the needles." She hoped the fact she wasn't allergic to cats or peanuts or anything, meant she'd be fine in this instance. "I have tweezers." She motioned to the bag. "I put them and the antibacterial spray and wipes in the small pocket in the front.

He pulled them out but stood looking down at Harper.

"Nick?"

"Barrett, these kinds of cactus have hairlike spines. They're hard to see and you slid through a bunch of them."

"I *feel* like I've fallen into a bunch of 'em."

"We can take the big spines out with the tweezers, but the little ones we need to use a knife and basically, shave the area they went in ... to get them out."

She nodded. "I have a knife."

"Harper, the little spines are probably in your clothes and going to be uncomfortable when you walk, even if we can get everything out of your skin."

"Nick," she held her hands out, "you said yourself, we need to go. Spray my hands. Let's get the big spikes out, give them a hit of spray and we'll take care of the rest later."

Nick gestured to a large group of trees that would help dampen the effects of the rain. He unzipped her hoodie and took it off, then nodded to her hands. Once they were sprayed she kept her palms down to keep them slightly dry. He turned her to study her side, grabbed an area of the cactus pad without stickers and pulled it hard.

"God!" Harper yelled. She could have sworn there were at least five long spikes that came out. She glanced down at her side, there were several long spines still sticking out of her shirt. Nick wiped the water from his face and hands, then slowly pulled each spike out. When that was done, he lifted her shirt and she understood what he meant about the tiny spines. She felt like he'd scraped her skin with a rough pad of sandpaper. "Shit," he said when he looked at her uncovered side.

A new bruise, and a bunch of off-white little hairy spines.

He took the knife, wiped it off with an antibacterial wipe, then closely shaved the skin. She hissed, "Seriously?"

But he came away with a blade filled with hairy spines. He wiped those off and did three more passes.

"I think that's the best it's going to get for now." He held up the bottle of antiseptic, the only warning she received before he sprayed the area and the stinging set in.

"Does it look really red or anything? A rash or bad welts?"

"*Are* you allergic?" he asked, concerned, kneeling in the mud to study the area better.

"I don't know. Though, I'm not allergic to anything else; but the way things are going ..."

"Can't be too careful." His face was drawn in concentration as he looked for a possible reaction.

She closed her eyes and tilted her face to the sky as he studied the area.

"It looks okay." He dropped her shirt and stood.

Nick pointed to a large rock further into the grouping of trees. "Let's wait out the storm for a little bit."

"You said they were coming back. That we needed to get moving."

"We can sit for a minute." He put everything back in the bag.

"I have a poncho ..." she shook her head, "too late now."

"I have a hat in the car." He smiled.

They arranged themselves close together on the rock, the trees stopping most of the rain. "So, we were being followed."

"We were," Nick confirmed.

"We don't have any information, do we? Other than whoever is pulling the strings here is doing it for a shit ton of money."

"See, we do have *some* information." He gently elbowed her. "Gael and Renee saw something in the past three weeks that, if they knew what it was, would lead them to the Tears of the Moon."

"The Tears of the Moon is the name of the treasure cave or temple that an army of men supposedly spent their lives hiding and booby trapping."

"We're on a roll," Nick joked.

Harper cocked her head. "And the treasure is housed somewhere in or near Choquequirao?"

"But we don't know if Renee and Gael ever went to that area," Nick filled in.

Harper used the back of her hand to wipe the water off her face. "So we really *don't* have any information."

"We know where Renee and Gael are headed. We know we were being watched. We know they think we're dead and that's actually going to play to our advantage."

"But we're not dead, we're waterlogged in the middle of nowhere waiting to see if I'm allergic to cactus."

"Exactly, you never know what kind of adventure life is going to take you on." He grinned and slung his arm around her shoulder, to pull her closer but she hissed in pain and stopped him.

"I think I found another spot where I got cacti-fied."

"Okay, Barrett. The rain will stop. We'll walk toward the one house we saw in the distance. We'll get dried off and have a snack, then we'll get back on the road."

"Nick ..." She wanted to ask: What if no one lives there, what if they aren't hospitable, what if their clothes never dry, what if—

"Harper," he stopped her thoughts, "it's gonna work out."

"Because you have a reputation of making sure the job gets done right?"

"Something like that." He gave her his cockiest smile.

And in an attempt to wipe the ridiculousness off his face, she leaned into him and brushed a long, breath stealing kiss against his lips thinking; *if it weren't for her friend's abduction, all the falling and stabbing and now cactus spine embedding, she would have jumped in bed with this man already.*

She frowned as she studied his lowered lashes. "This is weird," she admitted.

"Kissing me is weird?"

"The entire set of circumstances that have caused us to be in this moment is weird."

"True," He shook his head, whipping the water away. "But at least we're making the most of it."

Chapter Thirty-Eight

"I spent the night in jail, by the way," Renee said.

"Because of me?" Gael asked.

They were shuffling along the path, no idea how long they'd been at it. At first it had been wide enough for them to walk side by side, a comfort to be able to bump into each other's arms as they walked. But as the trail shrank, they had to walk single file and Gael let her go ahead of him.

"Not really because of you, it was probably more of how I handled the situation." She sucked in a breath. "I was a bit hysterical when you were taken, so I went to the police and demanded they help me." She blew out a laugh. "They weren't much help."

She stopped and put her linked hands on her head, to try and help the exertion from the grueling hike they'd been forced to participate in. Not only was she not in shape for this, she wasn't dressed for it either. She was wearing trekking pants, but they were lightweight. Her slip-on walking shoes weren't meant for this much mud or trail. Neither were Gael's flat canvas deck shoes. However, the hat, gloves and jacket she'd been given did help keep some of the warmth in.

"I can't imagine you in jail." He huffed, but immediately retracted, "Actually, I can imagine it."

"That's where I got the idea that if the police wouldn't help me, I would do it all myself." She started walking again. "Well, actually it wasn't me who had the idea. A woman in the cell with me asked why I was upset, and when I told her she said, 'you know, there's this dive bar you can go to and probably find some kind of mercenary who'll help you.'"

He reached out and touched her on the shoulder to get her attention, softly asking, "Did you do that?"

She looked over her shoulder, shaking her head, her eyes sparkling as she whispered back, "Didn't have to. One found *us*. Just hopped out of the jungle."

Scarface pushed Gael back into movement. Renee scowled at him before she started walking again, though was happy to see he looked miserable too.

"He's the guy Harper met," Renee supplied.

Gael chuckled. "At least she has someone to keep her company."

"Yes, while she continues my original work." She realized she wasn't doing very well speaking in code, but her life was being threatened and she'd been punched a few too many times already today. She didn't much care; in fact, she liked the idea that it would be a threat to know a mercenary was out there looking for her. "I have been thinking, though."

"Have you?"

"Mmmhmm."

"And what is bumping around in that amazing head of yours?"

She looked over her shoulder. "Leverage."

"What kind?"

"In the form of information."

"I agree."

It started to rain then. Renee stopped again to get her breath, looking around at the dark gray clouds that surrounded them along with the drop-off to her right. She took off the knitted hat, held it in her hand for a moment and turned to Gael. "Is it better to get wet and have a dry hat when it's over, or have a warm wet head?"

"Same difference?"

She put it back on as Kyle turned around to yell for her to keep going. Before she did, she shot Gael another grin as she quietly admitted, "I also brokered the purchase of an illegal gun."

"Of course. And how does one go about doing that?"

She started walking again before calling back, "Online."

⁂

Smith was a relentless taskmaster. Renee and Gael knew better than to complain. Not all the men had garnered that lesson, though. When one of the horsemen complained about the weather, asking if they could stop at the next covered overlook, Smith took a few steps so his height was on top of the man. When the guy craned his neck to look up at Smith, everyone held their breath; the confrontation ending when Smith threw a blow that toppled the man.

He turned in a circle and made eye contact with every man there, as well as Renee and Gael. In Spanish, followed by English, he asked, "Anyone else have a problem with our continuation?"

The only reply he received was a unanimous shaking of heads.

"Nos tenemos que ir. Let's go." He turned and led the way.

"Shit." Renee breathed, discouraged. If she and Gael tried to escape, they would only have one chance. That asshole would not give them a second one.

Heads down as the rain continued, the group put one foot in front of the other and trudged up relentless elevation gains, then slipped down muddy descents, as the path played out endless switchbacks.

The views were incredible, but it was hard to appreciate them when it felt like they were heading farther and farther away from civilization and deeper into a horrific nightmare.

"This is one of the Incan trails, right? The kind that connected the whole empire together?" she asked to keep her mind from spiraling.

To say she was surprised when Smith answered, was an understatement. "Yes, Miss Young. You are indeed following sections of the old Inca road system. These are the same landscapes that the ancient ones once saw. We are descending into the deep valley that was carved out by the Rio Apurimac over millennia."

Since he was being amiable, she asked, "Is that our destination? The river?"

"It is indeed."

"It seems pretty dangerous and slick, to take this path in the rain."

Again, he answered her, "This path is closed. No one travels here during the rainy season. Therefore, we will not be running into anyone."

She would have liked to ask him how much longer, but she had a feeling the question would be met with the same violence as the worker who'd just wanted a few moments out of the rain. So she decided to stick with history; thinking she'd hit on a topic he was willing to discuss.

"The Inca road connected all the different regions of their empire together for trade, right?"

"Oh, Miss Young. It was so much more than that." Since the path had widened again, he moved to walk beside her. Water rushed off the brim of his waterproof hat, and slicked off his new age, tech rain jacket. She hated how comfortable he looked in the downpour. And she wasn't too excited about having him walk with her, but like she'd told Gael, they needed leverage; with leverage came information.

He continued, "They built this road for travel through the empire, and we estimate it to have been over forty thousand kilometers. While the road was built for transportation, it was also used for communication. Inca messengers were called chasquis and we think the well-engineered road system, allowed them to cover up to three hundred kilometers a day."

"Relay runners, basically, right?" She hated how interesting this was.

"Yes, a series of runners who covered short distances would pass the messages."

"Knots." She thought about Victor's clothing and how he used fringed, knotted edges to represent the Incan form of communication.

"It would seem you have learned a few important pieces of history on your trip, Miss Young. The system of knots is called quipus."

"Key poos," she repeated phonetically.

Smith nodded. "We know it recorded numerical data and census information, but they have not been completely translated yet."

"Why are the paths so narrow at places? Is that because people were running them?"

"Actually, the Inca trail was made with the llama in mind. They were the main pack animal in the mountains."

Renee took a deep breath before asking her next question. She wanted to push him a bit, see what information he was willing to part with, but reminded herself that even though he was being congenial at the moment, this was not a nice man. "You said *we*."

"Did I?"

"*We* think they could have run three hundred kilometers in a day ..."

"It is a good hypothesis."

"We," she repeated, testing her theory about this British asshole accompanied by a lot of digging equipment, and traveling a closed path during a dangerous season. "Are you an archeologist?"

"Gael, this is a clever girl you've got," Smith called over his shoulder. "And what do you think an archeologist would be doing in the middle of Peru?"

Let's see. You keep asking us for the tears of the moon. You're an asshole. Men seem to fear you. You have an ancient map ...

She didn't say any of that out loud, but she did let one smartass comment slip. "Living your best Indiana Jones life?"

She thought she heard Gael groan softly, but it was drowned out by a large guffaw from Smith. "I am indeed, Miss Young. Living my best Indiana Jones life." He slapped a hand against his thigh. "And in order to do that, I need you and Mr. Torres to help me."

"Love to. Tell us what you need, we'll get it for you and we can all go back to our lives." Even as she said it she knew it was too cavalier.

She opened her mouth, but gave a shake of her head; stopped walking and narrowed her gaze through the rain. "I won't apologize. I hate the position we're in."

He put his hands behind his back and she had to force down the sinking feeling she was about to be hit again for some ridiculous 'manly' reason – to prove his dick was bigger than everyone else's.

"I have a map to a location that I think holds a vast fortune. I have reason to believe there are traps. I had an item that would have shown me exactly where the traps lay. But you and Mr. Torres don't know where it has gone. So you will help me. If there are no traps, you'll live. If there are, I won't die."

She could have handled being punched again. Because knowing that she was being marched into the jungle to be used as booby trap bait was worse.

"Vamos!" He prodded the group back into action. "Now, I will tell you about a great general of the Incan Empire, Rumiñahui. Some say he hid a great treasure in northern Peru. But I've found evidence that suggests it is much closer to where we are now."

Renee hoped that Gael was listening intently, because she was finding it difficult to concentrate on Smith's story. The intrusive thought that she and Gael were racing against time bombarded all her senses. And she continued to fight the internal hysterical screaming demanding, *you have to find a way to escape. Soon!*

Chapter Thirty-Nine

The rain wasn't letting up.

"Why don't you wait here," Nick said. "I'll follow this path and see what I can find."

Harper dismissed the idea. "I'm going to get wet just sitting here anyway. And I don't think separating is a good idea. So we might as well go together."

When they stood, Nick pointed in the direction he thought they should go.

Harper pulled her hair out of the ponytail and slicked it all back from her face, leaving it down. Who cared at this point. "How hard do you think it would be to get to the car? Should we go see what we can salvage?"

"I don't think that's a good idea. If the assholes who tried to run us off the road decide to come back, I don't want to be near the area or even have them seeing possible footprints leading away from the car," he rationalized.

Together they slogged through high grasses, trees and muddy paths. At least the rain washed all the mud from Harper's clothes, she tried to be grateful for that. She flexed her sore hands as they walked; reasoning it was more helpful to keep her hands limber, than let them get stiff.

Finally, they arrived at the structure they'd viewed from the top of the 'almost road.' An abandoned, one-story, one room house.

Nick had to lean against the door, swollen with years and weather; but when he pushed it in revealing a dry space, Harper groaned in delight.

Adobe bricks had been used to build the structure. The interior walls were whitewashed and the well-made roof still held back the rain. Five chairs – all of which looked suspect as to whether or not they would hold any weight – sat around a worn table. Across from the door was a square clay oven built out from the side of the wall, the cooktop charred from years of use.

In the opposite back corner, Harper spied hooks drilled into the wall, catty-corner from each other. Before they moved any further inside, she told Nick, "Don't drip anywhere but here." She stilled him as she formulated a plan. After a few seconds, she put the bag on a small table right next to the open door, fished out a dry poncho and paracord, placing them on top.

"Can you help me get out of these wet clothes?" She held up her hands. As he helped her remove everything while she held the dripping garments, she explained her idea. "I don't want to drip all over the dirt floor. If we get changed here, you can wring our clothes outside the door and then we can hang them up." She shrugged. "Maybe they'll dry a bit."

He nodded in agreement, but when she was down to her bra and underwear, she thought his eyes darkened a bit with want, but it faded as his finger lightly traced a new bruise on her side.

Fucking toothpaste and orange juice.

"I'll just go ..." She took the paracord to the back wall, strung it between the hooks as he wrung out her clothes.

⁂

Nick watched in appreciation as she hung up her clothes, then used the poncho as a tablecloth. From her pack, she withdrew a plastic bag, producing two dry, very warm looking sweaters. That's when appreciation turned to awe. The wind blew the rain in through the door, an obvious insistence for him to now take his wet clothes off.

In his boxers he hung up his clothes and gratefully accepted the dry sweater. Next, she pulled out a package of plastic wrapped tighty-whities, leaving him wondering what the next level above 'awe' was.

He changed while she averted her eyes. By the time he caught her glancing at him, he'd put the sweater on and was running his hands down the front. "This is a perfect fit, thank you."

"The color matches your eyes."

He pointed to her sweater on the table. "And you got green to match yours?”

She took out the knife and antibacterial wipes again. “Nick, there are more spines in my side and shoulder. It’s all I could feel while we walked.” She handed him the invaluable items, then turned her side to him.

He frowned at the number of bruises and scratches. “You okay, Barrett?”

“I’ve had better weeks.”

He opened the knife, the red angry welts on her skin a good indication of where the spines were. As he went over her side at all angles several times, the embedded spines would cling to the knife; he’d wipe those off and try another round. When he finished with her side and shoulder, he studied the rest of her body, trying to remain clinical. Satisfied, he said. “I think I’ve got most of them.”

“I bet there’s a bunch in my shirt and pants.”

“Can’t do much about those. At least you have a new sweater.” He helped her into it, and offered, “If you keep feeling like you’re being poked, we can try again.”

“I need to take a break. But it feels a lot better. Everything is throbbing, but it feels better.”

She retrieved the dish towel she’d wrapped around Renee’s computer and held it up to him. “It’s dry,” she announced triumphantly. He watched as she used it to squeeze out her wet hair.

Nick crossed his arms over his chest and leaned his hip against the table as he watched her work. The towel went over the back of a chair. Out of the pack came another plastic grocery bag; its contents, even though squished, revealed happily dry food. Two reusable bottles of water were added to the stack. But when she withdrew an emergency blanket, Nick asked in amazement, “Who are you?”

She glanced at him with a frown. “What do you mean?”

“If I asked you for ... a mint ...” He was trying to be a smartass but when she dove into the bag and fished out a pack of mints and placed it on the table with a twinkle in her eye; his grin grew. “Okay Barrett, impress me.”

She took the challenge and after rummaging for a moment, revealed a tin holding a candle and a bright orange tube with a whistle built into it. When she unscrewed the tube, waterproof matches slid out. “But wait, there’s more,” she said with a cocky lilt. Out came two brand new travel toothbrushes, a baggie with small salt and pepper packets, and lastly, she let a deck of cards fall onto the table; the equivalent of a mic drop.

"Damn." Nick beamed a smile of admiration at her. "You weren't lying when you told me you didn't need my help."

"I was a Girl Scout."

"One hell of a Girl Scout."

"I have *all* the badges." She made the brag, then scrunched her face. "Ew, I meant for that to be a bit more flirty, not so ... weird."

He winked at her. "I'm still impressed," he assured before going about testing the chairs. After picking the two sturdiest, he put them side by side in front of the table and covered them with the emergency blanket.

"I might have said I didn't need your help originally, but at this point, Nick ..." she cleared her throat, "I'm really grateful."

He reached out to slip his arm around her waist, thought better of it. There didn't seem to be a part of her that wasn't hurt, so instead, he brushed a kiss on her cheek then sat down with a crinkle in front of the table and patted the covered chair next to him. "Snack time while we regroup."

"Snack time," she agreed.

She pulled the pastries and tamales in front of them. They ate quietly, listening to the unrelenting rain. Harper finally asked, "So what's the plan?" Only the moment the words were out of her mouth, she groaned.

"What?"

"I feel like we've been running around for a month and the only question I've ever asked is 'what are we going to do?'"

"It's a valid question." He took out their smartphones and unlocked his. No signal; not that he was surprised. But because Harper hadn't closed the map, he was able to ascertain a rough estimate of where they were. "And if it helps you to ask it again and again, I'm more than happy to give you our step-by-step."

"Okay, Robbins. What's the plan?"

"Well Barrett, we're gonna wait for our clothes to dry a bit and hope the rain stops. Then, we're going to continue in a northerly direction until we find a signal or someone to help us."

"Someone who's not trying to kill us." She added the clause.

"Exactly."

"Is it safe to assume that whoever tried to run us off the road, are working for the same guys who took Renee and Gael?"

"Definitely."

He unwrapped another tamale and sat back after he took an appreciative bite. "If it weren't so wet out, I could try to find some firewood."

Harper unwrapped a pastry and waved it at the other three chairs. "They won't last long, but we do have a little wood if we need it."

"If we get desperate." He looked at his watch, then turned a thoughtful gaze at the worn walls, formulating a plan. Finishing the tamale, he lightly slapped the table. "Okay. It's a little after one. We have about five hours of light left. In one hour, whatever happens with the weather, we'll head out. If we can walk fifteen-minute miles, and try to cover at least eight miles, we'll either find something or someone. If we don't, we know we'll have time to get back here." He thought it was a pretty solid plan.

Harper raised an eyebrow. "I don't know if you're just really good at planning, or really good at spinning bullshit."

"Yes," he replied, opening another pastry.

"Yet, we keep sticking to your plans and they keep working."

With a mouthful of pastry he nodded. "Yesth."

She tilted her head and gave him an expectant look, waiting for him to elaborate.

After he swallowed he said, "Harper, when you move a collection, what do you have to do?"

"What do you mean?"

"I'm assuming you don't just get a box and toss a bunch of objects in and send it off."

"God no. There are lists and charts and spreadsheets ..."

"So you've been doing your job long enough that you know where to start with a plan?"

She nodded in answer.

He tapped her backpack. "You *know* your planning spills over into your life."

"Whatever." She waved his comment away.

"Plans are easy," he said. "I've been making plans to get out of difficult situations or to anticipate various entities' movements as part of my job. You just pick the most reasonable action and move in that direction. You'll most likely be knocked off course, so you take that into consideration and then make a new plan; but each reasonable, actionable plan moves you forward."

"You learned that in your job?"

He shrugged. "I wasn't taught that. It's something I learned more from observations of life, I suppose."

"But it's more than that, isn't it?"

He gave an interested *hmmm*. "Maybe I like to be in charge and make plans?"

She cocked her head to the side in thought, "But you're open to failure."

"Am I?"

"Not in a bad way. Like you said, you make plans, realizing they won't always go the way they should, but at least you're moving toward a goal. There is always the option for failure in that."

"I believe they call that a realistic optimist."

She gave a wobble of her head. "Or, you like telling people what to do. You've figured out a way to always have an answer at hand, and like it when people look to you for those answers."

"Could be." He wasn't offended by the judgement. "It's my way of always being prepared. Isn't that the Girl Scout motto?"

"That's the Boy Scout motto."

He frowned. "What's the Girl Scout motto?"

She bit her lip but the smile she was trying to stop spread anyway. "Be prepared." Then she rolled her eyes and pointed at Nick. "But girls are smarter so we didn't need the added adverb to remind us we *always* needed to be prepared."

He laughed and continued, "If I like having a plan to always be helpful, *you* like being prepared. And it goes way beyond Girl Scouts," he challenged.

"Of course it does. I like being the friend who always has what people need."

Nick gently elbowed her. "But Harper, after a while, doesn't that get a little heavy?"

He didn't know if he stepped over the line with the question; she'd frozen in place and he saw her swallow several times. Finally, she softly said, "It gets very heavy."

"I imagine ..."

"You've helped with that," she added.

"I'm happy to help." He reached out and touched the side of her face. "I'm going to offer you a bit of advice I was given years ago that I always think about. There's nothing wrong with carrying the burdens. You just need to make sure the people you are carrying all that crap for, are also willing to take the weight every now and then so you can rest."

She cleared her throat and gave his hand against her cheek an appreciative squeeze before she removed it.

"How are your hands?"

"Better. Sore, but better. How's your leg?"

"Well, we keep moving and that helps keep it stretched out I guess."

She took the cards out of the box and slid them to Nick. "So Nick, do you know how to play Gin Rummy?"

Chapter Forty

The rain became a mist once the treasure hunting excursion reached the edge of a rapidly rushing river and night washed over the land.

Tents were retrieved from packs on the horses and one was thrust into Gael's arms with no instructions.

Since he and Renee hadn't been separated in the past few hours and no one said anything different, they hurriedly put their tent up, assuming they would be able to stay together.

The lightweight, two-person geometric dome design went up quickly. They climbed in with their packs, happy to find the air pads and sleeping bags were dry.

Renee took off her shoes and outer layer of wet clothing, then shimmied into the sleeping bag, groaning when her body heat began to warm her.

"This isn't good," she whispered as Gael climbed into his sleeping bag.

"The tent?"

"No, my exhaustion." She wiggled in her sleeping bag, moving closer to Gael and softly said, "I thought we could try to escape tonight. But there is an exhaustion and ache in my feet I didn't count on."

"And they have horses."

She frowned, and he reached out and brushed her hair back from her face as he softly explained, "Mi reina, what if someone jumped on a horse to come after us? They'd catch us pretty quickly."

She shivered. "And that asshole isn't messing around."

Gael nodded at the obvious declaration. "I wish I knew what he was looking for. Truly. What the hell is the tears of the moon? I keep wondering if somehow I took a photo of it and didn't know ..."

"Did you see the map when he was looking at it in the van?"

"A little."

"There was a symbol at the top I thought looked familiar. But we've seen so many sun gods, serpents, birds and designs everywhere we've gone, that I keep thinking that's the only reason it looked familiar."

"I didn't see it."

Renee continued, "I don't think we should try to steal the map, though."

A soft chuckle rumbled in Gael's chest. "Were you going to try?"

"No." She sighed. "I'd like to. But we need to escape as soon as possible."

"Rest." He reached over and pulled her cocooned body against his. "And tell me about the horseback riding you did at summer camp."

Her head slammed into his jaw when she excitedly moved to look at him.

"Ow," he swore.

"Sorry." She freed her hand from the sleeping bag and rubbed his chin and breathed. "Do you have a plan?" He moved his jaw against the pain. She moved so they were eye to eye. "Gael, a lot of what I learned at camp came back when we went riding to the falls," she whispered excitedly.

Gael grimaced. "If ..." he took her face in his hands and repeated, "*if* we can get to the horses tonight, they won't be weighted down. But I don't know if they are used to riders. I don't know if they'll be happy if we ride them bareback. And I don't know if I remember how to ride bareback ..."

"That *is* a lot of 'ifs.'"

Gael gave her a little shake. "That's what I'm trying to explain, mi reina, we *cannot* just run into this situation wildly."

"I won't be going wildly. We'll be doing it together, sneakily."

He pressed his forehead against hers and closed his eyes as he muttered, "Por dios ..."

"Someone will be watching the horses." She whispered the obvious.

"Exactly. But we'd have to overtake that man. Quietly. Get the horses, *quietly*. And go as fast as they are willing to take us in the dark. And if we can ride them, if they'll let us. If they'll even go with us. And horses aren't great at seeing in the dark. But–"

"It's almost a full moon," she said breathlessly.

"*If* there aren't any clouds." He added another to the long list of 'ifs.'

"If we can't get the horses to cooperate, maybe we could at least let them all loose. It might hinder the opportunity for anyone to come after us quickly."

Gael groaned, "I knew you'd be too excited. I shouldn't have even brought it up."

"But I knew you were listening and studying the whole group and situation all day."

He gave another sigh. "This seems like the only plausible idea. But there are so many damn variables."

She brushed a kiss on his lips. "I'm not stupid. My body still hurts. I realize what a danger Smith is and that we'll only get one chance. But if we can make this happen, we're going to make it a resounding success."

Hmmm.

"You told me the plan because you wanted to hear that I understand the danger. I do." Before he could reply, she kissed him once more.

⁂

Harper and Nick renewed their walking. Nick insisted Harper wear the poncho, and he'd folded and tied the emergency blanket, like a bonnet, to keep what rain he could off his face. He also insisted on carrying the backpack.

They kept their heads down and trudged forward until the torrential downpour stopped, thankfully giving way to a mist. And finally, two hours into their walk, they stood on the crest of a hill and Harper happily pointed. "Civilization."

She had no idea how long it would take them to get down to the ant size grid layout of a town, but the visible destination reignited her energy.

"I've been trying not to think about what might be happening to Gael and Renee," she said as they began walking down a path Nick found (one more animal trail than human).

"Then hold onto the thirty-seven billion reasons they'll be okay," he soothed.

"The flip side is that there could also be thirty-seven billion reasons *to* worry."

"True, but at the moment, we've got our own problems, Barrett." Case in point – the large rocks and wild cactus he was picking his way around. She wasn't in the mood to fall into any more cactus. There were still some spines agitating her skin in her pants, side and shoulder. They hadn't gotten everything out.

She should probably be glad it was cold and rainy out, at least there wouldn't be any rattlesnakes. Although ... she stopped. "What kind of wild animals are in this area that might like to kill us?"

"Oh, all those animals are in the jungle," he promised, then attempted to wash any concerns away with a perfectly painted picture of the coming evening. "We're gonna get a nice hotel room. We're gonna take long hot showers. We're gonna find a lot of food to eat then we're gonna look at Renee's computer and see if there's some information that aligns with what Sophie gave us."

"That, Agent Robbins, is the kind of good time this girl needs."

Nick slowed to a stop. "And to add to that good time, I think I finally found an actual trail."

She stood next to him and followed his finger that outlined a zigzagging trail down the side of the mountain in front of them. She liked the look of it until he frustratingly muttered, "Shit."

"What's wrong?"

"It's pretty bare. That means it's going to be slick as snot."

"Shit." She reiterated his assessment. "But it's the only way down?" she guessed.

He nodded and instructed, "Try to hug the mountain, and walk on as much grass or shrubs or any growing thing you can find. It'll help with traction." He led the way.

The concentration needed to slowly pick their way down stalled any conversation. Harper slid every fifth step, and catching herself, engaged a lot of unused leg muscles; so she wasn't surprised when they began to feel like jello after a short time.

Nick looked back and checked on her often, but didn't ask how she was doing. She figured it was because he already knew and felt the same way: wet, tired and hungry.

She started reciting Nick's promises in her mind, and put it on a loop to get through all the slipping she was doing. A warm meal got her five steps before a slip. Hot shower, ten steps, slip. A bed to pass out in, twelve steps and two uneasy skating-like slip slides.

She eyed the horizon. "I'm comin'," she threatened the village, putting one foot in front of the other.

It was a slow slog until she could finally say with confidence they were about a mile out. Her shoes were filled with mud, her pants spattered up to her knees, and her socks were squishing with wet sludge every step.

Nick turned his head and called out a warning, "This next part is pretty steep, you might want to try and angle your way—"

Yeah, well, angling was what she intended to do, then there was what she really *did* do, which was slip. First, she tried to do a quick step to catch herself, then somehow found a last second twist, landed on her ass and was in a somewhat ideal position as the muddy mountain washed her the rest of the way down the steep side to the bottom, pushing the poncho up her back and somehow off half her body. She was accompanied by Nick screaming her name along with someone else screaming; though that might have been her.

The stop was abrupt, but she liked the fact that she was no longer falling and decided to lay where she was. Face up, misty rain trickling down onto it. Mud oozed into places she didn't want mud. Her behind throbbed from where she bounced it against the ground. However, a quick move of all the rest of her limbs verified nothing was broken. And she didn't feel like she'd impaled herself on any more cactus.

Nick's voice was increasing in harsh insistence. She held up a hand to accompany her loud scream, "I'm okay!" and wiggled her fingers in the air, the same way she had done earlier (the first time she fell down a mountain).

She muttered into the rain-soaked dusky night, "I'm not having the time of my life in Peru yet. But I'm okay."

She heard a litany of *'shits'* and *'damnits'* follow Nick down the mountain. When the sound of sloshing through mud approached, she called out again, "I'm okay." Then because she felt like it, and hadn't moved from the mud that was now squelching into her hair, she added, "I kinda hate that you didn't slip down too."

When he was in view, she blinked up at his abrupt stop. He screwed his face up as he stood over her, probably trying not to laugh and be sensitive at the same time. "Oh, Barrett ..."

She held up her hands for him to help her up.

"How are your hands?"

"Nick, they hurt. But it's a nice dull throb at this point so who cares," she said matter-of-factly.

When she was up, he began, "Are you—" but she held up a threatening muddy hand to stop him. "Do not even *think* of asking me if I'm okay. Just help me get the rest of the way into that town and get me a hotel room."

He curled his lips inward to stifle the laughter. She pulled her hands away from him and thought about pushing him into the mud, but decided marching toward the town was the best use of her energy.

It might be flat ground now, but it was still slick and she still slipped, so she basically began to skate her way forward.

Nick stood nearby for moral support, and when she slipped he would hold out his arm for her to brace herself against if she needed; but she didn't take the offer.

What she was trying to save – her dignity, her vacation, her self-sufficiency – she wasn't sure. But it backfired when she slip-skated into a re-creation of the fall she'd done in Ollantaytambo. Stumble, fall, slide face first into the mud. Only this time when she caught herself with her hands, it ricocheted mud into her face.

"Harper!" Nick yelled.

She turned her head and rested her cheek in the mud, closing her eyes. Her hands hurt, her knees hurt, her ass hurt. Her side, shoulders and legs hurt.

"Harper?" Nick whispered softly.

"Nick, I'm not having any fun," she mumbled.

"I know, Barrett."

"I was told there would be highs of seventy degrees. Not lows of cold and wet and muddy."

"C'mon, let me help you."

"I don't think anything is broken.

"Okay," he straddled her and helped her into a standing position, "here we go." He grunted.

When she was up, she hung her head. "The poncho is too heavy."

He removed it and dropped it on the ground. It didn't help her look any better. She was a walking monster.

"Let's take a break for a few minutes."

She shook her head. "I need to get out of this mud." She swallowed and began to walk, but this time when she slipped, she used his arm to steady herself.

Nick kept up a monologue of encouragement. Mainly – "We're almost there. About a hundred more feet ..."

With each step she took, her muddy body gave off an interesting orchestra of squishy, sloshy noises. The sounds were so ridiculous, when Nick said they had twenty more feet until they were on a paved road, she began to laugh at the insanity of the situation.

That's how they entered a town with no name, accompanied by laughter, misty rain and squelching muddy sounds. The town seemed to open its arms with welcoming amber lamplights creating a path down its sleepy main street, leading them directly to a blooming plaza – with manicured palms, what looked like burgundy bougainvillea trees and other bushes budding wisps of purple – all of it surrounded by majestic mountains.

But the grandest sight was a whitewashed two-story brick building, its set of green doors open with a sign above that read 'Hotel.'

"Nick." They headed straight for the door, but didn't enter.

Nick peeked in and caught the attention of a young man, late teens, who had been half asleep at the reception desk. His expression widened as he came around the desk to take in both Nick and Harper.

"Buenas noches." Nick gave one of his easygoing smiles. "We need a room, necesitamos una habitación." Though when he glanced at Harper, he added, "Y necesitamos ayuda." *And we need a little help.*

It took the young man several wide eyed blinks to shake himself free of his shock before he shuffled away from the door, calling, "¡Abuelita!" down a hallway.

The young man's grandmother walked quickly, in a no nonsense way, to the front of the hotel. When she was close enough to see Nick and Harper, she *tsked* and shook her head before she laughingly commented, "Esos dos se ven horribles." *You two look horrible.*

The obvious proprietress of the property, she came out into the street and walked around Harper, shaking her head, adding more tisking sounds as she assessed the situation. Then she made a few demands of her grandson who returned shortly after with a large basket.

"Put, la ropa ..." *the clothes.* She gestured to the basket set on the ground in front of Harper.

Across the plaza Harper glanced over at two elderly men, sitting and watching. When Abuela saw, she yelled at them, shooing them away.

"Gracias," Harper mumbled. Her shoes and socks went first. But she stopped when she was down to her pants and sweater.

The grandmother gave another set of directions to her grandson. He left but quickly returned with a few sheets.

The abuela held one of the sheets around Harper for privacy. Once she took off her sweater and bra, she was handed the sheet to tuck around her chest so she could remove the rest of her clothing. The woman clapped her on the shoulder, "good," then gave another set of instructions to her grandson, and gently urged Harper to follow him.

"Do you need help?" Nick asked as he removed his clothing under his own sheet.

Harper waved him away. "I'm fine. Everything's numb."

Up a flight of stairs, through a small, bright white hallway, Harper was shown to one of the rooms. Once inside, the young man opened the bathroom door, took the complementary products and put them on the edge of the counter, as if he needed them to be closer to her.

She thanked him, locked the door, then told the bottles, "I think it's gonna take every drop to get clean."

Chapter Forty-One

When Harper had scrubbed as much as she could and the water finally ran clean, she wearily wrapped herself in a towel and peeked out of the bathroom door, into the room.

Clothes had been laid out on the bed. A light purple knee length skirt made from heavy material, a yellow t-shirt, a dark blue button-down sweater and a pair of thick, long socks. Off to the side was a note from Nick: *Dinner downstairs when you're ready.*

Under the note, was a folded pair of clean, tighty-whities. She burst out laughing but was grateful; she was clean and would be cozy warm as soon as she was clothed.

Her backpack was on top of a towel on the floor next to the bed. It didn't look too bad. "Because it didn't slide through the mud with me," she muttered.

Her stocking feet were quiet on the tile floors as she retraced her steps through the hotel, taking in the details of the darling establishment she missed on her first walk-through. Bright white corridors, each door a different primary color. There were interspersed paintings of local flora along the walls. The stairs that led from the second floor to the small lobby, were surrounded by high windows, allowing her to see the final passing of dusky purples behind the gray, cloud-washed mountains.

The grandson was back at his station at the reception desk. When he saw her, he smiled in greeting – since she no longer looked like a monster from the Black Lagoon. He led her to the back of the lobby, pointed to the hallway on the right and instructed, "Dinner."

The hallway was connected to a restaurant. The same bright colors of the hotel continued throughout the establishment. On whitewashed walls were painted flowers and Peruvian designs in vibrant primary colors. The exposed beams were light wood and the large number of tables in the restaurant were crowded with diners. No one paid her arrival any attention, except a man sitting at a table by a window near the front.

Nick's face lit up when he saw her (so did hers if she was being honest). He was clean shaven, the shock of his strong, defined jawline a new revelation. His dark hair was still wet but combed into place. The slight jaundice he had when she first met him was gone, maybe replaced by a hint of exhaustion. Caught in his trajectory, she floated toward him. His eyes hooded slightly the closer she got, or maybe it was just a change of perspective? Either way, her whole body heated in reaction to him.

He stood when she was almost to the table. He wore a white t-shirt that was a little too tight (not that she minded). But his black slacks were a little loose and too short, ending at his calf, where she saw he wore the same thick socks she did.

Harper pushed past his personal space and slipped her arms around his waist, resting her head against his chest. She was clean and dry. She felt safe with him. And she wanted to be in the arms of a man who was so damn handsome he took her breath away.

Nick thankfully splayed his hands as he wrapped them around her and buried his nose in her hair, holding her with the same need she radiated. And as he held her, everything faded away. No friends were in danger. No rain fell in copious sheets. No strange mysteries twisted around her like the Sacred Valley roads. No mud. No threats. Even Peru was dissipating.

All that existed was Nick's breath echoing inside his strong chest, his hands warming her back, her body melting against his. She inhaled his scent, fresh soap and something earthy, warm and sure of itself.

"You smell good," she said.

"I was just going to say the same thing," he told her hair.

"Basta, enamorados." Abuelita's teasing pulled them apart, placing them firmly back in the middle of nowhere Peru.

Harper glanced over at the woman to find she held two plates full of steaming food. "Sit," she instructed.

While Harper only had eyes for Nick moments before, now she was happy to take in the warmth and spices of the plate in front of her. Even her stomach did several groaning rolls in anticipation. Roasted meat sat on top of a bed of purple and orange potatoes, with rice, large corn kernels, sliced carrots, diced tomatoes and onions on the side. The entire dish was finished with gravy.

"Gracias." Harper gazed up into the entertained face of the old woman who touched the top of her sweater and said, "Esto te queda bien."

"It looks good on you," Nick translated.

Abuelita cupped the side of Harper's face, leaned closer and said, "Y te ves muy bien sin todo ese barro. No mud, you look nice."

Harper gave another sincere, "Gracias."

"Okay." She motioned to the food and insisted, "¡Coman!"

Harper didn't need a translation for that one. She dug in and rolled her eyes as the delicious first bite exploded against her taste buds. Then she ate quickly; until her stomach was able to explain to her brain that it wasn't as desperate for sustenance and she could slow down.

Harper took a deep breath and sat back. "This might be the best thing I've ever had in my life."

Nick agreed, shoveling another bite. When he was finished chewing he said, "It's close. The best meal I ever had was a bacon cheeseburger and an ice-cold beer after a week of backpacking with some friends. The trail ended at a lake resort where we sat at covered picnic tables – dirty, smelling to high heaven, exhausted – but there were no more bugs and we were served hot food and cold beer. It was perfection."

Harper gave a gurgle of understanding and when she finished chewing, offered hers. "A cousin of ours got married in Vegas. It was a long weekend. Filled with rehearsal dinners, walking everywhere on the strip, random tours of the desert and staying up late drinking and gambling with family we hadn't seen in a long time. The last morning, we went to breakfast at the Bellagio. My brother-in-law told us to get whatever we wanted. And I don't know why, but I got filet mignon, which came with mashed potatoes and braised broccoli. It was *the* single best steak I've ever had, the *best* potatoes, and the broccoli was indescribable."

Nick held a forkful up in the air and appreciatively declared, "And this might be the second best."

"So the question is, what makes a great meal? Is it really the food or is it the situation?" Harper asked.

Nick raised an eyebrow. "Interesting question."

Neither really answered as they fell into silent concentration, finishing their meals.

"Great meal." A grunt of appreciation accompanied Nick's final satisfied bite before he fell back against his chair.

Harper nodded to her plate as Nick's voice lowered, catching her attention. "Harper ..." She looked up expectantly, but he didn't continue.

"Yeah?" she prodded.

He licked his lips and followed that with a shake of his head. "I'm tired."

"Me too," she tilted her head, "but I don't think that's what you were going to say."

"It wasn't."

Harper waited to see if he was going to expand on his original thought, but instead he said, "I used all my charm on Abuelita. She is going to try and get our clothes cleaned for us by tomorrow."

Harper gave a suspicious raise of her eyebrow.

Nick shrugged. "And I handed over a substantial tip."

"So these are loaner clothes?" She snuggled in the sweater and let a smile part her lips before she lowered her voice and inquired, "Even the underwear?"

"At least they're clean."

"At least they're clean," she agreed.

"I was going to be gentlemanly and not mention them, by the way," he teased.

She sat forward and propped her arms on the edge of the table. "Just in case you were ever taking a poll or anything, I prefer the black ones."

"You haven't even tried the black ones on yet." He matched her position as the temperature of the entire room changed. It was expressly heating up.

"From a spectator's point of view," she flirted.

"Oh," he slightly tilted his head, "if we're talking about spectator sports, then I have some notes on that lacy bra and matching underwear."

"Do you?" She tried to be nonchalant, but he had to know her pulse was rising, because breathing was becoming a little difficult.

"That bra ignites the imagination. All because of the way the lace hugs you and taunts me. It's suggestive and so damn alluring." He breathed.

Holy shit ... they were in it now.

"I hadn't anticipated what black boxer briefs could do for a man's impressive ... ness." A smile wobbled across her lips at her choice of words. But the only word that came to mind was 'manhood' and the idea of softly uttering 'impressive manhood' did not seem right for the moment. Her other option was to tell him that when she had pulled off his pants – within the first ten minutes of knowing him – not only had his legs caught her attention, but she'd felt his taut ass under her hand, and the rest of *him* had definitely *not* gone unnoticed.

"I too was impressed by your underwear." He inched across the table a bit more. "Do you know how hard it is to kneel at the feet of a gorgeous woman and be presented with a supple backside?"

"I know how hard it has been to focus sometimes, because your eyes are dangerously honey colored."

"That's been a problem?" He flirtatiously widened his eyes.

She gave a slow nod. "Oh yeah. The color brings up the idea of licking something sticky and sweet off of something hard ..." Her mouth wavered and she had to clear her throat. Nick raised an eyebrow and Harper forced herself to stand her ground. She grinned as she admitted, "I am not good at this."

"Oh, Barrett, you are doing *very* well. I'm quite uncomfortable and not interested in standing up anytime soon." He winked.

"Really?" she asked skeptically, not meaning to break the spell they'd built around them. "It's just been a long time ..." she tried to explain.

"What do you wear to work?" he asked, then wiggled his eyebrows, "I'm imagining your hair up in a bun, shirt buttoned all the way up to the top of your neck, long skirt. And please, tell me you wear glasses."

She tilted her head. "No-nonsense museum worker does it for you?"

"Oh yeah. End of the day, catch you alone in a dark corner, pull the hair out, unbutton that shirt to show off that white lace, and run my hand up a thigh to the other lacy half."

Her voice was hoarse. "Oh ..."

"Harper, you have to know how enticing a woman you are."

Oh.

In answer, she picked up her napkin, dipped it into her water cup and pressed the cool water to her cheek as she sat back.

Nick's face shadowed with a wicked triumph. "Harper, I thought you were sexy when I first saw you. Each moment we spend together, I find myself charmed. The more I get to know you, the more I'm drawn to you. You are mesmerizing and enchanting."

She didn't have time to answer, didn't know if she would have been able to. Abuelita returned and slapped Nick on the shoulder. "Estás calentando todo el restaurante." *You're heating up the whole restaurant.* Then she laughed, but took his arm and gave his bicep a squeeze. "¡Dios mío! Yo también necesitaría agua fría." *Oh my God! I could use some cold water, too.* She laughed and placed a resounding kiss on his cheek then picked up the plates. "¿Quieren comer más?"

"Do you want more to eat?" he asked Harper.

"No, muchas gracias. Delicioso."

Abuelita gestured toward the back of the restaurant that connected with the hotel and instructed them, "Go now."

Harper stood, but when Nick didn't, she frowned in question.

His slow grin spread. "I'm gonna need a minute."

She crossed to him, leaned down and in his ear whispered, "Nick, I find you distractingly attractive and if I'm being honest, I want to make bad decisions with you." She stood and was rewarded with a wide eyed grin that was something between shock, attraction and arousal.

She happily winked before walking away, slowly swaying her hips. But before she turned down the hallway, she glanced over her shoulder. Nick was stuck in his seat, his eyes laser focused on her.

She let the amazing feeling of having that sort of physical effect on a man wash over her. It had been way too long since she'd felt this way about someone.

Chapter Forty-Two

Renee and Gael were shocked awake from their brief nap when someone hit the side of their tent, demanding they come to dinner. The rain had stopped, the sun had set and the cold was a shock after the warmth of the tent, but Renee had to admit she felt better. What gave her the most hope was that her legs felt rested.

It turned out that the four guides in charge of the horses were also in charge of cooking and setting up the camp. One of the men was cutting up fruit on a portable table while another was busy with foil wrapped items cooking on the edges of a campfire. Most likely potatoes. Around the fire pit sat enough compact camping stools for everyone.

Since no one gave them any guidance when they arrived, they picked two stools next to each other and waited. Renee leaned over to Gael and offered her observation, "It's like a scared straight backpacking expedition."

The only notice that dinner was ready was a grunt. Renee and Gael followed everyone else, taking a plate from the table, putting some fruit on one side, grabbing a foil wrapped potato from where they'd been stacked on the side of the pit, then sliced them open and added some beans from the pot on the opposite side of the fire.

Renee grabbed two potatoes, as there was a mountain of them. She would force herself to eat two of the filling portions knowing her body needed fuel for what was coming, whether they continued with Smith or tried to escape.

The food wasn't half bad, it probably helped that she was starving. There was no conversation. And when she glanced at Scarface and Kyle, she enjoyed the miserable, almost pout, their faces wore. The driver sat by Smith, his attention only on his plate. The guides sat relatively close together and muttered a word or two every now and then, but the only other sounds of the evening were the flowing river, the snapping of the wood in the fire, and an occasional bird.

"How do you find the Inca trail, Miss Young?" Smith's voice carried across the fire. He was the kind of man who phrased simple questions in such a way it oozed with misogyny and a hint of racism and definitely a large dose of elitism. It made Renee seethe. She took a moment, breathed out what she really wanted to say and finally uttered the only word that really would describe it. "Wet."

He laughed, apparently delighted by the observation.

She shrugged and added, "Not exactly how I wanted to experience it, but interesting." She figured he was the kind of dipshit who would appreciate the truth.

"And the world-renowned photographer, your thoughts?" Smith asked.

"It's a shame I'm without a camera," Gael answered honestly.

Smith replied, "If I were doing a proper dig, I have to admit, it would be helpful to have such a keen eye along to document things." He gave a chuckle. "Isn't fate interesting? And such a waste of talent. Though I suppose the world will not mourn the loss of a hairdresser."

Renee's body sparked as she opened her mouth, but Gael pushed his elbow into her side, a silent 'it's not worth it.'

Instead, she muttered, "Where are the facilities?"

Smith gave a quick direction to one of the horsemen. He retrieved a small shovel with a roll of toilet paper on the stick handle; then handed it to her along with a flashlight.

Smith gestured to the area surrounding them and instructed, "Pick a bush, Miss Young."

She accepted the shovel, then glanced behind her at the dark shadows surrounding the gathering foliage. After a moment, she turned back, holding up the items, and said, "I have no problem using these. But since I wasn't planning on this adventure and haven't had a chance to educate myself on the area, are there any bugs or animals that might be a problem?"

"Possibly mosquitoes, but the rain and cold weather have kept them at bay." He shrugged. "However, it isn't unheard of to hear a Vicuñas or spectacled bears. And Andean foxes and mountain lions are around, but they stay away from fire."

His attempt to scare her was probably laced with a bit of forthrightness. Still, she kept any biting remarks in check and said, "Then I'll be careful."

When she was finished, she lingered to study the layout of the camp, such as it was. All the tents had been set up on the right side of the fire, the four horses on the left. She wasn't sure what to do with that information, but figured it wasn't a bad thing to have.

She tried to return the shovel and flashlight when she rejoined the group, but was waved away. "Keep them in case you need them in the middle of the night," Smith explained.

"Do I need to tell someone if I have to use the facilities in the middle of the night? Or will our guards know?" She nodded toward Scarface.

Smith laughed. "We're in the middle of nowhere, my girl. There is only one path. We have horses and would catch you before you got very far."

She kept a triumphant smile at bay. The cockiness of this bastard had let several important bits of information slide. She pointed to the potatoes on the edge of the fire, to change the subject. "Then you won't mind if I take two extra for a midnight snack?"

He glanced over the fire, and even though his words were light she could have sworn he snarled, "I'll allow it."

She picked up two more potatoes, gazed defiantly at him and added a third. He laughed as she pocketed them. "Since there aren't any smores or campfire stories that I'm needed for, I'll make an early evening of it." She didn't wait for an answer, but returned to the tent. Inside, she kept the flashlight nearby but didn't use it, to save the battery. She listened intently to the murmur of conversation between Smith and Gael, not able to catch what they were talking about, their voices muted by the rushing water. It wasn't a long conversation. Eventually, Smith's booming instructions washed over the camp and Gael returned.

Once he was completely inside, she reached for him and toppled him onto his back. They both grunted in pain, but she placed an excited kiss on his lips and felt his unmistakable smile as his arms slipped around her waist, pulling her against him.

"We're doing this?" she whispered into his mouth.

He bit playfully at her lower lip and whispered back, "Ojalá, we're gonna try."

"Ojalá?" she asked.

He nipped at her neck, then translated, "God willing."

Chapter Forty-Three

Harper stood in the hallway, with her back pressed against the wall.

Her body was sore. She had no idea where in Peru she was. Her friend had been kidnapped. And she shouldn't be feeling this way, but the momentary distraction was so enjoyable, she leaned into the way her heart was racing and butterflies performed a Formula One race around her stomach.

All because an unexpected man fell into her path.

An attentive, self-assured, intelligent, well-formed man.

Oh, but he was well-formed.

That t-shirt had outlined his sturdy chest as well as his arms to the point of distraction. And when he lowered his dark lashes and gave her those looks that rode the thin line between danger and desire ... well, it was a good thing there was a wall here to hold on to.

And what had come over her? Telling him she wanted to make bad decisions with him? But damn, she wanted to make some very distracting, steamy, indecent decisions with him.

Nick rounded the corner, as if she'd summoned him. She aimed a breathless, lopsided smile his way as he crossed the distance between them, propped his hands against the wall on either side of her head, then slowly, haltingly, tilted his head and lowered his lips toward hers. But he stopped when he was a breath away and met her eyes. This close she felt she could see into his soul; and knew what he was doing, giving her a choice.

It was only a slight distance, inconsequential really. A trivial span, all she had to do was raise slightly on her toes, which she did, and give into the gentle force of the rotating earth that would urge their lips together

... which she wholeheartedly did.

They kept their hands to themselves, allowing only their mouths to explore the moment. Tempting, enticing, taunting ...

Until the swat of a dish towel interrupted, followed by the playful exclamation, "¡Dejala!" *Leave her alone!* Abuelita's eyes shone bright as she swatted them once more. When she had their attention she put her hands on her hips and shook her head. "Oh Dios mío, vayanse a vuestra habitación. Go to the room," she insisted.

Nick reached for the short woman, pulled her to his side and kissed her cheek. "Gracias por todo. Buenas noches."

She swatted him away, then patted Harper's arm, wiggling her eyebrows – as if she was in on the conspiracy of emotions wreaking havoc on Harper's feelings.

A few steps away Harper admitted, "I wasn't sure what room I was going to, or if you wanted to be alone. Or, which room ..." Her voice faltered.

"I think we'd both feel more comfortable, under the circumstances, if we shared a room."

She happily leaned into that feeble logic.

"How are you feeling?" he asked.

"Better and awful. I think when I fell the second time, the way I tried to catch myself jammed my shoulders ... they hurt. But not too bad." She answered then had a momentary worry that hadn't been what he meant by the question. "Is that what you meant?"

He nodded.

"How are you feeling?" she returned.

"Well, my thigh hurts but I think it was all the slipping that tweaked different muscles. My shoulder is only slightly sore, probably from the finale of my snake bite, but at least my left hand doesn't hurt anymore when I make a fist."

Somehow, talking about all their ailments and what had befallen them, opened the door wide to fearful questions about Renee.

"Nick ... if that's what's happening to us, what could be happening to Renee and Gael?"

He slipped his arm around her shoulder, but paused before he put any pressure on the area.

"I used the washcloth and scrubbed the last of the spines from the cactus away. It doesn't hurt any more," she told him.

He finished the motion, pulling her firmly to his side as he began his pep talk. "You can't let your imagination get the best of you, Barrett."

"Kinda hard not to. We were supposed to be in the city that's used as a basecamp by now."

"Okay, then let's get to work." He opened the door of the room where she'd been taken to shower and began to lay out the evening's plan. "We're gonna pop some Advil or aspirin and we're going to look through Renee's computer at everything we can to see if anything resonates with the information Sophie gave us."

"Good plan." She retrieved the computer and Advil as Nick moved the room chairs next to each other in front of the small table.

She also checked her phone, and verified, "No service."

"Me either. Still, let's charge them."

They used one of the portable chargers then opened Renee's computer. It still had an almost full battery. Harper gave a prayer of thanks to whatever force made her think to ask for her friend's password. Then she opened the file Renee had told her she was putting everything in and they began to read.

A packed, three-week itinerary unveiled itself. Renee had made notes of what they did each day, from the moment she woke up until her head hit the pillow at night. Filling in what she could about everyone else in the group, as well as the models that were used; and where they had been located, who she saw them talking to, anything that stood out. She also made lists of things she purchased or recalled others buying, even meals and restaurant names. And in an eerie step, she had given a description of each person and model they worked with, something that would stand out in a photo so they could be identified by someone else.

"This is some incredible detail," Nick admired.

Harper agreed. "Renee is a powerful whirlwind. She's deeply interested in people and their stories, it's really helped with the business she's built and things like this. Her memory is built for names and faces and little details." Each word she spoke grew thick with worry in the back of her throat.

"You've been friends for a long time?" It was half statement, half question.

"Actually, no." A soft laugh escaped. "Although, I feel like I've known

Renee my whole life. She's that kind of person. Once you're in her life, you are *in* her life. But I've only known her for a little less than two years."

"Really?"

"Actually, my sister Luna met Renee first, when I sent her on a trip to Italy because she had agreed to marry this wet blanket of a man ..." she waved her hand, "but that's a story for another day. Anyway, while Luna was there, she met Renee, who was on vacation with her friends. Renee sort of ...." What was a polite way to say this? She eyed Nick. "Well, you've met Renee. You'll understand when I say she lovingly accosted my sister, then adopted her into her friend group."

Nick understood.

"I met Renee through my sister's social media and we immediately clicked. We started sending posts to each other because we knew the other would get a kick out of them. Then we started texting and talking and a friendship bloomed." She ran a mindless hand through her hair. "Last fall she came to visit me in New York. We took a few small trips to Connecticut and Boston and we traveled so well together, I think that's why she invited me to Peru."

"It must be hard ..."

She frowned when he didn't finish. He took a breath and admitted, "I was going to say how it must be rough having to step up this much for someone in such a new friendship, but–"

She interrupted, "You step up for strangers all the time."

"That, was exactly the argument I was going to make. Then I was going to say, we are going to get through this," he promised then gestured to the computer. "Let's see what we can see."

"How do you do this? For your job. When you're inundated with information and trying to make heads or tails of it?" Harper asked.

He raised an eyebrow. "Maybe I'm running around playing spy games most of the time."

She scoffed, "You forget you admitted that most of your job is information gathering. And I've read books and articles, I know all you do is sit around analyzing and assessing threats."

He shrugged. "Do you know how many people don't believe that it's really quite boring most of the time?"

"Unless you're running through forests with a knife in your leg."

"I'd call it limping," he muttered.

"What really happened?" she pushed.

He took a deep breath and sighed. "The bike I was given broke down. I was using the bushes when I heard someone pull up. I went to wave them down and found a teenage kid going through my pack. I yelled at him, and when I walked over to check my bag, I wasn't watching him and he took care of what he thought was a threat."

Harper blinked a few times then asked, "Are your friends going to give you a hard time when they hear that story?"

"Oh yeah."

"If I told Sean that story, would he tell all your friends?"

"Yeah."

"I need to call Sean real quick."

"No." He brushed a kiss on her cheek then glanced at the computer. "You said at *your* job, you deal with a lot of cataloguing items for scratches and knicks before you pack them to be moved, right?"

"Yeah." She didn't know what that had to do with anything.

"How do you work with a collection? What if some of the pieces look the same? What if you have two of the same thing?"

She looked back at the notes and in a surprised voice said, "We make a spreadsheet and cross-reference it all."

"I hadn't thought of a spreadsheet, but it's a good idea. It'll help us cross-reference people, locations and possible suspect issues."

Harper retrieved a pen and the notebook from her pack and made a column. "People, places, things."

He tapped the battery icon in the bottom right of the computer. "And not to add another layer of stress to this project, but we're racing against time."

They found the photos and Nick repeated the review he'd already given the work. "Damn, these are amazing."

Harper had filled almost ten pages, all three weeks with each location, who was present, what they ate and bought and where they slept. They'd also gone through Renee's photos from her phone that she'd uploaded into a file.

Harper scrubbed her face. "I didn't see any silver temples partially covered by overgrown jungle and no one ever got close to Cachora."

"That would've been too easy." Nick frowned.

"I mean, there was a lot of silver purchased and the models wore a lot of silver and gold." Harper pointed, eyeing the time that was left on the computer. They were almost out of battery. "This is shoddy work," she gestured to what she'd madly written, "but did we look at everything?"

Nick shugged. "Not with a fine-tooth comb, but with the time we had, we went through it all."

Harper turned off the computer and shakily sat back. After a few breaths, she got up and took out her Peru guidebook, the edges only a little wet. She turned to the map. "At least we can see their movements on a map."

"Have I told you how much I am loving your magic bag?" He practically twinkled. (She rolled her eyes.)

Harper shuffled the pages she'd written and flexed her hand.

"Shit, Barrett, I should have been writing everything."

She shook off the comment. "We needed your agent eyes on everything."

"Well," he stretched and gave a loud yawn, "these agent eyes are exhausted."

"Shouldn't we look at everything again?"

"Nope, we're going to let it marinate overnight. Get some sleep and tomorrow we'll be able to think more clearly."

"We still need a car," she muttered.

"That's a tomorrow morning problem," he soothed, "tonight's problem is going to be how to get rest in a bed with you in it." He stood and took a limping step across the room to the bathroom.

"You can't keep turning the flirting on and off like that ..."

He leaned back out of the restroom and grinned. "Sure I can. Can I have one of those toothbrushes?"

She got them both out with the toothpaste and joined him in the restroom.

He was clinical as he got ready for bed, which made it easier for Harper to do the same.

They turned the overhead lights off, and once again he left the bathroom light on and the door ajar.

Nick had his back to her as he sat on the edge of the bed and took off his shirt, followed by socks and pants. Her hands froze at the top of the sweater she meant to take off, but found she was closing tighter around her.

Nick arranged himself under the sheets, the blankets halfway up his chest, arms folded behind his head as he gave another loud yawn.

Harper's mouth was dry, she still hadn't moved and knew any second he'd give her a knowing look. Or a longing look. Or a seductive look. Or hell, he'd just look at her and she'd melt.

She opened her mouth, to tell him to put some more clothes on; she felt like they needed a few more layers between them. But then the last 'flirty' words she'd said aloud brushed against her neck. *I want to make bad decisions with you.*

That part of her, yeah; she wanted a lot less between them. With shaky hands, she removed her sweater, socks and skirt then slipped under the blankets and lay on her back.

"What do you want me to tell you about tonight?" he asked.

"What?"

He shifted, making the bed creak with his weight to face her. She rolled onto her side, mirroring his position.

"I told you about my folks and France last night. What do you want to hear about tonight?"

"Italy?"

"Oh, Italia. Where did you say your sister moved to?"

"Rome. Have you been?"

He winked in reply. "And not to brag, but I've also been to Florence, Venice and Milan."

"What was your favorite?"

He reached out and caressed the side of her face. "Florence."

She had trouble breathing out her question. "Why?"

"There was something charming about the city built by the Renaissance." He brushed his hand through her hair, "I like your hair down," the teasing smile was evident when he added, "and mud free." He shifted closer and continued explaining why he liked Florence. "I think I liked Florence because I was there the longest, and had more opportunity to explore."

"You're allowed to explore when you're working?"

His hand drifted down to her waist and pulled her against him, bringing her close enough to nip at her lips. "Who said I was working?"

She met his kiss, and because they were back under the spell of the quiet darkness and he might be helping her make good on her request to make bad decisions, she slipped her hand up his chest. When he sucked in a breath at her touch, she wondered if she'd ever felt this powerful in her life.

He was warm and hard, and she splayed her fingers through the slight hair, fascinated by the feel of him. She enjoyed how his racing heartbeat felt, and how the sound of his breathing grew shallow. All because of her touch.

It was her turn to brush her lips against his, but he caught her and intensified the kiss, allowing the flood gates to open while any remaining worries floated away.

Harper wrenched herself away to free herself from the t-shirt. He followed the shirt's path, running his hands up the exposed skin and moaning, until she pressed herself back to him and resumed kissing.

"I don't know if I like kissing you better with the beard or without," she whispered.

"Whichever you like best, I'll make sure it's always available," he offered breathlessly.

A phantom knock and the sound of a key turning in the lock wasn't enough to deter the increasing need.

The overhead light turning on did the trick.

Nick rolled his body over Harper, a protective move, as he looked over his shoulder to identify the intruder.

"Abuelita?" he called, confused.

"Abuelita?" Harper repeated, glancing over Nick's shoulder.

The woman was carrying a bag and holding her fingers over her lips, hushing them, putting Nick fully on high alert.

She put the bag on the bed. "Tienen que irse." *You have to go.*

"She said we have to go," Nick said, still holding Harper under his body. She slapped at his arm to get him to move and he apologized, moving into a seated position while Harper pulled the sheet up over her chest as she slipped back into the t-shirt.

"¿Qué está pasando?" *What's going on?* Nick asked.

"Dos hombres, look for you," she said quickly. "I say nothing. Pero, otra persona en la ciudad, they say you are here."

"We gotta go," Nick stated.

The woman dumped out the contents of the bag, their shoes still wet but clean of mud. "All clothes, todavía están sucios. No clean." She handed a pair of tights to Harper who was untangling herself from the sheets. Any embarrassment was thrown out the window with the new threat.

She handed Nick a sweater and then gave them both two alpaca wool hats and gloves.

"Tienen sólo unos momentos," she hissed. *You only have a few moments.*

Nick took to translating everything the woman said as they hurriedly got ready.

Harper hopped as she put her shoes on before shoving everything they'd taken out of her pack back in.

The old woman pulled out a set of keys and handed them to Nick. "La motocicleta de mi nieto." *My grandson's motorcycle.*

Nick accepted the keys as he asked Harper, "The money?"

Harper was glad she had all the money Renee had taken from Luis. "How much?" she asked.

"Most of it."

She took out a large wad of money from her wallet and handed it over to the old woman. Abuelita held up the money. "¿Este dinero es suficiente para ustedes?" *Will you have enough money for yourselves?*

Nick gave a hasty apology. "Lo lamento, we brought you too much trouble. Muchos problemas."

She waved him away. "I see you two," she grabbed both of their hands, "serán un problema dondequiera que vayan. All places you go, you are trouble. Con o sin hombres en persecución." *With or without men in pursuit.*

She pulled them to the door, put her finger over her lips as she listened, then peeked her head out.

Harper pulled out the gun when she wasn't looking and handed it to Nick. He quickly put it in his waistband.

"Vayan." She waved and they stayed behind her as she led them down the stairs and toward the back of the establishment.

Out the back door into the dark night, with a bit of light from the moon, was a motorbike being held up by the grandson, and three other bikes with couples (dressed more or less like Nick and Harper) sitting on each one.

Nick pulled the old woman into his arms and kissed her cheek. "You are amazing. Asombrosa."

"What's going on?" Harper asked, putting on her pack and the gloves.

"A little deception."

She glanced at the people surrounding them, helping them. She gave Abuelita a wide-eyed stare. "How do you know we're the good guys?"

Nick translated and she laughed and answered in a thick accent, "I know much more than you think."

Harper shook her head in wonder. "Gracias Abuelita."

The old woman patted Harper's arm. "Mi marido era un problema y mi vida mejoró gracias a el. My husband, he was trouble, and my life was good."

She waved her hands then pointed to the young man in front of the group, instructing, "Follow Sebastián. Él los conducirá al camino principal." *He will lead you to the main road.* "Pero primero, ustedes all ride crazy in all of town. ¿Sí?"

"Sí."

"What about her? Is she in danger?" Harper asked.

He repeated the question but she waved the concern away, "I tell them you leave. Let them check room."

Nick climbed on the bike and held out his hand to Harper. "Have you ever done this before?"

"Once." She settled as best she could on the back of the one-seat motorbike, which meant most of her weight was on the plastic fender.

The lead bike took off. Harper squeezed Nick around the waist to let him know she was ready. He gave her arm a pat, started the bike and they were off. No helmet, one seat, only a sense of dread and a wool cap to keep out the cold.

The quartet covertly rode the revving machines up and down the streets of the quiet town, trying to convince anyone watching they were friends being ridiculous, and possibly drunk in the middle of the night.

With her head pressed against Nick's back, she saw a car with two men standing by open doors, watching the parade. She thought she saw one of the men narrow their eyes, but when they didn't move to follow the parade, she gave a tighter squeeze around Nick's waist; hoping he understood the message she was trying to impart.

They went up and down several more streets, then the bikes peeled away from each other, and Nick stayed on Sebastián's trail until they reached the road. The man stopped his bike, and waited for Nick to pull up beside him.

"Go that way. Twenty kilometers. There is an old church on the right side of the road. Behind the church, there are many trees, but behind them you will find a cave. The bike will fit inside with you. It is a good place to hide for the rest of the night."

With a wave of thanks, Nick sped off into the night, led by the flickering headlight of a bike.

He tried to go slow enough to not put them in danger, but quick enough to keep a good distance between them and the men looking for them. He also needed to make sure Harper could grow accustomed to riding, and she did, naturally leaning with the bike as they traveled the curvy roads.

They had about twelve miles to go, and the heightened threat stretched the time. Finally, a road sign on the right announced a church.

Harper squeezed Nick, he figured to get his attention and make sure he saw the sign. He patted her arm confirming he saw it too.

They pulled off the road and slowed behind the church where the overgrown trees pushed against the parking area. Nick climbed off and helped Harper, then asked her to wait while he searched for the cave. He took out his cell phone and used the flashlight.

It wasn't obvious, more of an optical illusion and no one would have thought a path or cave was there. It was big enough for them and the bike. In fact, there was firewood, a fire pit and a tarp on the ground. He was pretty sure the distance from the road, the coverage, and the natural hole in the cave that led upward, would make any light and smoke invisible to a passerby. Even if they were looking for signs of life.

He went back and showed Harper the way as he pushed the bike over the path. Inside, he put the kickstand down on the bike and turned to

Harper asking, "You okay?"

"Honestly? I'm a bit punchy. We keep going from one extreme emotion to another."

"You mean being super turned on and then in danger?" He wiggled his eyebrows at the joke.

She gave a scoffing laugh. "Yes, all of that."

"First things first, are you ready to impress me some more? Show me what else that magic bag of yours can do."

Chapter Forty-Four

Gael urged Renee to get some sleep, but she refused. So they lay awake and waited, listening to the surrounding sounds of the night. A few nocturnal birds, the river and eventually snoring. When she felt like she would go mad from waiting, Gael insisted they wait a little while longer. Then he whispered that he was going to 'use the shovel' and for her to be ready when he returned.

And he took *forever*.

Renee was sure her heart was going to burst from her chest or the animated beat would wake up everyone in the camp. When Gael returned she was ready. He unzipped the tent, waved her out, then zipped it back up – his attempt to throw off anyone who might be listening for the exit and re-entrance zip of a tent.

Renee had three potatoes in her jacket and the flashlight. She'd never felt more unprepared or scared in her life, but she needed some sort of fortitude. Otherwise this wasn't going to work. She began an internal screaming pep talk; the same kind she'd given herself when she and Harper held Luis up at gunpoint.

The cloud cover floated back and forth across the sky, allowing a bit of moonlight to peek through every now and then. The fire had died down. The off rhythm sound of snoring men filled the night and it turned out the noise of the rushing river was going to be the element that made this whole attempt come together.

There *was* someone watching the horses, but the way his head was slung down on his chest, suggested he was asleep.

Gael put his hand on Renee's arm. They'd whispered this plan several times and they both knew what *had* to happen. They had one chance and they had to go as quickly as possible.

The horses all had a halter and a lead rope tied to a line stretched out between two trees. They loosened each horse's halter, and quietly slipped them to the ground. Gael had instructed her which was the lead horse (the one he would take), and the one that had been behind him in the line-up that day. Those two horses they untied and began to walk back toward the path that brought them inland, keeping as quiet as they could.

A few feet onto the trail, they tossed the lead ropes over the horses' heads and tied them to the halter to create reins. Gael bent next to Renee, holding his hands together for her to use as a stirrup. She propelled herself onto the horse, who sidestepped but thankfully made no noise.

Gael easily climbed onto the lead horse. He held out a thumbs up to Renee, the signal to gently nudge the horse with her legs to begin a trot. When both horses complied, Renee's heart hammered even harder. She mutely offered prayers to every deity she'd ever heard about and when Gael's horse picked up pace, hers did too. But then she heard a sound behind her; they were catching them, or it was another animal that Smith had not been joking about.

Fear gripped her, turning the blood in her veins to ice, yet she somehow made herself look behind her.

The other two horses were following them.

A lifetime had passed, or maybe only three or four minutes, but they'd put some decent yardage between themselves and the camp. The clouds parted, as if they knew what their part in this play was, revealing the path to Gael and the horses. He gave another encouraging nudge of his heel into the horse's side and picked up more speed.

They were nearing the top of the switchbacks they'd taken down, almost up to where there was a bend around the mountain, almost out of sight. But the alarm went up then, and it echoed beneath them. Yelling and screaming bounced off the surrounding mountains. Renee hugged herself against her horse and encouraged him, no need to be quiet now. "C'mon boy. You've got this. We can do this."

She squeezed her eyes shut when the reverberating sound of a gunshot choked her with dread. As if he understood the tense situation, her horse picked up speed and she squeezed her legs, holding on for life as the shots continued, trying to ignore the way her battered side ached and screamed in pain with the canter of her horse.

She heard Gael yell something, and saw a bend in the road, a trail they hadn't taken. Another shot but the horses kept trotting and once they'd turned, they were hidden behind the mountains. Renee sat up slightly but she and Gael let the horses continue their gallop to put as much distance as they could between themselves and Smith.

Without the weight of all the things they'd packed in, the horses were happy to keep going and going. They rode into the barren landscape and then down once again; it felt like they were going around the mountain completely. When they came to a flat region, it was Renee who asked if they could get off and sit for a few minutes.

"I'm not complaining, but my side, ass and legs are roughed up."

"I know, mine too."

They sat on the edge of the jungle cover and shared a potato in celebration. Renee checked her phone, no battery left.

"Well, I have no idea where we are," Gael admitted.

"We didn't go the way we came," Renee confirmed.

"No, but I think we put a decent amount of distance between us. But the men who were in charge of the horses probably know this area and there aren't that many trails."

She glanced at the horses that had meandered into the low grass and started munching. "And we have all the horses."

"I can't believe it worked."

"I'm having one of those worries, like this is what he wanted us to do." Renee voiced her worst fear.

"No, he was too full of himself. He thought the threats and what they'd already done to us would keep us from trying anything stupid."

"And this was definitively, utterly stupid," Renee agreed.

"It was."

But they both understood why they had to try. Renee asked, "What should we do? It's going to be sunrise soon."

"We'll rest for a few minutes, then keep going."

Chapter Forty-Five

Harper stared into the flames, the warmth was nice, but the way the light flickered and darkened the edges of the cave played games with her imagination. Nick insisted she show off her 'Girl Scout fire-starting skills' while he snuck back into the jungle to watch the road. She wasn't sure if it was a ploy to keep her distracted, but it was no longer working.

She organized the backpack, checking the computer to make sure it hadn't gotten wet, and the phones; full batteries, but no signal.

She checked her watch periodically. After fifteen minutes she was concerned. After thirty minutes, she was worried. Forty-five minutes, she started to pace. An hour later, some internal doomsday idiot was listing all the things that could have gone wrong and reminding her that she didn't know how to ride a motorcycle. Nick had the gun. And all she had was a bag of tricks.

She decided she'd give him ten more minutes before she'd go after him. Because fifteen minutes from now, she wasn't sure she could keep herself from spiraling, and at this point, she was not in the mood to continue this path of saving her friend alone.

She stood at the mouth of the cave, staring into the darkness, listening to the sounds of the jungle. Not sure what she was listening for, maybe Nick's breathing, rustling in the bushes? But there was nothing. And the wait time was up.

She decided to go left first.

She took slow steps, pushing her way through the trees, cringing at the amount of noise she was making. Only then, did her thoughts move from Nick's possible abduction to animals hiding in the foliage that could kill her with one little bite.

She pushed forward, still slow, trying to stop her loud breathing while listening for threats. She was surprised she didn't scream when arms slipped around her waist and a deep voice whispered, "whatcha doin'?" as she was pulled against Nick.

"Geez ..." She blew the word out, closed her eyes and tried to get the jump in blood pressure and heart rate down to more normal numbers. "You never gave me a timeframe and I started to worry that if something happened to you, I wouldn't know. I also think you probably need to teach me how to ride a motorcycle, just in case; and wherever the gun is, I guess I feel safer near it. Also, are there any nocturnal snakes I should worry about? And ..." she turned around in his arms and whispered, "do I have any spiders on me? Cuz I feel like there are spiders on me."

He kissed her, stealing her breath and the moment, replacing her firmly in the world of attraction, if not reason. She wasn't sure this was the time to get carried away, but when he let the barest groan escape when he pressed his body against hers, there was a small part of her that thought, why not get carried away?

Because the haunting, eerie sound of a bird shrieked, pulling Harper away from Nick. He kept a hold of her, and even though they couldn't see each other completely in the darkness, he cupped her face and asked, "Okay?"

She took a large inhale and once she'd breathed it out, replied, "Okay."

"Atta girl." He brushed his thumbs against her cheeks, when the sound of a car echoed. "Down," he instructed and she quickly dropped to her stomach, next to where he must have been earlier because the headlights of the car showed that they had an unobstructed view of the church.

They watched as a car slowed, turned into the open lot of the church, then drove in several large circles until the passenger got out. As he walked to the building, the sound of a gun cocking squeezed Harper's eyes shut. After several minutes, the man came stomping out. "Tendrían que estar delante de nosotros."

When they sped away, Harper asked what he said. "They think we're ahead of them," Nick informed.

"But will they keep going if they don't find us in the next place? Or will they come back?"

He stood and she started to follow him, but tripped. Luckily, he was there to catch her, slipping his arm around her waist. "The hope is they think we exchange the bike for a car and keep going."

"There's no signal yet."

"Okay."

"Nick ..." She rolled her eyes and asked, "What's the plan?"

He brushed a kiss on her cheek. "Glad you asked, Barrett. We're gonna take a nap. We're gonna get to the next town. We're gonna find breakfast and maybe a car. Then we'll make the next set of plans."

"Okay."

When they entered the warm cave, he groaned, "Oh that feels good." He eyed the crosshatch way she'd built up the firewood. "Good form, Barrett."

Mmmhmm. She added another few logs, not hiding a loud yawn.

Nick shared the yawn, set an alarm on the phone for two hours then stretched out on the tarp in front of the fire. He shifted to his side and patted the space in front of him. "C'mon."

Harper didn't need a second invitation. She batted the skirt into submission as she lay down. They squirmed to find a comfortable position on the hard ground and waited for sleep to find them.

"I can't sleep," Harper whispered, "I should be able to, but I can't."

"I get it." He gently kissed the top of her head. "You know, if something happened to me, you'd be okay, right?"

"I don't want to think about that right now."

"What would you do?" he asked.

"Nick."

"Harper, sometimes it helps to talk through stuff like this, to see you'll be okay."

"Well, I don't know how to ride a bike. So I'd start walking until I had a signal."

"Then once you had a signal, who would you call?"

She laughed, wondering if he'd been trying to set her up. "Ghostbusters."

"See, you don't really need me."

"I normally don't need anyone," she admitted to the cave. "I've been self-sufficient for so long, that even when I've been in relationships, nine times out of ten, they leave because I don't need them."

"I don't think that's right," Nick countered.

"You don't know my dating history."

"I don't want to know, I'm already jealous and hate them all." His sincerity warmed her. He went on, "I have a feeling the people you dated didn't appreciate your self-sufficiency. And I know for a fact, there are a lot of men who can't stand by a woman who can take care of herself."

"Nick, you aren't saying anything that my friends haven't said. It doesn't change the fact that they leave, even if they say they like a strong woman."

"Harper, you need someone who can appreciate how sexy you are when you field dress a wound, or hold a man at gunpoint. Just because you don't need someone to hammer a nail into a wall, or start a fire, doesn't mean you aren't worthy of being appreciated. Hell," she felt him shaking his head, "in my humble opinion, whatever idiots you dated didn't leave because you didn't need them, they left because they didn't realize a woman like you needs a partner. Someone who'll stand beside her for all the right reasons. Not run away because she won't follow or bend to their small dick energy."

The tears burned the back of her throat, but she laughed as he dismissed everyone she'd ever dated with one wave of his hand and the declaration that they all had 'small dick energy.'

"They weren't all small–"

His hand found her mouth to stop any further explanation. "Barrett, I already admitted I'm jealous of all the men you dated and I hate 'em all."

"Want to tell me about the women you've dated?"

"I could, but now that I've met you, I never realized how boring and lifeless they all were."

A small jolt of jealousy flared. "Yeah, maybe we shouldn't talk about exes."

He yawned again and Harper squeezed his arm. "Okay. We have a plan for tomorrow. So I'll tell you about the day in the life of a museum registrar."

He grunted his acceptance and she began to softly prattle about how she came to love museums and secured a job in one.

It was a matter of moments before his breathing turned even, and she allowed her own exhaustion to take over.

Chapter Forty-Six

It was mid-morning, at least it felt mid-morning *ish* to Renee. They rode for a while longer, until the aching in her body grew unbearable. Then they walked, Gael guiding the lead horse while the other horses instinctively fell in line.

Renee thought walking had never felt this good. Eventually, the path they followed became a wide dirt road with what they hoped might be fairly fresh tire tracks. Continuing onward, they reasoned they'd run into someone eventually; and hopefully, whoever that was, would be kind enough to help.

Renee shuffled to a stop and Gael followed suit, glancing over to see why she'd paused. Her head tilted to the side, her forehead furrowed in concentration. "Do you hear that?"

Gael tilted his head and listened, his eyes widening with shock. "Is that ... REO Speedwagon?"

She nodded when the music wafted over them again. "That's what I thought I was hearing. It was messing with my head, not something you think you'd hear randomly in the middle of the Peruvian jungle."

So they did the most common sense thing, and followed the music.

"I used to roller skate in my backyard to this song," Renee remembered fondly. "My mom had an extensive CD collection and still had a boombox with a CD player. I loved to play all her music while I roller skated." She whispered the chorus as the song grew in volume. "We built this city on rock and roll ..." She stopped and stretched her arms out wide, a leg behind her, the childhood skating routine ingrained in her body.

"I didn't roller skate until I was in college. When everyone in my dorm went through a rollerblading phase," Gael replied.

"I haven't skated in years." She smiled. "We should go, when we get home."

"I'm not very good."

"Good, we can hold hands and fall all over each other."

"It's a date," he agreed.

The music notes became breadcrumbs, floating ahead of them to follow. Renee wondered if they should be worried about what they'd find, but it couldn't be any worse than what they'd already been up against.

They rounded a bend in the road and came to simultaneous stops as they took in the scene before them. Off to the side of the road, in a cleared space of jungle, was what could only be described as a bar.

"Are you seeing this?" Renee asked.

"I think so. Or my lightheadedness, exhaustion and worry have me hallucinating some interesting stuff."

Trees had been cleared to form an area where pieces of corrugated metal and plastic had been strung together to create three walls. The top of the structure had mismatched tarps tied between trees at angles to allow rain to drip off.

"Gael, did we just happen upon a makeshift bar in the middle of the jungle?" She felt like she needed to say it aloud, to double-check what reality she existed in.

"Yes. Yes we did."

"Well then, I suppose I need a drink." She grinned at him.

Gael made a flourish of a wave in the direction of the bar and said, "Why not?"

They walked the horses to the side of the shanty bar, tied the lead to a tree, and entered a city built on rock and roll. A jovial jungle bar.

In each corner of the establishment, a contractor's extension cord light was hooked to the corrugated metal. Resting directly across from the open side of the alcoholic enterprise was a gorgeous mahogany bar, at least twelve feet long complete with a bored bartender, hip propped against the wood, cigarette topping his weathered fingers.

Large, soiled rugs created the floor. Mismatched tables and chairs sagged tiredly around the area. One table had two men slouched over drinks, another had five men in long sleeve sport shirts laughing while the unseen stereo played music over the telltale sound of a generator. No one looked up as they entered, nor seemed to think they were in a place they weren't supposed to be.

"Sure, why not …" Renee muttered her feelings about what they'd found as they sauntered up to the bar as large drops of rain began to flick themselves against the tarped roof.

"Just in time," Gael commented.

The bartender gave them a scowl in greeting, not really welcoming; but more wanting to know what they wanted so he could get back to his leaning.

Gael explained that they didn't have any money, but he had a horse he was willing to trade for dos cervezas. With a shrug that must have been the official 'horse for beer trade agreement,' he opened a small fridge and retrieved two bottles. After popping off the tops he slid them onto the bar.

A happy scoff rumbled in Renee's chest as she tapped her bottle to Gael's and softly toasted, "To escaping."

"To escaping," he agreed. They tilted their heads back for the first swig of the best beer they'd ever had.

The flimsy roof began to sway in the rain, but the setup hadn't failed the bar yet.

"So …" Renee said, glancing between the two tables and back to the bartender. They either needed to ask one of these men for help, or continue walking until someone else crossed their path, or they found a city.

"So." Gael eyed the prospects.

"If there is a makeshift bar in the middle of the jungle, maybe there is a city nearby?" she offered.

"Or *because* there is a makeshift bar in the middle of the jungle, there isn't a city nearby," Gael countered.

"¡Hola, amigos!" A man, who looked about their age, from the bigger group called, waving a hand for them to join his table.

Gael aimed a raised eyebrow at Renee. "Mi reina, you are a beacon wherever you go."

"Let's hope it's a good thing," she muttered before turning a grin at the man, greeting, "Buenos días."

He stood and stepped away from the table. He had high, defined cheekbones, and wore a backwards black baseball hat and a black long sleeve shirt with a Nike logo that hung off well-defined shoulders. Black Adidas pants tucked into tall rubber boots completed his look. His eyes were bright and he had a truly friendly look about him. "Buenos días," he replied, "you are Americanos?"

"I am," Renee answered, then touched Gael's shoulder. "He's Peruvian." She didn't need to explain that they were going to play up his citizenship big time here, because he laid it on thick. "Buenos días. ¿Cómo está usted?" Gael held out his hand.

"Estoy bien," the man said, taking the offered hand. "Soy Alejandro."

"Gael." After introducing himself he slipped his arm around Renee's waist. "Esta es Renée."

"Hi." She held out her hand this time. After he shook it, Alejandro motioned to the table where he was sitting with four other men around his age, all dressed in the same manner. He pulled up two chairs and invited them to join. "Sit with us."

"Thank you."

"I speak English. I do tours for the Inca trail," he explained, then introduced the rest of his friends; all tour guides in between tours at the moment.

"Do you only give tours of the Inca trail?" Renee asked, happy that they hadn't gotten to the part yet where Alejandro asked them what they were doing in the middle of nowhere, and why both of their faces looked like they'd been in a few fights.

He shook his head. "No, when it is the rainy season, we do smaller tours in the Sacred Valley and we work on Salkantay Treks and Lares Treks. Right now, we have a little vacation before we go back to work." As he talked, his friends didn't seem too interested in meeting new people, or in what Alejandro was saying, so had gone back to their own conversation.

Renee reached out to take Gael's hand. The best lie is the one closest to the truth, she thought and said, "Gael brought me to Peru to see where he grew up."

Alejandro smiled, sat back with his beer cradled against his chest, and glanced between Renee and Gael. He said softly, "This place is not easy to find."

"No, it is not," Gael agreed.

Alejandro tilted his head and quizzically raised an eyebrow. "I see a lot of people. I know how people are. Are you lost or are you in trouble?"

So much for putting off the inevitable.

Renee tilted her head. "That depends. Are you a good guy or a bad guy?"

The weathered skin around Alejandro's eyes wrinkled in delight as he let out a full-body laugh. He told the bartender to bring drinks for everyone, Renee caught the word 'pisco.' When seven shots were placed on the table, he held it up and said, "I think we toast to new friends who need some help."

"Why would you help someone you don't know?" Renee asked.

Alejandro pursed his lips. "We are bored." Then he threw back the shot.

Renee gave a half shrug toward Gael. He gently tapped his shot glass to hers and said. "When in Rome, mi reina." Then he tossed back his drink as well. She chased his shot with her own. Having had pisco several times now, she welcomed the light and sweet liqueur, as it warmed her empty stomach quite nicely.

"Okay," Alejandro clapped, "what happened?" He gestured to Gael's face.

"Are you really a guide for the Inca trail?" Renee asked.

"Sí, lo prometo," he offered.

Renee figured since the truth was absurd sounding, they might as well admit what sort of trouble they'd gotten themselves in. "We were kidnapped by a British archeologist but managed to escape in the middle of the night by stealing all his pack horses."

See? Ridiculous.

Only, Alejandro's face paled, his smile slipped and he straightened in his seat.

Renee's stomach gave a twirl of fear when Alejandro whispered, "A British man looking for a treasure?"

The twirl of fear rose into her throat. Gael put his hand on Renee's arm and she didn't know if that was an indication that they were in trouble or she needed to get ready to start running again.

Alejandro didn't wait for an answer to his question and stated, "That man is *no* good."

"No, he's not," Gael agreed.

Alejandro licked his lips, stood and motioned to a table by the front opening. "We should talk over there," he said.

Renee thought that at least they would be closer to a quick escape if they needed it.

Once they were seated, Alejandro gave them another study then leaned forward and asked quietly, "He is back?"

"He's in Peru, if that's what you mean," Gael answered.

"What name is he using this time?"

That wasn't quite the question Renee had been prepared for. "Smith, Jacob Smith."

"He used that name before." Alejandro gave a curt nod and asked, "Where?"

Gael answered. "We're not sure what town we left from, but we know we were headed to Choquequirao, but last night we made camp somewhere along the Rio Apurimac. And to be honest, we don't know where we are now."

"Choquequirao," he repeated. "If you camped where I think you did, you are about thirty kilometers away. This is good. You have his horses?"

"They're pack animals. We untied them all, meant to take two, but the others followed us," Renee replied.

Alejandro frowned. "So, who are you? Why did he kidnap you?"

"We're no one," Renee insisted. "He took Gael first, then me. He kept asking us for the tears of the moon, insisting we 'had it.' But we have no idea what he's talking about."

Gael added, "He said since we wouldn't give him what he wanted, we were disposable and we'd be used to test … traps."

Alejandro narrowed his gaze and shifted forward, lowering his voice even more, as if the raindrops had ears. "Did he find the lost city?"

Gael held out his hands. "All he told us was a story about a general of the Incan Empire and how he hid a treasure. And that most people think the treasure is in northern Peru. But Smith found evidence that says otherwise and he has a map to the location."

"Choquequirao." Alejandro blew out a breath, pulled off his hat and fixed it back in place. "I don't believe it."

"How do you know about him?" Renee asked.

Alejandro glanced around again, as if even the jungle was trying to intrude on the conversation. "Smith hired men three years ago. Twelve men. He said he needed them to help with an easy exploration. He said it was for photos and evidence. It was going to be a four-day trip. Ten days come and go, no men return. Two weeks. No men return. No one ever heard from one of those men again. And Smith is gone too. But last year," he held up his hand, "he came back. Used a different name, but people remember him. Still, he promises a lot of money and hires six men this time. The same thing happens. Men are gone. Smith is gone."

"Now he's back again," Renee said.

Alejandro aimed a level gaze at them as he admitted, "You are lucky to be alive."

The seriousness of the situation had not been lost on Renee, but the cold and hunger and overworked muscles and fear of the initial escape had kept her from thinking about it fully. Now that she had time and her bones were loose from the alcohol, she realized exactly what they had done and completely understood the sentiment that they were 'lucky to be alive.'

Renee filled Alejandro in on the group Smith had currently hired. "This time he had four guides working with the horses. A driver and two bodyguard types."

"They won't continue, you have their horses. They'll come look for you or go back to the cars."

"You really think they'd come after us?" Renee's voice had an unexpected shake as she asked.

"I think he is a very bad man. If he thinks you have something of his that has to do with treasure, it is a good chance he will come for you." Alejandro offered a sad, tight-lipped smile. "If you had gone where I think you were, there is one main trail and two side trails. Did you ride the horses the entire time?"

Renee looked worriedly at Gael who shook his head and supplied, "We rode most of the night and as long as we could this morning."

"If he sent someone after you, you are maybe three or four hours in front of them," he said.

The amount of time sounded so utterly small. But she didn't have time to think about that. Alejandro asked, "He has a map?"

"We only saw a little bit of it, but it looked like a copy of something really old." She scrunched her face, "But none of that helps really ..."

Again, he took off his hat and smoothed his hair before replacing it. "You said he was asking you about the Tears of the Moon?"

They nodded.

"Ay dios mío." Alejandro sighed all the air out of his chest as if he were being constricted. "Do you have it?"

"It?" Gael asked.

Renee splayed her hands on the table. "We have been in Peru for three weeks. We came because Gael was hired to do a photo shoot. We've been everywhere. And we don't know if he took a photo of something, if we talked to someone, if we saw something that has to do with the tears of the moon. But Smith thinks we have information that we do *not* know we have."

"You know what tears of the moon means?" Gael asked.

Alejandro thought for a moment, gave the room another study, and must have decided that he didn't need to whisper any longer. "There are many stories of our people that survived and many that were lost. When the Spanish came, they tried to burn and kill traces of the people. But they could never kill the whispered stories. But the stories that survived are sometimes difficult to interpret."

Gael understood. "Little changes to the stories over many years make interpreting oral traditions difficult."

A horrific game of telephone, Renee thought.

Alejandro continued, "My grandfather told us a story of the great general. He buried the treasure when he heard the Spanish had killed the emperor. But then he and his men continued to travel through villages with the baskets and containers; even though they were empty, they made it look like they traveled with the treasure. When the general was captured and killed, no one knew where he had hidden the treasure. Many people had seen him in many different locations." He took a sip of his beer. "The men who helped him bury it, they knew where it was. They gave up their lives, went back to the burial place and spent their final years creating traps and cursing the land where the treasure was hidden." He held up a finger. "But one man survived them all. In his last days, he made a map of how to get through each of the traps. If Smith has the location, what he was looking for was another map. A map made out of silver, out of the Tears of the Moon. *It* is not a place, it is a map."

"A map made out of silver," Renee scrubbed her face, "but we haven't seen anything that even resembles a map made out of paper, let alone one made of silver."

Alejandro shook his head. "That is all I know. The other thing I know is that you two need to go as far as you can from Smith."

"Well," Gael said, "We have three horses, maybe four; we can give them to you in return for a ride or directions to the nearest city."

"And a phone," Renee added.

"Oh," Alejandro reached into his pocket and pulled out a small flip phone, "use mine."

Renee's hands warmed as she took the phone. She felt tears spring to her eyes and had to swallow several times. "Where are we? Or, how far are we from the nearest town? Or, can you take us there? I'm gonna call my friend and need to let her know where to meet us."

Chapter Forty-Seven

I t started raining thirty minutes after Harper and Nick were back on the road. Harper yelled for him to stop. He did and when he asked what was wrong, she didn't answer. Instead, she slung the pack onto her chest and rummaged through it, finally producing a pair of sunglasses. "They'll keep the rain out."

"Barrett, I fucking love that magic bag!" He put them on and lowered the wool hat over the brim to create more of a shield. She patted his back to keep him from going, reached back in the bag and handed over the dirty dish towel. "Maybe you can tie it around your mouth and nose?"

He squeezed her hand and did as she suggested, and they were back on the road. Now as the rain tried to whip at them, Nick had some form of protection and Harper hid her face against his back, allowing her body to follow Nick's when he leaned into turns.

The roads were unrelenting in their continual twisting and turning climb into the altitude, only to zigzag back down again. Nick drove as cautiously as he could, and Harper wasn't immune to the slips of the bike's tires against the wet road; they were often followed by the reverberation of his curses.

When they were in a ravine between the vast mountains, she had to force herself not to think about things like flash flooding. Or mudslides. Or falling rocks.

They drove past groups of houses every now and then, but nowhere that offered a store, restaurant or even a covering to stop.

As he wound up another agonizing switchback, he spotted a sagging tarp-covered entrance of an uninhabited home and pulled over.

He climbed off and helped Harper, his attention on the fender where she was sitting. "I'm sorry." He scowled, taking off the glasses and lowering the sopping wet towel.

"What choice do we have?"

"You okay?"

She shrugged and repeated, "What choice do we have?"

Up on the top of the mountain, they should have had a better view, but it was gray clouds as far as the eye could see. And a lot of rain.

"I need to get us somewhere safe," Nick announced.

She took a few steps to loosen her legs and behind, then looked inside the house; it had worked before. "Do we wait out the rain?"

He shook his head. "It's too close to the road, and we don't know where those assholes are."

Harper pulled her phone out of the pack, still no signal.

"Okay," Harper repositioned the bag on her back, "sooner we get going, sooner we'll get there."

He climbed back on, held out his hand to help her back in place, and when she slipped her arms around his waist and pressed her head against his back, he gave her arms a comforting pat.

This time, Nick's words – *'we don't know where those assholes are'* – tried to keep Harper company. She played mind games with herself so she didn't worry about someone trying to drive them off the road, because she felt like it would be easier to get to them on a bike. And she didn't want to find out what jumping off a racing bike was like. Or a bike that lost traction and was sent sliding down the road, or one that slipped off the side of a mountain, for that matter.

She hugged Nick a little harder and muttered into his back, "I trust you."

The wet settled in her bones and she wasn't sure how long she had to fight the cold and discomfort. At one point it seemed that some of the water on her face might be from tears she wasn't successfully holding back. The heavy material of the clothing she wore helped keep parts of her warm, but they weighed her down as they collected more and more water.

She was lost in a heavy world with only Nick to cling to. She audibly scoffed at that thought, if ever there was a metaphor for what she was going through.

"Harper!" She heard him yell and tensed, but he slowed the bike and pointed to a sign announcing the inevitable arrival of a city.

They climbed another twist of road, and at the top of another mountain, he slowed and pointed again. A city, ten times larger than the town they (kind of) stayed the previous evening, opened up. But it was signage to their left that read *Casa B&B 1 Kilometer* that Nick dutifully followed.

A dirt road led to a short paved driveway surrounded by squat palm trees, tall spindly trees, blooming ferns, bushes and shrubs. Peeking out of the dreamy landscape was a large, two- story white house, with a terracotta roof and black window trim throughout.

He pulled up to the front of the house, put the kickstand down, then tiredly climbed off and held out his hand to help Harper.

"Is this a dream?" she asked.

He slid his arm around her waist. "If it is, don't wake me up." Their stiff legs hobbled them up the steps to the front door. "It's good there's a bigger town," Nick said. "A bigger population means we'll be harder to find."

She grunted in reply.

Shivering and sore (and feeling like a drowned rat), Harper was only half aware of the conversation Nick had with the owner of the B&B, who nodded sympathetically over whatever woeful story he was supplying. And she didn't care, because it wasn't that long before they were shown to a room on the first floor at the end of a hallway.

"Shower." Harper could no longer control her shivering.

She barely heard him say, "I'll plug our phones in."

She unceremoniously discarded her clothes, stepped into the renovated earthen tile shower, closed her eyes and stood directly under the showerhead as the hot water revived her. She wasn't surprised when arms slipped around her waist, and Nick's naked form pressed against her back while they waited for their skin to warm.

She rested her arms on top of his as she turned their bodies ninety degrees so they'd both reap the rewards of the hot water. He turned his head away from the spray, but rested his cheek against the top of her head. Neither moved, until Harper stopped shivering.

When she felt like she was human once again, and her brain was forming sensible thoughts, she slipped her hands down, reaching behind her to rest on the high side of Nick's thighs.

That was all the invitation she gave, and what she thought he'd been waiting for.

He dipped his head down and brushed a kiss against her neck. She let her head drop to the side, giving him more skin to tantalize with his lips, as his hands left the perch of her stomach and slid upward to fully capture her breasts.

She leaned into the sensual torture as a new heat replaced the cold. She turned her head to find his lips. He eagerly met her kiss, the first brush, another, and without breaking the connection, she turned in his arms and the dam of passion they'd been building up to this moment, broke in a deliciously, devastating deluge.

Hands searched and teased. Harper captured his moan of pleasure when she found him, hot and ready for her.

Nick reached between them and gladly flamed the building fire; enjoying each taste and touch. When Harper followed his fingers with her hips, offering herself to him, he growled appreciatively.

His yearning for her had been increasing since the moment in the jungle, when he stopped trying to rid himself of unseen spiders and focused on her. He knew, from just kissing her there was something between them, some unspoken connection, but he didn't know it would erupt in all this maddening desire.

They twisted and coiled around each other drifting among the exquisite building lust. But Nick was at a precipice and he was ready to jump.

He gripped Harper by her tantalizing behind, raised her up and pressed her against the shower wall. She instinctively wrapped her legs around him, her hunger evident when she reached between them to help guide him. She bit his neck and he moaned into her ear as he pressed himself inside her. He fought the urge to move, stilling himself for a lifetime, relishing the way her warmth felt and how she clung to him.

"Nick." Her sultry plea made him tighten his hold, press deeper and wait one more intoxicating, tempting moment. But Harper wasn't having any of it. "Nick," she demanded, insisting he move. Imploring. He let a ragged moan escape as he began to move with her. She let out a triumphant breath.

The hunger grew, she pushed at him and pulled, kissed him and into his mouth demanded "*bed*," but he answered with an animalistic "*no*." Because he didn't want to let go. He didn't want to stop. He didn't think he *could* stop. He was overcome with a longing to pleasure her, to let her hold on and let go while he conquered her body, because she had already conquered him.

She made demands that were savage sounds strung together against his ear. But he understood. He adjusted his hold on her, picked up his steady pace, the surge of desire cresting, too soon, too much, too thrilling. She fervently cursed his name as her body squeezed him. There was no holding back now, everything was speed and then thunder sparked and radiated throughout his body.

It took several lifetimes for their breathing to regulate, a few more for Nick to let Harper slip down his body and her feet to touch ground. Though they still clung to each other. She sought his lips and he caught her sigh of satisfaction.

Harper shivered in his arms and Nick gave a congratulatory grin, until he realized the water had gone tepid and was quickly losing what little heat it had left to offer.

He picked her up once more with a grunt of want that she echoed. They were a dripping mess of rousing entanglement as Nick tripped over the mess of clothes that needed to be wrung out, and into the bedroom to try and find the bed without looking.

There was a distinct ding sound, enough to stop their progress across the room. When it came again, the technological sound of a message was shockingly invasive. They fully stilled and waited. It came again.

Nick helped Harper down. She picked up a nearby blanket to wrap around herself, making her way to her phone.

"We have a signal." She glanced down at her phone in disbelief.

Nick stepped behind her, sliding his hands down her back where the blanket wasn't covering her, and began to slip his hands up her sides. He wasn't ready for her to hide this warm shapely body away from him; he'd just gotten started. He lowered his lips to her neck and she tilted her head, but continued to scroll through the conversations, listing who they were from. "Lena. Lena. Mom. Luna. Luna ..."

He watched her fingers work and when she paused at an unknown number then opened it, he was able to read what it said.

It's Renee. Gael and I got away. We're safe!

"Nick!" He slid his hand under hers and steadied the screen as he whispered a triumphant, "hot damn!" then kissed her soundly on the cheek.

Chapter Forty-Eight

"Harper?!" Renee yelled when she answered the phone.

Harper put the call on speaker and wiped another tear off her cheek. "Renee! You're okay? Really? You're safe? What happened, what ... where are you? You're okay? And Gael's with you?"

"We're at Alejandro's aunt's restaurant."

Harper nodded a smile at Nick then asked, "Who's Alejandro?"

"A friend we met in a jungle bar. He's one of the good guys. He knows Smith. Oh! This asshole, Jacob Smith, he's the one pulling all the strings and he's looking for a lost city of treasure and apparently at some point Gael and I saw this silver map and that's why he's been after us this whole time. But we still don't exactly know what the Tears of the Moon are. And, the reason we were taken is because this Smith asshole thought we had the Tears of the Moon."

The long-winded explanation that made no sense gave Harper déjà vu from when she picked Renee up from jail in Cusco. Thankfully, Gael said, "Mi reina, it's too much to talk about at once. First we need to find them."

"Where are you?" Renee asked.

"We're in ..." she glanced at Nick, "I don't know where we are."

Nick pulled up the map on his phone and told Renee the name of the town. They listened as Renee relayed the information then gave an excited squeal. "We're only two hours away from you! Okay, we're coming to you. Alejandro will drive us. Send me the exact address and I'll see you soon."

"We'll get you a room and ..." Harper shook her head. "You're sure you're okay?"

"We're okay." She punctuated her words. "Two hours. Use this number if you need anything."

"Okay, we'll get you a room," Harper repeated.

"Harper, it's really good to hear your voice."

"You have no idea how good it is to hear yours," she returned.

Harper held the phone loosely in her hand, staring wide-eyed at Nick. He gave her an encouraging grin, but it fell into confusion when she dropped the phone on the nearby chair, stepped into his arms and began crying. "I'm so tired, Nick."

He kissed the top of her head. "I know, Barrett."

"Nick, I've been to jungles, police stations and four hotels. The one time I went to *my* hotel room it was turned upside down. I bought an illegal gun, I've kidnapped someone. Half of the clothes I brought with me to Peru are in the back of a car which you pushed over the side of a mountain. I've scraped up my hands, jammed my shoulders, slipped down a mountainside – twice; been impaled on a cactus and fell into mud ..." She wasn't hysterical, she wasn't whining, it was more of a depleted delirium. "I haven't gotten a good night's sleep in what feels like months. I've spent most of my waking hours worried or," she gave a snort of a laugh and looked up at Nick, "turned on by you and all your Nick-ness. Because you're all appetizing and handsome." She pointed to the bathroom. "And that was really, *really* good. And now the word 'appetizing' is making me really hungry ..."

Nick leaned back, and still holding her around the waist, gently nudged her chin up with his other hand to give her a reassuring smile. She repeated her original concern. "Nick, I'm so tired."

"I know."

"This is just exhausted, verbal spiraling that's going on."

"I know."

She swallowed and tilted her head slightly. "Are you gonna kiss me again to settle me down?"

He raised an eyebrow. "I mean, it worked really well last time."

"Okay."

He seamlessly captured her mouth. She thought the kiss was meant to be gentle, reassuring. But something about touching each other – the recurring shock when they kissed – broke through good intentions, releasing a yearning to build up the passionate connection.

Still, Nick somehow managed to pull away. She softly blinked her eyes open, but didn't move. She soaked up his projected assuredness, happy to bask in their rays. He brushed a kiss across her lips once more then asked, "Want me to tell you the plan?"

"That's exactly what I need."

"Okay, first you're gonna take a nap because there isn't anyone to worry about. I'm gonna call Sean and get more money wired to town. He's gonna get us a car. We're gonna get new clothes. Renee and Gael will be here and we'll have a really nice long, drunken dinner to celebrate their escape."

"Renee and Gael are safe, but there are still people after us," she pointed.

He shrugged. "Yeah, there are still people out there who were willing to run us off the road without asking questions first. But we'll work that problem later, we're putting it on the backburner for now."

While she liked his honesty, she could have used a little less. She licked her lips and repeated the plan. "Nap. Money. Clothes. Car. Dinner. Drinks. And share all the information the four of us have found."

"That's the plan."

In an hour, Nick had moved mountains.

He apologized that Harper had to get back in her damp clothes, but he still had no ID for obtaining the money Sean sent. Though he did get a taxi to take them to town, so at least they didn't have to ride the motorcycle in the rain .

After stopping at the Western Union and with money in hand, the taxi took them to a clothing store next. The woman who was running the register gave a wide-eyed nod of understanding, when Nick explained they needed new clothes and asked if they could change into the clothing they purchased while there.

Harper picked out several items to try on and when she grabbed a beige bra and matching underwear, Nick, who was nearby, gave a dramatic deep sigh.

"What?" she asked.

"That's so sensible."

"Yeah, the way things are going, I kinda need something sensible. You know, for running around in jungles and sliding down mountains."

He closed the space between them and lowered his mouth to her ear, gently nipping at her earlobe before whispering, "But I need the kind that takes my breath away when I strip you and put you in a shower."

She cleared her throat, moved away from him, and subtly added a very sexy, very *un*sensible black lacy bra and matching underwear to her stack before turning back to him and gesturing toward the men's section. "It's only fair if you get some of those boxer briefs you were wearing when I first pulled *your* pants down."

"I'm on it." He backed away, but she added, "And pick out some clothes for Gael. He's about your height. I'll get some for Renee."

Dressed in new, clean, dry clothes – a pair of dark jeans, a t-shirt and jade green sweater, not to mention the new socks and undies – she felt more grounded. (Of course, the release of endorphins, a small nap and the snack Nick produced when they climbed into the taxi had helped round everything out.) She felt like she might finally be firing on all cylinders.

She added a black, hooded waterproof trail jacket and a pair of khaki, moisture-wicking pants. It was nice to have a new wardrobe, as long as they didn't end up having to leave yet another bag of clothing behind again — *because wild monkeys and rabid dogs decided to chase them ...*

Nick came out of the changing room in a pair of light jeans, and a tight white t-shirt showing off his taut chest and stomach. Her fingers tingled with the rush of sense memory, knowing well how his hard and warm body felt. Over the tee, he wore an open black button-down with the sleeves folded up. When he mindlessly pushed one of them further up to show off more of his forearms, her attention was drawn to his strong hands – hands that had gripped her so possessively she'd felt his desire for her radiate throughout her whole body.

She clutched her bag to her chest and licked her lips, and when he met her gaze, a grin creased his eyes and he winked. When he was close enough he breathed, "That color does something to your eyes that's twisting my insides up."

"Not so bad yourself," she whispered.

"Are you blushing?"

"No."

"You're clutching that bag a bit tight. Worried someone might steal it?" he teased.

"Yup."

"Or, are you as shocked to see me as I am to see you, even though it's only been a few minutes?"

"No idea what you're talking about."

He tilted his head. "That's a shame. Now that we have a little space to breathe, and we know Gael and Renee are safe," his voice lowered to that sexy octave, "my mind keeps wandering back to what you just did to me."

"What *I* did to you?" Now she couldn't deny the blush from the instantaneous memories, and Nick knew exactly what he was doing to her with those lowered eyelashes and slightly parted lips.

Thankfully, the young woman behind the cash register interrupted them. "¿Listos?" *Are you ready?*

"God, yes." Harper put all the tags from the clothes she was wearing, as well as the others she wanted to buy, on the counter. Nick did the same.

"What else do we need to do?" she asked him.

"Pick up the car and buy a charger for Renee's computer."

"Is the rental under my name?"

"It is."

"Did you get insurance?"

He leaned his hip against the counter and wiggled his eyebrows. "Barrett, I added shit they didn't even know they offered."

She winked at him. "Atta boy."

Chapter Forty-Nine

Harper and Nick sat on the covered front porch of the bed and breakfast in oversized patio chairs. When a car pulled up and Harper saw Renee, she gave a strangled sound of excitement as she hurried down the steps. The car hadn't even pulled to a stop, and Renee was already out and running toward her friend at full speed. They crashed into each other with grunts and laughter and tears as they fiercely hugged and talked over each other, recapping their worries and what they'd been through during their time apart.

"I was so worried," Harper said.

"I told you not to worry," Renee admonished.

"I was trying to help save you and worrying kept me going."

"We were fine."

"You're lying."

"Of course I'm lying. I was kidnapped, held captive, forced to go on a hike, had a relationship talk with Gael and stole a horse and rode it to freedom while being shot at."

"That explains the smell."

"I need a shower so bad."

"I'm not letting you go yet."

"Me neither."

"We have assholes after us, too."

"You and Nick?"

"They punctured all the tires in the rental, so we couldn't follow you."

"I saw that, not the guys but the flat tires."

"Then they tried to run us off the road."

"But you're okay?"

"Yes, I hid and Nick pushed the car over the side of a mountain. Then I slid down a hill and got impaled on cactus spikes."

"What?"

"I'm fine."

"I don't think Smith is going to be happy that Gael and I escaped. He's not a good guy."

"Smith is the name of the bad guy?"

"Jacob Smith."

"We're gonna figure this all out and take the bastard down."

"The secret agent man is rubbing off on you."

"You have no idea."

Renee laughed and lowered her voice as she asked, "Please tell me in the middle of all this crap you really did let him *rub off* on you."

"Renee," Harper chided, then admitted in a murmur, "Exuberant. So damn exuberant."

They finally released each other, allowing Harper to take in the tall, exhausted, bruised Gael. "Shit," she gasped as Renee introduced them. "Gael, this is Harper. Harp, Gael."

Harper didn't shake his hand, but instead stepped past his personal space and hugged him. "Sorry, hope I'm not hurting you. I need to give you a hug because I've been looking for you since I got here."

He returned the hug. "And I can't thank you enough."

Harper gave him one more squeeze before she released him. "I don't know how much it helped, you two seemed to figure out how to escape on your own."

"Nick!" Renee bounded over to him and threw herself in his arms; the force of her action pushed out an *oof* from his diaphragm as he hugged her back. Satisfied with her hug, she let him go, but kept hold of his arms, narrowing her gaze. "Have you been nice to my friend?"

He winked. "Very nice."

She wiggled her eyebrows in return, then grabbed his hand and dragged him the two steps to where Gael was standing.

"It's nice to meet you." Nick held out his hand. "I'm glad you're okay."

"Thank you." Gael gratefully shook his hand.

"And I have to say, I'm now a huge fan of your work."

Gael gave a slight nod of thanks.

The driver of the car got out and stood inside the open door. Renee pointed him out and explained, "That's Alejandro, he saved us."

"I only gave you a ride," Alejandro excused. "But I have to go. Because we stopped at my aunt's restaurant, she called my mother, and now I have to go to her house."

Renee and Gael returned to his side to offer their profound thanks for his help. "You have Harper's number, and she has yours," Renee reminded him. "If you hear anything, or if we have any questions ..." she trailed off.

Alejandro shrugged. "We will look out for each other," he reassured.

The vast amount of information that they all had swirled before Harper. It was going to be a long night.

"We got you a room," Harper said as the quartet headed inside. "And some clothes, they're laid out in your room." She cleared her throat. "Unless we should ..." She gestured between herself and Renee, but her friend waved her off and winked in Gael's direction. "I'm gonna stick with this guy."

Harper gave directions to the room and handed over the key. "Take your time. And when you're ready, Nick arranged for dinner in our room. We can talk and ... figure all this shit out then."

After dinner was long gone and all the stories and information had been rehashed, Nick sat back, draped his arm over the back of Harper's chair and summed up their current state of affairs. "Jacob Smith is an archeologist who isn't above kidnapping, threatening and beating. He has allegedly led eighteen men to their deaths. He has the location of the treasure of the century. The Tears of the Moon is a map made of silver, that either has the exact location of the treasure worth thirty-seven billion dollars, or a map of the traps to avoid so a person could *find* a treasure worth thirty-seven billion dollars. And without ever going near the area of Choquequirao in the past three weeks, Gael and Renee supposedly know about the Tears of the Moon."

Gael ran a frustrated hand through the slight curl of his hair as Renee scrubbed her face and asked, "What's the next step?"

"I think we need to do a background check on Smith," Nick replied.

"Is that part of the secret agent stuff you can do?" Renee asked.

Harper joked, "He's got friends in high places."

"Really?"

There was a knock on the door. Everyone tensed.

Nick retrieved the gun from the backpack and tucked it in the back of his waistband before he answered. It was the staff member who Nick had made arrangements with for their dinner.

"Señor, ¿cómo estuvo la cena?" *How was dinner?*

"Oh, muy buena." Nick smiled.

The woman pursed her lips and gave him an apologetic look. "I am sorry. I think you are all on vacation to explore Valle Sagrado?"

"Yes, we are."

Her face twisted more with an apology as she explained, "Lo siento, I did not tell you when you arrived, but I was not sure of the possibility. It has just been confirmed that they will be closing the road soon."

"The road ..."

"To Cusco? Several kilometers from here, they will close the road."

"For how long?"

"Four, five days?" She shrugged. "We have room for you to stay during that time. But, if you need to go, I think you don't have too much time."

"Thank you, we wanted to get back to Cusco tomorrow. How much time do we have before the road is closed?"

"I think if you leave before medianoche, midnight, you will make it," she answered.

Nick checked his watch. It was almost nine. "Gracias. We'll talk about it and make a decision soon."

"Again, I am sorry."

He waved the apology away. "Está bien, no te preocupes. We were able to take showers and have a cena maravillosa."

After he closed the door and made his way back to the table, Harper had already pulled up the map on her phone. "We're three hours from Cusco."

"I'm not ready to go back the way Renee and I came from. If we go the other way, toward the archeological site, we're bound to run into Smith," Gael reasoned.

Nick nodded. "I don't like the idea of being stuck here for four days."

"Looks like we need to adjust our plans?" Harper caught Nick's attention.

Nick gave Harper a knowing wink, lowered his voice as he softly aimed one word in her direction, "Okay?"

She caught her lower lip between her teeth as she took a breath then grinned as she whispered back, "Okay."

"Jesus ..." Renee laughed, "I'd say you two need to get a room, but you already have one. Maybe me and Gael need to give you a minute?"

Harper cleared her throat and playfully swatted Renee on the arm. "We should probably get going."

Renee loudly muttered, "Somethin' *already* seems to be goin'."

Nick gave a chuckle but stood, causing everyone to jump into action.

"My computer is charged. Gael and I can start going through all the pictures and everything in the car," Renee said. "We'll go get our clothes and meet you in the lobby."

"I can drive while you call your friends in high places," Harper joked.

"Sounds like a plan." They didn't have too much to pack up. Nick put the gun back in the pack and slung it on his shoulder.

Harper grabbed the plastic bag with their new clothing.

After saying their goodbyes to the receptionist at the desk and waving off another apology, Renee asked Harper, "Is the new rental car better than the last one?"

"Kinda."

"What does that mean?"

"It has four doors."

⁂

As they drove out of town, before they lost their signal, Nick put Sean on speaker phone, allowing him to set up Renee and Gael's smartwatches that he'd purchased earlier that day.

The last thing Nick did before hanging up, was to ask Sean to look into Jacob Smith.

"You are so cool," Renee said excitedly from the back seat. "Probably better than any mercenary we could have hired, huh Harp?"

"I suppose he'll do." Harper sighed, giving Nick a knowing sideways glance.

Renee turned on her computer and asked, "Do we just start looking at everything that's silver?"

"It's not the worst idea," Gael said.

Nick and Harper listened as every picture was scoured. A lot of the running commentary had to do with how talented Gael was, how beautiful the lines of the clothes looked on the models, how well she'd done picking out jewelry to go with everything and how great her hair and makeup work was.

Renee read signs out loud in the background of the photos, reasoning, "Who knows where we'll find something."

"Jeez, these photos taken in the market are like hidden object games," Gael said as Renee pointed out everything that looked silver. Plates, mirrors, statues. Snakes, bells, totems, moon designs, and even magnets.

"Damnit," Renee mumbled.

"What?" Harper asked.

"There are photos with stalls in the background and it's *all* silver jewelry. Everywhere."

"One picture at a time, mi reina."

They continued looking, discussing designs, reliefs on old stones in the background, bystanders and what they were holding in their hands.

Nick reached over and touched Harper's arm. "You good?"

"I'm sore, but I'm also napped, fed and warm. It's not raining and my ass has a soft wide seat." Nick slipped his hand to her thigh, causing her to grip the wheel tighter; that little touch sending millions of electrical particles pulsating through her body.

And maybe that shock jump-started something, pulling up a very tiny piece of information she'd read in a magazine about Peru, that she'd bought at the airport while waiting for her flight in Lima.

"Oh shit," she whispered, so stunned she took her foot off the gas.

"What?" Nick glanced behind them, but there was no one there. "Is it the car?"

"Oh shit!" she repeated and found a spot to pull over. She was shaking her head, trying to remember everything.

"Harper?" Nick gently called her name. In the glow of the dashboard lights, she grinned at him before turning around in the seat to see everyone.

"I read this article on the way here. About how the Inca carved plans of cities and important sites into large stones, effectively creating three-dimensional maps of their urban areas." She closed her eyes, trying to find the words. "The person who was being interviewed said that the Inca didn't see maps and mapmaking the way a European society would have." She shook her head and gave a groan of frustration. "It said something like they were all about combining art with the natural elements. What if we aren't looking for a map the way we understand it? What if it's hidden somehow? What if it's a piece of artwork?" She didn't think she was properly expressing the thesis of the article or her thoughts.

But when Renee parroted her earlier "*oh, shit!*" she knew she was onto something.

"Gael! The llama herding!"

He frowned, but she began to scroll through the photos and when she found the one she was looking for, opened it and turned the screen for everyone to look at.

A model wore a straight teal skirt that looked like it had been folded over itself at random angles, and a simple off-the-shoulder white shirt. The photo was taken at sunset and behind the model, a herd of llamas were walking away, into the mountainous terrain, while clouds gathered on the horizon, obstructing the light.

"It was near Ollantaytambo. I remember when she first tried this outfit on; the skirt was everything, but Victor and I weren't happy with the top and felt like she needed something ... I started looking around the market, I found the perfect necklace." She zoomed in on the collar shaped silver necklace the model was wearing. A large panel in the center was buffered on either side by a feathered panel, and in turn those panels were buffered by another detailed design, and so on. The whole necklace was a creation of seven panels. "It ah ..." she swallowed, "it actually folded over itself, and it kind of made an oblong shape ... and ..." She seemed to lose all ability to speak when zoomed in close enough to see enough of the symbol at the bottom of the center panel.

"That was on the top of his map," Gael whispered.

"Holy shit," Renee repeated.

"I think ..." Gael was having difficulty speaking, so had to clear his throat before he said the words aloud. "I think we found the Tears of the Moon."

Chapter Fifty

Harper barely recognized her own voice as she said, "We found the Tears of the Moon."

"What the hell?" Renee shook her head in disbelief. "I bought that from the same place I bought about fifteen other items." She frowned at Gael. "Were they just selling priceless artifacts? Did they know they were selling priceless artifacts? How did *they* get it?"

"All good questions, mi reina. With no answers."

"Do you have the necklace?" Harper asked, although she knew the answer even before Renee shook her head no. If it had been found, the men who tossed their room wouldn't have tried to run her and Nick off the road. (Or maybe they would have *because* it was found in the room ...?) And this Smith guy would have killed Gael and Renee to get rid of them for knowing where it was ...

"I gave it to Carla, the model in the picture. It really suited her and was gorgeous on her ..." Renee scrunched her face. "God, I feel like an idiot."

"Why?" Gael shook her worry off. "It's not your job to tell the difference between the replicas and relics."

"Still ...."

"Does Carla live in Cusco?" Nick asked.

Gael shook his head. "She was with us in Ollantaytambo then went with us to Aguas Calientes." His voice filled with excitement as he explained, "But she stayed there. She had two shoots back-to-back at Machu Picchu."

"So she still has the necklace with her!" Renee happily finished. "I don't have her number, do you?"

"No. Maybe we can get in touch with my assistant. Emily would have Carla's number."

"Emily's at her sister's wedding," Renee supplied. "I tried to get in touch with her to get some information about you, but she never got back to me. Or maybe she has, I haven't really had a chance to check my email lately."

Gael turned the computer back toward him, "I can't really make any of the symbols out on the necklace."

"So should we head to Machu Picchu?" Harper asked.

Gael grimaced. "It's a little difficult to get to. Every route has to go around the mountains. And the drivable road only goes as far as Ollantaytambo. From there we'll have to take a train."

"Then, since we know what we're looking for, should we stop for the night? Go back to the hotel in Cusco?" Renee asked.

"That's probably not a good idea," Harper said, "someone ransacked our room."

"Ransacked our room?"

"How far is Ollantaytambo from here?" Harper asked as she checked her phone, not shocked that there wasn't a signal.

"How are you feeling?" Nick asked, leveling his gaze at her.

She shrugged. "I had a nap."

Gael suggested, "We'll pass through several cities on the way, we can wait until we have a signal or stop off at one of them to find a place to sleep for a few hours."

Nick nodded. "It's as good a plan as any."

"What do we do once we have the necklace?" Renee asked.

"I haven't gotten that far in the plan," Nick answered honestly.

Gael looked at his watch. "It is almost midnight," he said. "The first train from Ollantaytambo to Aguas Calientes leaves at seven forty-five. Maybe we could try to get there tonight, then we'd at least get a few hours of sleep."

Harper started to drive again. "If that doesn't work," she offered, "I know a great cave behind an abandoned church."

At the first city they came to, after the car crawled up and down switchbacks lit by headlights, they finally had a signal. Ollantaytambo was a little more than two hours away, so Nick offered to drive the rest of the curving roads and allow everyone else the opportunity to close their eyes.

As he drove into the city, he saw the information sign that the road they'd been taking was a toll road. He began fishing money out of his pocket, then slowed the car as he neared the booth, its tired overhead lighting illuminating the area around it.

The window of the tollbooth opened, and a well-built man with light brown eyes, short brown hair, a blue worker vest and a smile leaned out and called, "Buenas noches."

"Buenas noches," Nick replied, but when he went to hand over the money, instead of an accepting hand, the operator produced a gun. At that point, a car pulled up behind them while another slipped in front, boxing them in.

"We need to talk," the man in the booth said.

Nick pointed to the car in front of them that looked very familiar. "Are you the asshole who tried to run us off the road?" Nick's voice was polite, almost playful.

Nick knew Harper was awake when he felt her hand squeeze his arm. He figured it meant she was ready to get the gun as quickly as she could. He reached for her hand and pulled it down between them, giving her a return squeeze, hoping to god she saw the slight shake of his head that meant *'wait.'*

The man in the tollbooth gave a frustrated sigh. "I've been trying to get your attention, to talk to you. We've been following you ... *all* of you, all over the damn place."

Nick's frown deepened as the man produced his other hand, holding a metal badge with the Peruvian flag and PNP logo. "Policía Nacional del Perú," the man spat.

Nick's eyebrows rose but his face broke into a wide grin as he thrust his hand toward him and said, "Mucho gusto, I'm Nick."

Chapter Fifty-One

Harper thanked the young man who placed a plate of food in front of her. He'd been roused to cook for the motley group sitting in the middle of his small restaurant, where four tables had been pushed together and the overhead fluorescent lights dulled the red and orange painted walls.

Nick, Harper, Renee and Gael sat on one side, the two men who had been following Nick and Harper, National Peruvian Policemen, sat on the other. The driver who pulled behind them to block in their car and make sure they didn't get away was the tollbooth operator who'd been coerced to assist. When the threat was over, he went back to work.

Officer Salazar was the man in the toll booth who'd pulled a gun on Nick. He was in his late fifties, broad shoulders, on the tall side, fit, but his face was drawn and he looked exhausted.

His partner, Officer Perez, might be in his mid-thirties. He stood a head shorter than Salazar and didn't look like he was prone to much laughter; the wrinkles around his mouth and on his forehead were all frown lines.

Harper started the conversation. "You tried to run us off the road."

Salazar tiredly shook his head. "No, lo entiendes. You do not understand. We were following you."

"Closely," Nick added.

"It was raining," he excused, glancing sideways at the man sitting next to him.

Perez shrugged and verified, "It was raining very hard."

"We were trying to get your attention," Salazar stated.

"Oh, you got it," Harper bit sarcastically.

"Después de ver el accidente, after we see the accident, we went for help. Two trucks came and I walked down to help you. But you were gone."

"I thought you were following us," Nick said. "I pushed the car over the edge so you'd think we were dead. You would have done the same thing."

Salazar gave a disdainful grunt. "It was a lot of work."

Harper filled her fork but before taking the bite, muttered, "That's what you get for trying to run us off the road."

"Are you working with the police in Cusco?" Renee interrupted.

Perez increased his frown lines, confused.

"Figured." She rolled her eyes. "I filled out a missing person's report on Gael and they said they'd 'get around to looking into things.' You're the only cops I've run into at this point."

Salazar sat back with a sigh and cradled his glass of water. "We investigate the looting of artifacts in Peru. We work to stop the theft and to stop any attempts made to sell the artifacts."

"Jacob Smith?" Gael asked.

"That's the newest name he's been using. He has been a problem for us for many many years." Salazar sighed. "We face many challenges because the archeological sites of Peru are many and very far from each other and difficult to get to. Es un trabajo muy difícil." He ran a tired hand through his hair. "We believe the man, Smith, has someone in our department that continues to inform him of our work. He has been like a phantom and leaves death wherever he goes."

"He kidnapped us," Renee informed.

Salazar raised an eyebrow. "We were trying to stop that from happening, but you were always one step ahead of us."

Renee smiled; even though it wasn't a compliment, but she probably took it as one.

"How did you find us," Harper gestured to her and Nick, "or know about us?

"You are con ella. With her." Perez pointed his fork at Renee before turning his attention back to his food.

Salazar cleared his throat. "The closest we've gotten to Smith was intel that two of his men were going to try and steal an artifact from a museum in Ollantaytambo. We had an operation watching for them, but when they came out of the museum, they spotted us and there was a chase. We caught one of the men, but he had nothing on him."

"We were gutted, the entire operation was a waste of time," Perez said with his mouth full.

"We could not keep the man detained for long," Salazar said. "Our operation was not very well supported." He raised an eyebrow, an implication that his 'operation' might not have been all that legal either.

"El hombre, he gave us no information anyway," Perez added.

"The men you were after. Did one have scars on his face? On his cheek and one above his eyebrow?" Renee asked. "And the other guy looked like he hasn't slept in years?"

Salazar nodded.

"That's Scarface and Kyle."

"Scarface and Kyle?" Harper asked.

"That's what I called them," Renee answered. "Oh," she sat forward as she slapped Harper on the arm, "you met them!"

"What? How?" She shook her head. "When?"

"When we were in the abandoned gas station, those two guys stopped and asked if we needed help? The guy driving was Scarface. The guy who got out to pee was Kyle."

"We had the man who looked very tired," Salazar interrupted, continuing his story. "While we had him, we had an idea. We released him and followed him. He was met by the scarred man."

"Scarface."

"Sí," Salazar grumbled, not willing to say the name. "We watched them. We saw them threaten a vendor in the mercado. But they left without doing anything else. When we were sure they were far away, we asked the vendor why he was threatened. He told us they were asking about a necklace, but he didn't know it was their necklace. He'd sold it to a white woman who was working with a famous photographer."

Gael sat back heavily as the realization of how he'd been found came to light. "I had *all* the proper permits in place, with dates and locations."

Salazar aimed a sympathetic shrug in his direction. "You were very easy to locate. And your photo is in many places online."

"So what did you want from *us*?" Nick gestured to himself and Harper.

"We could not stop the girl from being kidnapped," he jutted his chin in Renee's direction, "but we thought we could help you two before something bad happened to you."

Nick rephrased his question. "Now that we're all safe, what do you want from us?"

"Do you have the artifact?" Perez asked.

"What artifact?" Nick asked blandly, tilting his head slightly and narrowing his gaze on Perez.

Harper felt the change in his attitude and slightly turned her head to watch him out of the corner of her eye. She had been feeling strange about the entire interaction; she wasn't sure what it was, but something seemed off.

Regardless of what was going on, she did know Nick was getting ready to stare down Salazar and Perez. And she was sure neither of them had ever come up against anyone like Nick Robbins before.

The only sound in the room came from the back kitchen where dishes were being washed.

To his credit, Salazar didn't look unnerved by Nick's actions, but she saw Perez's eyes dart back and forth between his partner and Nick.

Salazar asked, "Do you know what Smith is wanted for?"

"We heard there were several guides who went out with him and never returned," Renee said.

Salazar gave a sad sigh then began to launder Smith's list of illegal actions. "He bribed local customs agents. Forged documents to gain access to protected dig sites. He partnered with black market artifact traffickers. He has falsified documentation to hide the age and origin of artifacts. He has operated ghost digs—"

"Ghost digs?" Harper asked.

Perez, still trying to gauge what Nick was doing, muttered the explanation, "Digging in areas that are kept secret with no official papers filed."

Salazar continued, "He has knowingly swapped artifacts with replicas, and bribed local guides to look the other way or assist with illegal digs. He has forged provenance papers and made deals with wealthy buyers who do not ask questions."

Nick didn't move his head, but it was obvious he'd moved all of his attention solely to Perez. "Your English is really good."

Perez frowned. "I worked hard to learn."

"It shows." Nick sat forward and turned his attention back to

Salazar, letting the growing tension fall. "I'm exhausted, man. We're all exhausted." He glanced at Gael and gave him a nod. "If we tell you where the artifact is, Smith and all of this nonsense and being followed is over, right? We can go home?"

Salazar gravely inclined his head. "This will all become my burden."

"We were on our way back to Cusco to get it." He gestured to Renee and Gael. "They put all the clothes and everything they purchased and used during the entire photo shoot in a storage unit."

Gael cleared his throat and expanded on the lie. "We thought, because the shoot was so important, at a later time we could create a showcase of the photos and clothing together. Stage a gallery show."

Perez pushed his plate away. As he stood he said, "It's probably best if we go with you to the storage unit."

Salazar seemed a little taken aback by his boldness, but stood as well.

Nick grinned, gave a happy declaration of "we're goin' home," then slapped his hand against the table; but he accidentally caught the side of his plate, which flung the leftover food onto his shirt. "Shit."

He pushed himself away from the table as everyone fumbled for napkins, levelling his gaze at Harper. "Can you give me that *dish towel* in your backpack?"

Her hands shook as she pretended to fumble through her bag, found the gun, took the safety off, and tried to figure out how she was going to hide the gun in the towel, while seamlessly handing it to Nick.

Thankfully, Renee understood what was going on and was quick to help. She bounded out of her chair, gave Gael a quick hug, then jumped up and down (ridiculously, but effectively pulling Perez and Salazar's attention to her ample, bouncing chest). "You have no idea how grateful we are." She clapped.

Nick stepped in front of Harper, and Gael must have seen the action because he did the same for Renee. Nick cocked the gun and aimed it at Perez. "Your English is really good," he reiterated.

Perez and Salazar both took out their guns and pointed them at Nick. But Nick was only paying attention to Perez, giving Salazar a perfect opening to shoot him.

Which was why Salazar didn't.

"Gutted," Nick leveled at Perez. "It's a simple word. No big deal really. Unless you just heard a story about a British archeologist who has no morals and is working with a mole. I have a feeling that all the conversations you've had with Smith have been rubbing off on you. Since you were so *gutted* that Scarface and Kyle didn't have any information to give you."

Harper watched wide-eyed as Salazar slowly aimed his gun at Perez.

"¿Qué estás haciendo?" *What are you doing?* Perez yelled. "He's talking crazy."

"Is he?" Salazar asked.

"¡Demonios!" Perez growled. "Me dijeron que eras estúpido." *I was told you were stupid.* He gave a disappointed *tsk* then quickly pointed his gun at Salazar and pulled the trigger, throwing Salazar backward.

Nick didn't wait for Perez to turn the gun on him, and shot him in the hand, causing him to drop the gun and scream out in pain.

"Check Salazar!" Nick yelled as he pushed the table out of his path to get to Perez who was screaming obscenities while trying to pick up his gun with his other hand. But Nick's fist connected with his jaw, sending him flying onto his back.

Harper was shaking even more as she knelt next to Salazar. Blood was pooling around his left shoulder, he looked stunned but was hissing in pain. Harper hoped that was a good thing. "We need to put pressure on your shoulder."

Nick yelled for Renee and Gael to get zip ties.

Salazar reached out with his right arm, gesturing for Harper to help him into a seated position. He wheezed through his teeth and demanded, "Find my gun."

Harper glanced at Nick, who'd heard the request and said, "It's okay."

She found the gun, but he was holding his arm out to her again. "In the chair," he directed. She put his gun on the table, then helped him into a chair with grunts and groans.

Renee and Gael helped Nick zip tie a half-conscious Perez on the floor. Legs together, hands behind his back.

"How did you know?" Salazar asked.

Nick said. "I didn't trust either of you. But when he used that word, I figured the best way to test my theory was to see what you did when you were between a rock and a hard place."

"I could have killed you," he said hoarsely.

"I had a hunch."

Harper stopped trying to help Salazar and slowly turned a wide-eyed gaze at Nick. "Did you say you allowed another man to level a gun at you because you had a *hunch*?"

Nick didn't answer.

"You have to go," Salazar said, pulling his phone out of his pocket. "I'm going to call for help." He dipped his head in Perez's direction. "If he works for Smith, I think someone else is coming to make sure you are all dead and to find out what you know about the artifact."

"Harper." Nick waved to the door, knowing she'd understand and hoped she would know it meant she needed to get everyone ready to go.

"Were you really going back to Cusco?" Salazar asked.

Nick gave him a devious smile and shook his head.

Salazar held up a hand. "Then do not tell me where you will go. But what are you going to do?"

"It looks like we need to go get the bargaining piece first, put it somewhere safe, then bring Smith to justice."

Salazar laughed, then sucked in a breath. "How are you going to do that?"

"Not sure yet."

The officer reached into his pocket and pulled out a card. "I'm going to have a lot of work to do. But I can still help." When Nick had a hold of the card, Salazar didn't let go but gave an apologetic shrug. "I think he might have been trying to run you off the road."

Nick gestured to his shoulder. "You okay?"

"Sí."

Nick studied him for a moment before giving a single nod then headed for the door. Salazar stopped him. "Wait, who are you?"

"What do you mean?"

"Were you in the military?"

"Something like that." Nick waved the card. "I'll be in touch."

They didn't need to be told twice to run to the car. Nick climbed behind the wheel and took off at a high speed.

Several long, tense moments passed as Nick twisted down the road. Harper was shaking enough for Nick to notice, so he reached for her hand. He brought it to his lips and brushed a kiss across her fingers before asking, "Everyone okay?"

"No," Renee answered honestly. "We're fine," Gael offered as Harper seethed, "You let someone point a gun at you because you had a *hunch?*"

He squeezed her hand and brushed another kiss against her fingers. "I had a plan."

She made a sound between a grunt, tisk and groan. Then she jerked her hand away and crossed her arms over her chest to keep from shaking. "If that guy really was the mole and he called someone, then they probably have the make and model of this car, huh?"

"And the license plate." Nick left off any sugarcoating. "How far are we from Ollantaytambo?"

It was Gael who checked and answered, "An hour."

"You have a plan?" she asked thinly.

"Get to Ollantaytambo. Hide the car. Take a nap. Go to Machu Picchu."

Hmph.

Nick reached out and dragged her hand back over to his lap. "You gotta trust me, Barrett."

Chapter Fifty-Two

They arrived in Ollantaytambo a little after five in the morning. Nick parked close to the hotel where he and Harper had stayed the last time they were here.

The mechanic, Rodrigo, was sitting outside the front door of the hotel with a hot beverage. He stood and greeted Nick, asking after the car and how his vacation was going.

Nick obviously refrained from telling him the truth. But he was happy to see Rodgrigo, because it crossed a few ideas off of the to-do list Nick had been making the past two hours. "Rodrigo, ¿Te puedo pedir un favor?" *Can I ask you for a favor?* He pulled out some of the money from his back pocket and revised, "A few favors?"

He wasn't asking for anything life-threatening. Nick simply wanted Rodrigo to hide the car somewhere out of sight for a few days. Could they have two rooms for a few hours (next to each other, just in case)? Also, they needed a ride to the train station and a wake-up call; the kind that, if needed, came with someone walking in and shaking them awake.

After Rodrigo checked everyone into a room, Nick walked him out to the car.

"Rodrigo, ¿El tren requiere identificación?" *Does the train require identification?*

"Sí."

Next came the biggest ask yet. He wasn't sure how it would go over, but he asked if there was anyone they could bribe to allow Nick onto the train with his friends. At least the story he told about his things being stolen had been the truth.

Rodrigo didn't think twice, but nodded and shared, "Claro. Tengo un primo que trabaja en la estación." *Sure. I have a cousin that works at the station.*

Nick handed over another grateful tip, then wearily made his way to his room. Harper was already in bed. He pulled off his stained t-shirt, shoes and pants, and crawled between the sheets, pulling Harper against him in the position they'd been working on perfecting. He buried his nose in her hair and took a deep breath. When he let it out, he asked, "You okay?"

"I don't know what I am."

"You mad at me?"

"Of course."

"Because I put my life in danger?"

"No," she defended, "because if you get yourself shot, I'll have to figure all this shit out alone. And your contacts are better than mine."

"But you have Sean's number now."

"Oh yeah." She wiggled against his body, trying to get closer. "Then by all means, proceed taking ridiculous risks, I'll be fine."

"Barrett–"

"You know what you're doing." She took a deep breath then blew all of it out of her lungs. "Nick, I'm not stupid. It's obvious you've had many, many years of training and been in difficult situations before. I don't like thinking of you in danger, and it's been easy to push the idea away, until tonight. Seeing it up close and personal ..." She ran her hand up his arm that was wrapped around her waist. "I had this idea that once we found Renee and Gael, everything else would go away. But it's gotten more complicated."

"I know."

"Nick, I'm exhausted and I know you are too. I've been trying to figure out how to settle down so I can get at least a few hours of sleep."

"How can I help you settle down?"

He heard the smile in her voice. "Stop rubbing up on me."

He chuckled. "I'm not the one rubbing up on you. Your ass is in my crotch."

She wiggled again, fully aware of his arousal. "I don't have any energy," she complained, before rolling over to face him. She reached between them and slid her hand into his boxers while she pressed her lips against his.

"You don't have the energy?" he breathed into her mouth.

"I can't even think about doing something like this right now," she returned between kisses as he rolled her shirt up toward her arms. "But it might help with all the pent-up anxiety from the past ... few ... million ... stressful years."

The heat built and rolled through them, fighting the exhaustion and new worries until everything disappeared. It was only Nick and Harper wrapped around each other, becoming one, reaching to the heights of the ancient mountains surrounding them until they both exploded into a million points of light to be added to the early morning sky.

The insistent pounding on the door was enough to bolt Nick up in bed. His sudden movement caused Harper's arm, which had been draped across his chest, to raise quickly; resulting with a slap to Nick's face as she rolled to the side of the bed with so much force, she woke up trying to stop herself from falling off the bed. "Shit!" It didn't work.

Harper stood, frowning at Nick, both of them rubbing body parts that didn't fare well from the abrupt wake-up call.

"Morning, Barrett," he muttered apologetically.

"Nicholas," she grumbled.

She collected her clothes and padded into the bathroom with her pack. Hair brushed, face and teeth cleaned, she left Nick's toothbrush out for him. Then she went to Gael and Renee's room to offer them the use of the items in her bag. It took everyone less than ten minutes to get ready.

Groggily, they made their way to the lobby where Rodrigo was waiting. "El tren parte en veinte minutos." *The train leaves in twenty minutes.*

It took them ten to get there.

Once they were aboard (Nick having no problems), they sat on the left side of the train in seats facing each other, with a large table between them. No one spoke until the train pulled away from the station, methodically building up courage to chug forward at a steady pace for the hour and forty-five minute trip.

Renee let out a breath that it seemed she'd been holding all night.

An attendant came by offering snacks and a breakfast service. The group tripped over each other asking for a 'café.'

Once all their food was delivered, Nick took out his phone. "I got an email from Sophie when we were getting in Rodrigo's car," he said. But after opening it, he frowned. "She's going to be unavailable for the next year."

"What?" Harper looked over his shoulder to read the message.

Nick shrugged. "She says she has some pressing matters lined up that will make her unavailable. And she urges us to contact Sonia Herrera, that director she told us about, if we find anything important."

Harper raised her chin. "Well, what's the plan today, Agent?"

"I think I should check on Salazar, and call Sonia Herrera and tell her what's going on. Then, we'll get to Aguas Calientes and find Carla and the necklace, and have lunch."

Salazar didn't answer; and he had to leave a message for Sonia Herrera.

"So those were easy calls," Renee said.

Harper took another sip of her coffee, frowning because it was finished – it had truly hit the spot. Nick noticed her reaction, stood and asked if anyone else wanted another cup. Gael and Renee gratefully groaned their requirement.

"That is one thoughtful and attentive man." Renee wiggled her eyebrows then moved so she could sit next to Harper as the train twisted along the tracks through the Sacred Valley. Spots of low clouds hugged mountain sides while the rising sun brushed sepia tones across the stunning landscapes.

The rushing Urubamba River kept pace with them out the left side windows and all the breathtaking vistas surrounding them were made visible by the panoramic windows of the train.

Nick returned with more snacks and coffees for everyone. He waved Renee to stay where she was when she shifted to move.

Harper hugged her cup to her chest as she watched the morning light play with the scenery. Renee hugged Harper's arm and let her head drop against her shoulder. "We were going to do this, take this train to Aguas Calientes. But not like this."

"Shhh," Harper whispered and lay her head on top of Renee's. She didn't want to talk right now. The mostly empty car was bright and clean, traditional Andean music played softly from the hidden speakers of the train car, and for at least the next hour, no one's life was in danger.

She was going to take the opportunity and steep herself as deeply as she could in the moment.

Though, she did tear her eyes from the passing scenery long enough to eye Nick. He was watching her and gave her a soft smile. That tempting smirk rising the left side of his mouth, the five o'clock shadow adding to his handsome allure. Even as he crossed his arms over his chest, her attention was brought to his strong hands; and the memory of how well he used them fluttered in her stomach.

"Okay?" He almost whispered the word that had become their shorthand for a multitude of sentiments.

She winked, toasting her coffee cup in his direction. "Okay."

Chapter Fifty-Three

Luis stared disbelieving at the two women that caught his eye. He sat at an outdoor table of a bar, drinking a beer, feeling pretty good about his life. He'd just pulled a great con and had his share of five thousand American dollars in his pocket. And no one got hurt. A job like that required a celebration.

He decided to pretend he was a tourist, sipping a cold one while watching tired families argue, and out of shape masses huff and puff as they passed. He actually thought he might do a quick snatch and grab on the way out of town; another small celebratory act.

Then, out of the corner of his eye, a few businesses up the small street from where he sat, he saw the blonde coming out of a hotel then joined by the brunette.

He didn't even realize he'd breathed out "puta madre" until the man at the next table grunted at the offense.

Luis slipped down in his chair. The last thing he ever thought he'd see in this small tourist trap of a village tucked in the middle of the jungle, were the women who attacked and kidnapped him at gunpoint.

He never told anyone about the incident. The only thing he ever mentioned to his contact that had hired him for the initial kidnapping, was that there were some women looking for the man. He wasn't about to go bragging that two women had *attacked* him. He frowned; okay, they didn't attack him, that made him sound weak. But he'd never admit it was a bruised ego that made him so angry and how easily he'd fallen for a pretty smile and big boobs. And maybe when he replayed the events in his mind, he exaggerated the level of the attack.

But that wasn't the point.

The point was that revenge was being held out to him on a silver platter.

The women were laughing and talking with some other woman, but he didn't care about her. He hurriedly took out his phone and scrolled to the contact who originally hired him.

"I found the women who were with Gabriel," he said without announcing himself.

"Gabriel?"

"Whatever the photographer's name was. Started with a *G*."

"Gael?"

"Sure. Look, I'm in Aguas Calientes? The Machu Picchu Pueblo place? They just walked past me. Are you still looking for them?"

"Why are you in Aguas Calientes?"

"Working," Luis hissed. "Are you still interested?"

Interested turned out to be an understatement. A very large sum of money was offered to him if he could detain the women for a few days.

"A few days?" Luis asked, unsure.

He listened to yelling and arguing for several minutes; something about road closures and difficult roads that would need to be traveled.

In English, a man yelled that he didn't care what it took, no one double-crossed him.

The evil rage made Luis second guess this move, but only for a moment; the amount of money outweighed his nerves.

Finally, his contact said, "There is a train from Aguas Calientes that goes to a stop called Hidroeléctrica Station."

"I know it," Luis muttered.

"From there take the bus to Santa Teresa, it is only twenty minutes away. Someone will meet you at the stop, take the women and give you the money."

"When ... should I get them by?"

More conversation in the background, this time muted, before he heard, "The last train to Hidroeléctrica Station is at eleven thirty this evening. If we leave now, we can be in Santa Teresa by the time the last bus arrives. Can you manage two little women for a few hours?"

"Sí, claro." Luis barely had the words out when the call was cut off. He interrupted the waiter to double-check when the last train to Hidroeléctrica Station left, and was told eleven thirty-seven p.m.

He fell back against his chair, maybe it wasn't worth it. To take them both, he'd have to make them cooperate for a long time. The image flashed of the woman with the dark hair pointing the gun at his crotch.

He would need to separate them from that damn gun.

His upper lip twitched as he watched the dark-haired woman, he hated her the most.

She turned her head suddenly, someone had caught her attention. Luis watched as a man came out of the shadows from the opposite direction, shining a grin toward the women.

Luis slipped down further in his seat as his snarl became audible. He hated that woman, but *that* man was worse.

Just then, the photographer, whose name started with a *G,* joined the group.

"¿Qué carajo?" Luis seethed. "Everyone is here?"

"Eh." The man who took offense the first time he swore held out his hands implying, *do you mind?*

He waved the man away, slipped a few bills onto the table, and took a long last swig of his beer, keeping his eyes glued to the little group.

Maybe this wasn't a job for him. Even if the money would tide him over for more than a year.

But then, the dark-haired woman reached out and touched the asshole's arm, looking at him in a way that was very difficult to misinterpret. They liked each other. And when the man brushed her hair back, Luis' face broke into a grin. Maybe he wasn't out of the game yet.

Luis could use those men to keep the women in line. Or at least the threat of them being in danger would keep them in line. He looked at the time, almost three in the afternoon.

He made a phone call to his partner who had gone back to his hotel room. "I've got another job. It's worth a lot." His eyes squinted. "And it might be fun."

When the four began to walk in the opposite direction, Luis followed at a distance. When they went to the mercado, he was grateful for the tourists who kept him concealed. And when he overheard them talking about taking the first train back tomorrow to meet someone named Sonia, he faded away and let the distance between them grow. Waiting until they went to a hotel, he called his partner again. They had some plans to make.

Chapter Fifty-Four

Gael groaned, unsure where he was. He forced his eyes open and squinted in confusion in the dark room. His face hurt; well, not necessarily his face, but his nose and head. He assessed his body for injuries and when he felt more or less like he was in one piece, he slowly pushed himself into a seated position.

Then everything came flooding back, not that there was much.

After dinner, he and Renee had gone to bed exhausted; when he held her it felt like everything was finally over. Then there was a knock on his door. He got up and opened it, and there was a man who ... slapped him? He frowned at the memory; it was a punch, but more open handed? He touched the bridge of his nose, it stung, immediately bringing tears to his eyes. The man looked familiar, but he couldn't be sure. He remembered stumbling before someone grabbed him and hurled him against the wall. Was that right?

"Renee?" he called, his voice hoarse. He felt like he was walking in quicksand with his head in a vice. Where was she? Gael slowly stood and called her again, hearing a muted grunt from the direction of the bathroom. He tripped into the room but when he turned on the overhead light, it wasn't Renee he found, but Nick laid out on the floor. Duct tape was around his mouth, his feet were zip-tied together, his arms bound behind his back, and he was wearing only underwear. There were two silver taser darts in his chest, the wires still connected to the gun they belonged to which was laying beside him.

"Nick!" Gael yelled, squatting next to him. After helping him into a seated position, he studied the tape. It went all the way around his head, twice. "It's gonna hurt." Nick gave a definitive nod.

Gael pulled up a section of the tape around Nick's cheek, ripped it apart there, and when he had a hold of it warned, "Here we go." Gritting his teeth, he ripped it off Nick's mouth. (They'd deal with the rest in a minute.)

"Fuck!" Nick yelled, then started coughing.

"You okay?"

Nick used his shoulder to wipe his mouth as he tried to get the coughing under control. But in between the rough wheezes, he said, "They took 'em."

Alarm flooded Gael's whole body as he confirmed, "Renee and Harper?"

Nick bobbed his head, clearing his throat to try and stop coughing.

Blood was forming where the tape had ripped off a few hairs and bits of skin. Gael stood to get him a washcloth, but when he saw his own face in the mirror – the bridge of his nose bruised, his forehead and part of his face caked with dried blood – he got two. After wetting them, he sat and held one in his hand so Nick could push his face against areas that probably needed cooling the most, while he fought the end of his cough; and Gael gently wiped the blood from his own face.

"I need to find something sharp," he said, referring to the ties on Nick's arms and legs. He did a quick search of the room, which was ridiculous because they didn't have anything. Everything they had, Harper kept in her backpack.

Gael tilted his head knowing it was a stupid question, but still asked, "Do you have the key to your room somewhere?"

"No." Nick finally cleared his throat. "But our room had wire hangers. See if you have one."

Gael found one and brought it back. Nick turned his back to him, instructing, "You just need to release the locking mechanism. Straighten the hanger head and try to use it to depress the bar under the loose end of the zip tie. If you can do that, then you'll be able to pull it back through the head."

It took Gael a few tries, and as he worked, Nick told his side of the story. "Renee came to the door, yelling; though I heard her before that. I was already out of bed. I told her and Harper to wait in our room and I took the gun. But the second I came in, the fucker tased me."

"Who?"

"Luis," Nick growled, "the asshole who kidnapped you."

That's who'd sucker punched Gael. "What the hell? How did he find us?"

Nick shook his head. "I have no idea."

Gael had the first ties loose enough that Nick was able to wiggle his hands out. He rubbed his wrists, accepted the hanger and began to work on the ties around his feet. "I dropped the gun. And then his partner brought Renee and Harper in here. Luis threatened up a storm and tased me again to make his point. Then the other guy fucking tied and taped me. My head was ringing pretty badly by then. The last thing I heard Luis saying was that if Renee and Harper didn't cooperate, his friend would kill us."

"You think there's someone outside the door? Standing watch?"

Nick shrugged, then gave a triumphant groan as he loosened the last zip tie. He straightened his legs and shook them out.

"Okay, now for these damn things." He glanced down at his chest at the raised red welts, under the fish hook barbs that connected to the taser.

"How can I help?"

"They're gonna rip the skin," Nick announced but didn't move. Gael knew he'd be just as reluctant. "Okay," Nick cleared his throat, "if you can stretch the skin around the area while I pull, it'll help."

Gael waited until Nick gestured to which one he wanted to remove first. "Okay, here we go." Gael pulled the skin tightly and Nick pulled it out growling, "Fuck." He sat back and took a breath before moving to the other side. Once the second one was removed, Nick tossed the whole taser into the tub.

He picked up the washcloth and rubbed the area, asking Gael, "You okay? When I came in you were passed out. Best I can figure it's been about an hour."

Gael gave a strangled laugh. "Nothing about this has been okay."

"No shit." Nick pushed himself into a standing position and when he wobbled, Gael reached out and helped him to the counter.

"Goddamnit," Nick hissed.

"You feel like someone tased you and continually made your muscles contract using electricity?" Gael asked sarcastically.

Nick gave a gruff laugh. "And my mouth hurts from where the tape ripped the skin away, but other than that ..."

"I just have a headache and my nose hurts," Gael said as he reached out a hand, just in case Nick needed it as he took several exploratory steps.

"I'm okay," Nick offered. They walked into the room and Nick glanced around. "What can we use as weapons?"

Gael hated the emptiness of the room suddenly. He shook his head and made his own assessment. "Chair and a fire extinguisher?"

"I think that's our best bet."

"I played baseball," Gael said, picking up the fire extinguisher and holding it over his shoulder.

"Ok, I'll look out; if someone's there, I'll open the door wide and you swing for the fences," Nick instructed.

After taking a breath, Nick peeked out the door. "There's no one there," he said quietly.

They both stepped into the hallway, Gael frowned. "Why all the threats if you're not gonna stick around?"

Nick gestured to his room across the hall, the door was cracked. When Nick was in position to open the door, Gale raised the fire extinguisher again.

Again, there was no one.

Gael quietly closed the door behind him and locked it while Nick went to Harper's side of the bed and found her backpack still there. He held it up. Gael was sure the confusion on his face matched Nick's.

He watched as Nick dumped the contents of the bag out, and when he held up the necklace, they both uttered curses.

"I don't think he knew we had the necklace," Gael said.

Nick nodded several times then shot a half smile at Gael. "Which means we have a huge bargaining chip."

Gael pursed his lips. "I suppose that's exactly what it means. So what do you think we should do?"

"Let's doctor our wounds while we call Sean and see if he can trace their watches. Then, we'll go from there." But he didn't seem happy about the plan, his frown was increasing.

"What?" Gael asked.

"Why leave us? Even if they think we're incapacitated, they know you're going to wake up at some point. And Luis was pissed."

"You think they're coming back?"

"Maybe." He hurried into his clothes. "Maybe we need to find somewhere else to patch ourselves up."

"Oh, well ..." Gael picked up the phone and called the front desk. In a very formal, curt manner, he explained they were going to get him a new room on the first floor within ten minutes. They could slip the key under the door of his room, and no one else needed information about the move, if they came asking.

He hung up and Nick gave an appreciative smile. "Or we do that."

"I've learned a few things watching and listening to models' agents over the past few years," he said tersely. "I'll watch for the new key to be slipped under the door across the hall, then we'll move."

Fifteen minutes later, they carefully made their way down the stairs to the new room on the first floor.

Chapter Fifty-Five

Harper frowned as she watched Luis use the palm of his hand to slick his hair, making sure the thin locks stayed in place. His other hand didn't falter from its job of holding the gun under the jacket draped over his arm, threateningly pointed at her and Renee from the seat that faced them in the last train out of Aguas Calientes. There was one other group in their train car, and Harper wondered if Luis had picked it because it was a family with three small children.

She and Renee wouldn't create a scene or try to do anything that might put the kids in danger. He must have known that. Of course, the other threat was working even better. If he didn't contact his partner every fifteen minutes, the agreed upon course of action was that his partner would kill Nick and Gael.

"All I can think about is the blood spilling from the cut on Gael's face," Renee whispered.

Harper squeezed her friend's hand, but she had no words of comfort. She'd had the same up close and personal view of Gael's lifeless body laying on the floor, and had to endure the look of twisted pain on Nick's face as Luis tased him to get them to cooperate. And they'd both screamed at Luis to stop, agreeing to comply.

When Luis stopped hurting Nick, he'd produced his own zip ties and duct tape with a victorious sneer, then led the women out of the hotel. Harper was thrown for a proverbial loop; why hadn't he ask for the necklace? Unless he had no idea they had it. What was this then? Personal retribution?

She should be happy he hadn't insisted on using her zip ties and duct tape. If he had, he would have found the necklace.

As they were marched out of the hotel room to the train station,

Harper didn't chance looking at Renee for fear Luis would somehow see she had a secret.

"How did you find us?" Renee spat the question.

Luis stirred the air with his hand. "Magic. I was celebrating with a cerveza and asking myself what could make this moment even better?" He narrowed his gaze. "And you two walked into view."

Harper squeezed Renee's hand to keep from asking any more questions or engaging with him. She turned her attention to the window. As it was dark outside, and inside the train was dimly lit, it was mostly her reflection she saw. But she knew there was an encroaching jungle keeping pace with the three-car train. Then, all too soon, they arrived at their destination.

Luis gestured for them to follow the family, using the kids to keep Renee and Harper in line. Harper hoped her hatred of him was palpable.

The Hidroeléctrica Station was more like a platform with a walkway that passed in front of closed up stalls. During the high tourist season, vendors probably offered fruits, drinks, and souvenirs. One stall was still open though, and as they passed Renee stopped.

"Go," Luis demanded.

"No." Renee picked up two pairs of gloves, two alpaca hats, two traditional felt hats, then turned to Luis and sneered. "Pay the woman."

"What? No. Put them back."

Renee handed one of each to Harper. The woman who was trying to make one last sale gave a price to Luis. He shook his head and demanded, "Put it back. Right now."

Harper repeated Renee's insistence. "Pay the woman."

"No."

Harper watched Renee's anger flare as she hissed at Luis, "If I'm being taken where I think I'm being taken, I will *not* be in the elements any more without the kind of coverage the locals have."

He called her a litany of names under his breath but pulled out money and tossed it at the vendor.

Luis gestured for them to continue. They trudged up a set of stairs to a dirt parking lot with a handful of cars, and two buses waiting for their last trip of the night.

He gestured to the bus they were to get on, and when they boarded, they saw the family from the train there as well. Harper gave a frustrated sigh. Again, Luis made them sit next to each other while he sat across the aisle, the gun still trained on them.

The bus driver called out the destination as he closed the door, then started up the tired beast and began to rock the passengers to their destination.

Harper refrained from touching her watch; though she squeezed her hand, flexing the muscles and tendons. The action allowed her to feel the weight of the watch against her wrist, and was calmed by it. "You have your watch?" she whispered to Renee.

Luis, hearing the whisper, leaned across the aisle and ordered her to be quiet. Harper matched his lean and met his vileness. "I was asking her if she was okay. Neither of us are by the way. But for some reason, asking and getting an answer — even if it's no — still feels good; like someone is in the middle of all the shit with you."

Renee gave an exaggerated "yes" in answer to Harper's real question before adding, "I'm okay. Just worried about Gael and Nick."

"What's to worry about?" Luis sneered. "My friend won't kill them if you behave."

Luis made a few phone calls then. Harper glanced at him several times, unable to really look away, trying to concentrate on what he was saying and who he was calling. And while she missed most of it, she hated the way the last phone call made him happy, his lewd grin growing.

"Hey Luis." Harper called his attention.

He jutted his chin at her and snarled as the bus rocked.

"When the time comes," she promised with everything in her, "I'm gonna kick the shit out of you."

He raised an eyebrow. "Not if you want your boyfriend alive."

She shrugged. "He'll be fine. He's been through worse." Dear god, she hoped her bravado was believable.

He cocked the gun in reply.

She looked away but kept her back straight as the bus finished its quick ride, pulling up to a stop in the main plaza square.

Knowing she was only about an hour away from Nick (by train and bus) was encouraging.

When they got off the bus, Renee's feet faltered as she grumbled, "Fuck."

Harper followed her gaze to where a man was sitting on the hood of a black, extended cab truck, chewing on his nails.

"Shit," Harper added, recognizing the man who had stopped the car near them that night in the abandoned gas station. The one Renee referred to as 'Scarface.' They both said the name at the same time.

He slid off the hood and inclined his head in a greeting as he opened the back door of the truck for them. Behind them Luis laughed as he gave the women their options, "Easy or hard way."

They climbed in, but sat close to each other in the center. Neither said a word after the door was slammed as they watched Scarface pull out an envelope and hand it to Luis. The man's body seemed to writhe with glee at the payment for his job well done.

There was no more pomp or circumstance. Scarface got in the truck, didn't tell anyone to put on seatbelts and pulled away from the plaza into the almost deserted midnight streets of the small town.

He drove exactly three blocks, pulled down a small alley of a street, angrily threw the truck into park then turned in his seat and scowling, yelled, "What the fuck, Renee?!"

🮲🮳 🮲🮳 🮲🮳 🮲🮳 🮲🮳

Renee pressed herself against her seat and blinked wildly.

"I thought you said you never talked to him." Harper said.

Renee shook her head, shocked into silence.

He turned around and gave a series of grunted yells as he pulled and punched the steering wheel. Finally, he stoppped. But hit it for what she hoped was the last time. Then took a deep breath, ran a hand through his dark curly hair before turning back around. "I'm a goddamned undercover agent. And you were supposed to have gotten away and *stayed* away."

"You speak English?" Renee sputtered.

"That's your take away?! I have been working for two years to get that asshole to trust me. Finally, we're getting somewhere and you buy a goddamn necklace." He scoffed and shook his head as if he were going insane.

Harper knew how he felt, especially when Renee threw an accusatory finger at him and yelled, "You beat up Gael!"

321

"*I* didn't do that." He rolled his eyes and muttered the clause. "Well, not all of it."

"You hurt him."

He leaned across the seat. "He would have been worse off if Raul had gotten to him first."

She shook her head. "Who's Raul?"

A slight smile tugged at the corner of his mouth. "Kyle."

"This is … oh my god. I can't breathe." She pushed her door open and toppled out.

"No." He frustratedly jumped out of the truck and grabbed her arm in an attempt to put her back in. She grunted, wrenching herself away from him, and bent over at her waist as she began to hyperventilate.

"Goddamnit!" he yelled.

Harper climbed across the back seat, got out and rubbed Renee's back, instructing, "Deep, deep breaths."

"Listen," he bent and tried to make eye contact with Harper, "we do *not* have time for this. Smith sent me to pick you up. We have to come up with a game plan and if I go back empty handed, everything is ruined. So as much as I want to let you go, I can't yet."

Renee stood and sucked in a breath. "He's not going to be happy to see me."

"No shit. How do you think you got away last time? I was on watch and saw you two tripping around, but I *LET* you go. I paid for it but I didn't lose my trustworthiness. And you were supposed to be gone by now."

"Well," Renee took a breath that forced her whole body to straighten, meeting his angry gaze, "I'm not gone yet because *we're* working with the CIA."

"Renee," Harper bit.

"What?" His frown deepened.

"And Harper was being followed by a mole from the National Peruvian Police Department who was giving information to Smith."

"What!?" he yelled at the same time Harper repeated Renee's name in warning and asked, "Do we need to show him all our cards?"

But Renee was possessed. She took a step toward Scarface, looked up defiantly at him and declared, "We also found the necklace."

"Jesus fucking Christ!" He took out a knife from his belt and opened it, compelling Harper and Renee to back away from him. But he wasn't concerned with them; instead, he punctured his back tire then turned toward them, motioning to the vehicle with the knife. "Get in the fucking truck and we'll talk."

Once they were all in, he continued to shake his head and mutter to himself at random intervals as he put the truck in drive and crept toward the main road. Renee wondered if he was doing it to give the tire time to leak out.

She decided to take a chance and asked, "Who are you working for?"

"Interpol," he mumbled.

"Isn't that in England?" Renee asked.

"No." He sighed and stated the organization's 'who we are' information. "We have a network of a hundred and ninety-six member countries that share information and coordinate efforts to track criminals, prevent terrorism, and address other transnational crimes." As he crawled along the street, the tire's flatness became an obvious issue. "Do you really have the necklace?"

"Not on us," Renee answered.

He gave a sadistic chuckle. "I should have made Luis come back with me. Smith could turn all his anger on him for taking you without the necklace." Two blocks later, he slowed the truck down to a crawl and pulled over to the side of the road. In a deadpan voice he said, "Oh no. We have a flat tire."

Renee aimed a wide-eyed glance in Harper's direction that seemed to ask; 'was this guy off his rocker or what?'

"Okay," Scarface said, "we all have parts we need to play in this little unfolding drama until I can get you to safety." He let his head fall back against his headrest and closed his eyes.

Renee caught Harper's gaze then pointed to her watch. *Should they tell him about how Nick was tracking them?*

Harper shrugged. "I have no idea what to do at this point."

Using the passenger seat headrest, Renee pulled herself forward. "What's your name?"

He let his head fall to the side and grinned. "I kinda like Scarface."

She held up her wrist. "So, not to add more problems to this big 'ol pile, but we're being tracked by a nonprofit security group."

"Of course you are." He reached his hand across the seat and introduced himself. "I'm Marcus."

"Renee," she said, "but you already know that. This is Harper."

"Okay," he took out his cell, "me and Kyle," he winked at Renee, "were sent to get you. He hates Luis, even though Luis is his contact ... Anway, I used that to offer to come pick you up so he didn't need to interact with that slimy asshole. Smith is three hours away. I need to call Kyle and let him know we have a flat. It'll buy us some time." He scrubbed his face. "That means the three of us will have about thirty minutes to come up with a plan. And I'm telling you, there are a lot of moving parts here." He frowned as he pulled up Kyle's number. "And you just threw seven or eight roadblocks in my way." He sighed and when Kyle answered, he angrily muttered about the flat tire.

At least Harper figured that was what he was saying, knowing he wasn't faking his anger.

Chapter Fifty-Six

"**D**amn, Nick. What the *hell* is going on down there?" Sean asked, when Nick answered his phone.

"I don't have time right now, but I'm glad you called. I need Harper and Renee's location."

"That's why I'm calling. *They* just called me."

"What?!"

"You are embroiled in one hell of a mess, my friend."

Nick squeezed the bridge of his nose. He felt like shit and his head was either trying to fold in on itself or explode. "No shit, now get to the part where you talked to Harper. Is she okay? Is Renee okay?" Gael's eyebrows shot up into his forehead when he heard the question, so Nick put the phone on speaker.

"They were taken by some guy named Luis, then passed off to Scarface? Renee said you'd know who that is?"

"Yeah." Gael's voice was barely a whisper.

"Apparently Scarface is working for Interpol."

Yup, Nick's head was going to explode. He sat down heavily on the edge of the bed. "Interpol?" He asked incredulously.

"Apparently under cover," Sean explained.

"Sean," Nick licked his lips and wished giving his head a slight shake would help ease the growing tension. "We have a criminal archeologist who's not above killing people. We have a stolen artifact. A police investigation with a mole in the Peruvian police department. We have, what I can only assume, is a petty criminal who keeps kidnapping people. We were supposed to meet with the director of the National Museum of Archaeology, Anthropology and History of Peru tomorrow. We had the shit kicked out of us, and now you're telling me that our girlfriends have been kidnapped but they're okay because they're with Interpol?!"

"Girlfriends?" Sean asked.

"Wilder." Nick barked.

"They are being taken to Cachora. You are supposed to bring the necklace and meet them there. And it was demanded that I relay to you, 'get them the hell out of the evil bastard's clutches.' But you also need to know that Smith is going to call you and probably try to trade their lives for the necklace. When that happens, you can't let *him* know, *you* know … all of this. He needs to think you're still in Aguas Calientes."

Nick looked at Gael. "How's your head?" he asked.

Sean answered, "What? Fine."

"Not you …"

Gael held out a shaking hand, a tangible display of how he was feeling. "I feel like I was thrown against a wall and everything hurts and my head is really fuzzy, and judging on how insane all of this is sounding, I keep thinking I might be stuck in the Matrix. So, not great?"

Nick nodded. "Okay good. I wanted to make sure I wasn't the only one that felt that way."

Sean interrupted, "So Scarface, aka the gentleman from Interpol, said they will probably be in Cachora by tomorrow night. Then they'll leave for the ruins first thing the following morning."

Nick frowned and asked Gael, "Did Scarface help beat you up?"

Gale thought for a moment and slowly shook his head. "Not really. He was always interrupted. But the few times he did get some punches in, I thought I was lucky because they weren't bad." Gael's eyes widened and Nick shrugged as they both said, "He was pulling his punches."

Somehow that made Nick feel slightly better. Not much, but it was something.

"What's the plan here, Nick?" Sean asked. "I don't know how to help you. Shaw's team is already gone. It would take me at least forty-eight hours to get someone installed."

Nick laughed as he muttered, "Wilder, didn't you know there are bars you can walk into here and find a mercenary, sitting around, waiting to help?"

"What the fuck are you talking about?"

Nick narrowed his gaze in thought; he was being facetious, but having made the claim he had an idea. And since Nick wasn't the only one working the problem, he wasn't shocked when he and Gael aimed smiles at each other and said, "I know who we can call."

"Great." Nick took a deep breath. "Okay Sean, look, I need a satellite phone, asap. I have no idea how you'll get it to me, but that's what I need. We're also gonna need tickets for the first train out of here to Ollantaytambo. I have no ID and had to bribe my way onto the last train, but if you could clear the way for me, that'd be great. We'll try to intercept Sonia ..." He was listing the half needs and random thoughts aloud to Gael who was nodding along, while

on his phone looking up information.

"First train out is at three twenty a.m., in two hours," Gael stated.

"How long is it to Cachora?" Nick asked Gael before continuing with Sean. "We're gonna need cash and we need you to keep watch on the women's movements. If Renee and Harper are separated even for a moment, we want to know."

"C'mon Robbins," Sean muttered, "give me a hard problem." But Nick heard him on the computer and the dial tone of another line.

Gael piped up, "It's four hours from Ollantaytambo, plus the train ride."

"I'll send you the ticket information for the train shortly, and the rest as I have it in place," Sean said. "And I have a few personal notes to pass along as well. According to Renee, Harper wanted me to tell you she is more worried about her magic bag than you."

Atta girl, Nick snarled a half prideful smile.

"And Renee also wanted me to tell you that kidnappers might not have to sleep tonight, but they are driving for hours, you shouldn't worry."

"Good to know," Nick said the same time Gael offered, "Oh, mi reina."

The messages did what they were supposed to; refocused Nick, settled him slightly, and pulled all his attention back on the larger picture.

Chapter Fifty-Seven

"Miss Young, I'm sure you hoped our paths would never cross again," Smith called from the chair he sat perched, as she and Harper were lead across the large sitting room of the house. The sign on the front of the place said it was a hostel, but there had been no trace of anyone else since they'd been prodded through the front rooms.

Renee tried not to shake, she tried not to show fear, and she tried not to reach for Harper's hand. Though it helped that as they were pushed into the room, they were forced to stand shoulder to shoulder.

The conversation they'd had with Marcus (Scarface) began to merge with the moment.

> *"I can't save you from Smith's anger. He's pissed, and he wants retribution. He had a schedule to try and stay under the radar of the Peruvian government. With you getting the necklace, trying to find you and then getting away; in his eyes, you have cost him a lot of time."*

Smith's eyes were dark as he turned his attention to Harper. "I'd ask you to introduce me to your friend, but I've already been made aware of Miss Barrett. It's good to see you looking well, after that tumble your car took off the side of a mountain."

> *"If he wants you hurt, I'm going to be called to do it. I don't know how to express this enough, I cannot blow my cover. The best I can do is pull my punches."*

"I do wish your man friend was here too. He has caused me more obstacles than I anticipated. And all because of a sad comedy of errors." Smith nodded, which was all the notification the women were given before fists found their stomachs.

Renee wheezed out Harper's name as they both fell to the ground. Kyle had been holding Harper.

"Kyle won't hold back and I can't always stop him when he's instructed to 'take care of things.' You have *to dissuade Smith as quickly as you can, turn his anger on someone else."*

Renee forced air to fill her lungs and spat out, "We have the Tears of the Moon."

Smith stood, frowning as he crossed the distance to Renee and gestured to Marcus, a silent instruction to pick her up.

"Where is it?" His voice had a deadly edge.

We need him to be single-minded in his anger and put it on to Luis and his mistake. Luis needs to be the punching bag and scapegoat for everything. We need to pour all Smith's extra anger and energy toward Luis.

"In the hotel room Luis kidnapped us from. Where he never checked any of our belongings," Renee said, winded.

Smith's face turned to stone. "What the fuck do you mean?"

"Luis took us. He never looked through our things," Harper added, she'd been coughing badly on the ground. Renee was relieved Harper could gather herself enough to sit back and speak. "The necklace is in my backpack. In my hotel room in Aguas Calientes. The room Luis abducted us from. It was sitting right next to the bed and he never even looked at it, let alone in it."

Smith moved to Kyle and growled, "¿Luis es tu contacto?" *Luis is your contact?*

Kyle met Smith's snarl with his own and after a staring contest, Kyle gave a slight curl of his upper lip in defeat. Smith demanded, "Call the asshole and find out where he is."

Kyle pulled out his phone as he walked toward the back of the room to have the conversation.

When he passed Renee, she thought *I'm never referring to you as Raul. You'll always be Kyle.*

> *The only good thing about Luis, is that he's a rat, and even over the phone they can sense danger. He'll crawl under the nearest rock and be difficult to find. And Kyle will be tasked to find him, and while he already hates him, this will be a good distraction for him too.*

"Jacob," Renee sighed, "I'm sorry, do you mind if I call you Jacob?"

He held out his hands, palms up; she assumed that was permission.

"Why didn't you ask me if I knew where the necklace was? If one of you had the decency to simply ask, 'hey, do you know where a silver necklace that looks like this is?', I would have been like; *bitch I bought over a hundred of them during this trip. Let's look through some pictures and find it.* But you had to be all cloak and dagger and punch and scream 'where are the Tears of the Moon?' We were looking for a mineral deposit, a bank vault, in the fucking sky ..."

Harper cleared her throat loudly as she finally stood, interrupting Renee's tirade.

Renee muttered her personal views once more. "I would like to pass along a little advice. Perhaps next time you kidnap someone for information, go ahead and be a little more forthcoming."

"I will take that into consideration," Smith condescended.

Kyle returned with a single shake of his head, Luis hadn't answered.

"I want him found," Smith instructed. Kyle sighed, the only emotion he'd shown that he wasn't happy. Then he left with his phone to go work through the bad guy phone tree.

> *The map on the necklace would make everything much easier for Smith. He's been looking for this treasure for ten years. When he found where the necklace was, he was fixated, with a fearful concentration. But his attempts have*

*been thwarted and his system is slowly being dismantled.
He's out of time; so now he's a dangerous animal, with no
scruples.*

"If we get you the necklace, will you let us go?" Harper asked
blatantly.

*"If you offer the necklace for your life, don't beat around the
bush or try to be cute or even cry. Put it on the table with as
little emotion as you can."*

"How rude of me, you've been traveling for hours. Are you hungry?
Please, sit down." He nodded to Marcus to go get food then walked to
the head of the table that sat on the right side of the room.

"I've been looking for a substantial treasure that was no more than a
myth for centuries, and now that it is within my grasp, the last obstacle
in my way are the Inca and their ingenuity." He tilted his head to the
side and pursed his lips. "Not to mention a few ridiculous American
tourists, but—" He shrugged. "Did you know the necklace was handed
down as a wedding gift for years? Brought out to only be worn for special
occasions. No one is able to recall where it came from. The family, having
lived in Ollantaytambo for generations, decided to create a museum.
They do demonstrations of how textiles were made and sell postcards
and magnets." He shook his head in wonder. "The map I found several
years ago had a crude drawing of the necklace. And then, a serendipitous
fortune dropped in my lap. Since I am well known, I was invited to the
opening of a little nothing and nowhere museum. The pamphlet that
was sent to me had photos of the collection that would be on display.
And there it was, the Tears of the Moon. A forgotten map, reduced to a
generational hand-me-down, a pretty piece of artwork and mine for the
taking."

Renee bit the side of her cheek, her hatred of this man made her want
to lash out and point out the obvious.

He smiled. "I suppose all great men have had obstacles to overcome.
You added another layer when you scooped up the necklace like it was
nothing and absconded with it."

Remember, when men who think they are all-powerful are cornered, they are at their most dangerous. Don't goad them or mock them, the only thing you can do is bide your time, put all the proper pieces in place until you can pull the trigger and completely destroy them.

Marcus returned with two plates of food. Rice, beans and meat.

"Oh good, please." Smith gestured for them to start eating. "While you eat, let's begin playing our little game, shall we? Trading your beautiful lives for a priceless artifact." He repeated his declaration in Spanish to Marcus and then instructed him to get a phone.

"This will help move our situation along." When a phone was handed over to him, he said in both languages, "Did you know that one's boyfriend works for the CIA?"

Marcus seemed as genuinely shocked as Harper looked. He took a step toward her, in what appeared a false angry sense of show, but Smith stopped him. "No no."

Renee watched Harper freeze with her fork in mid-air.

Smith tilted his head to the side, almost delighted. "Oh my dear, did you not know where he works? Granted, the two of you just met, but," he narrowed his gaze, "it would seem he's already made an impression on both of us." His mouth twisted into a snarl. "Nicholas Robbins contacted people who have put quite the roadblocks in my operations. He has brought a lot of unwanted attention to the work I've been doing so quietly for a very long time. You could argue, he's ripped out the beating heart of what I've built."

Renee tensed. Marcus had said to turn Smith's anger elsewhere. His fury at Luis was one thing; but letting him rage against Nick brought a new concern – what if he used Harper to take out his anger on Nick?

"I think I want Miss Barrett to call her agent and set up the trade."

He's not going to let you live. If he finds out about the necklace, he will let you live long enough to use your lives as an opportunity to lure Nick and Gael to a trap and kill you all at once. If you are going to have any chance, you need to warn them and hope they can stay one step ahead of Smith.

Harper hated how her hands shook and how long it took her to recall Nick's phone number.

He answered on the first ring.

"Nick?"

"Barrett?" The way he released her name over the phone was filled with the relief he must be feeling. Then he asked her one question, "Okay?" She knew he wanted her to be emboldened by the word, but it shook her off steady ground for a moment. She had to swallow hard before she was able to blandly force the word out. "Okay."

"Okay," he reiterated in that intimidating voice he'd tried to use on her twice now, the one that didn't work. But she was grateful for his use of it.

She unemotionally explained the current situation. "I'm here with Jacob Smith who would like to arrange a trade. Mine and Renee's lives for the necklace."

Smith snapped his fingers and Marcus took the phone, handing it over to him.

"At last, Agent Robbins. While it's nice speaking to you, I can't wait to put a face to the name," Smith said.

"When and where?" Nick answered.

Smith tisked several times. "Now Nicholas, is that any way to treat a new friend? I was told you have the necklace. That is of some great value to me. And I have been told that I have what is of great value to you." He beckoned to Marcus then put the phone on speaker.

Marcus squeezed Harper's arm, hauled her out of the chair and punched her in the stomach.

She fell forward and wheezed, but it was mostly shock as she had just been met with the realities of what 'pulling a punch' meant in relation to Kyle's brutality.

"That was Miss Barrett, if you are curious. Now, if you would please send me a photo of yourself and the necklace. If you have another phone in the room, as I'm sure Mr. Torres is with you, that would move all of this proof of goods right along."

It didn't take long for the photo to be taken and sent.

Smith nodded. "Very good. Now, it's late and we all have long days of travel ahead of us. It's almost four in the morning. Let us say we'll meet tonight, at eleven past eleven, for kicks. We will see you and the necklace at Casa de los Antiguos in Cachora."

He hung up and grinned at the women. "Have a good night ladies." He inclined his head to Marcus, who this time pulled Renee out of her chair.

"There are times when I'm left alone to work. If that happens, I can make everything look like a show, but you have to react as if you're truly being hurt."

Renee resisted and grunted when the fake punch came. Harper added her reaction, demanding, "Leave her alone." They played their parts, no celebratory grins slipping through, but that was because Smith had gone beyond unhinged and delusional. He was firmly planted in mentally disturbed. And it was safe to say they were both scared shitless.

After two fake punches, Marcus instructed them both, "Up."

He grabbed them each by their upper arm and dragged them through the house. Marcus came to a room, instructed, "Abrir la puerta." *Open the door.* He pushed them both inside and said "sleep," before slamming the door.

"Did you go with Smith on the other explorations? The ones where those men died?" Harper had asked Marcus.

Guilt flashed in his eyes. "No. I was working on earning his trust. Making it look like I was creating black market relationships and other grunt work. When you escaped, it forced that expedition back to the drop-off area, and that felt good. Lives were saved that day. But I need you both to understand this. I cannot save you. I can do very little, because I must stay on the inside. If he finds out my truth, he'll never trust anyone ever again and we'll never get anyone in the position I've earned. I will do what I can, it helps that you found a real government agent. When I can help you I will, and in return, I'm trusting you both with my life."

Chapter Fifty-Eight

After sleep that amounted to yet another catnap, Harper and Renee were unceremoniously ushered into the back of a van for the most monotonous ten-hour ride. The fear of what was to come was jarred out of their bones after a few hours of being in a vehicle that bounced up and down dirt roads. The road attempted to follow the river, but sometimes it rose up the sides of smaller mountains before dropping back into neighboring valleys. After the first three hours, Harper began to wonder if the road construction was somehow a wronged civil engineer's devious payback.

Then the rain started, the clouds lowered themselves to brush up against the mountainsides, bringing mud and poor visibility – which Kyle met by continuing to drive like an asshole.

Renee whispered, "We won't have to worry about being beaten to death or choosing the wrong booby trap; we're gonna die in a car crash."

Thankfully, when they came to a part of the road that was flooded from the waterfall rushing beside it, Smith growled, "slow down," which corrected the speed for the remainder of the ride.

The women took turns watching out the windows, trying to figure out where they were; or watching Smith, who spent most of his time in the front seat sleeping, with his jungle hat over his eyes. Even Marcus nodded off a few times. He sat in the center, his arms crossed over his chest, a scowl in place. He never looked at the women, never made eye contact in the mirror. But that was to be expected.

Another harrowing climb up was followed by coming back down in torturous zigzags. Once they finally reached the paved roads, Kyle stopped at the first gas station.

"Thank god, I need to use the restroom and throw up," Renee

announced.

"I just need to throw up," Harper added.

Marcus was in charge of them. He led them around by their upper arms, which gave the viewer the illusion that he was being rough; when in fact, he was barely holding on.

They both knew not to engage with him. After a supervised trip to the restroom, he walked them into the small convenience store and grunted as he gestured toward the snacks.

Renee instructed, "Try to get something that will stick to your ribs for a while and give you energy."

Marcus waited by the cashier. Finally, when Renee placed her snacks and water bottles on the stack of purchases, Harper added a pack of disinfectant wipes and babywipes. This time, she didn't hesitate to add two of the 5-hour Energy drinks. She eyed Marcus; his expression didn't change, but he winked at her.

Harper didn't quite understand why, but that stupid wink gave her a shot of courage she desperately needed. The variables and 'what ifs?' were lurking so heavily; granted the tedious drive kept them at bay, but that didn't mean they had gone away completely.

They were shown back to the van and presented with more twists and turns. More rise and fall. More rain. More clouds. More green landscape. Then the sun set on the lost day and, being on a paved road once again, the number of houses and small towns and villages they drove through began to grow.

The fear that had been packed away for the duration of the drive, slammed back into place when Renee reached for Harper's hand.

"What?" Harper asked.

"Cachora," Renee whispered.

Harper snuck a glance at her watch, a little after eight p.m. Three hours until Nick and Gael were supposed to be here. For all she knew, they were already there.

Please let them already be here.

Kyle stopped the van and Renee had difficulty keeping a snort of laughter at bay.

"What?" Harper asked.

"I swear we're parking in the same exact spot as last time." As they were escorted through the street washed in unforgiving rain, Renee pointed,

"Same dark street."

The door opened and they were led inside the hotel.

"Same hotel," she said to Harper. And when they were offered dinner, she added, "Same table."

Harper reached out and took Renee's hand, trying to comfort her friend, but the food was delivered quickly.

After several bites, Renee said, "You know what I've been thinking about?"

Harper wondered if she was making small talk because of the way her hand was shaking as she ate. "Tell me."

"Even deodorant commercials are stacked against women."

That was some good small talk. "How did you get to deodorant?"

"I stink. The van stinks. I wish we had deodorant, then the jingle for one of those commercials jumped in, 'confident, dry and secure, raise your hand if you're sure.' A woman has to be confident, secure and assertive. Otherwise she isn't deserving of the little things in life like deodorant."

Harper countered, "I think the point was to say, even if you aren't confident and secure or assertive, if you use their product you will somehow obtain those things."

"Maybe," Renee shrugged, "but they also have the underlying theme that you aren't a real woman unless you're confident, secure and assertive."

Harper tilted her head in consideration. "Either way the deodorant companies are out to get us?"

Renee laughed. "I think that's my thesis, but really, I think I just wish I had some deodorant."

Food finished, Marcus gave a grunt and gestured for them to stand. He showed them upstairs to a room, waited until they were inside, before unceremoniously slamming the door.

Harper didn't need to ask what they should do, because now they were in the middle of a waiting game. Renee insisted they both take showers. After, they sat on the bed waiting and listening.

But nothing happened.

The arranged time came and went.

There was no Nick.

No explosions.

No gunshots.

No splintering of doors.

As the minutes passed, with still no sound of intrusion, Harper's worry built and boiled over. Her worst fears came to fruition when Marcus opened their door and stood aside, allowing Smith entrance.

"Your boyfriends seem to have abandoned their mission to save you," he angrily spat. "We leave tomorrow, you will be tied up, separated, and you will be the first to test each trap until you perish." He crossed his arms over his chest and aimed a slight raised eyebrow in Marcus' direction.

Marcus turned an unreadable gaze at the women. Renee stepped in front of Harper and said, "No."

"Wait!" Harper yelled. "Can we call them? Can we at least try to call them?"

Smith shook his head. "I've had enough."

Marcus slammed his fist into Renee's stomach, and when she wheezed and fell to the floor, Harper reached for him to get him to stop, but he backhanded her.

Smith grinned. "I'll see you in the morning." He closed the door, leaving Marcus in the room with them.

He looked at Renee and with wide eyes whispered "no," an indication of the word he wanted her to scream. She did, then he pointed at Harper, who was holding her face and didn't have to be told to yell. "Fucker!"

Marcus set his mouth and gestured for them both to come closer. "He's gonna want bruises. Proof."

Harper gritted her teeth and began shaking her head. He held up his hand to calm her and pulled out restraints. Then he explained, "Sometimes, being left alone to think about what's coming might be enough, though."

Harper swallowed hard as Marcus brought the only two chairs in the room into the center and motioned for the women to sit.

They shakily followed the silent instructions and Marcus whispered for them to cuss him out as he worked on tying them to their chairs.

Finished, Marcus stood in front of them, clenching his jaw, as if he was trying to decide on something. Finally, he whispered, "Sorry." Before either Renee or Harper could ask what he was sorry for, he gave them each a soft, yet effective, punch around the bridge of their nose.

"Asshole!" Harper yelled.

He leaned between their chairs as they blinked back tears and harshly instructed, "Do *not* stop the tears. Let them fall."

He went to the door, opened it, and once again stood aside for Smith who had been in the hallway waiting. With his hands behind his back he walked around them, nodding in approval.

"Maybe there is a good reason your little boys aren't here. Maybe Luis found them and disposed of them. Maybe they finally did run off the side of a mountain in all this rain." He laughed as he snarled, "Maybe you aren't worth it."

As he left, he gave Marcus instructions in Spanish which he then repeated for the women. "I told him if they do show up, I want Agent Robbins killed on sight. But maybe we'll make the photographer take a few pretty pictures for us before we kill him." He winked at Renee. "It'd be a shame to waste all that talent right away."

They left and even though Marcus quietly closed the door behind him, it had a deafening sound in Harper's ears.

The exact thing Smith wanted done was realized. Harper imagined another snake, poisonous tree frogs, a fall down a mountainside that could break a bone, no way out of a trap they fell into. Luis finding Nick again with another fucking taser, his body in convulsions, the grunts of pain—

"Stop it," Renee hissed, watching her friend's face contort. "They're fine. This is on purpose."

Harper gave Renee a sad smile. "I'm trying."

"Are you only thinking of bad reasons they aren't here?"

"It would be safe to say I am spiraling," Harper admitted.

"Quick, top of your head. What's one *good* reason they aren't here yet?"

She stuttered, shaking her head, looking for words. "They got a helicopter and can't fly in the rain."

"Ohhh, I like that one." Renee tilted her head in thought. "Shithead Smith didn't realize there are like five towns nearby, all named Cachora."

Harper gave a soft snort of breath. "They stopped to buy us presents and are waiting for them to be properly wrapped."

"They stopped for a beer and are too inebriated to find us." Renee laughed.

"There was a group of baby alpacas crossing the road, they had to save them and help find their mother first."

Renee gave a soft snort then whispered, "Wilder is sending in a lot of firepower."

As that was the most plausible, and it radiated with hope, Harper clung to it by repeating it out loud, "Wilder's sending in a shit ton of firepower."

Chapter Fifty-Nine

Renee recognized the driver. He was the same man who had driven her and Gael; coincidently enough, it seemed he would be driving her again in the same weather and at the same time of day. The asshole remembered her too, going out of his way to step in front of her and spit at her feet as he passed.

She and Harper were pushed into the back seat of the van again, as Smith and the driver were in front, with Kyle and Marcus in the center.

The rain had stopped, but the low clouds dispersed a fine mist that accompanied them up the mountain. Renee looked beyond Harper, who had the perfect view of the vast landscape, the steep drop-off a few feet from the side of the road.

"We have seen some amazing views of Peru, huh?" Harper asked, as if she'd read her friend's mind.

Renee blew a half laugh out of her nose. "I suppose we have."

"I got to ride on the back of a motorcycle."

"You did? Did you feel badass?"

"No, I was freezing, fearing for my life and had to prop myself on the fender."

"At least you'll get to hike some of the Inca trail now."

"Oh good." She held up her hats. "And properly attired this time. Did I tell you when I rode on the bike I wasn't wearing a bra?"

"Is that integral to the story?"

"Not really. I had a nice shirt and a very heavy sweater on. I liked that sweater."

"You got to see Machu Picchu." Renee began to build on the list.

"Lots of tourists," Harper reviewed. "The train was fun, though. And I've had some great Peruvian food."

"Have you had cuy yet?"

Harper frowned. "I don't think so. What is it?"

"Guinea pig."

"The pet?"

"Well, yeah, but not here. It's kind of a celebratory food, but guinea pigs were raised to be eaten in the Andes for centuries until the Europeans arrived."

"I don't think I've had cuy." Harper shrugged.

After a few minutes, Harper leaned her head toward Renee and whispered, "At least I got to experience some *exuberance*."

Renee took a deep breath and sighed. "Thank god for small miracles."

"Not *so* small," Harper muttered, and Renee let an unexpected laugh burst forth.

Smith tilted his head to the side, his one-eyed warning and scowl enough to stop the conversation as they let the gurgling of fearful laughter die out.

They arrived at the campground that doubled as the starting place for the hike Renee had been on once already. Smith nodded to Marcus before he climbed out of the van.

Left alone, just the three of them, Marcus turned in his seat and quietly ordered, "Hands." They held their hands over the back of his seat. After he finished tying her hands, Renee frowned but easily twisted out of the bindings.

"Damnit," he seethed, "don't do that. Keep your hands pulled apart. Be a damsel in distress."

"I *am* a damsel in distress," she shot.

He pulled Harper's hands apart, a silent invitation for her to keep them where they were. She did, but in a lilting southern voice said, "Why I do declare, I am tied up at my wits' end."

Renee snorted then told Marcus, "This is what happens when the fear grows."

He rolled his eyes. "Stay here," he demanded, then got out of the van to join Smith – flanked by Kyle and the driver – talking to the men who were in charge of pack horses. Five men this time.

The campground and beginning of the trail hadn't changed since the last time Renee was forced to visit. To the right of the van were the A-frame cabins. Next to those, the convenience store was still closed.

So the three trailers — that had brought five horses — weren't blocking anyone from shopping. A covered picnic area was beside the store, along with two storage sheds. And to their left was a small building with a wooden sign in front that said Toilet.

Renee scanned the scene in front of her and frowned. "Funny, that man looks like ..." She squinted and gave an internal scream of *HOLY SHIT!* before she grabbed Harper's arm and excitedly whispered, "That's Alejandro."

Harper grabbed Renee's arm back. "And is that Salazar?"

Renee watched the man, whose arm was in a sling, walk up to Alejandro; she'd just shared a midnight dinner with him and watched him get shot.

They both whispered, "Holy shit."

"What do we do?" Renee asked. "Do you think we should let the ropes go yet?"

"Not yet, not until things start happening."

They both glanced around the area that had been carved out of the mountain. With only a handful of buildings and a few places to park, Renee didn't want to point out that this was an awful place to stage a rescue. Where were they all supposed to go? She supposed the buildings offered a little cover. But there was a sheer drop down the side of the mountain if anyone got too close.

Marcus returned to get them. Renee tripped over her feet getting out, causing Marcus to catch her. Frowning down into her face, she widened her eyes, hoping to convey the question; *did he know what was coming?* Though she realized her look could also mean she was scared and worried, or had to go to the restroom.

"Bathroom!" she yelled. "I need to go to the bathroom before we go."

The corner of Marcus' mouth gave a slight twitch and he turned toward Smith with a questioning look. Smith waved that it was okay if Marcus took them.

"No soy niñera." *I'm not a babysitter*, he muttered as he passed Kyle, who sniggered. "Hoy eres tú." *Today you are.*

The small bathroom was opposite the convenience store, against the mountain side. It had two single-room toilets available, but still Harper followed Renee into one; if Marcus cared, he didn't say anything.

Harper locked the door, then turned to Renee to ask in a rushed whisper, "What are you doing?"

"I don't know, buying time? I felt like we should do *something*. Once we start on the trail, there isn't room for anything and it's a sheer drop-off one side..."

"I'm assuming there is a plan. Why else would ..." Harper gestured with her head twice rather than saying their names, "be here?"

"You don't think we should stall?"

"Renee, I have no idea what we should do." Harper took off her wrist bindings and handed them to Renee. "Hold these, I really do need to go."

Renee turned her back to give Harper privacy as she said, "Then we'll just keep our eyes open, mouths closed and wait for the signal."

"Signal?" Harper asked.

Renee grinned as she explained, "There's always a signal."

Chapter Sixty

Renee was disappointed there was no signal.

As Marcus led them back from the restroom, the five horses were lined up, ready to go, with Alejandro holding the lead of the first horse.

The driver was talking with the four other horse handlers, and Salazar was handing out breakfast empanadas to everyone.

Kyle and Smith stood in the rear, adjusting their packs.

And Renee and Harper were led to where three packs were waiting, packs they'd be forced to carry.

The horses neighed nervously as Smith loudly explained that Renee would stand in front of Marcus and Harper in front of Kyle.

Renee held out her hands. "How would you like us to get the packs on?"

Another nervous neigh from one of the horses before it broke rank and headed back toward the group waiting to get on the trail.

"What the hell is going on?" Smith yelled, repeating his question in Spanish as a second horse moved out of line, following the lead; both horses coming back to the gathered group.

"Lo siento, señor," Alejandro said, "ellos estan nerviosos." *They're nervous.*

"I don't give a shit if they're nervous. Let's go. ¡Vámonos!"

Salazar, having given everyone an empanada, moved next to the driver, standing slightly in the man's blind spot; not something you'd necessarily notice unless you knew who Salazar was. Renee also noticed that Salazar had a pack on his back, but it wasn't buckled around his waist.

The horses continued walking away, heading to the grass. Alejandro jogged after them, calling out his apologies as he went.

"Jesus Christ!" spat Smith. "I'll go first, shall I? You can catch up?"

He'd taken a few steps when a man stepped from behind the van that was parked on the opposite side of the road from the horse trailers and said, "You havin' horse troubles?"

Smith turned slowly, snarling, his gun at the ready.

Gael was wearing a bulletproof vest as he held out his hands, one empty, one with a necklace draped over his fingers. "Better late than never, right?"

"And here we were worried you had *died*." Smith bit the word.

Renee gasped when she saw Gael's bruised face. She called his name, but Marcus grabbed her around the shoulders, pulled out his gun and pressed it hard to her temple to get her attention. Pressing his mouth against her ear, he whispered, "Almost there. Stay calm."

She saw Kyle grab Harper in reaction.

"There's the necklace." Gael tossed it on the ground and gestured in Harper and Renee's direction. "Let them go."

Smith shook his head, keeping his gun trained on Gael as he walked over to where the necklace landed. He picked it up and studied it for several seconds; it was the real thing.

Finally! Smith thought to himself as he gingerly folded the necklace in on itself to form the map. The detail was small, laborious work had gone into it. The map was a mixture of Latin and Quechua and symbols.

He closed his hand around the necklace. This was it. It was all within his reach now. He was merely a few days away. He'd sent fifteen men ahead, to the site they would use as a field camp. They were waiting for him. With the map, he could excavate just enough. He still had enough contacts in place to falsify the proper paperwork and get out of the country. He could cover his tracks, silence a few dozen men, but that was fair in the grand scheme of things. When billions of dollars were at stake. Then he could come back once things cooled off and get more out. He snarled in glee, he was going to steal an entire ancient Peruvian treasure.

No ridiculous women, no photographer, no fucking CIA agent was going to stand in his way. They were all going to litter the side of the road.

Smith leveled the gun at Gael. "Where's Nicholas Robbins?"

Two of the remaining horses, with no lead to follow, nervously trotted between Smith and Gael.

"Bloody hell!" Smith screamed, aiming his gun in the air and shooting off a round. That only frightened the horses more, as they neighed and pressed against Smith, trying to get away.

He shot again and that prodded the horses out of his way, but it also sent the other hired men running down the path, not interested in what was happening.

He focused once more on the area where Gael had been, but the man was gone. "Goddamnit!" He leveled the gun in the space where Gael once was and shot.

❊❊❊❊❊

Harper glanced down at the hand that was holding her; why Kyle had thought to cover her mouth with his hand, she wasn't sure. But when attention slipped to one of the horses brushing past them, pressing in on them, he had to use his hand with the gun to push against the beast's side to get it to move.

When the hand over her mouth slipped down, Harper took the opportunity to bite down on the soft fleshy part between his thumb and pointer finger, *hard*. He was so shocked, when he swung the gun back toward her head, she had time to block him with a fist against his wrist. Astonished, he dropped the gun and she bit down harder, making him roar in pain. His fist came swinging her way, but she released his hand and ducked, causing him to swing at air. Then, she jammed her hand into his windpipe. He dropped, grasping his neck as she spit and wiped at her mouth, stepping away from him. When another gunshot erupted, her eyes wildly scanned the area. Renee was being held by Marcus, and even though Harper knew Marcus was 'on their side,' her anger at him for sucker punching them was still fresh; she kicked him from behind, between the legs. He turned a frown to her, gripping his crotch as he dropped to his knees. Though Harper could have sworn, through the twisted look of pain on his face, he gave her a nod of approval.

She tugged Renee's hand and they headed away from the fray, toward the van. But a lithe man in a tactical vest, holding a firearm close to his body, stepped out from behind one of the horse trailers and said, "Not that way, ladies. Behind the building." He walked backward, keeping himself as a shield.

Behind the building was Gael, along with Alejandro and Salazar — also in bulletproof vests. All three stood over the incapacitated driver. Renee gave a shocked squeal and threw herself into Gael's arms. "Are you okay? Oh my god, when I saw you on the ground at the hotel—" She pulled away and gripped his face in her hands, looking like she meant to study his wounds, but couldn't stop her lips from tasting him, reassuring herself he was real.

"Where's Nick?" Harper asked the man who must be on their side. Instead of answering, he told her to stay put.

Gael gently pulled away from Renee and bent to a duffle bag on the ground, where he pulled out two more tactical vests. "Put 'em on."

"Nicholas Robbins. I know you're here. This whole little ridiculous play has CIA stink all over it!" Smith screamed.

"Now that's just mean," Nick yelled back.

Harper thought her legs would give way simply from hearing his voice; it sounded like it was coming from behind the restroom.

Harper quietly asked Gael, "Is there another gun?"

He shook his head.

"Damnit." She should have grabbed Kyle's.

"Hey, Smith. Wanna put your gun down and give up peacefully?" Nick's voice echoed.

"Counter offer," Smith replied, "how would you like to put your gun down? I promise we can talk politely with all civility."

"No thanks."

"Then it would seem we're at an impasse," Smith snarled.

"Are you sure about that?"

There was a large explosion then. Harper fell to the ground with Renee, both of them covering their ears, but Gael tugged on them. "C'mon. We have to move."

They were up, just as Alejandro gestured to the driver and explained to Gael, "He threw them over."

"Who threw what?" Renee asked, then hugged Alejandro. "It's so good to see you again."

He looked shocked that she was using this time to hug him, but smiled down at her. "You too. The driver, he threw the keys to the van away. Over the side of the mountain."

"We take the truck?" Gael said.

Alejandro nodded.

Gael frowned. "It would be better without the trailer, though."

Alejandro wiggled his eyebrows. "I unhooked it already, in case …"

"You're a legend, Alejandro."

"What's happening?" Harper asked.

"The first plan was to get the keys to the van and escape that way, but it seems that asshole …" Gael pointed to where Salazar had the now handcuffed driver sitting on the ground, "he tossed the keys."

"The back-up plan is a truck," Alejandro supplied.

"It might be difficult to use as a getaway because of the shooting going on out there."

"It will be fun." Alejandro jogged the few feet to Salazar to explain the situation.

"When did you get here?" Renee asked.

"Last night." Gael tugged on her vest to make sure it was on the right way.

"Who's the other guy?" Harper asked.

"A guy we hired." He tugged on Harper's vest next.

"A guy you hired?" Harper asked as Renee squeezed his arm and said, "Please tell me you found him in a bar."

He pressed his lips together, but gave an affirmative nod.

Another explosion.

"Okay," Gael said and moved to the left side of the building. "We wait for Alejandro and Salazar to get the truck and pull up behind the van; then we run."

They were stacked up looking around the corner, Gael, Renee, and Harper, watching and waiting for the truck; which is why Harper never heard Kyle approach.

He grabbed her around the shoulders this time, incapacitating her arms and pressing the barrel of his gun against her temple again.

"Tranquila." *Stay calm.* He forced Harper backwards, quickly. Renee yelled, "no!" and took a step, but Gael quickly grabbed her and stopped her progress. Harper yelled as she struggled, watching Kyle turn the gun on Renee, Gael's eyes wide as he pulled Renee around the corner just as the shot went off.

"No!" Harper screamed, not sure if Renee had been hit or not.

Harper tried to fight, but the angry breath against her ear and the replaced barrel of the gun against her temple suggested she not piss him off any more than she already had.

He pulled her into the road and yelled, "Tengo a tu mujer!" *I have your woman.*

Smith's laugh echoed off the cars and mountainside. "All I have to do is give him the order."

"Okay!" Nick yelled and Harper wanted to yell back for him to stay where he was because they needed someone to have the upper hand (or, the ability to *eventually* have the upper hand).

But she was shaking and could feel the anger seeping out of Kyle. He pushed the gun harder against her temple, and as her head tilted as far as she could to the side, the pressure followed.

Then *he* appeared, in the middle of the road, in the middle of the cars; and it was Smith who was ducking for cover this time as Kyle used Harper as his own shield. Nick looked directly at her, his face void of any emotion, but she was scrutinizing him so thoroughly, she thought she saw his jaw clench in anger.

"Put the gun down, Nicholas," Smith called.

"How about we both have a civilized, face-to-face conversation at least." Nick did *not* put his gun down.

"Oh, Agent Robbins. You are merely trying to save your girlfriend. But you have no idea what you've stumbled upon. You have no idea what's going on here. This is all much, *much* bigger than you could ever imagine."

"That sounds like a great place to start a conversation then. You could lay out what problems I'm up against, I could tell you what my favorite Peruvian dish has been and we can share our weekend plans ..."

Harper scrunched her face. Was he really playing his smartass card right now? When she had a gun to her head?

The sound of a helicopter erupted through the air, as did the sound of another gunshot; resulting in a jerk of Kyle behind her and the loosening of the gun against her head. Then his whole body began to crumble. Harper turned her head as far as she could and found a shocked look on his face. He'd been shot, and it was muscle memory that had taken over, his arm wrapped around her shoulders, dragging her down with his toppling body.

"Nick!" she yelled. But it was the new mercenary who slid to her side and pulled her out of Kyle's lifeless grip. While righting themselves, they both caught the movement of Smith running from the cover of one of the trucks, toward one of the sheds beside the closed store.

Her rescuer bellowed, "Robbins, he's on the move!"

Nick must have seen it too, because he followed, steadily, his gun leveled at any threats in front of him.

The mercenary helped her behind one of the nearby trucks and told her to stay hidden until he was back with their ride.

She caught sight of Marcus then, steadily following the direction Nick and Smith had gone.

Even though everything inside her screamed for her to stay put, concern for Nick trumped those emotions and compelled her to follow in the direction he'd gone.

✺✺✺✺✺

Nick tackled Smith, wrenching his gun away, but in the struggle, Smith landed a blow. Nick used all his brute force to slam his fist into Smith's kidneys, making the man grunt in pain. Nick wanted to keep their grappling on the ground, in the hopes it would be easier trying to empty Smith's pockets. And when he felt the necklace, he freed it, then rolled Smith away. When Nick stood, he made sure he had Smith's attention on him, rather than on the ground or what he might have lost. Smith struggled to his feet, giving Nick time to get into a crouching position; a slight smile pulled at his lips, he was going to enjoy kicking the shit out of this asshole.

So he was shocked when he was tackled from behind.

Nick scrambled to throw his attacker off and get to his feet, but by the time he was able to get his legs under him to get rid of his assailant, Smith had climbed into the helicopter. Nick turned all his anger on Marcus who held up his hands, beckoning Nick to fight him.

Nick roared, head down as he slammed into Marcus' chest. Marcus immediately put him in a headlock and wrestled him so their backs were to the helicopter.

"Marcus?" Nick yelled over the noise.

"I need to be on that helicopter," was his confirmation that he was indeed Marcus. He threw Nick off and they took predatory steps around each other. Nick growled, "I saw a bruise on her face." It was a question; *did Marcus do that?*

One shrug of admittance and Nick flew at him again, got several punches in before it was his turn to incapacitate Marcus by holding him in a front headlock. Marcus said, "There was a number she used to contact you. Will that be good for a while?"

"Yeah," Nick said, then added, "and it's already encrypted." Then he let Marcus slip out of the hold.

Nick dropped his hand slightly, the only hint he gave Marcus he'd let him get the upper hand and escape.

He took the punch Marcus threw on his chin, stumbling back far enough to give him time to get to the helicopter. Nick bellowed in frustration as he got to his feet and the helicopter took off. He took out his gun, poorly aimed it and shot wide several times, missing.

"Nick!" Harper came screaming around the corner the same moment Smith was handed a gun from the pilot, who turned the helicopter slightly, allowing Smith to reach his hand out the small window of the passenger side and follow Harper with the barrel of the gun.

Nick's scream was real this time as he hurried to place his body between the threat and Harper. It was enough of a hindrance that he saw Smith's frustrated snarl, and the muted sound of the gunshot echoed inside his head at the same moment he was hit and forced in a stumble backward. Another ricocheted sound of a shot filled the air and cracked against wood. Nick could have sworn he heard Smith's angry howl as the helicopter sped away.

Chapter Sixty-One

"Nick!" Harper yelled.

When he jumped in front of her and the shot caught him, his body slammed against her, forcing them onto the ground. She scrambled from under him, yelling his name again. "Nick!"

He lay on his back, eyes closed. Blood formed around the bicep area of his shirt. When he took a deep inhale, she yelled his name again, a mixture of relief and anger at him putting himself in harm's way. "Nick!"

"Barrett, I'm okay," he mumbled, blinking his eyes open.

"You're bleeding!" she accused, kneeling over him to assess the situation.

He reached out his right hand and touched the side of her face. She pressed the hand into her cheek, cradling it, her eyes glassy. "You're bleeding," she gently repeated.

He sat up with a grunt, took off the vest and unbuttoned his long sleeve shirt. Harper helped him take it off, and he used the shirt to mop up some of the blood as he studied his arm. "The bullet just grazed me," he tried to reassure.

"Just grazed you?"

"I brought your magic bag, you can fix it."

"You know Nicholas, patching you up isn't my idea of a good time." She wanted the remark to be biting, but it came out wobbly. "Jesus, Nick..."

He slipped his hand around the back of her neck and pulled her to him so he could swallow her concerns and anger with a kiss.

"Robbins?" someone yelled.

Nick pulled away with a frustrated sigh, turned his head and loudly called, "Clear."

"Are you really okay?" Harper asked.

He touched the bruise on her cheek. "I've been more worried about you."

Everyone arrived then, Salazar, Alejandro, Gael, Renee and the man in the tactical vest.

"You have to go," Salazar said.

Harper helped Nick up. Not that he needed it, but she needed to help him. He rolled his shirt and handed it to her. "Can you wrap this around my arm?"

"Smith got away," Salazar declared, frustrated.

"The necklace, it should be over there." Nick pointed.

Renee went to retrieve it, calling out when she found it.

"You *have* to go," Salazar insisted again.

"Go?" Harper asked.

"When we're back in Cochora, Salazar will call this in. We can't be associated with this in any way," Nick explained.

Nick held out his hand to Salazar. "Thanks for the help."

"I'll be calling you," was the man's reply. Then he stopped Renee with a gentle touch on her arm. He looked guilty, and it took him a few attempts to say, "I am very sorry. It wasn't my idea to ruin all your makeup."

"What?" Renee frowned.

"We were looking for you and the necklace, we went through your room. I didn't know how much damage Perez was doing."

"Okay ..." Renee's frown deepened.

Harper patted Renee's arm. "I'll tell you in the car."

"Robbins. Thanks for a good time." The other man nodded to Nick. "I'll stay and help."

"I'll drive." Alejandro waved to the dwindling group that would head down the mountain because they were 'never there.'

In the truck, Harper sat in the back to help Nick with his most recent wound. And once cleaned, she saw it really wasn't that bad. She held up the duct tape. "For old time's sake?"

A grunt was his reply.

Renee and Gael sat in the front next to Alejandro. "What about Smith?" Renee asked. "You got the necklace but he got away."

Nick shrugged. "He'll be angry. But Marcus is still watching him.

And the mole that Salazar has in custody has been sharing all sorts of information."

Renee ran her hands through her hair as she blew out a breath. "What do we do now? Are we still in danger?"

Gael hugged her to his side. "We're fine. Now that Salazar is no longer being obstructed, he can work a lot more efficiently. We're going to give the necklace to Sonia Herrera, the director of the museum, then get some sleep and heal."

"Why didn't you leave the necklace with Salazar?" Harper asked.

Nick shrugged. "At this point, I'd feel a lot better if we handle this. I trust *us* to get the necklace to the rightful owner. The country of Peru."

"How did you get away from Luis?" Harper asked. "He told us his partner was watching you and if we did anything, if he wasn't able to check in, his partner would kill you."

"I think he was lying," Nick replied. "His partner was gone. Never showed up back at the hotel."

Harper opened her mouth then shook her head. "I was going to ask if we needed to worry about Luis or his partner, but Marcus said rats like Luis know when to hide. And he knew people were pissed at him."

"Exactly, we don't need to worry about Luis or his partner. And we don't need to worry about Smith."

"Really?" Harper asked as Smith's words echoed around her. *You have no idea what you've stumbled upon. This is all much, much bigger than you could ever imagine.*

Nick squeezed her thigh. "Really."

"Nick," Renee asked, "who was that other man?"

"No one. He was never there."

She turned fully in her seat and aimed a bright smile at him. "Did you go to a bar and hire a mercenary?"

He didn't answer her, but gave a very slight raise of his left eyebrow.

Her grin lit up the entire cab of the truck. "You went to a bar and hired a mercenary." She turned back around and, mostly to herself, muttered, "Good to know it would have worked."

Chapter Sixty-Two

As exhausted, traumatized, and beat up as the group was, they decided to drive the four hours to Cusco anyway. The promise of being in a place they could stay for several days in a row and recover sounded like a dream.

After thanking Alejandro and promising to contact him the next time they wanted to go sightseeing, when lives weren't in danger, they climbed into the new rental car. The nicest one yet; one Sean had obtained for Nick and Gael to get from Ollantaytambo to Cachora.

Nick called Sean to relay the events of the morning.

Gael called the hotel and had them moved into two large suites, his reasoning that they all needed a little space. The long conversation was punctuated with his occasional declaration of "gracias." When he was finally off, he said, "The receptionist told me she felt guilty for allowing the room to be ransacked. She washed all the clothing, folded it and organized everything for you to take account of what might be missing."

When they shuffled into the hotel, the receptionist's eyes bulged.

As a group, their clothes were tattered and muddy, everyone was sporting a visible bruise or cut. Their hair was disheveled and they were wearing fatigue like a cloak.

"Should I get a doctor?" Her question came out in a shocked whisper.

"Maybe tomorrow," Gael said. "I think right now we just want to shower and sleep."

"Do you want your passports?" she addressed Harper, but retrieved and handed them over anyway, unable to stop blatantly starring. She shook her head in wonder as she finally cleared her throat enough to hand over directions and keys to the new rooms.

First they went to the old room, and since the clothes were

already folded, Renee and Harper made quick work of gathering their belongings.

Harper handed one of her graphic t-shirts to Gael, then aimed a smile at Nick before glancing toward her backpack he had slung over his shoulder. It was all the instruction Nick needed to pull out a pair of clean underwear from the dwindling six-pack.

In their own room, Nick dragged Harper into the bathroom, turned on the hot water, quietly undressed her himself, then stepped into the elongated shower and held out his hand for her to join him under the spray of water. She slipped into his waiting arms and began to shake. Nick tightened his grip, resting his cheek on top of her head and allowed her to grieve; expelling the close calls, the horrors, the fears and the danger of the past few days. However they needed to leave her body, he seemed happy to hold her while she worked through it all.

"When Luis kept using that taser ... I would have done anything to make him stop," she whispered, looking up into his eyes, her tears flowing freely. "I would have done anything to get him to stop hurting you."

"I know." His soft understanding echoed around the shower.

"Nick," she swallowed several times to get out her confession, "I wanted him dead. Kyle?" He nodded in understanding. "I bit him, like you said and that's how I got away the first time. But when he had me again, and used me against you ... when I saw you ... I wanted him dead and I've never felt so helpless in my life. I hated it."

"You were amazing." He cupped her face. "You *are* amazing." He used his thumbs to brush the tears away while he held her. "Babe, you did great. You are a survivor and you survived." He narrowed his gaze and she nodded in agreement. He finished, "That's exactly what you do in those situations."

"I didn't like seeing you in danger," she reiterated.

"I didn't like seeing *you* in danger," he countered.

She lay her head back against his chest. "I'm so tired, Nick."

He adjusted their position, opened the shampoo and gestured for her to get her hair wet.

"I can wash my own hair," she muttered, still following directions, turning so he could wash it for her. Slowly, attentively.

When he was done, he moved her by her hips to quickly scrub his own scalp.

"I could help you," she mumbled.

Nick took the soap out of the small package, liberally lathered it between his hands then held it out to her. When she took the bar, he turned her and with her back to him, he began to massage the soap into her shoulders and rub her back. He worked his way lower, squeezing and cupping her backside, before he ran his hands up her ribs to cup her breasts.

She turned in his arms, her hands properly lathered now, and splayed her hands on his chest, all across the muscular expanse. "See? It's better if we help each other."

They worked diligently to make sure every body part was seen to. Finally, when the soap had all been washed off and the pulsing of their need was an offbeat rhythm shortening their breathing, steaming up the small space more than the available steam was able to; she rose up on her toes, slipped her hands through his dark wet hair and tugged him to her. When her lips were a breath away, she took a step back, and he followed. She took several more.

His hooded eyes opened and he grinned down into her face. "What do you need?"

"A bed." She smiled.

When he bent to pick her up, she wrapped her legs around his wasit, giving his hands a way to cup her behind. She laughed, holding on tighter, as their wet bodies slipped them against each other. Nick made quick work of moving them into their room and lowering her onto the bed, but when he followed with his weight, she sucked in a painful breath.

He pushed himself off. "You okay?"

"My side is sore." He sat on the side of her body and let his hands drift to where she had pointed. The skin had turned purple and yellow from the bruise that was fist size. She watched his eyes darken, so she touched his face, urging him to meet her eyes. "The guy who did that is dead."

He reached up and touched the bruise on her cheek.

"That was Marcus," she muttered.

He slid up beside her and brushed as gentle a kiss as he could near the edge of the bruise as he said, "I already got him for that."

"So did I."

Nick raised an interested eyebrow.

"I kicked him in the balls." She grinned.

"Atta girl." He awarded her a smiling kiss.

Soon the smile faded, quickly replaced by the heat of need that hadn't gone too far. Nick was a man possessed, having decided to build that heat into a roaring fire. He began at her shoulder and traced each inch of her body with his fingers. When he came to her bruises and scratches from the past few days, he would linger, brushing his lips against them. By the time he finished his circuit, she was desperate for him. She knew that was exactly how he wanted her.

He eased into her and she sighed, pulling his head down, but before she kissed him, admitted, "I was gonna kiss all *your* bumps and bruises."

"Barrett, we don't have time for that," he replied, and agonizingly slow, he showed her exactly what they did have time for.

Chapter Sixty-Three

Incessant, rapid pounding on the door woke them, but it was Renee's muffled voice yelling that propelled them into action. "They took Gael!"

"Jesus Christ." Nick tripped over himself getting out of bed, grabbing the comforter on his way to the door.

Harper glanced at the bedside table clock, 8:21 a.m., as she pulled the sheet around her, following Nick.

When he opened the door, Renee's eyes were wide with panic. "They took him."

"Who?" He pulled her into the room.

"They barged in and barely let him get dressed, and they got a good eyeful of me because you can bet your ass you don't get to come into *my* room and boss me around."

"Renee." Harper said her name sharply to force her story onto any sensible track.

"The cops came and took Gael! I don't know if we need to call Salazar or if you need to call someone or why they took him but we need to go *now*, before they get away." She was tugging on Nick as she reached for the door.

"Renee," Harper said sternly, "let us get dressed. You go get your phone and your passport."

She held up her phone. "My passport is in your bag."

Harper threw on jeans and a t-shirt, grabbed her backpack, and slipped into her shoes in record time. Nick had done the same.

They rushed to the reception desk and the same woman was shaking her head in greeting. "I have never waited on guests who are this full of adventure."

"The cops, where did they take him?" Renee asked.

"The comisaria. Where you went." She grinned. "Do you need directions?"

Renee shook her head and grabbed Nick and Harper's hands, tugging them behind her. "I got it."

Outside, Harper helped liberate their hands from Renee as they walked.

"Nick," Renee's voice was shaking, "shouldn't you be calling someone?"

He tried to ease her concern, "As soon as we figure out what's going on, I'll make whatever calls I can to help."

When they got to the police station, Harper forced her way past Renee. She was still in charge of Renee and didn't want to go to jail because her friend started screaming at the cops again. Although, she was pretty sure Nick would be able to get them out if they ended up in that predicament.

Harper pasted a sweet smile and greeted the frowning gentleman at the information desk. "Buenos días." The man's frown increased.

Smile in place, she realized she wasn't the one who should be doing the talking, so she grabbed Nick's hand and swung him in front of her. His turn. But before Nick had a chance to say anything, the man pointed at Renee. "Te recuerdo." *I remember you.*

Nick made the mistake of translating, causing Renee to seethe from behind Harper's shoulder. "Of course you do, you never believed me when I came asking for help."

Nick caught the man's attention and began one of his calm, relaxed conversations.

After a few moments, the desk clerk gave an exaggerated sigh and clicked around on his computer; made a call, then looked at the group and asked, "Renee Young?"

"Yes?" She stepped in front of Nick.

"Wait there." He pointed them to the benches against the wall. Harper and Nick sat, Renee paced.

A few minutes later, Renee nodded the officer coming their way. "That's who I talked to about Gael's abduction the first time."

He arrived, beaming a smile. "Señorita Young. I have good news. We found your boyfriend!"

Her face scrunched into something between frustration, quizzical anger and a silent *'what the fuck?!'*

"You are not happy?"

"*I'm* the one who found him, you piece of–" Harper slapped her hand over Renee's mouth before she could finish the sentiment as Nick stepped in front of them and asked, "Can we see him?"

The officer frowned but jerked his head that they could follow him. Gael sat at the man's desk, filling out paperwork.

Renee hurried to him and took his face in her hands, studying him to make sure he was okay.

"I'm fine, mi reina," Gael reassured. "I just have to finish some paperwork. They found my bags and passport from the taxi. Lucky, huh?"

"You all look awful," the officer said suspiciously, having studied everyone in the group.

Gael didn't look up from the paper but loudly explained. "I told him about our car accident."

"It was bad," Nick chimed in.

Renee stood with her arms crossed over her chest, suspiciously regarding the paperwork.

"Señorita." The officer gestured for her to sit down.

"I'm not moving until he stands up and can walk out with me."

The cop rolled his eyes and muttered to Gael, "Ella es un problema."

"Did he call me a problem?" Renee raised an eyebrow.

"Eh," Gael waved the comment away, "she saved my life. We should all be that lucky; to have a woman who can cause that kind of trouble. Hará de ti un hombre."

Nick chuckled, and when Harper looked to him for a translation, he repeated, "It'll make a man out of you."

⁂

"We're going to get breakfast, want to come with us?" Harper asked Renee as they all walked out of the police station thirty minutes later.

"No, you two go. Maybe we'll meet up for dinner tonight?"

A time to meet was agreed upon before they parted ways.

Harper slipped her hand in Nick's and as they walked, she was once again able to focus on little wonders, like her inability to get used to the elevation. "You would think after all this, I wouldn't be so out of breath."

"Barrett," he leaned down and whispered in her ear, "it's okay if you want to admit I take your breath away, I won't let it go to my head."

She tilted her head so she could meet his eyes, and in the same tone he used, said, "I'm already in your head, Robbins."

He gave a slow nod, "You have no idea."

She delighted in the shiver that ran through her body and laughed; and loved how good it felt.

They settled on the first restaurant they came to. Seating inside was limited, but they were led to a large courtyard, surrounded by brick walls and potted flowers blooming red, maroon and yellow. Swags of lights and flags floated happily all around the edges of the walls with umbrellas covering every angle to keep the obtrusive sun at bay.

And it was a glorious bright morning.

They ordered and with coffee in hand, Harper snuggled back in her chair and asked, "Is it really over?"

Nick nodded. She took a deep breath and slowly let every last ounce of it out over her lips.

She held up her coffee cup. "Then welcome to my first, official day of vacation. Though I'm going to have to call work and see if I can get some more time off ..."

Nick had been considering her words, and when she trailed off and took a drink, he stood up and walked away, back into the restaurant.

She tilted her head and pursed her lips. *What just happened?* She jumped to the most logical excuse, perhaps he needed the restroom.

But when he returned a minute later, he didn't look at her. Instead, he nonchalantly studied the area as he walked through the crowded tables. When he was a few tables away from her, he finally made eye contact.

She watched, baffled inquiry etched on her face.

Nick looked behind him, then back at her and pointed at himself. "Me?"

She smiled, even though her brow furrowed in confusion.

He sauntered over to their table. "Hi. I'm sorry to be so forward, but I couldn't help noticing you when I walked in. I have this overwhelming feeling we've met before."

She sat back as she realized what he was doing. Starting over. She licked her lips. "That's your big opening line?" She shook her head, she didn't like it.

He tried again, "I can't explain it, but when I saw you from across the room, I was drawn to you. You must get this a lot, but you are the most beautiful woman I've ever seen. I just couldn't leave without asking the name of the woman whose enchanting green eyes will forever haunt my dreams."

"Stalker?" she offered, even though a few butterflies flipped around.

"Really?" He scratched the new shadow of a beard that had begun. "I thought that one was good."

"Hmmm."

He cleared his throat. "Hi, I'm Nick. I hate to bother you, but I saw you from across the room and I was enchanted. I told myself I couldn't leave here without asking if you'd allow me to buy you a cup of coffee and sit with you and talk about ... anything. Even if it's only the weather."

"Interesting." She cocked her head to the side.

He did a backbend, then twisted from side to side. After considering her for a moment, he held out his hand. "Hi. I'm Nick Robbins. Can I buy you a cup of coffee?"

She offered him her hand. "Nick? I'm Harper. I saw you when you walked in. I was hoping you'd come over. I can't explain it, but you seem like the kind of guy I'd like to get to know."

He held her hand in his and they heard her phone beep with a message. But that was no longer important. He let her hand go, cupped the side of her face, then leaned down and brushed a soft kiss against her lips; when another message beeped its arrival.

The waitress returned and asked if they wanted more coffee. Nick sat down as their cups were refilled and another beep sounded.

"I bet it's my sisters. I haven't really told them anything about my trip, they've probably decided it was time for a proper update."

But it wasn't a message from her sisters.

It was several messages from an unknown number.

When Harper opened them, her body heated at the same time a horrific chill ran the length of her spine. Nick was acutely aware of the change. "Barrett?"

Her hands were shaking as she raised the phone to him. His face paled.

The message read: *Tell your boyfriend it would be a shame if something happened to his little sister. She's a real beauty.*

The next message was a screenshot of an article that had run in the *San Francisco Chronicle.* The headline: "Nina Robbins' groundbreaking art has a permanent home." Under it was a photo of Nick's sister standing in front of her art gallery.

The final messages drained all the life out of Nick's body.

You ruin my treasure, I'll ruin yours.

Who can get to her first? Let's find out, shall we?

Ready, set, go.

Shadows
of the
MOON

Note to the reader

I hope you enjoyed the *Tears of the Moon*!

I'd like to thank you for gifting me your time and attention. In this day and age, your time is one of the most valuable things you can give to someone and I am honored to be the recipient.

—I started dreaming about Peru years ago, and when I read the book *Turn Right at Machu Picchu* by Mark Adams, it solidified the dream. I have not been yet. *Yet!* But this book was a great way to keep the dream alive.

—The lost treasure of Atahualpa is true, to a point. I made up a lot more of the legend and the general's actions. That is, after all, what the fiction writing game is all about.

—I've been traveling with a 'magic bag' for years. But it was a friend who coined the name. On a 17 hour road trip, I continued to pull items needed out of a travel bag I always carry: eye drops, a bandaid, allergy pill, nail file ... when the trip was over, the friend asked if I could make him a 'Magic Bag'. Thus, the name was born.

—I'm pretty sure much of the area my characters were traveling has better cell service than I let on.

—PSA: Don't bribe your way through Peru. Don't purchase illegal firearms in Peru. And don't kidnap Peruvian men to get answers to questions. These tasks are for fictional characters only. That is all.

—Why yes I do know a little bit about motorcycle maintenance and repair. After I learned to ride a motorcycle, my husband thought it would be a fun 'couple's activity' to rebuild a motorcycle engine together. At least I learned enough to sound plausible on paper.

—The road from Cusco to Quince Mil is not littered with nefarious bad guys hiding kidnapped photographers. The road actually has a lot of population and is well traveled. According to an article in *Time* magazine, "Quince Mil sits at a strategic point on one of the final legs of a new highway that will link Peru's Pacific coast to Sao Paulo on Brazil's southern Atlantic coast."

—As of the writing of this book, the director of the National Museum of Archaeology, Anthropology and History of Peru is Sonia Elizabeth Guillén Oneeglio. Looking up her name was the most contact I had with her, but I liked the idea of using her first name as a nod to her work.

—"Don't you dare talk about my friend that way." For the life of me, I don't remember where I first heard this. I searched the interwebs to no avail. So I just thought you should know, that I know, someone else should get credit for using it first.

–When I began writing the character of Victor, I did a lot of research on designers in Peru. I based his clothing and designs on two real people - Annaiss Yucra and Mariella Gonzales - who are using sustainable practices and old techniques in their work.

—One of my favorite meals was indeed a cheeseburger and ice cold Miller Light after backpacking in the Sawtooth Mountains for a week. It wasn't the greatest food in the world, it was simply *the* best meal for an exhausted moment.

—I have my artist daughter to thank for designing my page break. When I explained I found what I wanted from a photo of an ancient Peruvian textile, but I wanted it a little more free flowing, she first (rolled her eyes at me because she's a teenager) and quickly created it and handed it over with the explanation, "It wasn't really that hard."

—A very tiny list of my google searchers for this book: Dear Google, how can you knock someone out without doing brain damage? How do you get out of zip-ties? How long does it take to come back into consciousness after being choked into unconsciousness? (Only 10 seconds by the way...) What is it like to be bitten by a pitviper? Do you spell pitviper one word or two? How much weight can the plastic fender of a bike take? Are there really over 3000 varieties of potatoes in Peru?

Acknowledgements

First, I'd like to thank my ARC readers and my beta readers. I hope you know how much I truly appreciate your time and support!!!

There are three women I consider the heart of my indie writing team. My editor: Ariane Kimlinger, my cover designer: A. M. Rasmussen, and my Alpha reader: Michele Tomlinson. All three amazing, invaluable women have fortified and championed each of my books. They are the glue that holds me together, the cheerleaders, and sounding boards that help me drive these stories to the bitter end. Their work and friendship has bolstered, encouraged and all the other synonyms there are for the word 'support'-ed me. This book would not be in the world without them. I hope you three know, from the bottom of my heart, how much I appreciate you.

Thank you to my friends who would hire the mercenaries: Amy, Gina, Jewell, Kaite, Sophie, Shannon, Ariane, Michele and Ash.

And thank you to my friends who would bail me out of jail: Crystal, Barbara B, Adam, Keith, Jeremy, Amy B, Josh, Vanessa, and Alison. (And those I've forgotten, could you let me know? I need to make sure your number is in my contacts. You know. Just in case.)

Thank you to the Book Broads: Elaine, Margo, Lauren, Cheryl and Mary.

Thank you to my family for their love and support, and because they like to see their names in print: Nat, Daniell, Katie, Piero, Cameron, Ashelee, Bryan and Tammy.

A huge thank you to Hildy who just happened to be going on a motorcycle tour of Peru when I was thinking about writing this book. For some reason when she told me about what she was going to do, EVERYTHING fell into place in my imagination.

Thank you Brigitta C. for the help with the Spanish.

All my love to my husband and my 'A' for your support and patience with me when I disappear into the worlds of my own creation.

And always, I wouldn't be the woman I am today or have the stories I have to tell without the fierce support of my parents. Mom and Dad, at this point you really do know how much I love you and am thankful, right? I mean, this is book number 11 and I've mentioned to the world how much you mean to me in each one ... Are we good now?

Visit NicoleSharpWrites.com for more entertainment.

Want to read more by Nicole Sharp?

Another jungle adventure, perhaps?

Maybe try an Italian holiday

or get started on

The **Simply** TROUBLE *Series*

Legend has it that Nicole Sharp was born to hippies during an ice storm in Stone Mountain, Georgia. While confirmation of said events cannot be agreed upon, one fact is for certain, it was a Tuesday.

By age twelve, Nicole was sure of two things: 1) She wanted to be a writer and 2) She wanted to travel. She begged her parents to allow her to voyage alone to exotic lands. They permitted her to go from California to Boise, Idaho to visit a great-grandmother.

After muddling through her college years, Nicole graduated with a Bachelors in History (think Greeks and Romans). Why not study English if she wanted to be a writer? There were better stories in history class.

Nicole is Italian. According to Ancestry.com it's a rather low percentage, but she feels she is at least 51% Italian. She's visited the homeland a handful of times, studied the language and loves the Italian cappuccino.

Nicole's first concert was to see the bluegrass group The Seldom Scene when she was a fifteen-year-old, thanks to her parent's bluegrass phase. However, she never admits it, and instead tells everyone that They Might Be Giants, whom she saw in college, was her first real concert.

Her first car was a yellow Chevy Celebrity and her favorite job was working as a docent at a museum in an old Colorado mining town. She has written extensively about both.

Visit NicoleSharpWrites.com for more entertainment.

MOSSWOOD APOTHECARY

JP RINDFLEISCH IX

9th Publishing